Hense R Ellis
30 June 2012

LAW S...

A Novel

Hense R. Ellis II

OrphansNoMore Press

YOUR PURCHASE OF *LAW SCHOOL* BENEFITS TWO WORTHY CAUSES

Please know that, when you purchase this novel from an online source, in print or as an e-book, the net proceeds will go to two worthy causes: half to the Alabama tornado relief effort via a reputable charity, and half to help orphan children and adoptive parents via OrphansNoMore II. Profits from print copies purchased offline will go to both charities and toward the book's substantial promotional expenses, all of which the author funded.

TWITTER @lawschoolanovel
www.LawSchoolANovel.com
www.Facebook.com/LawSchoolANovel

LAW SCHOOL, A Novel by Hense R. Ellis II
www.LawSchoolANovel.com

OrphansNoMore Press
P.O. Box 397
Fort Deposit, AL 36032
OrphansNoMore Press is a division of
OrphansNoMore II, Inc.,
an Alabama Non-profit Corporation.

First Edition: February 2012
ISBN-13:978-0-9852024-1-5

Printed in the United States of America

ABOUT THE AUTHOR

Hense [*hen(t)s*] R. Ellis II is a small town guy, a 1985 graduate of the University of Alabama School of Law, and a former Assistant Attorney General who spent ten years fighting the bad guys . . . until some of them began to remind him of certain fellow members of the bar. He now works with a private lender and focuses his efforts on providing low interest rate church loans. He likes to write, to help kids, and to travel.

AUTHOR'S NOTE

When I wrote LAW SCHOOL, I sought to add some new ingredients to the legal thriller format. Hence, as you read this story, you should find unique characters (a curious protagonist, an anti-hero with a sense of humor), a unique setting (LAW SCHOOL may be the first mystery ever set in and around a law school.), a unique genre (a legal thriller blended with a coming-of-age story), and a healthy measure of themes and morals, e.g., "The first thing to learn about the real world is that it's mostly fake." Hence, when you're in LAW SCHOOL, it is wise to stay awake; it is wise to pay attention.

ACKNOWLEDGEMENTS

A real world thank you to mum, Jo, F.G., Cindi P., Nat K., Mike G., Elaine A., to S.K. for *On Writing,* and a special real world thank you to the only invisible, omnipresent *cohorte'*

DEDICATION

For Clara Rose, the ideal little sister

CHAPTER ONE

September 16, 1985. Tuscaloosa, Alabama, a university town. A good place. And as good a place as any for bad things to happen.

A huge law school classroom auditorium, filled with first year students. Contracts Professor Patrick Dooley stood below; he spoke in legalese. Seth Sentel sat on the back row, and, even from that distance, he noted the undetectable air of import in the Professor's tone, an air Seth found unimpressive.

Seth was lean, dark haired, handsome, athletic . . . and bored. Then, his head rose. His eyes flew open. His lungs seized. His hands grabbed his ears. His face winced. The double metal doors to Professor Dooley's right had burst open and slammed against the auditorium walls. The loud, metallic sound had torpedoed Seth's ear drums.

A strange man was there. His scream was straight out of hell, "*Hey you*!" He stabbed a finger at Dooley. "Yeah, *you*!"

Seth focused back on reality. He saw the man's old gray overcoat, out of place on a sunny September day, noted the faded jeans, the running shoes, and a white ball cap that was circa 1960. The intruder's bushy black mustache was peculiar, his stalking type gait the only familiar image.

His voice unleashed itself again and jolted Seth to the core. "You *blackballed me* out of here. Now, you're gonna *die*!"

Seth spied the gun: chrome, semi-automatic, a .45 caliber, ivory-handled, a Colt Government Model. It came from a left coat pocket, was horizontal in a flash. Seth's mind retrieved the photo of Jack Ruby leveling off on Lee Harvey Oswald.

Dooley, who had been drawling on about, *oddly enough*, a book entitled *The Death of Contract*, froze in mid-pronouncement.

The intruder further intruded. "She's *my* wife, *not yours*. You had to have her, so you ran me out of here. You should've stopped, but you just couldn't. *Could you?*" Dooley's eyes widened. His arms dropped; his jaw followed. So would he.

The gun spoke, jerked up: once, twice. Dooley gasped, jerked back: once, twice. His arms folded, almost as if he was a cheap metal chair. He twisted right, crash-landed on his face behind the podium. The gunman walked out, that same stalking gait.

Students jumped up; some dove down. A girl seated below stood and yelled, "No!" Another screamed, "Oh my God!"

Seth heard two guys cursing out of mere comprehension. He saw Susan Longshore's hands atop her lowered head. Her eyes closed tight, she gripped that pretty head as if it hurt. Students on their knees peeped over countertops. Seth heard the rumble of feet, as five more scrambled for the upper exit above his left shoulder. Leading that herd were two guys Seth knew from the Legal Beagles intramural football team: Rentzell and Hays, two guys who could run like deer. The door rattled. Seth knew it was locked. They'd run no further.

Seth stood, changed his focus. He saw the blood on Dooley's shirt expand from the exit wounds in his back. He found the eyes of his new friend, H.R. Garrison. They asked if Seth was going after the shooter. Seth ran down the red stairs to his left, ignored his fear, pointed at Dooley, leaving H.R., a surgeon's son with vicarious medical knowledge, to examine the body.

Seth breathed in the smell of gunpowder, hit the door running, running out of sheer principle and sheer naiveté:

Killers just weren't supposed to get away. He winced at the second abrasive clang of the door.

Too scared to be scared, his eyes flicked right, where a glass side exit door was closing. He aimed his frame toward it. He ignored the line of silver-blue light beneath a wooden closet door to his left. He stopped short of the exit. His back against the left wall, he peered out. Did the same from the right side, saw nothing but scenery.

He crept outside, took two snapshots, one of each side of · the brick entranceway, then took two steps out for a better view. Outside, he heard nothing, saw nothing. Not even a squirrel or a tardy student ran across the green lawn before him. His hands twitched. He stepped back, remembered the big brown closet door now to his right. His breath surged. His heart raced. His eyes blinked, and his ears took in every stray sound an empty foyer could muster. He was too scared to die, but too curious to walk away. A stout broom leaned against a nearby wall. He grabbed it, smacked the door open, hugged the wall, clinched the broom handle. He saw the gray trench coat on a hook and the Colt Government Model on a shelf beside it, dropped the broom, grabbed the gun, held it out front. He heard a voice, a voice now familiar.

A voice now methodical, it rolled out of a mouth he could not yet see. "Well, I can't *honestly* say I was expecting company."

Seth exhaled, glared right, grasped why that stalking gait had seemed familiar. His face flung off a child's amazement. He took one step in, one big step, then asked on reflex, "Wull, does that mean you could *dishonestly* say?"

♦

Moments before, Seth had sat in the back of the class. Professor Dooley was prattling on about a finer point of

Contract law. "The rule of this . . . Section 24 of that." Seth's law school was a double torture: fear with a boredom chaser.

He didn't know change was coming, change for the worse, but he did know something was wrong. His mind had been running for cover from a funny feeling he didn't belong, an inner suggestion he was out of place among halls both hallowed and ambiguously unpleasant. But his old diversions were failing him: the scent of coffee from the law center Coffee Room 75 feet away, the sight of Susan Longshore massaging her neck as she gazed at a banned commercialized case summary, the oddball look from H.R. the magnificent, pretending Sue had inspired yet another heart attack.

Seth had emitted his typical shy smile, but he'd needed new cover. *Section 24. That number: 24.* He'd just recalled Chapter 24 from the New Testament Book of *Matthew*, something about flashy false prophets who would deceive people. That image had been worth his thoughts. That image had made his hand twitch.

And now he sensed that change, vague as it was, had arrived early.

CHAPTER TWO

A room with a dead body on the floor has an eventual tendency to get really quiet. The dispersed crowd of collegians stared down at law school history sprawled out on the floor below them. A few, such as Susan Longshore, just couldn't look. Instead, they took in close up views of the red carpet, the white ceiling, or the gray walls. All were silent, with nothing left to do but fear, cry a few silent tears, and wonder who their substitute teacher might be.

H.R. Garrison leaned down to Dooley's stilled person for a look. Something didn't fit. The professor had somehow fallen with his head inside the full-length podium. This was odd: the shots were fired from Dooley's front right and should have propelled him in the opposite direction. Dooley was truly one bloody mess, even though the clotting had apparently set in fast. A body with exit wounds meant the bullets must have stopped somewhere else, but H.R.'s quick scan of the surrounding walls yielded no sign of lead.

He kneeled down, checked for a pulse, then rose and shook his head. There was Susan's little cheat sheet out in front of him, about three feet from where Dooley last lectured. He took two long steps, scooped it up with one hand, and offered it upside-down to Susan.

H.R. whispered, "He's going to get up in a minute. You might want to put this somewhere."

Sue, apparently overcome by the day's felonious events and perhaps expecting the paramedics to make it all go away, peeped between her hands, took the illicit volume, and shoved it down her backpack. H.R. choked back a laugh at her sudden recovery. Seconds later, she looked up at H.R., curious about how he'd raise Dooley from the dead.

H.R. stepped toward Dooley, then whispered, "Sir, I think it's okay for you to get up now."

Dooley cringed a bit, adjusted himself. Sue's eyes followed her ears. The man with blood on his shirt was moving and pushing up to his knees. Dooley, the dead professor, gave his head a tiny shake, adjusted his glasses. With an air of prominence, he eased to his feet, straightened his tie.

For Sue, sensory overload was mere seconds away. Dooley opened his mouth to speak, and that was enough, Sue blacked out for ten seconds. No one noticed.

Before anyone else could faint, Professor Dooley spoke. "May I have your attention? Please remain calm. No one is dead here."

Only Seth's shell-shocked soul had left the room. The upper exit door had held firm, and only Seth had followed the gunman out the front. H.R. was still at floor level, and he looked up at the wide-eyed faces of the disassembled. No one said a word, but after several girls drew in deep breaths and one guy cursed in a whisper, someone emitted a little laugh of release. Several others joined in. That the laugh would spread like kudzu in July was inevitable. Dooley stood silent and allowed it to run its course.

He even smiled a little himself. As he did, the clanging metal door opened again, and Dooley, now receiving a little round of applause for his Oscar-winning death scene, opened an arm of fanfare to his right. "And here is your mystery shooter."

◆

Seth crept in, his cheeks red as a Chianti. He negotiated the stairs of the room, along with the stares of the curious. Another wave of laughter struck, then a surprised Dooley looked over at Seth. Seth looked at the crowd, then quickly away. Surprised at his feat of bravery, he felt he'd just negotiated an out-of-body experience. His embarrassment was joined by an entire family of other emotions. First, the fear he'd felt when he'd gone after the shooter hadn't yet subsided. Second, he felt somewhere between angry, confused, and insulted that he'd just been jerked around. Fakery was one thing, but a fake murder? Finally, he empathized with his classmates, most of whom likely felt confused, scared, or insulted. For this many emotions, there wasn't enough time, but emotions had their own schedule.

Seth heard a light tap on the door. Instantly, he was grateful someone was behind him to take the limelight. Dooley looked again, suspicion in his eyes, and said, *"This,* I presume, is your mystery shooter." More laughter erupted.

In "the shooter" ambled, wearing faded blue jeans, Converse low tops, and a Cal-Berkley sweatshirt. The mustache, overcoat and weapon were all missing, but the old baseball cap was still there. The now familiar shooter seemed to have a gift for understatement, and today was no exception. The students applauded.

Dooley raised a left hand and interrupted, "Isn't this the *last* man on earth you'd picture as a murderer?"

And it was. Professor Barry Goodfried, affectionately known as "Your good friend Goodfried," was one of those laid-back, curly haired, beginning to gray, faded Levi-wearing products of the sixties and early seventies. The only professor who socialized with students, Goodfried had a natural ability to relate, to empathize with the oppressed law student.

Dooley scratched his head, looked at Goodfried, and continued. "Tell us, Mr. Shooter, would you even know the difference between a revolver and a revolution?"

7

Goodfried hung his head and shook it with a grin of admitted ignorance. Knowing him as a teacher for only two weeks, the class somehow must have already viewed him as an older brother, and they clapped and laughed again. Dooley raised his hand to silence the crowd, then gestured for them to sit.

He spoke like a true Georgian product of higher learning, his voice shifting into erudite. "Allow me to pose this question. Did it even cross any of your bright young minds that this unassuming character to my right might be masquerading as our angry, jealous gunman?"

No one uttered a sound, though Seth recalled the familiarity of the "shooter's" walk.

An unkempt, overweight male student spoke up. "Actually, I thought it was Asst. Dean Thurow, except for, you know, the look of purpose on his face."

The class went "Ooh" in unison, then laughed.

Dooley jumped back in. "Now, now, Mr. Farrior, careful, careful."

To Seth, it was difficult to discern whether Dooley also agreed with the subtle commentary on law school Asst. Dean Ashley Thurow, a man with an acute inferiority complex, but without apparent respect from anyone.

Dooley then prodded. "Anyone even have a hint?" Seth sat mum in his back row seat, recalling the shooter's familiar gait but too nervous to take credit. No one answered. "Someone must at least recall the color of his coat?"

A few guessed black. One said, "Dirty beige, you know, like Colombo's." Seth knew the answer, but, embarrassed at his knowledge, said nothing. H.R. sat still, but Seth saw his eyes glance over toward Sue.

"Are you certain he even wore a coat?" A short disagreement ensued over that point too.

"How about facial hair?" Many recalled the mustache, but some thought he had a goatee as well, and the disagreements abounded over length, style, and color.

"Now, what about our good friend's weapon of choice? Sawed off shotgun? Pistol? Revolver or automatic?"

Because his classmates failed to agree on even this detail, Seth was tempted to state the answer, but his reticence held sway. Instead, he jotted down the correct answer to every question, his hand still shaking.

Finally, Dooley shook his head and concluded, "Fine group of eyewitnesses this lot would make."

Still high on diversion, the class even laughed at itself.

Then, Goodfried spoke. "In case you blokes are missing the point of what must be a marvelous escape from the entangling arms of the law, eyewitness evidence isn't always perfect, or even reliable. Sometimes, other forms of proof are actually more indicative of the truth, although not necessarily more convincing to a jury of mortals. Circumstantial evidence can be powerful these days, and it's much less subject to all the assorted biases we human beings possess."

Dooley let him finish his point, but he took a step forward and looked over at his colleague. To Seth, Dooley was hoping to add his own enlightened generalization. Goodfried raised a finger, but to Seth's eye, Goodfried didn't recognize Dooley's step, and Dooley appeared resigned to the result.

Goodfried went on. "Second, I hope you've realized through this eye-popping event that truth is a highly elusive prey. It is often not as it appears. People play roles in the real world, just as they do upon the stage."

He concluded. "No one has a monopoly on truth. No one really knows what it is or whether it exists . . a lesson I hope you'll all remember." He paused to scan the room, and Seth could sense the doubt decorating his countenance. "Well, at least past your first semester."

Caught between a smile and a wince, Seth froze. His eyes narrowed; he felt confused. For a rare moment, law school was joy, but something in the air was stoking the weird uncomfortable feeling that stirred within him. Something wasn't right.

CHAPTER THREE

Dooley's 'class to remember' was over. Seth left for the men's room, right behind H.R. The men's room filled up fast, but with its long rows of white commercial grade sinks and other facilities, the place could accommodate a rock concert. After the morning's excitement, Seth's sensitive sinuses led him to search for tissue paper, so he took a stall two doors down from the left. He noted how the toilet seemed to have the initials "KK" indelibly stamped upon them in light blue ink. He wondered what "KK" stood for.

A few moments later, Seth and H.R. stood before a long horizontal mirror to wash up. Seth looked at his face and thought, *I'm twenty-two, and I still look like a teenager.*

He then considered his new best friend. H.R.'s eyes were blue, and Seth correctly surmised the red splashes were from the previous night's drinking. H.R. stood for Henry Richard. His dad was Henry, and after a four-year-old H.R. bristled at the nickname "Little Dicky," he became "H.R." Though the nickname sounded instinctively Texan, H.R. didn't look the part. His red hair with the cowlick in front was from Ireland. His line of charming bull was about two miles long, so then again, maybe he was part Italian.

The clever chap wasn't attending the University of Texas's renowned law school because, between playing football and playing the field--and also decking a dean's son in a fraternity brawl--H.R. had skipped something important at U.T. undergraduate: studying. H.R. had a top twenty percent entrance exam score and a surgeon father who knew how to make a well-placed phone call, yet his C+ grade point average had banished him to a middle tier law school like Alabama.

Seth broke the awkward silence. "H.R., what time is tomorrow's intramural game?"

"A little after four, shortly after we've watched the next episode of 'Susie Loves Susie' in Civil Procedure class."

They walked out. Seth smiled. Their banter often reminded him of Hawkeye and Trapper John on MASH.

They crossed a hallway toward the Coffee Room, the morning-place-to-be for the socially minded law student. Seth stopped. His eyes riveted on a sight moving right to left. It disappeared in the jostling wave of the student body. His eyes raced down the hallway and picked it out again. H.R. walked on, speaking with his usual eloquence and metaphor.

Seth focused on the vision, narrowed it down--a girl, with medium-length blonde hair, light-colored skirt, white blouse, some type of stylish handbag, and pearls. Her head turned left a moment. The face was sharp, but not severe, somehow magically softened to perfection. The nose was feminine, the lips full and pouty, like Natasha Kinski's. Then, her true uniqueness hit him. The cheekbones were classically high, the kind that rendered a woman captivating well into her fifties.

Overwhelmed by beauty personified, Seth mumbled a thought about its cheekbones. "They'll look even nicer when she smiles."

H.R., having just finished an expose' on the artistic nature of Sue's expertly sculpted bosom, released a small laugh as they entered the Coffee Room. Clueless about what H.R. had laughed, Seth mustered a small fake laugh of his own.

Inside, fresh coffee was both available and popular, so they lined up to keep waking up. The Coffee Room, officially named the Ryals Coffee Room, was unofficially non-academic square footage. The place was all small talk, all the time. Seth overheard some second-year students in front of him.

"Hey Mark, do you know the difference between a good lawyer and a great lawyer?"

"No, Brad, what is it?"

"A good lawyer wins when he's right. A *great* lawyer wins when he's *wrong*."

A modest, sleepy laugh spread through the line. Seth's eyes narrowed, and he and the man pouring the coffee weren't laughing.

H.R. was somehow inspired to utter Shakespeare. "Man, proud man, drest in a little brief authority, plays such fantastic tricks before high heaven as makes the angels weep."

Seth tilted his curious head, looked at H.R. with a bit of respectful surprise. H.R. threw off a minute and insightful smile. Seth didn't miss it. Now, he knew something new about H.R. H.R. was more than he wanted you to know.

The man pouring the coffee was Mozz, an older black man. He'd run a coffee service for the school for years. Mozz poured hot "Eight O'clock" brand and handed out change, doughnuts, and sage advice to the future barristers of the great State of Alabama. Mozz had that venerable look many black men assume as they age. His face was full and rounded and framed with a beard both dense and gray.

The coffee was fifty cents and the doughnuts a quarter. Mozz·was there every morning, plus, on Mondays and Thursdays, he ran a shoeshine stand in an upstairs corner. Seth enjoyed the banter with Mozz. He relished the cadence of Mozz's baritone voice. The voice had a certain rhythm and accent, not unlike that of a black minister.

"So, my good man Mozz, who did you have your money on last Saturday? Alabama or Southern Miss?"

Mozz winced and shook his head. "Why you even ask such a question, *Sixth Sentel?*" Sixth Sentel had been Mozz's nickname for Seth since day one. Mozz nicknamed all of his favorites. "I knows you," he'd say, "and now I gots to nickname you."

Mozz continued. "You know a man should never go against the Crimson Tide of *Alabama*. A man always better off going *wid* the Tide. Besides it'd be *sacrilegious* to bet against Bama. Duh Man might come out of his *tower in the sky* . . and make Mozz pay for his sins."

"Duh Man" was Coach Bear Bryant, and Seth, who had played for the deceased legend, pictured him standing in his old observatory tower. If he was climbing down it in the middle of practice, it was bad news for somebody below. Coach Bryant died over two years before in 1983, but Seth was still scared of him.

H.R. handed over a dollar for coffee and a doughnut. "Well, Mr. Mozz, you think if The Man found out you're charging fifty cents for a twenty-cent cup of coffee, he might come down and make you pay for that sin?"

Mozz gazed up from the change in his hands. "Listen here, H.R., *Holy Rogue* Garrison, a man like *The Man* would know my coffee is worth mo than any *twenty cents*." Mozz lowered his voice to a whisper. "Besides, Mozz don't see nobody selling coffee heah for less."

H.R. and Seth refused the change Mozz offered. They smiled and walked on. Seth overheard Mozz parceling out wisdom to some poor schmuck still hung over from a weekend of fun. "Now listen here, mister party boy, the bottle be good to yuh in the nightlight, but *mighty mean* when daylight comes."

H.R. arranged seating for two at a window table where three girls were gathered. They weren't about to decline company with two local heroes. Seth sat at the head of the table facing the wall and the portrait of Kathleen Ryals, a former student who'd died a few years before. H.R. just happened to sit near Sue.

Sue was there in all her sorority girl-ness, sporting her own God-given cute, plus all the additional cute her daddy's money could buy. Beside her was Bea Hostilson, a poster child for the radical feminist movement, sporting all the obligatory short, unflattering hairstyle and dark, masculine wardrobe that her daddy could abhor. The third girl, Lesley Peace, twirled a huge set of keys she'd found outside. Lesley was the picture of normality.

Seth recognized the picture and realized the law school needed a lot more of it. Her hair was a medium length dark brown, her khakis nicely pressed, and her short-sleeved polo shirt a perfect white.

Around him, Seth could overhear talk about the morning's events in Contracts class. At least one mentioned him. Now, he'd feel self-conscious the rest of the day.

Lesley asked him, "So, why did you to go after Goodfried? That was unbelievable."

Seth was too humble for his own good. "I don't really know. I just did it."

H.R. helped out. "Because he's a genuine American hero-- that's why."

Seth shook that one off and added, "I just can't get over how they jerked us around that way. One second, we think we just witnessed a murder, and the next, we realize we've just been had."

Lesley and Sue nodded.

"Makes me feel as if *they* don't respect *us*," Bea offered.

By the way she accentuated the words "they" and "us", Seth sensed she meant "those men" and "us women".

H.R. added, "Yeah, it was one helluva con job. Then again, it all made a good point. Life *can* be a con."

Less tilted her head and made the observation of the day. "Then again, this isn't seminary."

A quick silence ensued as they all looked at each other. Then, they all had a good laugh at themselves. No. It wasn't seminary.

All complaints aired and a good laugh had, H.R. brushed off the questions about how he'd stayed calm enough to examine the body while everyone else was diving for cover or running for their lives.

Lesley picked the keys up again and dangled them just above the table. "What do you think? I found them in the flower bed near the back entrance."

Sue commented on the obvious. "Wow, so many keys."

H.R. added, "Someone will be looking for those, mostly because they miss the sheer weight of them."

A polite Lesley concluded, "I guess I'll turn them in to the Dean's office after coffee."

A polite Seth asked, "Would you mind if I look at them?"

Less raised her polite manner another notch. "Sure."

Seth raised the fist-full of keys by their stainless steel ring and allowed them to hang a few moments between his absent eyes and Less's not-so-absent.

Obviously perplexed, H.R. asked, "Seth, you're not trying to hypnotize our new friend, are you?"

At first, Seth seemed not to hear him. "What? Oh, not at all. I was just wondering what type person would own these particular keys. I mean, for one, there are so many of them, and several are padlock keys, so, to me, the owner probably lives in a rural area. You know, where there might be gates and sheds to keep locked and plenty of reason for this dried red clay to be on this Ford vehicle door key. Either he doesn't live in the city, or he's entrusted with someone else's property, or maybe both. And see how worn some of them are. To have keys like this, the owner is probably at least fifty."

Seth sensed everyone staring at him as if his preoccupation bordered on the unusual; everyone but Less, who merely stared.

Less asked, "What else do you see in those common looking keys?"

Seth's eyes refocused on their target. "Well, there's an old gasoline cap key likely purchased in the early 1970's during the oil embargo, and it's still here despite cheaper fuel. Perhaps his vehicle, probably a Ford F-150 truck, is over ten years old. Who knows? He might also have been a theft victim a time or two in his day."

Bea responded with attitude. "Why did you assume the keys belong to a man?"

"Oh, sorry. I didn't mean anything. There's a worn lucky charm of sorts here on the end. It shows a bull rider with the lone star of Texas in the background. There might be female bull riders in the world today, but I doubt there were any at all when this old piece was made. The lone star emblem could also mean he's from Texas."

Bea mentioned she had an appointment. Her face afire, she stood, snatched on her backpack, and left.

H.R. appeared to appreciate the process as well as the reference to Texas, and the blessed exit of Bea. He shook his head and asked, "Anything else, Sherlock?"

"Not really, unless maybe he's forgetful. This set is for a Ford, but it's not the original pair. These were probably copied from the original as a spare set."

Sue spoke in the manner of the flabbergasted, a cute, sweet, flabbergasted. "How do you keep up with so many ideas at one time?"

"I'm not sure I do. Law school makes it difficult to keep up with anything."

No one dared argue that point.

H.R. then turned his attention to Sue and proceeded to put on a charm clinic, the likes of which a begrudgingly impressed Seth had never witnessed. Realizing meaningful conversation with H.R. was now impossible, Seth excused himself. It was if H.R. pretended not to notice, maybe to prove his devotion to Sue, who surely didn't need to pretend.

Less stood as well, and to ease their unplanned exit, Seth said, "It seems you also know when a group discussion is no longer possible."

"Yeah, I guess maybe love at first sight really does exist," she said in a gentle attempt to converse.

"Love, or something arguably like it," Seth replied with a warm, winking smile. He turned right and headed to the law library via the downstairs hall.

♦

Less's senses were about to abandon her. She opened the door to the back foyer and promptly bumped into Dean Daniel Clay, the school's 55-year-old facilities manager. He excused himself, turned to walk away. Less saw his cowboy boots.

"Pardon me, Dean Clay, did you lose some keys today?"

He said: "Matter of fact, I did. I was just outside looking for them." His accent said: *once a Texan, always a Texan.*

Less produced the keys and inquired, "Is this them?"

Dean Clay's mouth dropped, then formed a smile. He replied on reflex, "Damned if it ain't." Less's eyes widened a little, and Dean Clay tilted his head down and put his hand over both eyes. "I'm sorry. I was just so surprised to see those lost keys that I lost my manners. Hope you'll forgive me."

Less was actually a little tickled and charmed at the sight of a grown man being alternatively coarse and apologetic. "It's fine, sir. I'm just glad I found the owner."

"Well, thank you. I'm not sure this place could operate without these keys, not to mention my little spread outside of town."

Less remembered. "Excuse me, Dean Clay, so you have a place outside town. You mean out in the country?"

"Well, yeah I do. It ain't big, but it's home."

"Do you have barns and gates you keep locked?"

"Yes." He seemed curious at the questions, but this girl had found his keys.

"Is some of the soil there red clay?"

"Yeah, some is, but there's good black dirt too." His face scrunched.

"By any chance, do you drive a Ford truck, an F-150 model, I think it's called?"

Amazement leapt into his eyes. Maybe this girl was psychic. He nodded quickly, likely wondering what she'd ask next. "Well, yeah, matter of fact I do. I don't drive it here. It's about twelve-years-old, and I just use it as a work truck."

"Did you lose the original keys?"

"Actually, about eight years ago, I forgot them at a bar."

"This is the one you're really not going to believe. Does it have a gas cap lock, maybe because someone stole your gasoline?"

He nodded. "You're *some kind of something*. How could you *possibly* guess all that?"

She walked away backwards, wandering amid her own cloud of amazement. "I didn't, and I don't think any normal person could."

CHAPTER FOUR

Seth hit the law library, studied till his eyes wore down, then started home for a quick meal and a bitter Property Law dessert. Professor Jacob Myerson's Property law class was at 8:00 a.m. the next morning. "Jake the Ache" Myerson, as H.R. had renamed him, was famous for one simple statement: *Any student unprepared for class will be removed from the room forthwith, and shall theretofore be banned from it for life.* Seth blocked the words out of his mind, focused on the road ahead, considered supper, kept driving.

He resided in the garage apartment of the University Chancellor at Number 9 in the old-moneyed Pinehurst neighborhood. The Chancellor was head of the University of Alabama System, informally known as "The System." The System was comprised of all three University campuses, the main campus where Seth was, the medical school campus in Birmingham, and the high-tech branch campus in Huntsville.

As a well-reputed former member of the football team, Seth had good references, so Chancellor George Bausch allowed him to live on the premises. In return, Seth walked the Chancellor's venerable Basset hounds, Harvard and Yale, made an informal security check each night, and served as bartender and chauffeur at various System functions. When the Chancellor was out of town, Seth had the run of a two-mansion paradise.

H.R. had nice living quarters as well: He lived in a small log cabin in a wooded area outside town. It belonged to his cousin, a reputable Birmingham insurance agent, who meant to use it for hunting, but never had time. His only neighbor was a shy, uneducated woodsman named Lymon. Despite his serene, low priced "cabin in the woods", H.R. had labeled Seth's setup the "sweetest gig in the free world." Seth wished they could trade.

Seth turned right into Pinehurst and coasted past the front of the estate. Both houses were painted white, with Number 9 made of heavy stucco and Number 11 fashioned of brick. The twin two-story homes were tied together by the landscaping, which included a beautiful array of impatiens and azaleas, and the large patio resting among them.

He parked at one end of Number 11 and followed his appetite toward the kitchen, then overheard the System chef, François Bernaut', pontificating in his usual expressive, French-accented state.

"Dinner for six, and I get one hour's warning. Who do these people think I am, Chef Superman?"

Needing relief from an overdose of case law, Seth glanced in and smiled. François was only 35, but to Seth, he might as well have been 55. He seemed to know everything, yet worried about nothing, except food.

The Chancellor's social secretary, Stacey Coalson, attempted to placate him. "Now, François, I know it's short notice. The two board members and their wives arrived unexpectedly. They can't help that their Mercedes broke down. You know there are no suitable hotels in this town, so Dr. Bausch insisted they stay overnight. He doesn't expect a seven-course meal--just something simple, yet appealing."

"Simple? I cook no simple fare. There's not one good meatloaf in me!"

"Well, they weren't expecting meatloaf. Can't you just prepare the seafood dish we served last week to those legislators? You still have most of the ingredients in the fridge, and I'll call Kroger and have them wrap up the snapper and shrimp."

Seth heard a guttural noise, saw a hand slap down on a tile counter. "Seafood Tricia in one hour! Never would I insult my ex-girlfriend by assembling her favorite entrée with such haste."

"You named a dish after your ex-girlfriend? What if Marnie found out? She'd have your head."

"You speak as if Marnie is my queen. Besides, I name new creation after her, Chocolate Mousse Marnie. Ah! It is as delightful as she." He closed his eyes, looked toward the ceiling, and shivered his head. "Smooth, delectable, so *irresistible*."

Stacey, impatience bursting from her eyes, responded as any true boss would. "Look, François, you're paid big bucks to take care of the Chancellor and his wife, so let's see you earn it. I don't give a rat's behind what you do or how you do it, but I want it on the dining room table in one hour!"

François scrambled toward the dining room, un-tucking his shirt as he walked. "You want it with François on the table, eh? Well, why not I make love to you? And now that I know you care, why wait an hour?" He sounded as if his repressed desire had finally seen its vent.

Stacey's face registered somewhere between shock and flattered, but once she'd regained her composure, labeled François a "culinary imbecile," and popped him lightly on the head with a spatula, she left through the patio door.

When Seth entered, his face showed something between shock and laughter. "François, sometimes you remind me of the cartoon character, Pepe Le' Pew."

"Oui, Monsieur Professional Student, but I fear, like Pepe, I am disappointed." The Chef cast a frown in the direction of his shoes.

Seth got to the point. "So, what's for supper?"

"Time is scarce. Any bright ideas from the student-assistant?"

"Sure, and I'll show you just the dish, if you'll promise to prepare the usual quantity of leftovers."

"As long you assist with the cleanup."

"Agreed. Now, do you have eggs, some aged cheddar, a few bread crumbs, some sausage, and a little buttermilk?"

"Yes, and the best homemade yeast rolls known to man."

Seth proceeded to teach the chef an old family breakfast recipe, which took only thirty minutes to prepare. By the time the cleanup was complete and the wealthiest two men on the System's twelve-member board had repeatedly complimented the chef, it was 7:30.

Pleased with the result, François asked, "So, young Seth, what do you call this breakfast-for-dinner dish?"

"I think mom called it 'cheese doings'."

"Nnnuh. Ze dish, she needs new name. You have girlfriend, young Seth? Perhaps you've taken her to Number 11 guest room as François does Marnie?" The Frenchman's eyes gleaned with curiosity, as he leaned forward in anticipation of the answer.

Seth first looked away, then mustered a weak French accent. "No, but I've fallen for a most beautiful Mademoiselle with perfect high cheekbones, like those of a fashion model."

François nodded: He had enough to work with. "All right then, we call dish 'Eggs le Vogue'." Seth shrugged. "Now, out of my kitchen before François tires of poor impersonators."

Seth left the kitchen with the smile of innocence, cut through the empty dining hall, crossed the patio area in the dark, and trod a stone-paved walkway to his apartment entrance. He stopped to overhear the high-powered front-porch conversation between the Chancellor and his guests. Eventually, he caught himself eavesdropping. His guilt overcame his inclination to investigate. He bounded up the stairs and unlocked the door to his room.

Now he had less than three hours to read twenty-five pages on property easements, and he'd need every minute of it to avoid the potential wrath of Jake the Ache. Myerson served double duty as coach of the law school intramural football team: the Legal Beagles. He was as tough on the field as he was in the class. Already, he'd chewed out H.R. for dropping a pass at a rainy day practice. H.R. had played tight end for the Texas Longhorns, but any receiver could drop a wet ball on occasion.

Myerson shunned modern textbooks. He preferred his own package of materials, including several English cases, some from the 1800's that read like Chaucer. H.R. had agreed. His comment? *At least The Miller's Tale was a fun read.*

Tonight, there were two primary cases to read and summarize: *Ackroyd v. Smith*, an 1850's English case, and *In re Ellenborough Park*, another English case, but at least penned in the twentieth century. Seth felt he needed more than *Black's Law Dictionary* to get through these readings. He needed a translator. Thankfully, Pinehurst was the quiet neighborhood that absolute focus required.

He read the following passages from *Ackroyd* at least three times before he could comprehend them:

> . . . that, long before any of the said several times of committing any of supposed trespasses in the declaration mentioned, and before and at the time of making the indenture of release and grant hereinafter

next mentioned, to wit, on the 27th of September, 1837, one Ellis Cunliffe Lister was seized in his demesne as of fee as well of and in the soil of the road in this plea first mentioned. . .

then therefore paid by the said John Smith to the said Ellis Cunliffe Lister, did bargain and sell the last mentioned lands, tenements and premises, with the appurtenances, to the said John Smith; . .

. . . the rule, noscitur a sociis, therefore, applies.

Seth pleaded with the ceiling. "*Why*? Why does this man *hate* us?"

There were thousands of intelligible U.S. easement cases, yet Myerson forced them to read old English drivel. With obscure cases like *Ackroyd* and *Ellenborough*, case briefs required a long labor of mental pain to even extract the pertinent facts. He consulted his *Black's* fifteen times before the night was over.

It was 11:30 when Seth completed the readings, two hours later than he'd planned. He'd hoped to catch up on his sleep. He leaned back in his chair, shell-shocked into what every law student eventually realizes: Law school could be grueling, confusing, boring, and--particularly for Seth--frightening. There had to be a more pleasant way to make a living.

The realization was different and more powerful for him, however; it was more disconcerting, more alienating, and it made sleep even more than the usual chore. It was enough that there was some strange stealth virus evolving in his subconscious life.

He rolled over to try the other side of the bed, wished the unnamed enigma would play fair and show itself. His life would be simpler without such inexplicable inklings of trouble. He fell asleep frightened of Myerson, frightened of the future, frightened of this new sense that some vague evil was at work.

♦

The speedy Rentzell and Hays were roommates. It was one a.m. They walked toward Hays's car in an empty parking lot outside The Sidetrack, a college bar near the railroad tracks. They didn't enter Hays's car. Instead, they and a large bald-headed man dressed in black entered the panel van parked behind it. Getting inside strange black panel vans at one a.m. was never a wise idea, but when there was a pistol or a sawed-off shotgun jammed into one's spine, Rentzell considered it the reasonable thing to do.

During the short drive to an empty warehouse, Rentzell changed his mind. The blond Rentzell glanced at Hays, a black student with cropped hair and zero body fat. Hays's eyes registered comprehension of a plan. Rentzell was certain Hays knew what they both could do so well. They wouldn't make it easy on their two captors. The van stopped a moment, idling while they heard the sound of a large door sliding open. The van edged forward and stopped. Rentzell heard the door sliding back into place and the driver re-entering the cab. The van eased forward again.

A second passed. Rentzell dropped a handful of change from his coat pocket. The thug looked down. Hays kicked his jaw. His head bounced off the wall. Rentzell kicked the gun. It came loose. Hays grabbed it, slammed its stock against the thug's head. Rentzell had the door open. The van stopped. They both jumped out into a huge, unlit warehouse, the only light from a small row of windows set five feet off the floor.

Rentzell was indeed fast, Hays even faster, but Rentzell had the head start. Both accelerated down the center corridor. Hays still had the gun: He tossed it aside as they cut right down an aisle. Rentzell set his eyes on the windows ahead, Hays two strides behind him. In seconds, they were halfway down the aisle.

Rentzell yelled, "Zigzag, Hays, zigzag." Both darted left and right.

Rentzell heard the first "crack", knew it was a small caliber weapon, knew the bullet went past his right ear. They ran faster. The windows were only 15 feet away. He heard the second "crack". Hays flew in front of him to the cement floor, a small hole in the back of his head. *No one shoots like that*, Rentzell thought, as he zigged and zagged even more. There were the huge windows, now only four feet in front. The panes seemed thin enough. He ran straight at them, left his feet at the perfect point.

He wouldn't remember the third "crack".

A thin red-haired man holstered his .22 caliber pistol, retrieved the shotgun from a shelf, backhanded the bleeding thug, then drove them both home.

CHAPTER FIVE

After six hours of relatively peaceful sleep, Seth reached the law center by 7:00 a.m. He went by his cubicle for a quick review of the previous night's property readings. Maybe it would somehow make sense if he slugged through it one more time. At 7:50, H.R. dropped by on his way to class, his eyes promising the imminence of good theatre.

"Sethster, did you read Myerson's Swahili law last night? I needed a mental machete just to make a path through it. Who does he think we are, monk-scholars in Latin and Middle English? Holy Prima Donna, Batman! There's nothing worse than a sadist with tenure."

H.R. paused to reload his lungs with fresh air. Seth leaned back and clasped his hands behind his head. This dramatization promised to be a needed diversion.

H.R. continued. "You think maybe the jerk is paining our brains just for a few fiendish laughs, or does he do it to benefit some formal psychological experiment?"

"I don't know, H.R. Why don't you ask him in ten minutes while the question is still warm?"

For a moment, H.R. hushed, appearing ever-so-slightly humbled. Seth stood, and they both began to walk toward the classroom.

H.R. raised his head and answered his own question, "Well, if it were the latter reason, at least he'd have a justification, albeit a twisted one. Say, Seth-boy, looks as if you have some voluminous notes on our new friends *Ackroyd,*

Smith, and Ellenborough Park. Any idea what the cases mean? Any idea what your notes mean?"

With H.R.'s endless good humor, Seth's feeling of distraught panic was slowly becoming ordinary fear. They walked down the long inner front porch toward the classroom, and H.R. continued the monologue. "Over a beer last night at The Nasty Tap, a third-year swore that, ten years ago, these two cases drove a timid first-year bonkers. After eight hours of preparation and thirty minutes sparring with the Ivy League obsessor, um professor, the guy finally jumped up and declared, *I'm an Easement Appurtenant! I'm an Easement Appurtenant!* Then, he ran away without his books . . . *and was never seen again.*"

A man could always count on H.R. returning to poison-free humor. Smiling, Seth posed the return question. "So, what about you? If today is your date with destiny and he calls upon the house of Garrison to explain these two *fine examples* of judge-made law, would you be ready?"

"Ready? Hell's bells, he's got it rigged so a guy can't be ready. A poor schmuck can't even anticipate all the questions he'll ask, much less know the answers. Besides, the third-year I drank beer with late last night was a little fuzzy about how it went when he took Myerson's class, and it was a little noisy in the place with Madonna on MTV singing *Like a Virgin*. By the way, don't you wonder if she was *ever* a virgin?"

Seth avoided a digression on original sin and instead asked, "You anticipate questions, too? I feel less insane knowing I'm not the only one to invest so much time in these meaningless cerebral gymnastics."

"Take solace, pal. From what I've heard, the heavy workload of Ole King Nefarious is breaking the spirits of *all* of his loyal subjects. Next thing you know, he'll ask us to interpret cases from the fifteenth century that he hasn't even handed out .

. . you know, a new twist on the ole bricks-without-straw deal the Egyptians gave the Old Testament Hebrew slaves."

Seth's smile was perfectly calibrated. "You know something about the Old Testament? Call 911. I'm in hyper-shock. How were you ever exposed to it? Was it inscribed on a motel headboard somewhere?"

H.R.'s sheepish grin was perfect too. "I was raised Baptist. My mom took me to Sunday School every week until I was old enough to drive myself and play hooky."

"Really? Me, too, except I grew up next door to the church, so I couldn't play hooky, well, even if I'd wanted to. What's your favorite Old Testament book?"

"Proverbs is fine reading, but I'll go with the Song of Solomon."

Seth shook his head. "Why did I bother to ask?"

"Really, it's so poetic, like when it says, *For love is as strong as death.*"

King Solomon's sentiment struck Seth, but there was no time to ponder it. They were now just twenty feet from the classroom, time for Seth to confess his latest fear. "I'm not sure I'll be ready if he calls on me. I feel like I'm strolling toward the gallows."

Without warning, H.R. stopped and went into his Foghorn Leghorn imitation, "I say, I say, Boy! You wurrrry too much. Beats anything I *ever* seen. Maybe ole man Myerson hates us, but he ain't so bad. He's just a human being like you and me. Of course, I'm actually a chicken as you might notice, and he's more of a chicken hawk. Anyway, the man ain't gonna' tear you limb from limb. In fact, I've figured the odds of him calling on one of us today are fifty-to-one against. Besides, even if he do call yo name, the wust he can do is throw you out 'a class and ruin yo legal life. It's not like he's gonna cutchuh peckuh off. Peckuh. Ha. I made a funny. I'm a chicken and I called it a peckuh."

Seth smiled, exhaled, then replied, "Well, I'm glad you've decided to take this medieval law with a grain of corn." Then, he nodded his head. "You know, H.R., you might never make a great lawyer, but you sure make a great friend."

CHAPTER SIX

They walked into Myerson's room, found their assigned seats. Myerson soon followed. The room became an instant funeral home.

The balding, yet stately man of letters and wool suits adjusted his glasses and Phi Beta Kappa key, then opened his seating chart on the table in front of him.

To Seth's right, a girl named Jill LeDoux was wearing an Atlanta Braves baseball cap. A Catholic girl from Mobile, she had no Southern Baptist background to regulate her intake of taxed beverages, not that such a background was always effective. Anyway, H.R. had once observed, "Jill could drink the Gulf of Mexico if they'd just put the right amounts of vodka and vermouth in it." She'd already been before the Dean to explain a drunken driving arrest.

Myerson put a finger on a location in the seating chart and stated, "Miss LeDoux, would you kindly remove your hat?"

The class looked over in frozen horror.

The already petite Miss Ledoux shrunk to the size of a six-year-old, but still managed to eke out an objection. "But, um, Professor, I'm having a bad hair day."

The entire class seemed to be caught between dread, fear, and the temptation to laugh out loud. Seth felt like a balloon being slowly overfilled with helium.

"Well, I see, but you must understand, Miss LeDoux, about the rules which govern decorum and proper behavior. When you enter the practice of law, firms and judges expect compliance with certain standards. You must now become accustomed to living in a professional environment. I prefer to begin the process of maturation in my classroom. Hence, I must ask you again to remove your head covering."

Jill somehow cowered down another six inches and slowly removed the cap, placing it in her lap for a quick replacement at the sound of the bell. Jill was a lush, but she was no liar. Her hairstyle was ghastly. Unwashed, it protruded in four different directions, and Seth noted three different shades.

The room was now a morgue, everyone stiff and silent. Myerson did a double-take stare, the second of which, to Seth at least, reflected a comical disgust.

Finally, he managed to say, "Perhaps, in this one instance, I will grant an exception to the rule. Please, Miss LeDoux, replace your hat upon your head."

Seventy helium balloons broke at once into laughter, and even Myerson failed to completely restrain himself. Humor belonged in a Myerson classroom like it belonged at an execution. Once the outburst dissipated, Myerson resumed his standard undertaker's tone, examined the seating chart as might a surgeon, then announced the daily sacrifice.

"Mr. Hays?" There was no response: Hays's desk was empty. Myerson glanced up, then, with a hangman's stare, noted Hays's absence on his attendance sheet.

"Mr. Rentzell?" Another dose of lethal silence arose, followed by another empty desk, another dead stare, and another mark on the sheet.

"How about Mr. Garrison? Might you assist the class in understanding the case of *Ackroyd v. Smith?* "

Seth sneaked a sympathetic look of disbelief over at H.R., who was on the same row, but six spaces to his right. H.R. shielded the front of his face with a notebook and mouthed the words, *He can't cut off my pecker.*

Myerson continued, "Please, Mr. Garrison, grant us a brief rendition of the facts from this instructive case."

H.R. cleared his throat, hesitated a moment, scanned his notes. "Well, there were these two guys named Smith and this one guy named *Ackroyd*."

Myerson interrupted, "More detail, Mr. Garrison. What were the first names of the Smith brothers?" Most students in their right mind wouldn't recall this detail.

"I think one was a Sam and the other a Tom."

Myerson added, "Samuel and Thomas to be precise, but continue, Mr. Garrison."

"Anyway, the Smiths were trespassing like mad on *Ackroyd*'s property, both on foot and with their *divers* wagons and horses. It was even to the point where a road had been formed by the passage of the Smiths."

Myerson said, "Again, Mr. Garrison, more detail. From whence did the Smiths and their various carts and horses originate, and to whence were they bound?"

Seth noted the class seemed to be holding its collective breath for H.R. The detail Myerson wanted seemed irrelevant, so no one had noted it.

H.R. paused, but seemed undaunted. "The road the Smiths took across *Ackroyd*'s property joined two other roads, a certain turnpike and a Legram's Lane."

"The turnpike's name?"

"I don't remember", he stated with a shrug.

"Perhaps you could take a moment to review the case."

Maybe H.R. couldn't discern if Myerson was serious. With head down, Seth flipped his eyes up to surmise Myerson's expression. There was no clue. It could take five minutes to locate such an inane fact. H.R. whipped through two pages and read the text aloud.

Seth detected an undetectable impudence in H.R.'s voice. "The easement was, quote, 'for all purposes, in, over, along, and through a certain road running between the Bradford and Thornton turnpike and Legram's Lane', end quote." H.R. could just as well have asked, *Is this specific enough for you, you anal-retentive jerk?*

The exchange became a contest of wills that lasted over twenty minutes. It was a match of two skilled boxers, bobbing and weaving. H.R., sometimes irreverent--sometimes appropriately so--and sometimes comical, certainly took a few shots, but he gave as well as he took.

Myerson inquired if a certain argument about the easement in *Ackroyd v. Smith* could be made.

H.R. replied, "A creative lawyer can make most any argument . . . and make it sound good."

The class released another smaller tension-relief laugh, but it was silenced by a Myerson doomsday stare.

In the end, Myerson delivered a summary, and seemed to despise doing so. "Mr. Garrison has made some interesting points for the class to consider, one of which is that courts are tempted to make end runs around rules to suit the necessities of the times, or that of their consciences. A valid case on point might be *In re Ellenborough Park*. Who might assist us with that dispute?" Then came the last two words on earth that Seth could then bear: "Mr. Sentel."

Seth's eyes came alive with terror. His heart rate leaped. H.R. glanced at him as if regretful that *Ackroyd* hadn't consumed the entire class period. Seth calculated the odds they both would be called upon in the same day by the same teacher, about three-thousand-to-one. He felt the perspiration in his hands.

Seth noticed Myerson's voice had lost some of its edge. Seth's was still creaky. "Yes, sir. *In re Ellenborough Park* concerned a right to use an open area as a park. The rights were created in the 1850's when the original owners sold home lots surrounding the park. Each sale included a conveyance of the right to use the park as a pleasure ground. The homes were eventually transferred to new owners."

Myerson interrupted. "And the primary issue that arose before the 1955 court decision, Mr. Sentel?"

Seth's left hand twitched. Fear was gaining on him; he switched to block-out mode, his voice suddenly robotic. "Whether subsequent homeowners retained the right to use the park."

Myerson assisted. "Or whether the right to merely walk about a property or picnic upon it can be legally transferred. Now, using the old rules about easements we applied in *Ackroyd*, would such a unique easement *run with the land*?"

"I don't see how, Professor, especially given that Court's narrow view of transferability."

"Ah, but you're already escaping into policy considerations. Let's slow down and dwell upon the rules."

Seth changed mental gears. "The rules speak in terms of supporting the land, but how could this be when the lots didn't require the park for access or septic lines."

"True, but how many years had passed between these two cases?"

"Over one hundred."

"By 1955, was there not less countryside in England, and more cities, with more people living within them?"

"Yes, sir."

"So wouldn't an open area in the city have more 'usefulness' to surrounding lots than say an open area in the country?"

"In a less agrarian society, a park could be viewed as meeting the *Ackroyd* test."

"Good, Mr. Sentel, but think back. Is that how the court approached the situation?"

"No sir. The court asked if the right was *overly unique*."

Myerson interrupted, "Ah, and what did the court conclude?"

"It used some indirect precedent to hold that use of land as a pleasure ground wasn't a, um, *modern novelty*."

"This court is having a little fun here, but we must venture on. Time walks among us. On what else did the court lean to make its decision?"

"How the original grantor's intent was to preserve the open space as a park."

"Could the court have been sure this was their intent?"

"No sir."

"Of course it couldn't, but it *thought* it could, which is a lesson in and of itself. Finally, Mr. Sentel, is there any chance you might tell us what modern real estate construct exists which would have prevented the *Ellenborough Park* dispute?"

Seth couldn't possibly know this. This modern "construct" was slated for second semester Property. His mind wandered off, as was its custom. It turned to more relaxing thoughts, his usual escape mechanism kicking in. He drifted off to Destin, Florida, a clean, sleepy little beach village. He considered the resort where his family would stay, with its three neighborhood pools, all surrounded by grassy areas belonging to no one owner, and . . .

"Correct, Mr. Sentel. Condominium law provides explicitly for common areas. You must be reading ahead. Our time has expired for today. The wise among you will rethink these two cases and thereby glean many valuable lessons. Class dismissed."

CHAPTER SEVEN

H.R. bolted out of the classroom, stomped past a stunned Seth without a word, and blasted through the door. Seth grabbed his books and hurried behind him, still unnerved by Myerson's inquisition. Less, who was seated across the room from Seth, stood to trail him.

He caught H.R., who turned and whispered in anger, "He was gunning for me, couldn't you tell?"

Seth spoke rapidly. "Are you sure?"

H.R. walked faster, heading toward the spiral west staircase.

"That Jew jerk is after me. He's trying to humiliate me. I'm not saying he treated you with kid gloves. I'm just saying he treated me with rusty iron ones."

"H.R., you should watch your word choice. You could-"

Then, there was that voice, right behind Seth. It jolted him down the spine, might as well have been from God.

"Mr. Garrison. Is there a problem?"

Seth saw H.R.'s face. It snatched up and over toward the class room door, then morphed from shock to resolution.

"I'm tired of you badgering me, Professor. You do it in class. You do it at football practice."

Afraid, Seth managed to pivot toward Myerson standing five yards behind him. The professor's words bore into H.R. "A measure of special attention can build character, Mr. Garrison, and more character never hurts anyone, does it?"

Myerson's implication was clear. Seth could see H.R. was physically biting his tongue and could sense the power intensifying in his friend's long right arm.

Suddenly, the hand attached to that arm pointed at Myerson's face. "Now, you may be my teacher and my flag football coach, but I've got my daddy's permission not to take certain varieties of BS off anyone."

Myerson replied, "Calm yourself, Garrison. Don't get yourself into a hole you can't escape."

H.R.'s voice climbed the ladder of anger. "You're the one in a hole, Professor. You stepped in it when you insulted my character."

"You're taking this too seriously."

"When my character is attacked, nothing is too serious. Maybe I laugh more than your hard ass can stand, and maybe I have a little more fun than you're accustomed to, but, don't dare suggest that's a character flaw."

Seth calculated the data pertinent to a fistfight between these two. H.R. was certainly younger and bigger, but he'd hurt his shoulder lifting weights. Myerson was in great shape for his age, still stocky, still mean. Seth knew he had to stop this before it started.

"H.R., this would be a good time to just walk off. I think you've made your point." Seth's last sentence seemed to break H.R.'s concentration.

Seth started to breathe a sigh of relief, but Myerson spoke. "No, let him finish. I want to hear the rest of his unrefined thoughts."

Seth went mute. H.R. also seemed surprised, but regained his train of words. "You've been riding me like a scrub horse since the day I got here. You *don't know me*, and how *could you*? You ever had a heart-to-heart talk with old H.R.? You ever sat down over a beer with him? Of course not, nor would you, because you're a pompous, elitist sadist. I've had all of you any reasonable man can take. If you really want a piece of me, this is a perfect time to try and take it."

Myerson smiled . . . knowingly, it seemed to Seth, then said, "You really like to push it to the edge sometime, don't you, Garrison? The day approaches when such will cost you."

Myerson turned and walked toward the faculty elevator. He appeared neither frightened, satisfied, nor angry, a man undecipherable, even to Seth. H.R. turned his head: To Seth he appeared to do so in frustration at himself, but Seth actually stood in a strange awe of his friend.

Seth looked around at the small crowd gathered behind him, still there, likely wondering if H.R. would charge Myerson.

Seth tried to say the right thing. "Maybe it seemed as if he was after you, but don't let him get to you like that. I think you stood up to him well enough in class, H.R. You weren't scared stiff like I was. Maybe you even earned his respect."

H.R. stopped halfway down the staircase, looked Seth in the eye. Seth looked back and said, "It's true, and you may be the first to stand up to him."

"Thanks, Seth." As he walked on, H.R. added over his shoulder, "You know, Seth, you may never make a great lawyer, but you sure make a great friend."

Less, who had watched the entire exchange from behind Myerson, froze, stared at Seth, her mouth slightly open. She took in a deep breath and hurried out the side exit.

◆

Seth walked three steps down the staircase, then decided to give H.R. some space. He stopped, let H.R. continue to the downstairs foyer and out the back door. Seth's instincts said he needed space, too.

He sensed someone behind him and turned. It was what he needed: that perfect face and that golden blonde hair, only a glimpse, but enough. He raced back up, then stopped. If she was heading to the library via the second floor breezeway, he could use the first floor hall and arrive ahead of her. He hurried down the stairs, dodged random students, galloped up the east stairwell, turned left, and took in a quick view of the upstairs.

She wasn't there. Maybe she stopped at the registrar's desk or the Dean's office, both upstairs in the middle of the breezeway. He saw a white BMW pull out of the faculty lot in front of the building. The driver's hair was the same shiny blond. The car zipped down the curved cement driveway toward Bryant Boulevard. He stared at the vision, his eyes wide.

He admired her parking courage, knowing he'd never have it. He was jealous of how she relished driving that BMW, knowing he'd never experience it. The familiar alienation was nowhere to be found, for the moment.

CHAPTER EIGHT

At 7:00 p.m. the next Thursday, September 26, the phone rang. Seth was in the Number 11 kitchen, dining on François leftovers from a luncheon for academic department heads.

It was H.R., and his first five words hit Seth like a truck: "Rentzell and Hays are dead."

"*What*?"

"They found 'em both shot in the back of the head in a warehouse near the tracks."

"Geesh, you sure this isn't just more bogus law school gunplay?"

"Uh-uh. This time something real finally happened around here."

Seth stood. He felt his knees weaken. He muttered, "Man, just when I'd finally realized everything in law school was fake."

"By the way, don't think the world outside law school is any different. In fact, the first thing to learn about the real world is that it's mostly fake."

Seth closed his eyes: he had to let that one settle. He shook his head, then muttered, "Good God."

H.R. replied, "Well, he wasn't good to Rentzell and Hays."

"Really; they weren't law review material, but they were good students. Hey, did you say in the back of the head? Isn't that mob style or something?"

"Yeah, the cops are already thinking drugs or unpaid gambling debts."

"Those two? They were *really good* guys, H.R., from good families, raised in the Mobile suburbs."

"Well, they're *really dead* guys now, Seth, and you know what? I've seen plenty of good family types with a taste for the nose candy. Maybe daddy's allowance ran out, and some dealer with unpaid trade credit got impatient."

"Man. They played receiver on the intramural team with us. Both of 'em were *so quick.*"

"Whew, and now both are *so dead*. I guess we'll have to play every down now, Seth."

With death out of the way, H.R. changed the subject. After all, no H.R. conversation was complete without a discussion of women.

"Hey Seth. Remember that femi-nasty girl from the Coffee Room? Talk about 'Bark first and ask questions later'."

"Yeah, I'm all for women learning the law, but must they learn to hate us men in the process?"

H.R. added, "Now, Sue and the girl-next-door type, I wouldn't mind them as law partners, particularly if they liked to mix law with pleasure."

Seth's eyes came alive, right before his entire face scrunched in concern. "So, you also saw her as a girl-next-door type. Thinking like you troubles me, H.R. Where should I seek counseling?"

"Good one, Seth, real good. And isn't she as wholesome as apple pie? Might make a good mate for you. What happened when you two waltzed off together?"

"We weren't waltzing."

"Really? I thought yall had some kind of eye thing going."

"There was no eye thing. Besides, how could your eyes have noticed, glued as they were to little Suzy's big bosom."

H.R. declared, with an air of officialdom that made Seth smile, "To the charge of first degree scamming, I plead guilty as sin. Actually, I'm meeting the darling Miss Sue tonight. How 'bout you? Did you get off your shy keester and ask out little Miss Take-Me-Home-To-Your-Parents?"

"Don't even recall her name."

"Too bad. I can just picture it: The All-American Boy and the Girl-Next-Door, a marriage made in small town America."

"Sorry to whiz on your grand vision, but she really doesn't have that elegant quality I like in a woman."

"Oh, you mean the old instant raw attraction test? Well, I can see your point, but remember sex ain't, I mean, looks ain't everything."

Unconvinced, Seth replied, "Unless it's six a.m., and her hair is in curlers, and she's leering at you across a bowl of shredded wheat."

H.R. concluded, "Just remember, there's a definite connection between the beautiful and the bizarre."

H.R. then proceeded to magically talk Seth into meeting him, Sue, and Cindi Vicari, a third-year student and Sue's sorority sister, at H.R.'s favorite local dive bar, The Nasty Tap. Sue remembered she had a previous commitment to hang out with Cindi and felt an uneven girl-guy count could make her friend feel uneasy.

Seth avoided blind dates, mostly because he was scared to death of them, but H.R. casually mentioned Cindi had won a beauty pageant, and Seth convinced himself he could read two Civil Procedure cases on *inpersonam* jurisdiction in time to make it.

On the short drive over, the uneasy feeling struck him again. He sensed it was somehow tied to the notion there was too much about law school that wasn't real . . . and too much about himself that didn't belong there. Yet, now it was getting real in a hurry, and despite his alien status, he was there. It was too much negativity with which to deal, and H.R. was talking gorgeous women, certainly a more pleasant subject than "CP."

Beauty on the brain, Seth read the two uninspiring cases in record time and headed for the Jeep.

CHAPTER NINE

Seth whipped the Jeep through Pinehurst to University Boulevard, turning left toward the infamous Nasty Tap. It was upstairs in a two-story building on the strip, across from the Sigma Nu fraternity house. The bottom floor was unoccupied, with boarded doors and windows, but it was painted and well kept.

The Tap half of the building looked miserable. The white exterior enamel flaked away, and the shingles were weathered and cracked. An interior stairwell split The Tap building from an adjoining structure on the left that housed a copy shop.

Luck found Seth a parking space out front. He jumped from his Jeep, and his heart jumped with him. He saw it, the same white BMW, again courageously parked in a reserved space situated two buildings to the right. This time, he noted a personalized tag, declaring the sedan was ALLMINE. He looked the pristine coupe over, then ran up the stairs to The Tap. His footsteps made a hollow sound, so he stopped, wondered what was under that stairwell, tapping it with his foot to gauge the emptiness below. He thought a second, then continued up.

Inside, he scanned The Tap's interior. The management allowed students to write on the walls, and, over the decades, they had taken full liberty, using paint, Magic Markers, crayons, and even lipstick. The place was at least twenty-years-old, and scant creative writing space remained. The messages were as varied as the writing instruments, informing one of which fraternities were cool and which weren't, which girls did and which didn't, which professors could drop dead and which could be bribed. Apparently, except Goodfried, every law professor could do the former.

For the place's live music, there was one word: loud. Tonight's band called itself The Lowest Priority. Seth concluded that band practice was just that. The racket made him uneasy. He stood well away from the speakers, yet the noise still pained his sensitive ears.

A smoky haze slow-danced through the air. He panned the room, but failed to locate H.R. and Sue. He did see two pool tables, both in use and both with at least two sets of quarters on the ledge. He also noticed three dartboards, two pinball machines, and a downsized basketball goal where a cute brunette was holding court. The precocious gal sank every shot, taking money from would-be suitors, and reminding Seth of Scarlet O'Hara's opening scene in *Gone With The Wind*. He also saw Lesley Peace, "The Girl-Next-Door." Her eyes met his, then darted away.

The joint's four bartenders and three waitresses worked like firemen to insure nobody remained sober. Seth drank precious little; he didn't have much tolerance for the stuff, and it didn't seem worth the hassle and the wait just to become irrational. As he surveyed the smoky scene, it all felt uncomfortable and childish, the atmosphere, the music, and the women. He didn't see one girl he felt right about. He couldn't discern the beauty, depth, and strength he instinctively sought.

Then someone changed the subject, just by being. She walked right at him from the restroom area, and for once, there was a decent view of her. The smoke, the dim lighting, and the crowd made it a twilight view, but this time, he could see more than a profile. She was simply styled and simply beautiful. Her true blonde hair still shone like a precious metal. She wore a blue jean skirt, and, even in this light, he could see she had the lines to wear it. There was a white, sleeveless, pullover top revealing a perfect Florida tan, a womanly skin shade that perfectly colored those perfect cheekbones. She wore white Keds and white socks.

She glided along as if at home, and, after taking a quick look around, she moved right to a group of three girls chatting at a booth, two of whom Seth knew from law school. The smiling girls exchanged the obligatory hugs and seemed to admire one another's outfits. She sat down and leaned in to speak.

He ignored his vibrating heart and initially ignored the soft tap on his shoulder, but then heard a soft feminine scream over the "music." "What's a pseudo-intellectual like you doing in a place like this?"

He couldn't imagine who knew him well enough to ask, but when he turned, it was Sue. His head tilted, and he saw H.R. hiding behind her. His big grin stretched the limits of his face.

Seth knew he'd been had. "H.R.! You *told her* to say that."

"I'll bet she surprised you when she did!"

"Yeah, she did, coming out of nowhere like that. Oddly enough, I was just asking myself the same question."

"Well, the answer is to meet one terrific woman." H.R. said, as if this Cindi was a vibrant vixen, a woman poised to put some serious loving on him.

Sue waded in, "Oh H.R., she's just a girl. You make it sound like she's Madonna or something."

H.R. tweaked the subject. "Madonna. Now go figure that babe. America's most famous, and most active, floozy." H.R. tilted his head sideways as he injected the aside. "Yet she makes millions singing about virginity."

Seth and H.R. finished it together. "Sometimes, I wonder if she was *ever* a virgin!"

48

All standing within the five-foot hearing range paid the remark a deserved laugh.

H.R. saw Seth's empty right hand. "Hey Seth, let me get you something cold for your empty drinking hand."

Afraid to appear impolite, Seth didn't object. H.R. edged through the crowded bar, ordered three tall boys and left the bartender a five-dollar tip. He didn't like to wait on his brew.

Seth restarted the conversation. "So, where is this friend of yours, Sue? I thought she'd be coming with you."

"She said she'd come on her own, something about having to meet with a few other law students somewhere in this mixture of bad music and bad penmanship."

Seth smiled at Sue. He already liked her sense of humor, a necessity to hang with H.R.

"Listen, you guys stay here by the bar. I'll go look for her. Okay, H.R.?" She was almost screaming at the top of her lungs.

H.R. almost screamed back, "You don't have to ask me twice to wait by a bar."

She gave him a *you are way too much* expression and eased through the crowd.

Seth eased up to H.R. and asked, "Aren't you a little worried she'll meet another guy while she's away? Every decent girl here gets hit on within minutes."

"Not really. She tells me too many things with her eyes. Besides, it wouldn't take long to find a more permanent temporary girlfriend."

"Most of these girls are taken. I wish I had your confidence."

"It's a simple thing, Seth. If you act like you've got it, people think you've got it and respond accordingly. Once they do so, then you've got it for good."

Seth absorbed the interesting pearl of wisdom, breathed deeply out of respect for it, then asked, "You mean you already see Sue as temporary? How do you know she won't last at least a few months?"

"Other than the fact she's a woman and thereby would get on my nerves within two weeks?" he came back light heartedly.

Seth rolled his eyes, an act now a habit around H.R. "Yeah, other than that."

"Well, let's just say." He paused. "Aw, good lord, I can't pinpoint it. It's just something I know. Maybe it's because she loves a good time too much."

Seth responded, "In that case, she sounds perfect for you."

H.R. laughed at himself, and as he did, he saw Sue walking through the crowd with company. H.R. was taller and could see who was with Sue. "Ooh, Seth, you're knee deep in luck. Sue may be cute, but her friend *is gorgeous*."

Seth's head jerked around. "Where?"

H.R. pointed, but Seth still couldn't see the girls. A few more seconds went by. Then, his eyes froze. A rare feeling grabbed him, like someone powerful was looking out for him. He couldn't believe those tanned legs, that shiny hair, those cheekbones. He'd guessed correctly. They looked even better when she smiled.

Sue spoke up. "Seth, I want you to meet my friend, Cindi Vicari. We were in the same sorority, and now she's a third-year."

Cindi extended her hand with perfect control. He touched it, and, as their eyes connected, the pressure felt perfect too. The night before, he dreamed that, when he finally met her, it would be a disappointment. It wasn't.

He mustered his courage and spoke. "I'm Seth. I guess you know I'm a first-year."

50

"Yes. Sue told me. It's nice to finally meet you. Hope the first-year blues aren't getting you guys down."

"H.R., anything getting you down?" Seth asked, a vague reference to Myerson.

"Who, me? The only things gettin' downed around here are these Bud Lights."

Amid mild laughter, they worked their way over to a rare empty booth. Seth watched Cindi walk in front of him. Her curves were impressive from every angle. Plus, she had to be intelligent because she'd made it into law school and through the first year. She had a sense of humor, too, not to mention a zest and confidence Seth had never witnessed, particularly in himself.

Once seated, H.R., ever the perfect facilitator, noticed Cindi needed a drink. "What can I get you from the bar, Cindi? You look thirsty."

"You mean you can tell I'm thirsty just by looking at me?"

"Sure. It's a medical thing. My dad's a doctor, and he taught me there are certain outward indications of thirst."

"For example?"

"When a guy has a fear of commitment in his eye at a bachelor party, he's likely thirsty. When a beautiful girl is situated in a bar and has no drink in her hand, then she must be thirsty."

Cindi thought a second, then said, "Okay, because there's a compliment somewhere in there, and because it's warm in here, I'll have a rum and Coke on the rocks. Just don't make it with that New Coke."

Everyone but Seth simultaneously twisted their faces and went "Oooh."

Seth was busy soaking in Cindi's presence. She was so perfect, yet so down to earth. He asked himself if this could get any better.

Then H.R. had to bring up murder. "I guess you ladies heard about Rentzell and Hays."

Sue nodded, but Cindi responded, "What do you mean?"

H.R. continued. "They found them both dead today, inside a warehouse near the railroad tracks. They had been at the Sidetrack, but somehow wound up shot to death."

"It happened last night?"

Seth noted the expression on Cindi's face. He noted true surprise, but of a variety somehow misplaced, as if she was surprised at the wrong thing.

H.R. answered her question. "Actually, it happened a few nights ago. They just now found them."

Cindi appeared to gather herself, then Sue seemingly changed the subject. "Cindi, how's your mother?"

"Well, it's been a year, and I think she's finally back to normal. They say it can take longer for some women, so she's doing well, under the circumstances."

Seth was in the dark. "Was your mother in an accident?"

"No, it's my father. He was murdered last year."

Seth felt stupid, horrible. He mentally kicked himself as his face went flush. "Oh. Sorry. Are you okay talking about it?"

She went on. "I guess so. Talking sometimes makes me feel better."

H.R. observed, "Man. My whole life, I've never known anyone who was murdered or anyone who did. Now I'm faced with three in the same day."

Seth shook his head, then, as H.R. and Sue visited the restroom, he ventured in gradually, and considerately, and, of course, nervously. He and Cindi talked a few more minutes, with her being graciously open and Seth being graciously understanding: of her beauty, her brains, and her manner. The smoke, the noise and the crowd weren't there anymore. He saw and heard nothing but her and her attributes.

H.R. returned with three longneck beers in one hand and Cindi's rum and real Coke in the other. After ten more minutes of small talk, the drinks were history.

Seth was beginning to resemble an obedient puppy. H.R. had no choice but to change the subject. "Hey, guys, how about some *free* booze? I hear there's a great keg party somewhere tonight."

"It's at the Kit-Kat House," Cindi said. "It's not too far from here. Let's go in my car."

They weaved through the crowd toward the stairs.

♦

Lesley left her table of friends and followed them, her eyes full of determination, broken-heartedness, and a sudden dislike for blondes.

♦

The newly formed fab-four headed down the inner stairwell.

Seth asked, "Yall ever wonder what's under a stairway like this one? I mean, um, you can tell it's hollow under there."

H.R. smiled. "You ever wondered whether you have one strange imagination?"

Seth stopped in the middle of the stairwell so he could blush and shrug. Everyone laughed.

CHAPTER TEN

They arrived at the Kit-Kat House. The party had hit its stride. The place was in an older area of Tuscaloosa between the law school and the main campus. The small wood frame had a big front porch, a great place for a keg, the same place where ten people stood with empty plastic cups. Seth smiled: They resembled baby birds waiting to be fed.

Seth gazed a bit more. Cindi seemed to know everyone. Girls approached her for the sorority girl hug routine. Seth liked how she went through this girlish rite with more authority than the other girls, and how they responded to her. She seemed to join the ritual because it was expected, and because to refrain would be to risk hurt feelings or reduced popularity.

H.R. interrupted. "Hey, Seth. Stop snoozing. This ain't a wake. Then again, with two students dead, maybe it is, but, hey, in my book, wakes are about forgetting."

H.R. spoke directly into his ear. The music was too loud for Seth, though the possibility of neighbors phoning the police limited the volume to that of a mild thunderstorm.

"Oh, sorry. Guess I was daydreaming."

"You do too much daydreaming at nighttime, you know. You might miss something that's actually transpiring." H.R. pointed to his right. "Take that sultry, calculated babe over in the corner. She's definitely transpiring!" A girl with a head of long, permed, dark hair was swaying in the corner, looking to Seth like she was fishing for attention. H.R. added, "Now that, my friend Seth, could rule the world."

Seth tried to suppress a laugh, but he felt better when he couldn't. "I suppose she could rule the world of most men, at least for a night or two."

"Yeah, and once she ruled it for two nights, she could rule it forever!"

"Think so?"

"Uh-huh, and, if she could do that, she and a few girlfriends could rule all of us."

"You know, H.R., I never thought of women as being so powerful. It's interesting when some of your more outlandish suppositions seem to have some warped grain of truth in them."

"Maybe they aren't as outlandish as you might surmise, my overeducated friend."

"What's *that* supposed to mean?"

"Just be sure to allow yourself a little life outside the printed page. You'll see."

While Seth's face was busy contorting itself, Sue and Cindi joined a crowd gathered inside around Professor Goodfried, who was at yet another student party.

Seth peered at him, the only teacher who taught two sections of two first-year classes. The professor had enough tenure to decline the load, but he seemed to embrace it out of a love for the students. Seth focused on him. Barry Goodfried, the counselor to the troubled law student, actually kept reverse office hours: There were only certain brief time periods when he *wasn't* available. Sometimes, the female students affectionately referred to him as "Good-Freud."

Intrigued, Seth stuck his head in the door. Goodfried reclined on a couch. Students stood and sat all around him, firing questions and comments at him about Rentzell and Hays. Seth gleaned the competing moods. There was disbelief--"This kind of thing just doesn't happen here, Professor", fear--

"Could it be a serial killer who has it out for law students?" and shock--"I only know I need another drink."

Sue fell into the shocked category. She walked toward Seth, who still stood at the door. "Everyone's asking Goodfried about the murders," she said. "Murder makes me nervous, and I'm losing my face buzz. Where's that keg?"

"I hear it's a great tasting foreign brew," Cindi added.

"If it's free, then it can't taste too bad," H.R. reasoned.

They made their way to the porch in a single-file line. Sue led the way. As they reached the door, two third-year guys ambled toward them. Seth recognized them from the Legal Beagles. They were big, slow, and boorish. They approached the door heading in, just as Sue walked out. They didn't stop and let her pass; they barged ahead like self-important barbarians. The lead oaf wore a black beard and a black shirt boasting of his attendance at a Hank Williams, Jr. concert. Sue looked over her shoulder because H.R. looked over his at the private dancer still swaying away.

The missing link took a slug of beer from an oversized bottle. One second later, he collided with Sue. Beer sloshed everywhere, some on the floor, some on Sue, and a lot on Hank, Jr.

He swallowed what sloshed in his mouth and asked, "Hey dumb blonde, what's your problem?"

Sue stood there drenched and stunned. She wasn't tipsy enough to laugh. Finally, she saw the ounce of Hell in the big guy's eyes and mustered an instinctive apology. "I'm sorry. I guess I wasn't looking where I was going."

"No joke, dingbat. Now who's gonna' get me a clean shirt? You gonna' launder this one while I wait?" He poked her just above her breasts. The beer dripped down his beard and sprayed out his mouth.

H.R. attempted diplomacy. "Look, this ain't a big deal."

56

"I'm sure it's not to you. You're not the one this klutzy bimbo just tripped into."

"Well, whatever she did, she obviously didn't mean it. She wouldn't intentionally make an enemy out of a guy like you."

"What do you mean, a guy like me?"

"Nothing. Here." H.R. opened his wallet. It was full of cash. H.R. took out a twenty and held it out toward the guy. "This really ain't worth arguing about. Why don't you just take this, then I'll get you another beer, and we'll all be happy."

The guy took the twenty, then as H.R. was about to walk past him, he said, "Hey, rich boy, see if it's a big deal now." He splashed beer in H.R.'s face with his right hand then took a wild swing with his left.

Giving H.R. a warning was a mistake. He leaned backwards and slipped the punch. The jerk followed through, hit Sue in the right shoulder blade, knocked her and her head against the house. H.R. retaliated. He hit the slob five times in the head, a full measure of drum music on a skull. His boorish brother joined in and caught H.R. a good one on the forehead and backed him up a pace. He seemed focused on H.R.'s reaction, another mistake.

Seth had never been in a real fight. With no time to think or fear, he forgot to do both. His football instincts seized him. He dived into the brother's beer gut and drove him into the porch railing. The rail cracked, splintering into his back. The redneck yelped. Seth drove through him. The rail broke. Seth kept driving, right into a holly bush below. His target screamed; Seth rolled away.

Frightened he'd killed the guy, Seth mumbled, "I'm sorry". Surprised at his own aggressiveness, Seth looked at H.R. Their eyes switched to the lead brute, now somehow sprawled flat on the porch, blood matted in the back of his bushy head. H.R.

and Seth looked at each other again. It made no sense. H.R. had only hit him in the face.

Their focus moved to a feminine hand. It held a small wooden lamp. The unplugged cord dangled on the floor. They stared wide-eyed. Cindi looked down at the big guy on the floor. Lying in a puddle of beer, he began to stir, writhing a bit at the extremities. Seth watched Goodfried examine the situation and give his head a little shake of disbelief, or disappointment, certainly not of disinterest.

Cindi shrugged the slightest shrug, the corners of her mouth bent downward. "Maybe I shouldn't have hit him so hard, but he was about to hit H.R. again. You'd think nothing could hurt him, and this lamp was sitting atop this end table, so I just, just, um-"

"Clocked him a good one?" H.R. helped her out a little, as that big smile began to trek across his face. "Heckuva blow for a beauty queen."

"Well, I didn't hit him too hard. It probably barely broke the skin."

"Probably." H.R. said, still smiling.

Thoughts of assault and battery from Criminal Law were running through Seth's mind. Because the troglodyte had been the aggressor, however, he wouldn't look too good in court as the victim of a girl.

Cindi stood poised with the lamp, looking to Seth as if she could use it again. The guy Seth tackled gathered himself, reached down to assist his buddy, who was showing weak signs of existence. He was on his knees. He grimaced, rubbing the blood on the back of his head.

The crowd had become still and quiet, but no one had thought to turn off the music. Duran Duran's *Hungry Like A Wolf* played in the background. Several students peeked around Cindi, who still stood at the door gripping that lamp. Others looked out the front windows toward the porch. Those on the porch stared at Cindi with an apparent drunken awe.

H.R.'s sparring mate murmured, "My aching head. What kind of truck was that?" Judging by his tone, he'd been here before.

His buddy said, "Come on, Scott. Looks like we lost this one. Get on up, and we'll get the hell outuv here."

H.R. approached the Brutus twins and extended a hand, "Nothing personal, guys. Look, we're all on the Legal Beagles team together, and I don't want any hard feelings."

"None taken," Skeeter said with a moan. "Man, you guys fight like you do it all the time."

"Well, you just had the misfortune of running into a couple of ex-jocks. Seth and I both played college football, me at Texas and Seth right here. If ole Sethster hadn't blown out a knee his Sophomore year, he'd be in the NFL and already a household name."

"No kidding," Scott added.

Seth shook his head in denial, knowing it was H.R. who merited the flattery. "Thanks, H.R., but I think you're overdoing it."

"I dunno," Skeeter managed to say. "That broken railing is saying he ain't."

H.R. then checked on Sue. She'd be sore the next day, but she didn't need an ambulance.

◆

Lesley Peace watched from a distance. She was falling more for Seth with every bashful move he made, even when the move involved inadvertent property damage.

◆

Lisa Golson, one of the Kit-Kat House tenants, made her way out the front door. She spoke like a true veteran of parties interrupted. "Alright, everyone. The show's over. Just relax. I see no actionable injuries, and it ain't a party till someone hits the floor." The crowd obeyed. "Someone grab a mop and we'll crank this thing up again."

As the crowd dispersed and the noise level returned to ninety decibels, she placed her hands on her hips and turned to the two troublemakers. "You two again? When are you going to learn to party like adults? Look, if you come over here, you're going to have to at least *act* like you're civilized."

The first guy was off the floor now, looking like a whipped puppy. "Sorry, Sis. I guess we had a few earlier and were a bit worked up already."

His cohort added, "Yeah, Lisa, didn't mean no harm. You know how it is when you're feeling a little pumped."

"Well, next time you two are feeling pumped with testosterone, go pump some iron, but stop making a mess of my parties. If you can't even show up sober, then don't show up at all."

The two defeated pugilists repeated their apologies and drug their humbled selves off the porch.

Lisa brought a glass of hunch punch to Sue, who took two gulps of the pink, intuitive concoction.

"Easy on that stuff," H.R. warned. "It could power a space shuttle."

Lisa intoned, "He's right. It's potent, and I added a little extra splash of vodka to hers for-"

"Medicinal purposes," everyone said together, right before they laughed away a little tension.

Seth asked Lisa, "Did one of those guys refer to you as Sis?"

"Yes. My poor misguided twin brothers, Scott and Skeeter. I was hoping law school would grow them up, but over two years later, no such luck. How they passed their first year is beyond me."

"You never know. They might make great criminal defense lawyers someday," H.R. said, trying to give her some hope.

Lisa's eyes brightened. "Yeah, they could make a good living keeping each other out of jail."

They all laughed, then decided to call it a night. Cindi was sober enough to drive back to The Tap. No one else was. Unaccustomed to alcohol, Seth had consumed four beers. He felt he was in a trance. They walked to the BMW. Sue and H.R. climbed into the back. Seth and Cindi glanced back at the two lovebirds, then at each other.

CHAPTER ELEVEN

It was almost midnight when they dropped off H.R. and Sue. H.R. swore he was able to drive. Sue kept the ice pack to her head.

Cindi drove to Seth's Jeep. Seth noted a hint of little girl in her voice. "That whole thing with that Scott guy shook me up a little. Would you mind if we went for coffee before you go home?"

Seth remembered Contracts was at nine a.m. "I'd like to, but it's just getting so late."

"Please. It won't take long. There's a little place near my apartment and not far from here. They have great breakfast."

The usual empathy immersed Seth's being. "Well-"

"It'd really make me feel better. I need to relax a minute, clear my head."

Seth wanted her to know he was worried about her. "Okay, but just for a few minutes. I'm a little hungry." Seth's metabolic rate was off the chart.

"It's the booze," she said. "Alcohol stimulates the appetite."

"For me, just existing stimulates the appetite."

"Me, too. Let's bolt!" she said.

She drove with a lot of conviction, he noted, same as when she'd left the faculty parking lot. When they arrived, she whipped into the last space out front, just before another car could reach it. She looked at him, the smile of parking success on her face. She opened the door for him and marched in, her eyes straight ahead, her enthusiasm still intact. Seth guessed she must really like the restaurant. Inside, the New Orleans atmosphere enveloped him. The smooth jazz music within was almost indistinguishable. Seth noted every note. The lights were low. Seth had trouble seeing through the booze.

Acting as her own hostess, Cindi seated them against the back wall. When a waiter arrived, Seth ordered a pecan waffle, link sausage, and a decaf. Cindi ordered a three-egg cheese omelet, grits, and a cappuccino.

"I didn't get the decaf because I'll stay up 'till two, either reading *Cosmo* or watching Showtime. I don't have class until a seminar at ten. I'm a night person, anyway."

The conversation continued and was as fluid and natural as any Seth had known. The forced and uneasy feeling he'd grown to expect on dates was less apparent. They compared childhood notes about Christmas mornings and family housekeepers.

When the waiter returned with their orders, Cindi whispered something in the guy's ear. He returned with a pint bottle produced from an apron pocket and poured a generous shot of Irish whiskey in her cappuccino and, without asking, did the same for Seth's decaf. Seth knew he'd had enough to drink but didn't wish to complicate the mood by declining. He decided he'd sip it slowly and hope the waffle absorbed the effect.

Cindi looked at him with the slyest of smiles. "Lance here is my buddy. He takes care of me. A little something extra in your coffee will make it taste better and help you sleep." Seth the born insomniac wasn't going to object to any form of sleep assistance.

They continued to talk. Cindi did most of it, but Seth never noticed. She could discuss any subject, and, with her tone, mannerisms, and knowledge of human nature, she could make it enjoyable. "My mom sure seems to do more shopping in

Birmingham since daddy passed on. I don't know if it's because shopping is effective grief therapy or because dad's not here to audit the credit card bills. Maybe it's a little of both."

Then, "I wish I was at the beach instead of here. Oops. I didn't mean I wish I was away from you. I only wish we were having this great time in Florida. We've got this house mom bought with the insurance proceeds at a place called Seaside. It's so quaintly classy." After wondering why she was with him, Seth knew Seaside was the newest, most exclusive beach community in northwest Florida. "Dad was such a good-hearted, responsible person. I just wish he were here to enjoy the results of his planning. I guess that's the problem with life insurance. Someone's gotta die for you to get it." She shrugged and smiled with nonchalance.

Though she filled the air with lively discourse, she finished her meal in record time, seemed to savor the omelet. The alcohol blunted Seth's usual incisive focus, but he was still struck that Cindi was different. When he considered why, she'd distract him with a wink or a cute smile. Or, he'd just look at her and her perfect face: that was enough.

She grabbed the check, paid it, and left a large tip for Lance. Courtesy of the Irish whiskey, Seth knew he shouldn't drive home, and if Cindi took him home, he'd have to explain why his car wasn't in its usual space at Number 11. Cindi interrupted his dilemma.

"Seth, you look tired. Like I said before, I live nearby. Why don't you stay on my couch? First thing in the morning, you can call a cab to take you to your car. You'll be in before the Chancellor ever knows you were gone."

Seth rubbed his eyes. He didn't have many options. He hesitated. His parents, and probably the Chancellor, wouldn't like it if they knew he'd slept at a girl's apartment. On the other hand, she was a good girl from a good Montgomery family.

Besides, she lived nearby, and he was exhausted. His tired body won; it didn't want to wait another minute to collapse.

"Okay, sounds good."

"I have a big queen-sized foldout and some Egyptian cotton sheets that are *so comfy*."

It sounded enticing. His body yearned to melt into those sheets and escape.

She lived in a new condominium development with a peach colored stucco exterior. It was the first of its kind at the University. Well-heeled parents would buy them, then, when their last child graduated, they'd sell them at a profit. She drove through a security gate that sealed off the basement parking area. He followed her to an elevator and noticed a curious look on her face as she stared straight ahead and clipped along.

On the elevator, she explained that she lived on the top floor. "It's an okay view from up there. You can see the law school lights and even see Bryant-Denny Stadium. I love how they decided to name the field after Coach Bryant, don't you? He was such a nice, grandfatherly man."

Seth laughed a little to himself. Bryant had to be the toughest coach to ever field a team. "Well, yeah. I guess he could be a big old teddy bear at times."

"I heard you played a few years."

"Really?"

"I think I just overheard it, maybe in the Coffee Room."

"I guess you could overhear about anything in there."

"Yeah. An aspiring law student with open ears might learn some *highly useful* information there."

Seth half-drunkenly wondered what she meant. They entered the hallway, carpeted in crimson, and made a short walk to her door. She gained entry with a computerized card and opened the door to a high ceiling with washed pine beams.

There was a large fireplace to the right and a big Sony in the right corner. It looked like a decorator's showcase.

"My decorator is gay. He's funky, but he's a natural." She walked toward the back and said, "I'll get your sheets, then I'm going to take a bath. I love a bubble bath at night." She returned shortly with an armload and dumped it into his lap. "Here's your stuff. I have a new toothbrush you can use. It's back in the other bath. Help yourself."

She clipped down the hallway. He busied himself moving the heavy marble coffee table and making his bed. He heard bath water running, then heard it stop. He needed to whiz. He walked down the hallway in only loose white boxers, his faculties still well intoxicated, his mind in need of a tune up. He stopped a second, counted four doors. He guessed the first two doors opened to baths and the last at the end were a bedroom and an office. He saw a light on under the first door to the left; it must be the master bath where Cindi was. He turned the knob on the opposite room's door and stepped in.

His heart surged. His eyes widened. Her uncovered back was to him. She wore nothing but her whites, and they fell across her bottom like supernatural cloth. There was only one large candle on each side of the tub, but her form was unmistakable before the glistening mound of bubbles, so rounded where it was meant to be, and so sculptured everywhere else. The legs and arms were long and toned, the proportions perfect. Her fine golden hair flowed to her shoulders, seeming so free.

Time began its escape. Her turn was slow, un-reflexive. She covered her upper self with her left arm. Her eyes glowed in the candlelight and said something Seth had never heard. He responded involuntarily, seemingly detached from his conscience. A deep, quiet breath swelled her chest.

He took in air quickly, more noticeably. "I chose the door with no light under it."

"I like candles."

"They glow."

His voice became weaker and hers softer, but he didn't notice. A pulling sensation co-opted his senses. It held him in place, then tugged at him.

Her left arm eased down. His chest heaved once. She sat upon the edge of the raised tub, took her right hand, and slid it into the water, gripping his glance. She let her arm sway gently, dragging it back, caressing the water, the sound caressing his ears. She turned, gently brushed her bangs away. Her eyes pulled at him. Hiding his shaking right hand behind his back, he took one small step forward, and she placed her right leg into the water. He moved again, and she'd slipped beneath the cover of the glistening white foam. Her eyes rested on his face until he was totally immersed, her wet everything against him.

He gasped as he sensed her clutching him like a child alarmed, with arms reaching under his, clinching the tops of his shoulders, pinning him. He sensed the soft cushion of her between them. He felt strange being there, but he wanted her to feel safe and wanted. The bubbles clung and swayed atop the water as they clung and kissed. She rolled over him. The bubbles moved. A blink revealed the contrast of her taut shoulders and soft orbs. Another showed skin that glowed like a setting sun. A wealth of sensations conveyed rapidly all along his torso and limbs, seeping into every crevice of his being, into places he'd never sensed. Seth was overwhelmed.

Now he rested his back against the tub and cuddled her in front of him. He stared at the red-tiled walls and thought past the alcohol. The uneasy, alienating feeling came, then left again. Then it sneaked back, but this time, seemed different as if he wasn't just alone, but alone on the hot sands of a desert.

She whispered to him. The feeling faded with each word.

CHAPTER TWELVE

He arose early from Cindi's bed. He felt guilty, unworthy, and more generally uneasy than ever. He left Cindi still asleep. A taxi dropped him at the Jeep around 7:00, and, by 7:30, he'd shaved, showered, and delivered himself to the big Number 11 kitchen.

François was whipping up his famous French Toast Charlemagne. Livened with at least two liqueurs, it was named for the Chancellor's cat. The regal male feline was under a table drinking the leftover mixture.

"Charlemagne the great!" declared François. "King of the Franks and master of Pinehurst. *Eat hearty*, and strengthen your mighty frame for battle."

François looked Seth over and frowned. "Young Seth, I see shades of red dashed amid the whites of your young eyes. No doubt, a night of revelry preceded your waking!"

François proceeded to fashion a family hangover remedy brought over from the "old country": Pepto-Bismol mixed with Alka-Seltzer, orange juice and a multi-vitamin, then chasers of coffee a latte' and Visine.

He looked Seth over and seemed pleased with the results. "Now, take two French toasts with you for the trip over. They'll give you energy to survive the day."

François put them in a paper towel. Seth thanked him and left through the Number 11 office.

François called from the door, "Young Seth."

Seth turned. François perused him as if a poisonous spider was crawling up his shirt. "Yes, I thought I saw it."

"Saw what?" Seth inquired with complete self-awareness, moving toward his car.

François laughed and followed him, stopping at the stoop. "You have rendezvoused, have you not?"

"What?" The response was tossed over an escaping shoulder.

The chef spoke with a knowing, yet congratulatory tone. "She of the high cheekbones. You have met her, and her bones have made close contact with yours. No wonder your spirits have rapidly recovered from those of The Nasty Tap! And what of this slightly more mature visage? You must be living well to have deserved your dream girl."

Seth's red cheeks looked away, and he shook his head at the Frenchman's keen perception. He hoped his classmates weren't so perceptive. He looked at the floorboard, considered how he'd been living, and how she was above him, then doubted he deserved her.

CHAPTER THIRTEEN

Seth blinked, and it was November 30, 1985. The last days of summer had secretly blended into the first days of fall. Then, his October evaporated into the thin air of one job, one law school, one Cindi, and two murders. Time to ponder what was wrong with him and his life had been scarce.

His incurable soul sickness still weighed him down. Maybe the great escape of football would help. In Alabama, football had a welcome way of stealing the agenda. A good football game could make any problem disappear.

And, when Alabama met Auburn in football, a special feeling overtook Seth's soul, a feeling borne of history, love, and faith. Seth woke up to it, took it in--the anticipation, the memories of a coach who'd been a second father, the hope of victory, a hope Seth often tainted with the fear of losing. His thoughts of Cindi trumped it all. He reveled in the notion of her pending presence, his greatest escape of all over the great wall of law school.

H.R. at the wheel, Seth rode the feelings all morning, all the way up Interstate 59 to Birmingham. The girls had stayed there Friday night after some post-Thanksgiving shopping at Brookwood Mall.

Seth had more serious things on his mind. "H.R., have you heard anything new about Rentzell and Hays?"

"Yeah. Two baggies of cocaine were found in the attic of their little campus rental house."

"Huh? What have the cops said?"

"They're not saying there was a necessary connection. They're not saying anything at all, but that's not gonna' stop every wanna-be lawyer at school from speculating as much."

"What do *you* think?"

"I asked around, found out their parents will have the bodies exhumed for drug testing. What does *that* tell you?"

"Tells me this is serious business."

"Yeah, I've heard murder can get that way."

They drove on, but said little else before arrival. Soon, they stood with their gals in a long line outside the stadium, fifty feet from the elevator that would deliver them to the President's Box, for which Seth had secured last-minute tickets from the Chancellor. They chatted, trying not to appear as if they didn't belong.

H.R. motioned toward the statuesque man in front of them and whispered, "Isn't he Hound Dog Hampton, the big time plaintiff's lawyer who used to be attorney general?"

Seth nodded. He didn't much like plaintiff's attorneys, but there was a casual confidence about Hampton that he appreciated.

Seth could overhear an apparent non-lawyer telling Hampton a lawyer joke, the stale, ancient one about lawyers, sharks, and professional courtesy. He observed that Hampton was humoring the humorist.

The punch line thankfully over, Hampton replied, "You know, there's a funny thing about lawyer jokes: Lawyers don't think they're funny, and no one else thinks they're jokes."

Seth smiled and marshaled the courage to speak. "You're Mr. Harry Hampton, aren't you?"

"Indeed, I am. It's a pleasure to meet you, Mr.-?" Hampton extended Seth a hand.

"I'm no Mr.; I'm Seth Sentel, a law student at Alabama, as are my friends here: Cindi, H.R., and Susan."

Once H.R. had removed his eyes from the gorgeous woman in front of Mr. Hampton, who might have been a daughter, H.R. said, "You may not believe this, sir, but I see you every day without your even knowing it."

Hound Dog appeared pleasantly puzzled. "And how exactly is that?"

"Your class composite hangs on the wall facing my cubicle. The class of 1961."

"Is that so? It's amazing you recognize me. My appearance has likely changed since those days of academic grief and weekend revelry."

Seth mustered some social courage and observed, "Even so, you appear much wiser for any wear there may, or may not, have been."

"Thank you, young counselor. Apparently, you've already graduated from diplomacy school." Everyone smiled. "If you'd like to compliment someone who actually deserves it, meet my wife Lacey." Lacey Hampton, who could've passed for twenty-four with her long, blonde hair and long, tanned legs, had been speaking with the couple in front of her. "Lacey, these artful young law students are Seth and H.R., and these are their friends, Cindi and Susan."

Lacey's accent belied how she'd spent most of her life in East Coast private schools, but her words hinted no arrogance. "It's a pleasure. How long have you known my new husband?"

Sue answered, "We just met in this long line, but we feel like we've known him for years."

Lacey nodded. "He's so friendly they should have nicknamed him Stray Dog!"

A good laugh, then they continued to converse until they reached the elevator. Hound Dog handed out business cards and encouraged them to call if he could be of assistance.

Inside the President's Box, they discovered a buffet fit for a thousand benefactors. They dined on prime rib, chicken breast filets in light cream sauce, yellow rice with slivered almonds, and sautéed vegetables. Priester's pecan pie and soft-serve frozen yogurt were available for dessert.

An open bar was operating off to one side. Seth stepped up and recognized the bartender. "François!"

The Frenchman flashed an enormous grin. "Hmm, I see that Monsieur Seth is in heaven today."

Seth smiled, his voice too polite. "If this is heaven, then what are *you* doing here?"

François tilted his head up and remarked, "Ah, my student-assistant friend is sharp today, but to answer, I'm saving for a new Motobecane racing bike; thus I toil on a Saturday."

After François asked Seth to taste the cream sauce for balance, Seth introduced the infamous chef to his friends. François mixed Old Forester with cola and ventured a guess, "You must be the lovely mademoiselle Cindi. Young Seth does not exaggerate your *beaute'*." Cindi seemed flattered. "Well, thank you. He also raves about the wondrous things you do with seafood."

"Flattery will get you a free cooking lesson!"

As Seth relayed beverages, and Cindi, Susan and H.R. turned to leave, François whispered to Seth, "A mademoiselle of the highest order, *mon jeune ami*." Seth smiled, an innocent pride swelling in his young eyes.

The young lawyers-to-be sat in cushioned cinema chairs on the bottom row. Seth leaned back and drank in the atmosphere. The temperature was mild, so the box windows were open to invite the crisp fresh air and the ambience of the crowd. The University's band struck up the fight song and brought half of 74,000 people to its feet. Spirits ran high, and it promised to be a competitive contest. Auburn featured a particularly adroit running back named Bo Jackson, and Alabama had an undersized, left-handed quarterback named Mike Shula. Normally, Seth didn't trust southpaws, but he knew Shula personally, knew he was cool, knew he was smart.

Cindi nudged Seth. He shook his head and said, "Oh, I'm sorry. I was just a little lost in the atmosphere."

She moved closer, cut her eyes at his, and baby-talked. "Alright, just don't forget that the rest of us are part of it." Within minutes, she and Sue, who were seated between the two guys, were off and running on a female talking spree. They only broke for the national anthem, and, ten minutes later, they were still covering the full array of Southern-girl conversation topics: shopping, beach trips, debutante balls.

After the kickoff, they discussed the wardrobes of various law professors, then Cindi raised the issue of which male professors were attractive. H.R. leaned back and looked at Seth behind the two girls, then with comic hopelessness at the ceiling. Seth smiled and focused on the game. Bo Jackson tried the left side, but he ran into an Alabama linebacker named Cornelius Bennett. The crimson crowd went wild.

After the teams exchanged punts, Seth discerned a change in Sue's tone of voice. "I feel as if I'm doomed once finals begin. I study so hard, but I never feel like I'm keeping up. Sometimes, I just don't think I'm getting it."

H.R. reached over and gently touched her right shoulder. "Don't worry about it, Sue'ster. I won't allow you to miss five more semesters of highly fulfilling social life. I'll not only help you study, but also provide the needed comic relief."

Seth observed, "That's a nice thought, H.R."

"Plus, what I can't handle, we'll delegate to our friend Seth the legal prodigy, not to mention Cindi here, who came through her first year of prison with a 3.5 average."

Sue still resembled a deer in the headlights. Cindi tried next. "He's right, Susan, and to be exact, it was a 3.6, so don't worry. Like I said before, I'll help you get through this year." Sue exhaled. Cindi looked at her, spoke at her. "If you'll just trust me, you'll have nothing to worry about." Cindi's words grew softer. "You're going to be fine." Sue managed a weak glance into Cindi's eyes, the way a three-year-old looks at her mother. Cindi's glance held firm. Sue nodded one notch up and one down, then leaned back in her chair, tried to watch the game.

Seth rose and offered to refill everyone's drink. Cindi volunteered to help.

They walked up the carpeted steps, and Seth whispered in her ear. "What was the last comment about?" Behind them, Bo Jackson was stopped again for no gain, and the crowd noise covered their voices.

Cindi responded without looking at him. "Oh, just an attempt at assurance. If I can make her believe I can help her, then maybe I can."

"I hope you're right. Sue may not have a graduate level mind, but she certainly has a graduate level attitude."

"There's more to law school than raw brain power. If you really *want* good grades, you can *get* them."

A few good drinks and a little good football later, the half-time score was Alabama 16, Auburn 10. The foursome made their way to the private restrooms. Naturally, the girls waited in line while the guys entered, finished up, then waited outside. Sue emerged in a much better mood. She walked straight to H.R. and planted a big kiss on him.

H.R.'s eyebrows bobbed. "Wow, Miss Sue! What was *that* for?"

"Just for being you."

"In that case, I'll make a point to be me more often."

"When we win this game, I'll suffocate you with kisses."

"In that case, Go Bama! Beat the Aubs!"

They were walking toward the dessert table when Seth saw a familiar face at the other end of the large room. "Look, there's Professor Goodfried."

H.R. added, "Who's that babe with him?" Sue punched him gently. "I mean, who's that homely girl with him?"

Seth saw Cindi's eyes turn and lock on Goodfried's companion. "I'm not sure, H.R., but I think she's an Alabama law school grad. Now, she practices with a big Atlanta firm."

Seth was curious. "How do you know about her?"

Cindi waited a moment, and Seth saw the tight focus in her eyes.

"She was in my sorority, but at Auburn. I saw her photograph in a sorority publication. Anyway, she's much better looking than Goodfried deserves."

Sue's new bliss remained. She smiled and said, "Maybe, but he makes up for it by being so considerate. I wish all the professors were as nice."

Goodfried spied them, waved them over, and said, "It's good to see you students aren't always suffering under the iron hand of the law."

Seth replied, "Well, Professor, it's only a diversion, but at least it's a pleasant one."

"Please, Mr. Sentel, call me Barry."

"Excuse me?"

"Not to worry. Speaking of names, this is my friend Heather Anders. She graduated from the law school three years ago and now practices in Atlanta. Heather, these are four current students: Seth, Cindi, H.R., and Susan."

Seth looked at Cindi. Her guess about Heather had been right. Cindi shrugged.

H.R. couldn't help himself. "Nice to meet you, Heather. Any chance you might advise us neophytes on how to survive our first year?"

"It's not so bad. Just don't make it more difficult than it is, and if you're attending this game instead of studying, you may be on your way."

H.R. opined, "We may just be seeking a diversion from an acute lack of confidence." H.R. smiled big, and everyone laughed but Sue. Seth saw her weak smile and how Goodfried noticed it. He could see the sympathy in the teacher's eyes. Seth looked over at Sue, but Goodfried's gaze had moved to Cindi. Seth saw his eyes twitch once.

H.R. risked a follow-up question. "So, Heather, what's life like at a big Atlanta firm?"

"It's like hard work, and a lot of it, but the money is more than I could ever hope for."

H.R. inquired nicely, "I wonder what the salary range is with Atlanta firms?"

Heather tried to sound helpful. "It probably falls within the decade in which you were born. There are also some fringe benefits. The firm flew me over here because a big Birmingham client invited me and a guest to a nice pre-game party."

There was a curt playfulness to Cindi's response. "It's a good thing it was a pre-game party. You Auburn graduates may not be in the mood to celebrate afterwards."

"Well, it's not over until it's over."

That was a good line for an exit. The teams took the field for the second half. The foursome left for their seats, then Goodfried softly called Seth over. "That was unfortunate about the finding at Rentzell and Hays's home. I mean, I suppose you heard."

Seth's face wheeled around to meet Goodfried's. He gathered himself and replied, "Yes, I heard." He hesitated. "It is unfortunate, *I guess*."

Goodfried shrugged. "I suppose the evidence is difficult to argue with, but perhaps it means nothing. What do you think?"

"I've heard they weren't the type."

"Maybe yes, maybe no. Maybe it belonged to the tenant before them."

Seth nodded and walked away wondering why Goodfried had spoken with him alone about it and why he'd wanted Seth's take on the matter. He felt as if he was in the professor's confidence now, a good feeling, but for a Seth, an out-of-place one.

Seth caught up with Cindi and asked, "Wasn't that Auburn comment a little dicey?"

"I didn't like how she talked down to H.R."

"I didn't catch that."

"Besides, she was a bit enamored with herself with that talk of salaries in the sixties and big Birmingham clients. She could've gloated less conspicuously."

Seth shrugged. "Maybe so."

The second half football action was too intense to allow much socializing. Auburn's Bo Jackson was now doing what he did best--gradually obliterating an opposing defense. Auburn drove the ball methodically down Alabama's throat, and about ten plays later, scored their second touchdown of the half. Alabama was forced to counter with finesse. Shula pitched the ball to a little tailback named Gene Jelks, who sprinted to his right. Seth yelled for him to cut left. A half second later, Jelks cut left, then scored on a beautiful open-field 74-yard run. Seth smiled deeply. His friends examined him, awe in their eyes. He looked away.

Auburn's long drive had consumed about seven minutes. Jelks's imaginative gallop had taken about seven seconds. Nonetheless, Bo Jackson's one-man demolition derby wasn't finished as Auburn responded with another punishing scoring drive. With time scarce, Auburn held a one-point lead. Seth sensed vibrations in the air as the Auburn faithful went bonkers.

For Alabama and little Mike Shula, there were only 57 seconds, and one time-out to delay their expiration. Soon, there were just 37 seconds, and the time-out was spent. Two plays later, Alabama was only at midfield. With fifteen seconds left, Shula scrambled for survival and somehow found a receiver, who somehow dragged a defender out of bounds at the Auburn 35-yard line. Only six tiny seconds remained, just enough time for a big attempt by a tiny kicker named Van Tiffen. An odd thought struck Seth: Tiffen stood only five-feet-seven-inches tall, but the happiness of an entire state's populace rested on whether his tiny foot was true, or false.

The kicking team scrambled onto the field and set itself. The snap was good; the hold was good, and somehow Tiffen's tiny foot propelled the kick into the air. Instantly, Seth heard true silence in the arena. The ball floated amid the glow of silver Southern lights, drawing the crowd inward as it tumbled. Seth extrapolated the kick's trajectory and knew it would be good, but some strange sensation suggested something else wasn't. It was that same mental virus, dogging him, even on the weekend. He sensed the discomfort, then shook it off, blamed it on the Old Forrester.

The ball passed over the horizontal crossbar. With a haste rarely witnessed on earth, 37,000 Alabama fans shifted mode, from still to pandemonium. An inexplicable energy hurled crimson voices and bodies upward and toward the field. Half of the arena became a human hurricane, squalling around in waves of crimson and white.

Seth didn't jump or cheer. Instead, he watched everyone screaming and saw Sue smothering H.R. with kisses. His glance was tugged toward Goodfried and his date. Goodfried pointed a playful finger at Heather, but the good professor's eyes almost seemed to be returning from Seth's direction.

Seth knew a great football game had ended. He sensed a vague something else had begun.

♦

Riding home, Seth took another jab from the same odd queasiness, as it resumed its relentless progress against him. Something about being in law school still just seemed wrong. He conveniently avoided analyzing what or why, but his mood declined a sleepover at Cindi's. She frowned at his decision, and he sensed he'd spoiled some special plan. Once home, he dutifully read his *Bible*, flipping it randomly to the Twelfth Psalm: "Help, Lord, for the godly are no more; the faithful have vanished from among men. Everyone lies to his neighbor; their flattering lips speak with deception."

He closed his eyes, shook his head, and turned out the light. He tossed around beneath the sheets for over an hour, considering Rentzell and Hays, picturing them hit, taking their last breaths, wondering who got it last and thereby knew what was coming. Then came the familiar ever-encroaching evil sloshing about inside his head. He still considered not its cause. Finally, he moved his pillow to the foot of the bed, just as he'd done as an eight-year-old. Ten minutes later, he fell asleep, backwards.

CHAPTER FOURTEEN

Another week blew by, and now it was Sunday, December 8, 1985, two days before final exams began and time for the annual Football Team Appreciation Day at Calvary Baptist Church. Seth, the rare student who realized football wasn't the only god on campus, was a regular at the comely, campus area church. He liked the Spanish architecture, which lent the church a solemnity that typical red brick Baptist churches often lacked. H.R., despite a full weekend social calendar, agreed to meet Seth there at 10:45. Seth invited the two girlfriends, but Sue was studying and nursing a cold, and Cindi stayed in to watch taped soap opera episodes.

At 10:57, H.R. arrived, definitely hung over, and if the lingering scent of Scotch was any indication, possibly intoxicated. Surprised that H.R. had agreed to show, Seth gave him some gum and directed him to the seats he'd saved on the aisle in a back row. Seth settled into the pew and looked around. He sensed a temporary relief from his own inexplicable mental hangover, the one still hiding out within every crevice of his being.

Seth whispered, "H.R., your drinking may catch up with you someday."

H.R., in a lucid trance, mumbled, "That's the problem with living. It'll eventually kill yuh."

Seth closed his eyes and smiled, then focused on the pulpit, where long-time pastor Karl Volton recognized two sororities and the football team as the day's special guests. The latter received a standing ovation for their miraculous comeback win over Auburn. After the typical Baptist order of worship: a few old hymns, a scripture reading, the offertory, a special choir presentation, and a long, coma-inducing prayer, Dr. Volton introduced the day's guest speaker, University Psychology Professor and Therapy Program Administrator Dr. Roland Whitehurst, who was also an ordained minister.

Dr. Whitehurst began with a good joke, one with the required hint of truth. "In heaven, a group of Baptists gathered in a large hall. There, they ate, sang, and celebrated. Saint Peter stepped in and requested a reduction in the noise level. Billy Graham agreed to comply, then asked why it was necessary, given how they were quite happy about being in heaven. Peter replied, 'I understand, but the Catholics and Presbyterians are in rooms across the hall, and they both still think they're the only ones here.'"

The assembled had a nice laugh at the expense of their competition, but Whitehurst was setting them up. He went on to preach an original sermon about the practical aspects of love. Seth looked over and noticed how, for H.R., to close one's eyes was to sleep. Dr. Whitehurst made an interesting comparison between the idea of eternal life for mankind versus the expiration dates on driver's licenses and dairy products. Everyone smiled at the illustration. H.R. smiled too, but maybe more out of a well-honed sense of camaraderie than of comprehension.

Whitehurst returned to the nature of love. "Nowhere in the *Bible* does it say love is impatient, love is overaggressive, love is iron-eared, or love is prideful. *On the contrary*, it instructs that the greatest love involves giving one's life for one's friends."

Seth saw H.R.'s eyelids blink and considered that, if his ears had had lids, they'd be doing likewise.

Whitehurst kept sailing along. "Allow me to delve into the world of specifics. If we wish to communicate our ideas about the subject of *forever*, should we not treat our employees and employers, our spouses and family, and our college girlfriends and boyfriends, with the respect and gentility our faith commands? Should we not attempt to see their viewpoint, to stand in their shoes? Should we not show empathy toward those weaker or less fortunate, mercy toward those who have wronged us, and patience toward those who try us?"

The speaker paused and adjusted his glasses. H.R. appeared to be in the midst of a heroic effort to remain awake.

Whitehurst broke the pause with the precise measure of authority in his voice. "Show me one living without empathy, and I shall show you one living without faith. Show me one living only for self and only by self, and I shall show you one living without a present and without a future. I might also show you one living without the serious consideration of his audience. And, if one considers himself to be a preacher, a teacher, or just a messenger, that form of disrespect is a most fatal complication."

Seth blinked, realized he'd become lost in the good Dr. Whitehurst's spoken thoughts. Dr. Whitehurst concluded with a few light-hearted summary comments, then Dr. Volton took the microphone to close the service and remind the congregation of what a great honor it was to have the football team as guests.

After the service, Seth and H.R. spoke to a few football players and a few Tri-Delt sorority girls, three of whom H.R. had seen out on the town. Numerous people spoke to Seth and his now sobered guest, including Dr. Kenneth Falls, Seth's knee surgeon, who invited him, H.R., and their girlfriends to be his guests at the North River Yacht Club for dinner one evening. H.R. observed that he'd never seen so many nice Baptists in one place.

They both then wandered into the pastors' greeting line. Dr. Whitehurst asked Seth what was new, and Seth told him about Cindi and introduced him to a trailing H.R.

Dr. Volton spoke to Seth like an old friend. "Hello, young Seth. Are you finding law school an adequate substitute for college football?"

Seth smiled with the customary reticence and shook his head. "Only in that it consumes the same amount of time."

Seth saw H.R. with Dr. Whitehurst, leaning down to speak into the good man's ear, then saw Dr. Whitehurst nod and respond, concern upon his face. Seth found himself somewhat shocked at the sight. He hoped the gum had covered the whiskey.

CHAPTER FIFTEEN

Murder. Fights. Women. Football. A sermon. Law school life was getting interesting. There remained a lot of boring law to learn, however, and Seth lost himself in it. On Monday, December 9, 1985, the two-week exam period began. The typical first year student now had zero mental downtime, but H.R. wasn't typical. He still hit a bar after each exam and on weekend nights.

When time is short, time is quick, and the first semester thus ended with a rush. The students sprinted into the Christmas season.

Over the long Christmas break, the Legal Beagles won the National Flag Football Championship in New Orleans. The speedy, sure-handed Seth was named Most Valuable Player, but kept it as another humble secret. On the sideline, Myerson had berated Seth and H.R. for discussing Rentzell and Hays. "We're here to play football, not to play detective," he'd said. At a post-game team meeting, Myerson blasted H.R. again, this time for staying out on Bourbon Street until four in the morning . . . more business as usual.

Come early January, the first semester exam results were posted on the Wailing Wall. This sheet of glass beside the rear entrance had earned its nickname when a maniacal first-year broke a bottle of Jack Daniels across it. The poor guy had scored a .5, a big fat D, in Myerson's Property class.

With telegraphic efficiency, students with parents in Tuscaloosa retrieved and phoned exam results all across the state. Seth had made three 4.0's--including one in Property--a

3.5 in Torts, a course whose Marxist bent severely irritated him, and a 3.0 in Borland's technical, uninspiring Civil Procedure class. With a 3.7 average, he was at the top of his class, but he whipped his self-worth for a week for not making all 4.0's. H.R. had muddled through with a 3.2, slightly above the middle of the pack.

Sue's 1.8 had left her on academic probation. H.R. and Seth assisted her all they could, but Cindi hadn't been able to help as much as she'd promised. She said her mother wanted her home for shopping on pre-Christmas weekends. Sue had one semester to raise her average to a 2.0. Otherwise, she'd have to leave H.R. and head home to join the Junior League sooner than she'd planned.

The murders of Rentzell and Hays remained unsolved. No update was found in the newspapers, none even within the law school grapevine. Seth couldn't grasp the slippery subject of how two well-behaved law students had gotten themselves executed, but his mind couldn't help trying. He'd been around the two guys on the Legal Beagles team, and, although he found them inquisitive to the point of irritation, he certainly sensed nothing indicative of delinquency. Seth knew nothing of drug dealers, but he figured most kept a lower profile. He was unable to shrug off the seeming contradiction between their curiosity and their rumored illegal dealings.

♦

H.R. knew something concrete, as drinking establishment patrons often do. There was a Sidetrack bartender named Polina Klimenko, a leggy granddaughter of Ukrainian immigrants who came to Alabama from Chicago on a volleyball scholarship. Via his usual generous tips, H.R discovered that Rentzell never ordered more than two beers, that his dad was an Asst. U.S. Attorney, and that he and Hays behaved like Southern gents. Neither had hit on her. Both had classy girlfriends.

H.R. combined these tidbits with information from a few Legal Beagles teammates and realized that the deceased seemed nothing like the druggies or the dealers he'd encountered in Austin. He wanted to know what their girlfriends might add. Polina gave him the two girls' names, writing them down, of course, on the same cocktail napkin as her phone number. H.R. called the girlfriends, but never called Polina.

CHAPTER SIXTEEN

At seven p.m. on Wednesday, January 8, 1986, Seth parked his Jeep in the law center lot, then began a high-energy, seventy-yard walk to the back entrance. He'd done well his first semester, and the Legal Beagles had won in New Orleans. All the big law firms were rushing him to join their summer clerkship program at the rate of $1,000+ per week. Add the fact that he was making love to an art form on a regular basis, and he had every reason to move like a high-spirited spaniel. Over the break, he'd slept with Cindi so many times that he no longer felt so awkward about it.

Nonetheless, that same undefined malicious malady still weighed on his brain cells, but today he was in no mood to wrestle it. Why allow some unknown suggestion of perniciousness rain on his happiness parade? Why engage in self-scrutiny when life seemed so objectively perfect?

The sprinkler system was on, watering the shrubbery that lined the wide, rock-trimmed walkway. The water was spraying on each side of the walk. To test his reflexes, Seth darted from side to side, just to see how close to the spray he could step, yet still avoid the water. Beside the door, he saw a girl taking notes in front of the Wailing Wall. She looked at him via the corner of her eye, then seemed to look away from him too fast. He realized it was Lesley, the "girl-next-door" he'd met at the Coffee Room in September.

They re-introduced themselves, and Seth made the obvious inquiry. "May I ask what you're doing?"

She replied, "I'm copying all the first-year grades so I can run statistical analysis on them."

"You're kidding. What for?"

"Just curiosity. I wanted to calculate everyone's average, find the shapes of the grade curves, then maybe run a few regressions."

Seth tried to cover his instinctive impression that she was peculiar. "Running regressions? I've forgotten what that means, but it seems like an interesting diversion."

"Maybe it'll be informative. You never know what you might see when you play around with numbers."

Seth rubbed his chin. "How'd you become so interested in Statistics? It seems like a curious diversion."

"Just something I picked up in my undergrad studies. So, how did you become so interested in dodging sprinkler heads? It seems like a curious diversion." Her smile was wry, yet cute.

Embarrassed, Seth zipped toward the door. "Just something I picked up playing football."

Classes were over for the day, and Seth headed to the library for a dose of uninspiring Decedents Estates precedent. He walked into the Coffee Room to check his message box. As he approached the long rows of numbered boxes, he noticed two second-years playing a round of no limit Canasta. They discussed the wonderful future day when luck would deliver the first quadriplegic to their law office.

He also saw a man in a nice gray suit seated with his back to the window. His tie was a dark red, a shade almost equal to his hair. The man in the suit pointed something out on a table, then glanced at Seth. Seth did a double take. The man reminded him of someone, someone seated opposite him.

Seth looked over and asked, "Hey, H.R. What are you doing in the building at this hour? Isn't The Tap open yet?"

H.R. turned and answered with a smile meant for wise-mouthed friends. "Hey, Seth. I want you to meet my cousin, Thomas Garrison, from Birmingham. He's the guy shortsighted enough to rent me his cabin."

The introductions and handshakes were over only a moment when Seth noted some complex printouts on the table. They were insurance illustrations, each with neat columns and rows of numbers. The columns had headings with strange phraseology like "Total Paid Up Ins."

Seth squinted. "This doesn't look like law."

H.R. replied, "It looks like confusion to me."

"Gee, H.R. you're not buying insurance, are you?"

"Just a little. I thought it would be smart before Thomas changes careers. I don't trust anyone else in his business."

Seth smiled, winked. "And no one else would take a bet on your lifespan."

Thomas laughed and added, "Plus, it's not a bad idea to buy a little when you're young and healthy and the premiums are still cheap."

Seth nodded, then backed away smiling. "Well, I'm sorry to interrupt. Thomas, I'll look you up whenever I feel a fatal disease coming on."

Seth walked on, but felt like he'd just made some kind of Freudian slip. H.R.'s cousin laughed. H.R. didn't.

CHAPTER SEVENTEEN

At three a.m. on the cool evening of Thursday, January 16, 1986, a normal person would have been sleeping like a baby anvil, but Seth's tight hands grabbed his frustrated head, which again argued with whatever was making him so mentally woozy. Other inspiring topics also delayed his slumber, such as who had killed Rentzell and Hays and whether they had any life insurance before they were shot. Lusting for the Sominex bottle located a ten-foot walk to the lavatory, he already felt guilty for opening it thirty minutes in the future.

The phone rang. It was an obnoxious old alarm clock of a phone, and at this hour, a normal person would have attacked it like an alligator. Seth looked at it like it was a friend. A friend it was.

"Hey, Seth, my old partner in legal misery. I figured you'd be awake at this hour." H.R. seemed a little drunk, which was the obvious explanation for the late call on a weeknight, but, at the same time, there was something pleasant in his voice.

"If you had figured wrong, we'd be *old* friends."

"You ever tried sleeping pills?"

"I was pondering an entire bottle of them when you rang."

H.R. hesitated. Seth sensed H.R. knew he was only discouraged. "Look, I'm sorry you have to deal with the whole insomnia curse, but look at it this way, you could be a narcoleptic instead. I mean, wouldn't it be tough to make it as a narcoleptic lawyer, or politician, or whatever you wish to perfectly be?"

Seth noted again the new tone in H.R.'s voice. There was something upbeat and empathetic about the way H.R. sent the compliment his way. "Actually, I think I'm a nobody who can't do *anything* perfectly."

H.R. never missed a beat. "Think about it, Seth the Great. You're in the middle of the end of a brilliant oration, then you pass out into the microphone with the entire audience listening to you snore."

Seth shook his head, again reminded why he was forced to like his always-encouraging, always-pontificating pal. "I need to drink more, H.R. Where are you? The Tap?"

"Just closed her down. I'm over at Sue's. She's sort of closed down, too. My darling girlfriend. Out like Rip Van Winkle."

Seth noticed H.R. was now referring to Sue as his official girlfriend, but figured it was just the booze talking. "Hey H.R. You ever wonder why they call it The Nasty Tap?"

"I wonder why they don't call it worse. If you hang around there long enough, you begin to spot every version of nastiness the world has ever known. Don't you just hate how there's so much evil about and so many evil people purveying it?"

Seth squinted. "I need to start drinking less. What particular version of nonsense are you talking tonight?"

"There's a realization I've seized upon, Seth. We're different, but about the important things, we're alike. We'll always do *the right thing*. Man, don't you despise knowing how evil always preys on the weak? And how having everything amounts to nothing, if you have to whore out to get it."

Seth was confused. "I thought we were discussing a local dive bar where the young pool their egos just to see what will happen."

"Man, you got a way with words. What are you doing with yourself, Seth? Aren't you weary of lazing around in the lobby of destiny? It makes no sense that you don't have more confidence in yourself. Who put all that hyper-humility in you anyway? You should *already* be famous, or something similar."

"My demanding dad and my sometimes barbaric hometown probably put it in me: both often seemed to tell me I was nothing. By the way, about now, I'd settle for just being well-rested, or something similar."

"And, maybe you were born humble, and, by the way, speaking of well rested, consider young Sue here. I hate to admit it, but I haven't seen another girl in a month." He stopped just a moment, which seemed to give his conscience a chance to catch up. "Well, I've seen them, but not as much as a double-take; well, no triple takes anyway. Double-takes don't count; they're reflexive."

"Agreed."

"Look, Sue and I are going hunting in the morning. It's almost the end of deer season. After class, why don't you and I grab a late Storyville breakfast at about ten?"

Seth was concerned. "Good plan, H.R., except for the fact you'll be hunting on less than three hours sleep."

"I'll sleep in the tree stand. Besides, it's not your ordinary hunting excursion."

"You mean you may actually slay a trophy buck?"

"Something like that. Hey, Seth, remember the time we were at the Burger King, and I had a serious discussion with the manager, then you and I started talking about things that matter, then we just looked dead at each other?"

"That manager and I will never forget that day."

"I wondered then about who you really are."

"H.R., what in the name of God do you mean?"

"Have you ever considered that you're not who you're supposed to be? You are your completely gifted self, yet you're so naïve, so polite, and so reserved that *you'll never even realize who you are*, much less be it."

"Aw, c'mon, H.R., you're talking BS."

"We're always going to be friends, right Seth?"

"Of course, man."

"No matter what happens. I mean you'd defend my honor even if I were dead, wouldn't you?"

"Yes." Seth's voice couldn't conceal his hurt.

"And I can bring my kids over to play with your kids."

"Kids? Gee, you've been drinking *way* too much."

"Maybe so, because I've been seeing these visions when I look at Susan in her sleep. These little redheaded H.R.s and Sues looking back at me like they need help. It's so scary and cruel. Wonder how a man could just leave her for someone else, or for no one else?"

Seth was a little too quiet for a little too long. "H.R., did you ever feel *you* might be lazing around in the lobby of destiny?"

Now it was H.R. who was a little too quiet for a little too long. "Well, maybe I'm tired of being lazy, but I'm not so sure about you, Seth. Meet me for breakfast and prove me wrong."

Seth answered. "I'll be there."

"Good."

Seth put a hand over his eyes and shook his head. "A friend of yours just never knows what's next, does he?"

"Guess not, but then again, that's the fun of it. See yuh there."

Seth hung up, stared at the wall. He knew H.R. was a certified clown, but there was something unique about the guy. He'd make a great character for a movie, or a novel. One never knew about him. He had a thirst for good booze and good women, but then he'd show up for church and take the minister aside for a private talk. One minute, he'd verbally assault a Myerson, then, the next, he'd get all responsible and buy some life insurance. *Life insurance?* Seth wondered. *To benefit whom?* And now H.R. was talking future children with Sue, the same girl he planned to dump at the first sign of boredom.

Sure, H.R. was, in common speak, *unreal*, but at the same time, he was completely real, a guy with a strong grip on reality. With H.R., Seth could sense something steadfast and true, something reassuring, something--in this new world of fabrication and alienation--that his inner Seth needed. Seth mused aloud. "Thank God for H.R., for H.R. and football."

He glanced at his *Bible,* flipped to Proverbs 27: "Wounds from a friend can be trusted, but an enemy multiplies kisses." What was *that* supposed to mean to him? Who were his friends and who were his enemies? He inhaled, attempted to corral the stray invaders that galloped within his head: realizations about how Rentzell and Hays spent plenty of time at The Tap--just as H.R. did, realizations such as *Holy Rogue Garrison indeed.*

Then, he sensed the same internal doldrums that had become a permanent and unwelcome mental roommate. Tonight, however, there were just too many ideas to round up-- too many vague, yet troubling, distractions. His overactive brain waves soon wore him down, and ten minutes later, he fell asleep.

CHAPTER EIGHTEEN

The next morning, Friday, January 17, Seth sat in Dooley's Contracts class, looked at his watch. It was 9:05. Dooley noted the absence of H.R. and Sue on his attendance sheet. H.R. dreaded any class starting before ten, but he'd rarely been absent. Dooley and Myerson only allowed two unexcused absences before imposing sanctions. Seth scratched his head and wondered where H.R. and Sue were, ignoring the return of the usual strange psyche sensations, of which he'd just about had enough.

After watching Dooley skewer a liberal over the legal concept of *quantum meruit*, explaining simply that "A deal is a deal", Seth hurried to the student phone in the back corner of the Coffee Room. There, his ear had to compete with a third-year girl quoting with approval the partner for whom she'd clerked over the holidays. "He said, 'If you don't have the facts, argue the law. If you don't have the law, argue the facts. If you don't have either, throw up the biggest smokescreen your client can buy!'"

Her words were like static, but on the other end of the line, there was no answer. It was just H.R.'s usual trick outgoing message beginning with a live-sounding "Hello?", then explaining to the fooled caller he was talking to a mere machine. A call to Storyville indicated no tall red-haired guy. He tried Sue's apartment, but her roommate hadn't seen them since they left the afternoon before.

He had a Mozz coffee alone at a window table. Mozz had commented that Seth looked as if his brain was run down and

97

had given him a large cup for the price of a small. He gazed out at the back lawn and began to rummage through a few thoughts: about Cindi, about the law, about Dr. Whitehurst's sermon.

It seemed so quiet outside. Only a weak breeze flowed through the tops of the trees, and only a pair of flicking Cardinals added movement to a still landscape. Twenty minutes later, he could hear the morning train that ran behind the school, realized how silence was too often fleeting. Seemingly frightened by the train, the Cardinals fled to a chinaberry bush. Seth's head snatched upwards. The familiar eerie feeling jumped him again. Then, it slid away.

He swallowed, stood, glanced around, and left for Pinehurst.

♦

It was 10:45 when the phone rang in his little garage apartment. "Seth, this is H.R.'s father, Henry Garrison."

"Hello, sir. It's a privilege to speak with you."

"Well, I don't know about that. I'm just a humble doctor." Seth smiled. There sure weren't enough of those left. "Anyway, Seth, I have surgery on a burn victim in fifteen minutes and wanted to be certain I reached you first."

"Is something wrong?"

"Oh, it's nothing, but we expected to hear from H.R. because his mother was born this date in 1937, and he always calls in the morning to wish her Happy Birthday. There's been no call yet, and I was curious if you've seen him."

"I haven't, sir. He wasn't at class this morning, and there was no answer at the cabin, except for the usual outgoing message."

"Cute message, isn't it? From whence does he get that sense of humor? Some people say it's from me," he added, in light-hearted confession.

Seth laughed a little. "It's the best, sir. Anyway, I also called his girlfriend's place, and her roommate said she hadn't seen H.R. or Sue since yesterday afternoon."

"Sweet, cute girl, that Sue. Can't fathom what she sees in old H.R. In any case, please don't take me for a paranoid parent, but would you mind checking on him at the cabin? Maybe he's still asleep, and he and I'll both be happy if he remembers to call his mother."

"Glad to, sir. Torts class was cancelled, so I don't have class again until this afternoon."

"Glad Torts is cancelled. The thought of more law students learning to sue doctors is enough to inspire my retirement. Anyway, thanks, Seth. Hope you can come out to Texas and visit."

"I'd be honored, sir."

CHAPTER NINETEEN

It was 11:30 a.m. when Seth reached the Garrison cabin. He touched the hood of H.R.'s Jeep: cold. He knocked on the front door. The sound was solid off the rustic oak, but the return echo from the lonely woods was hollow. Seth looked behind his back. He waited to detect noise inside, but heard nothing. Risking the wrath of the dead, he banged on the door with the side of his fist. Still no response, no movement, no sound. He walked around and peeked in a few windows. His footsteps crackled through the dead leaves and twigs. He saw a dim light in the kitchen.

He retrieved the spare key from its hiding place beneath the back steps. He opened the door and walked inside. The silence disturbed him, made his eyes shift. It seemed he'd entered an empty concert hall--no people, no music. The potency of emptiness pounced upon his senses. Two items of H.R.'s were gone: no heavy coat, no shotgun.

H.R. and Sue were missing.

It was almost noon. A rush of fear raced to Seth's center. He gathered himself and called his old friend Walter Rushton, who sat in the office of his small timber management company.

"Walter, this is Seth. Guess I was lucky to catch you out of the woods."

"Hey, Seth. How's the student life treating you? It's raining here, so we're catching up on paperwork." Walter's slow drawl still gave him away as the reliable, plodding country boy Seth had known since they were both toddlers.

"I'm fine, but I need your help with a small problem."

The tone of Walter's voice downshifted to concern. "What is it, and where are you?"

"Two of my friends are missing. I'm at my buddy H.R.'s cabin fifteen minutes outside Tuscaloosa."

"What can I do?"

"How are the dogs, Barney and Buford? Can they track humans?"

"They're still the best, and they track what I tell them to."

"Can they do it *now*?"

"Just a minute." The pause lasted two minutes. "Give me directions, and I'll be there in about three hours."

"I have a bad feeling about this. Could you make it in two?"

Seth hung up, then dug out a phone book from underneath a pile of law texts. He found the number for the Tuscaloosa County Sheriff's Office. A receptionist answered with a Southern accent that could melt an iceberg. Seth then spoke with a Deputy Kenny Dolton, who seemed to take a missing persons report almost too seriously. The deputy's eager, dramatic demeanor made Seth nervous. The deputy promised to drive out pronto.

He looked in H.R.'s backpack, found his address book, and turned to the letter "G." Below the names of three girls, he located that of H.R.'s first cousin Thomas, the life insurance agent who owned the cabin. He explained the situation to Thomas and asked him to contact Dr. Garrison. Thomas told Seth where H.R. would likely hunt on the 300-acre tract.

When Seth hung up and looked outside the window, he saw bad news. The clouds had been sparse when he left Pinehurst, but now they were numerous and gray. He closed his eyes and cursed. The tracking dog's worst enemies were water and time.

CHAPTER TWENTY

Seth figured Deputy Dolton would be punctual but was surprised when, twenty minutes later, the officer sprang out of the squad car and shoved out a uniformed arm. "I'm Deputy Ken Dolton, Tuscaloosa County Sheriff's Department."

The sun was almost hidden, but Seth still had to squint when the sheen from Dolton's badge and belt buckle hit his eyes.

"I'm Seth Sentel. I spoke with you on the phone."

"Nice to meet you, Mr. Sentel. You won't mind if I take a few notes, will you?" Dolton pulled out a small black leather pad holder and a Bic pen, which he clicked before Seth could answer.

"No, I guess not."

"Good. I wish to note every important detail for possible future reference. You never know what could be important a few weeks, months, or years from now."

Seth didn't think there were many details to add to those he mentioned via telephone, and he hoped to find H.R. within hours, but he nodded in comprehension. Seth told him everything he knew about the disappearance and supplied every relevant fact, including Sue's address, phone number, hometown, and roommate's name.

"Roommates are always informative sources," Dolton declared with more authority than the observation deserved.

Seth nodded again as his bewildered eyes took in Dolton's military-style haircut and spotless deputy hat.

"Precisely what time did they disappear?"

Seth thought a moment. The question somehow seemed odd. "I suppose I don't know."

"Your statement over the phone was that the two individuals went hunting early this morning."

Statement, Seth thought. He didn't know he'd made anything so official. "Well, his gun and coat are missing, so I think they went out for a quick hunt at about five-thirty this morning, then planned to be at the law school in time for Contracts class at nine a.m. Not even H.R. cuts Contracts."

"I see. Can I take it from your wording this H.R. might not be the most responsible of individuals, and that it's possible the parties are not technically missing?"

Seth didn't feel a yes was the perfect answer to either question. "I suppose so."

The deputy pulled back his left sleeve and took an official look at his watch. "It's 12:30. If we give them ninety minutes to hunt and return, it would mean they walked out of this residence six hours ago. That would leave four hours unaccounted for."

Seth breathed in at the realization that, as more hours passed, the situation became less explicable by good news. He wished his mind could somehow avoid such realizations, that he could tune it like a radio to pick up only pleasant thoughts. He exhaled, rubbed his temples and blamed the cold, dreary weather for his morbid thinking.

The deputy went on for his audience of Seth and trees. "Six hours may be too long to run a promising dog search, but I'll consult with the Sheriff about the possibility. Under wet conditions, we'd be limited to a search party." He looked up at the sky as if to drop Seth a subtle hint there would be no dog search this cloudy day.

A worried Seth made a low-key plea. "Is there anything else I can do?" Dolton's face appeared intentionally blank. "What will your office do next?"

"I have your statement, Mr. Sentel, and I'll report back to the Sheriff. We'll have a sit-down to discuss the situation, then develop an action plan."

"Does that mean you'll be back today?"

Deputy Dolton was walking to the squad car. "You can count on it."

Seth acknowledged the commitment, but his face must not have reflected any assurance. "Now, don't you worry, young man. This will be *my* case. I'll personally oversee it and insure it receives all the benefits of regulation and protocol."

He drove away at regulation speed. Seth crossed his arms, started feeling alone. Then, somehow, out of some evolving miracle of fate, he began to realize he was weary of people calling him "young."

Inside the cabin, he resumed the wait for Walter, Mister Dependable, Mister Dependably Late. There was no point in searching alone. On a 300-acre plot, he could look the entire afternoon and still leave plenty of ground uncovered. What he avoided realizing was how his instincts compelled him to wait. They didn't want him to search for H.R. alone.

Instead, he looked for coffee and cream. A red bag of Folgers and a carton of Half-&-Half sat in the fridge door. As he checked the expiration date on the cream, the corner of his eye caught an oddity. Something stood out. Under a twelve-pack of Budweiser was something white. His head turned like a robot's. Both eyes focused on this thing that didn't belong. He pulled an envelope out from under the red box, took a deep breath. His name was on it. He sat down to read.

My Good Friend Seth,

For the last eight weeks, something has been going on at school. If you're reading this, it may be too late for me to do anything else about it. It took me over five weeks to almost figure out what was happening. It's like they say: sometimes the answer can be staring you right in the face, yet you don't see it. Sometimes, it's also right under your feet. And isn't it funny how those who seemed like something great, were great nothings instead . . . or great evils? People should be more like you, Seth: thinking they're nothing, yet being a lot.

I want you to talk to an attorney at Hound Dog's law firm named Elliot Gaston. He'll give you the details I have so far. In a way, I'm happy I won't be me telling you. Remember, I didn't want you to know until I knew pretty much for sure. It's enough that Sue and I are in danger. No point in you being in it too, unless Sue and I couldn't get out of it. Well, you won't like what Elliot will say, but I think I can trust only you to get to the absolute bottom of things, so to speak. By the way, rumor says that Rentzell and Hays passed their posthumous drug tests.

Well, I hope you have the guts for this because I don't know who else has the character, not to mention the weird imagination. If so, may your luck be as good as your instincts.

Goodbye for now,
Henry Richard Garrison III

The coffee was too hot to drink. Seth swallowed two gulps anyway. He stared out the picture window. His eyes looked left, then right. He didn't know what to feel or think. He read the note a second time, but the peculiar collection of words and vague references were no relief. He placed it in his pocket, its second sentence lodged in his mental 'In' stack. The usual inexplicable negative tide rolled toward him, but now it was joined by some sharper individual waves. Some distinctive unknown was wrong. He sat and thought. Eventually, he napped off a few minutes.

♦

Thunder brought him to. His watch read 1:05. He walked to the window and focused on the clouds. They looked still, gray and heavy. That second sentence tried to sneak up on him. He felt his pulse quicken, sensed the short breaths coming on. He tapped his right foot. The phone saved him. It rang like a fire alarm.

Seth snatched it. "Hello?"

"Is this H.R.?" The woman's voice was hurried, nervous, terse. Seth cringed and backed the receiver off his ear. "No. This is his friend, Seth."

"Where is my daughter Sue? Why are you answering?"

"I'm waiting on them to arrive. They should be back soon."

"I just received a call from Sheriff Ray Gibson. My husband has known him for years. I'm worried sick. What did that H.R. think he was doing by going hunting on a school day near that cabin? Anything could've happened in those woods. They could be trapped, or that madman could have them. *My God! I can't believe* this."

Seth focused on calming her, but he was getting more nervous himself. "*Who* are you afraid may have them, Mrs. Longshore?"

"That Lymon, or whatever his name is. I understand he just roams the woods like an animal."

"I've heard he's harmless, just kind'a peculiar. I promise you, Mrs. Longshore, if you'll give me your number, I'll phone you when I know something."

"There's no need. I'm already on my way there. I'll arrive in less than two hours."

She hung up. Less than ten minutes later, Cindi called.

"Seth, it's me."

"Hey."

"I heard the bad news from Susan's roommate. Have you seen or heard from them yet?"

"Well, it's not bad news yet. An old friend of mine and I are going out to search for them in a few more minutes."

"Oh. I see. Well, I had called Sue's place to speak with her about something, and her roommate said no one knew where H.R. and Susan were. She said Sue's mom had called a bit upset." Cindi sounded hesitant.

"A lot upset. I just spoke with her. She's on her way here."

"Okay. Well, I have studying to do. Even we third-year students must study. Bye." Seth glanced at the phone. His head moved from side to side.

A second cup of coffee further sharpened Seth's senses. Fifteen minutes later, Walter arrived. The stocky guy eased out of his truck. Seth shook his oldest friend's steady hand and recalled Walter's sense of resolution, his way of pursuing things to a thorough end. The lines in Seth's face relaxed a little.

"We'll need a base scent, Seth. Do you have some of their clothing?"

Seth retrieved H.R.'s U.T. sweatshirt and a sweater of Sue's. Walter placed them on the ground behind the truck where two shiny-coated Beagles clawed at the wire door of a plywood dog box. Walter opened the box, and after a quick tree break, the dogs returned at Walter's call.

He attached two long leashes, then introduced them to the clothing. "Take it in boys. That's your men."

Seth admired the hound pair as they made muffled snorting sounds while they drew in the relevant scents. When the Beagles turned away and tugged, Seth's eager eyes lit up in appreciation.

Walter looked at Seth. "They're ready."

Thomas Garrison had described four hunting spots on the property. One was where two deer trails intersected in the thickest part of the woods. Near Lymon's property, it included a tree stand large enough for two people. Another nearby spot overlooked a deep ravine with a small stream at the bottom. It had a ground stand. Two other places were at small fields planted with winter wheat and oats. Thomas thought the green field stands were too small for two people.

The dogs didn't seem to pick up any scent near the cabin, so Seth had to choose which way to direct them. He knew there would be a wealth of assorted wild animal activity at the stream below the ground stand. Sue was a photograph lover with a Minolta. It was the most likely spot. The dogs loped along, pulling at their leashes, but they didn't strike, not even when they reached the ground stand. Seth looked inside the black plastic walls. The only signs of life were a couple of Snickers wrappers and three empty soda cans.

He turned to see Walter return a can of Skoal to his back pocket. "Nothing inside indicates they were here."

Walter inspected the forest floor. "No footprints since the rain last week."

Seth felt something contact his left shoulder. "Speaking of rain, I just felt the first drop."

"Let's move. Time is after us."

Seth took out a rough map he'd made from Thomas's property description. They needed a shortcut from this stand to the one in the deep woods. They agreed on a path and started out again.

Two hundred yards later, the dogs grew frisky, whiny, pulling their handlers forward. Buford looked back at Seth like he was a bothersome impediment. The two canine noses worked the air, pointing downward intermittently to gauge any ground scents.

Walter looked at Seth. He knew the dogs were onto something. "Time to let 'em run, Seth. The rain's almost here, and they act like they're on the edge of a trail."

The leashes were taut when the two men unhooked them. The dogs bolted and turned right.

To a man of sounds such as Seth, the trailing cry of a hound was like nothing on earth, and nothing on earth could replicate it. A lonely, rhythmic, high-pitched noise, it mellowed as it pulled away in the distance. Seth and Walter began a slow run, and as Seth's eyes beaded in on the echo of the wails, he realized dogs never made this same noise in a pen or yard. This cry was reserved for the chase.

And the chase was on. Walter was out front now, whipping out a machete from a scabbard. He slashed left and right, cutting through thorn bushes and leaving low pine limbs on the floor of a new path. Seth followed close. When the brush dissipated, they broke into a full gallop, dodged trees both large and small, high stepping it over rotten logs and briar clumps.

The dogs were out of sight. Seth and Walter directed their feet by sound. They stopped twice to wait out pauses in the call.

For ten minutes, they ran without a word, then, between breaths, Seth exhaled a question. "Walter. How will we know when they've found what they're onto?"

Walter yelled forward to the faster Seth. "You'll know if we're close enough. The problem is that Beagles are so low to the ground that they'll leave you behind in the thick stuff, but we're keeping up now that we're on a path."

Seventy-five yards later, the call of the wild changed. Seth noticed less time between the wails and less yearning to their tone. Then, abruptly, it halted. The hounds were out of sight. Both men stopped. Seth could only catch feint whimpers. The men continued at full speed. In ten more strides, Seth got a distant glimpse of a white paw.

Walter stopped, turned to Seth, looked straight at him. "Should I check this out alone?"

Seth couldn't bring himself to speak. He felt his heart rate jump another gear. The dogs had stopped. He managed a nod.

Walter plodded on, marching toward two small patches of white. Soon, he too was out of sight. Seth was drawn to ease forward, but only made it five steps. A few minutes later, he saw the outline of a dog moving a few paces toward where Walter should be. He thought he saw Walter kneel. He convinced his brain Walter was rewarding the dogs or attaching their leashes.

The longest minutes of his life ticked by. Seth sat on the trunk of a big hardwood that had been downed by the last hurricane. When Seth prayed, he always asked that God's will be done, but not this time. He pleaded with God to let it be a wounded deer on the ground or a piece of clothing. He begged God to make it as if H.R. and Sue were nowhere in these woods, not on the ground, not even with this Lymon man. He pleaded with God to make right everything that was wrong, to fix it all as if it never happened.

The sound of panting and tiny footsteps broke his prayer, More rain tickled the leaves at his feet. He could now see Walter's outline through the limbs and the drizzle, but Walter's face pointed toward the ground. When that face lifted, he was only three feet away, and his coat was missing. Then, Walter said it without a word: He moved his head, horizontally.

Seth's lower lip curled under. Before he could utter a sound, or even lean in the direction where Walter's coat now lay, Walter raised his right hand between his sternum and Seth's. "You shouldn't look, Seth. Not now."

Specificity was unnecessary. They'd been close friends long enough to know what Walter meant. Walter paused to take in Seth's reaction. Except for a bracing of Seth's face, there was none. "Let me stay here, Seth. Why don't you go back to the cabin and call the Sheriff? He may already be there anyway, and it's beginning to rain."

Seth's lips trembled out a word. "But-"

Walter shook his head again as his words grew somber. "Staying here won't make this any different. Walk it off. Take the dogs with you. They make good company."

Walter had chosen good words. Seth took the two leashes and turned toward the cabin, fighting reality with every step. The energy of his avoidance, and the feeling someone was following him, found its way to his legs. He broke into a full sprint. If it hadn't been a time most ugly, it would have been a run most beautiful, a run born of escape.

He slowed at the cabin when he saw the Sheriff's car. A white Cadillac was there, too. The short, blonde-haired lady standing beside it had to be Sue's mother. She wore her edginess like her bright red coat, both of which stood out in the dead, damp woods. She was looking up at the wet sky and didn't notice Seth, but when he was near, she snatched a knot in him with her eyes.

"Sheriff!" she yelled and beat on the window of the patrol car. "Sheriff Gibson. There's a boy out here with two dogs." Her tone spoke fear and frustration.

Seth stopped as Sheriff Gibson stepped out of his car and asked, "Can we help you, young man?"

"I'm Seth. My friend Walter and I found them." Seth pointed behind him.

The cruel eyes of Sue's mother looked at him. "What do you mean?"

A strange tone enshrouded Seth's voice. "Something has happened." He stopped, sensed a welling up of something unknown inside. "They aren't here anymore."

Seth noted Sheriff Gibson's gray hair and the way his face fell. He looked into the old lawman's eyes. They reflected comprehension and sad surprise. Likely, Gibson had thought this was about two silly college kids who were lost in the woods.

Mrs. Longshore's voice sounded panicked and perplexed. "What are you talking about? Tell the Sheriff and me what you mean, son."

Seth had said all he could. He walked straight to Walter's truck, poured water for the Beagles. His hands shook. He put the dogs in their box. Mrs. Longshore charged behind him, the rain gathering atop her red coat.

Sheriff Gibson tried to stop her. "Mrs. Longshore, I think you should sit down. "The patrol car is warm and dry."

She walked at Seth, now speaking louder. "What are you saying, young man? My Susan's fine, isn't she?" There was a tremor in her last two words. She persisted. "You mean they're out there, but are camping, right?" Her voice grew louder, but no less weak. "I want to see my little girl. Take me where she is. You know where she is, don't you?" Her words were breaking up as Seth closed the tailgate and stared at nothing.

"She's close by, isn't she?" The woman was right behind him. He stared away harder. "Tell me everything is okay. Tell me!"

Seth turned. She was two feet away. His face was like chiseled stone, the white stone of a tomb. He said it with anger, fear, and hurt. "She's dead. H.R.'s dead too. It ain't right. They're both just dead."

She backed away, still looking at him, then turned and walked to her car. Sheriff Gibson watched her until she reached the door handle, then grabbed his microphone and called for the coroner, two deputies, and a four-wheel drive. Seth would have to wait to lead them.

Leaning against the truck, drenched by the rain, Seth knew nothing of this death thing, though it felt akin to the peculiar inner curse still circulating inside him. He realized first that, whatever it was, it didn't belong there, and next, that he didn't belong in law school, yet somehow had to be there. He tried to make himself cry, but something inside him felt like a cement dam. He stopped trying and looked up.

He stared at the depressing sky, but from the corner of his eye. Now, H.R.'s church appearance, life insurance purchase, and talk of a future with Sue began to make sense, innate sense, but sense nonetheless. He looked at the ground. What didn't make sense was why H.R. hid the note.

CHAPTER TWENTY-ONE

The same day H.R. and Sue died, Therapy Program Administrator Dr. Roland Whitehurst was a busy man. There was a quick lunch after teaching two classes and seeing two patients. Then, there was a session with a female student, a research assistant for a law professor. At 2:15, the session was over, and Dr. Whitehurst dictated his first impressions:

Session One; Friday, January 17, 1986

Patient is a white female law student complaining of an eating disorder, specifically a tendency to fast, then binge. Patient exhibits no severe current body weight abnormality, appears to pay attention to appearance and style, and, objectively speaking, is attractive.

Patient is of well-above-average intelligence and, when asked about her high scores on standardized tests, reports she "always makes good on those tests." Patient reports an undergraduate GPA of 3.4 and a current standing of "top third or so" in her law school class. Patient volunteered there had been a "few academic goof ups" in undergrad because she claims she was bored with the subject matter, hated the teacher, or chose the "wrong stuff" to study. Patient agreed to release her transcripts for review.

Patient reports enrolling in law school because she "doesn't wish to rely upon some man for money to spend." Patient is an only child and reported a stable family background with but one serious negative event, the death of her father a few years before. She described him as "a good man," then added, "maybe too good." She mentioned being closer to her mother after her father died and how they now spent more time together, e.g. shopping and watching "chick flicks."

Patient's eating habits first began to change five-six years ago. She doesn't believe anything is wrong with her and only met with me to make her mother and favorite professor happy. If she had been more careful, her mother would've never noticed her eating habits.

Patient agreed to meet again the following Friday at one p.m. and also agreed to bring some family photographs and her high school yearbooks.

Dr. Whitehurst looked out the window at the campus quadrangle and drummed his fingers on his desk. Nothing conclusive came to mind, but he suspected something soon would.

CHAPTER TWENTY-TWO

The next day, a Saturday, January 18, 1986, Seth found himself driving back to the cabin. For once, he'd slept well enough, his body without a quick soul to awaken it. H.R.'s father had called and asked him to check on the place, to make certain H.R. hadn't left on an iron or something, and to cut the water off in case of a freeze. Rain dropped lethargically on his windshield as he drove and grew frightened about returning to the cabin. He inhaled. He sensed some steady, unknown force pulling him there. He wished it would go away.

Upon arrival, he noticed the lack of crime scene tape and related door notices. It seemed strange that the Sheriff's Office hadn't considered the cabin relevant to its investigation, but he was relieved he faced no moral quandary over whether to honor the tape.

Once inside, he straightened the room and checked around. H.R. was the slob one would imagine him to be, but Seth didn't expect to find a *Bible* and *The Writings of Plato* under a *Field & Stream* and a *Sports Illustrated* swimsuit issue. The burst Budweiser bottle in the freezer was more characteristic, as was the restroom, which was a biological catastrophe. Seth cleaned it before tackling the kitchen.

As Dr. Garrison had feared, a dangerous household appliance had been left on, namely the coffee pot. Seth then remembered that he had used it last. His attempts to assuage his own guilt and to remove the tar like-sludge from the bottom of the pot were futile. He tossed it in a big green garbage bag with the rest of the trash.

Seth turned his attention to the rustic great room. He folded an afghan and a sleeping bag and took some insect-ridden firewood outside. When he returned through the back door, he saw the blink from the corner end table. He looked down at H.R.'s answering machine, a modern convenience, but somehow not out of place in H.R.'s rural bachelor pad. Most would have pushed the play button out of mere curiosity, but Seth felt something more, something not unlike the pull of moon upon ocean. Seth ignored the distinctive nature of the feeling, but still followed it.

The first message was from Asst. Dean Thurow, who, way out of character, had returned H.R.'s call. Seth doubted his ears. H.R. held the standard disrespect for Thurow, and Seth couldn't imagine why he'd have called him. The next message was from H.R.'s mom, who had apparently grown weary of waiting for her birthday call. It was one of those motherly *I'm worried, so I'm calling to tell you how to live your life* messages. Then, there was a message from Elliot Gaston, the attorney mentioned in H.R.'s note.

Elliot's voice was deeper than an oil well, further distinguished by the unmistakable penumbras of privilege. "Mr. Garrison, as we discussed when you visited to sign your will, I've researched and considered all possibilities of meeting your tax and estate planning goals. Please phone me at the office or at my Mountain Brook home this weekend to discuss your additional options. My home number is 205-871- . . . ."

That same strange pull smothered Seth's hesitancy to call. He picked up the phone, then a few moments passed, but something dialed the first number for him.

"Mrs. Gaston, my name is Seth Sentel. One of your husband's clients sort of referred me to him. Is it possible to reach him?"

"Well, he's at the club for his usual Saturday doubles match."

Seth made a snap decision. He felt awful about it, but he resolved not to lie. "Oh, yes, his usual doubles match. I haven't visited his club recently, would you mind giving me directions?"

Mrs. Gaston provided directions. It struck Seth she might be naïve, then that she reminded him of himself. He was in too much of a hurry to beat himself up. He ran out the door.

CHAPTER TWENTY-THREE

He and the Jeep converted the eighty-minute drive to Birmingham into sixty-five minutes. He arrived at the Birmingham Country Club in another twenty. He inquired at the tennis shop and was directed to a clay court where Elliot's doubles match was ongoing. The match was a fast paced affair, complete with spectacular reaction volleys and overhead slams, along with several arguments, which Elliot graciously seemed to lose on purpose. Elliot and his playing partner, a white-haired man who never committed an unforced error, won in a tiebreaker.

Elliot was a gentleman of a winner. The mid-thirties attorney complimented his opponents, downplayed his own impressive skills, and directed the credit to his partner. Seth introduced himself as a friend and classmate of H.R.'s. Elliot seemed pleased to make the acquaintance.

"I was struck by his untimely passage. I heard it was a hunting accident."

"Or so says the Sheriff."

"Ah. Well, I suppose we're not dealing with the investigative equivalent of Oliver Wendell Holmes, are we, counselor?" Seth remembered the lack of yellow crime tape.

Elliot continued. "When Mr. Hampton broke the bad news, I was struck not only by a sense of loss, but also by one of coincidence. A law student in his early twenties not only desires a rather unique will, but also expires soon after its execution. It's not what my practice typically encounters."

"A unique will?"

119

"Yes, it contained- Oh. I almost forgot. As past counsel for H.R., and current counsel for his estate, I'm not at liberty to reveal this type information until the will is probated, not even to you, Seth."

"Not even to me?"

"Let's just say today wasn't the first occasion I've heard your name." Seth saw the telling look in Elliot's eye.

Seth volleyed back the look and replied, "I've also stumbled on some interesting information. There was a message on H.R.'s answering machine from Asst. Dean Thurow, who was returning H.R.'s call. Thurow wasn't H.R.'s favorite pompous academician, so H.R. wouldn't have called him without a serious reason. Also, H.R. just purchased some life insurance, and he left me an out-of-character note recommending I contact you. This stuff would puzzle anyone who knew H.R., but the faster I can gather the pieces, the faster I can put them together."

Elliot peered at Seth a little more thoroughly than light conversation would dictate. He turned his head an inch to the right and said, "Come along, Seth, and I'll show you some real tennis players."

They walked two courts over to a mixed doubles match. Thirty other spectators watched with interest. Seth noticed that the players on one side were relatives.

Elliot confirmed the notion. "The two on the left are siblings from old money. The girl is two years younger than her brother."

The girl of sixteen wore a classy-cute ponytail, and it swished to and fro like that of a thoroughbred mare. Seth watched her hit a delicate drop shot down the right side, a certain winner that caused the member audience to smile and raise their hands to applaud. They were premature. From the left, a blaze of brown hair and red shirt cut to the net and hit a backhand slap shot. The now-stilled ponytail never even prepped her racquet. Her brother flung a hard forehand of blame right between her eyes.

"Interesting, isn't it, Seth? There's still no substitute for speed. He's a Hoover kid. It's a new money suburb south of town. He trains on public courts, yet has a gift all the old money on the globe could never buy."

A few points later, the pony tail's brother blasted a hot, solid-sounding first serve, but, as it curved out of the reach of any mere human, the Hoover kid made a reflexive dive to his right, his racquet stretched out so far that it threatened to unhinge his arm. He was parallel to the ground when the yellow ball struck it, then flew like a yellow ribbon by the charging server's head, spinning it from self-congratulation to disgrace. The pony-tailed sister looked at her bewildered brother, enjoying her turn to fling the blame. Seth smiled.

"It's interesting, Seth. At times, the unexpected happens, and the game goes to the one with the gift, not to the home club favorite. Seth saw Elliot make a futile attempt to subdue a revealing smile. Seth was quick too, but he had to study Elliot a second before the full meaning of the match settled in.

Once it had, his face revealed his wonderment. "So, what *is* the prize for this match?"

Elliot suppressed a chuckle as he marveled at his successful circumvention and at how Seth recognized it.

"Details are difficult to communicate with sports analogies, but let's just say the winner takes all, with only a few prizes for the others, most of whom are without need anyway." Seth's pupils expanded as he thought about H.R.'s wealthy family. "I'll call you after the funeral, Seth. There are a few important and confidential details to discuss. For now, I'll only say, as the next Bjorn Borg out there will soon discover, that great responsibilities often accompany great gifts."

♦

Seth drove home. It was as if his Jeep's interior was filled with a sense of honor, something that terrified him, yet empowered him, too. He'd never been the beneficiary of a will.

Asst. Dean Thurow had asked Seth to speak at a memorial service for H.R. and Sue, and now, writing a eulogy seemed no longer a task. The idea of discussing H.R.'s murder with a Sheriff, on the other hand, worried him.

CHAPTER TWENTY-FOUR

Elliot hit the showers and drove a Volvo to his Mountain Brook English Tudor. His wife had prepared his favorite: roasted salmon in champagne sauce. He read a bedtime story to his little girl, Mary Catherine, and tucked his nine-year-old son Little Elliot, "little E", into a bed shaped like a Piper Cub airplane. He made love to his wife, but only after reminding her she made the finest salmon in champagne sauce on the planet.

He fetched a drink of ice water, then, intelligent man that he was, wondered about H.R. and Seth. He still didn't quite believe H.R. was dead. He'd thought the big redheaded kid was kidding or maybe taking something too seriously, but the lad had been persistent, not to mention willing to pay his usual big firm fee. So, he'd done the will and taken possession of his sealed documents addressed to another law student named Seth Sentel.

He realized he wasn't surprised that Sentel had shown up today. H.R. had said Sentel was a principled, trustworthy, inquisitive type. This opinion H.R. had offered in response to a question about why family members received such a small slice of his surprisingly large net worth. And then there was that look in the Sentel kid's eyes, like he was on a mission from God.

He swirled the ice in his glass and considered whether there was something else he was, as an ethical attorney, obligated to do. Should he notify the authorities? Elliot made a mental note to discuss the matter with Hound Dog Hampton and the other senior partners Monday morning.

At midnight, he was still awake. His contented wife snoozed beside him. He switched his thoughts away from death. He'd fly tomorrow. The weather would be clear and cool, perfect for a 500-mile round-trip to Gulf Shores in the Beechcraft Baron twin-engine his father had sold him on the cheap. He'd take little Elliot with him. The persistent youngster had begged to fly with daddy for months, and Elliot had promised to take him on his fourth birthday. He considered the image his son's face would have when they flew over their house and saw how small it appeared from the air.

Elliot fell asleep smiling.

♦

At two a.m., it was quiet around the metal hangar housing Elliot's Beechcraft. The same man who'd followed Seth to the Club had more tasks on his to-do list. On this cool, silent night, this intruder made barely a sound. The simple burglar alarm had been easy enough to disarm. He found the correct plane and got busy.

It didn't hurt that the red-haired man in the dark jumpsuit had been both an airplane mechanic and a foot soldier during the Vietnam War. They'd kept him a year in the Army Special Forces, but after that, his airplane mechanic experience got him out of the jungle. North Vietnam merited bombing at an increasing level, and more men were needed to keep the jets flying.

Sabotaging a plane was a little trickier with a twin-engine, but he knew the secret. *Just a few minor adjustments to the fuel line where it ran near the heater*, he thought, and he'd create an equipment malfunction, a handy fire hazard. Besides, once a plane like this exploded, there wouldn't be much left for the FAA boys to investigate.

♦

Earlier that evening, a portly young law student had assumed the role of pest control specialist in charge of the monthly spray-down at Birmingham's Financial Center, the same building housing Hound Dog's law firm, Hampton and Hellums, the same firm where Elliot was a partner. The usual exterminator had suffered an unfortunate blow to the head and, wearing only boxer shorts imprinted with bowling pins, slept in the back of his van, minus his keys, uniform, and equipment.

Another law student had clerked at the firm two summers earlier and knew the floor layout by memory. The fat impostor proceeded straight to the file room and removed a sealed envelope from the H.R. Garrison file. Then, he made a photograph of H.R.'s will. He sprayed down two of the forty-five rooms on the way out, walked away, and drove back to Tuscaloosa.

♦

Nothing but blue sky ahead, Elliot glanced over at "Little E", whose little face was pinned to the window of the Beechcraft as they flew over their Mountain Brook home.

"Wow, dad. Everything looks so small, kind'a like everything's a toy!"

Elliot agreed and smiled. *These are the moments*, he thought, the moments that made all his high stress, high-priced lawyer work worth it.

He throttled the Baron up a bit, and within moments, they'd cruised over all of suburbia: Homewood, Vestavia Hills, and Hoover were all behind them.

Little E had another comment. "I smell gas, daddy."

Intrigued, Elliot looked over and asked daddy-like, "Hmm. Did you do a tootie, little E?"

"No, daddy. It smells kind'a like the gas that goes in the car."

"Really son? I don't smell any-"

Elliot didn't smell gas. He smelled smoke. Then, he saw it. "What the-"

"Daddy, something's burning."

Elliot already had the headset on. "May-day. May-day."

Little E cried out his next words. "Daddy, I want to go home."

Elliot coughed out his. "It's time to pray, Little E. Time to *pray* we get home."

Little E clasped his hands together to pray, just like his daddy had taught him.

Elliot had other things to do. "May-day. May-day."

CHAPTER TWENTY-FIVE

At 4 p.m. Monday, January 20, 1986, Seth opened the door to Sheriff Ray "Pork Chop" Gibson's office behind the Tuscaloosa County Courthouse. He saw a disputably attractive receptionist talking on the phone, flipping through a *Frederick's of Hollywood* catalogue.

She addressed an apparent girlfriend. "No, he's just not your type. He's too uppity of a lawyer. You need someone who's more country." She paused to listen. "That's not true. Some folks from the country are loaded. You take my Uncle Josh. He's got so doggone much timberland that he never has to work. He just sells a few more trees whenever his second wife wants another Jaguar. Can you imagine? Buying a Jag just so you can run it up and down a damn dirt road!" There was another pause to laugh. "Hang on, someone just came in."

Seth saw an opportunity to advantage himself, and, despite his conscience, couldn't resist politely doing so. "Hello, I'm Seth Sentel, and coincidentally, my family is in the timber business, too."

Her left hand disappeared under the table, but there was no missing the one-carat flash. She was about twenty-seven, wore a white blouse along with hair both dark and big. She also had two of the brightest eyes which had ever lusted.

"Yes, Mr.-"

"Sentel. Seth Sentel."

"May I help you?"

"I'm a law student at the University and was hoping to see the Sheriff a moment about something."

"Oh, like maybe a school project?"

Seth considered whether to lie. "You might call it that."

"Okay. Maybe I can arrange a meeting," she said, as if hinting she could also arrange one with her.

"Great. Is this a good time?"

"Well, he's on the phone with his wife now, but he should be off any hour now." She smiled and giggled at her sense of humor. Seth returned the smile part. She pointed to the chair in front of her desk. "Why don't you sit in that chair while you wait?" Seth took the hint.

She stared and said, "So, you were saying your family's in the timber business. Where abouts?"

Seth stared back. "You know where nowhere is?"

She shook her head playfully, her eyes lingering. "I guess."

"It's on the other side of there."

They smiled together, and she added the expected giggle until Seth said, "It's just south of Montgomery, in Fawnlund."

"Yeah, I know that place. It's on the way to the beach."

"Right. It's close to Greenville, where we went for fun on the weekend," Seth said with twisted lips.

"Sounds like an exciting place, this Fawnlund."

"Yeah, a real Las Vegas of the South."

She kept smiling and preened a bit. Seth noticed all the phone lines in front of her had cleared. The Sheriff had finished his *Yes dears* for the day, but Seth didn't have the heart to mention it just yet.

"So, Mr. Seth Sentel, tell me more about your family in Fawnlund."

"It's also into politics, banking, and entrepeneuring."

"Entrepeneuring! What's that?"

Entertained by the wide-eyed, emphatic way she formulated her inquiries, Seth continued the banter. Three minutes later, as if he'd forgotten why he was there, he asked, "Is the Sheriff available yet?"

She looked at her unlit phone and replied with genuine surprise, "Oh. Yes, he is."

She reached the Sheriff on the intercom, and with a more professional sounding lisp, announced, "There's a nice young gentleman from the law school here to speak with you. May I bring him back? His name is Seth Sentel." A slight pause ensued. "You're already acquainted? Really?" Seth had stood, and she was gazing up and down his solid frame. "Well, he looks like he played football. Okay, I'll show him back." She latched her bright, green eyes onto his brown ones again. He noticed she had removed her engagement ring.

"So, you played football for Bama?"

"For a few years."

"Sheriff Gibson says he remembers you playing."

"Well, I'm flattered."

They reached the Sheriff's Office. When he saw Sheriff Pork Chop again, Seth realized the origin of the nickname, the massive man must've consumed a ton of them. Deputy Dolton was seated to one side of a massive desk. They became reacquainted. Seth had been sufficiently fortunate to have avoided his company since the bodies were found.

The Sheriff seemed cordial. With a self-congratulatory grin, he said, "I knew I'd heard of you before. You played for the Bear a few years back."

"Right. Until I was hurt."

"Made a good tackle against Auburn on a kickoff return, right?"

Seth's humility answered. "So they tell me."

Seth's heroic status established, the Sheriff offered some county budget coffee and asked him to have a seat. "So, Seth, how have you been? I know it must've been tough losing a good buddy like H.R., and the girl Sue, too. I've heard she was a sweetheart."

"I've been okay, I guess. The good thing about law school is that you're too busy to dwell very much."

"Yeah, I guess so. I know I never could've made it through law school. Lord, it was all I could do to get through undergrad, right Kenny? And in Criminal Justice at that." The Sheriff and his chief deputy enjoyed a law enforcement insider chuckle. Seth wondered if the Sheriff had flirted with decadence during his college days. "Anyway, glad you're staying busy, Mr. Sentel. Idle hands is the devil's workshop."

Deputy Dolton spoke as if he couldn't wait to do so. "And if that's true, he's got a well-equipped one in our receptionist, right, Sheriff?"

Another law enforcement laugh.

"You know, I've gotta find more meaningful tasks for her or else she'll get us *all* in trouble. Since she got engaged to a rich defense lawyer, it's just been worse. The woman's like a cat in heat, except she's that way all year long."

They were still laughing, even as the Sheriff spoke. Seth smiled a little to go along. Sheriff Gibson settled down and asked, "So, to what do we owe your visit?"

"How is the investigation going? Any leads?"

"Leads?" The Sheriff seemed a little confused by the word.

"Right. Are you on the trail of any particular suspect, and have you talked to the city police about a possible connection with the Rentzell-Hays murders?"

"Oh, of course. I guess we're used to using the word *lead* only in cases of intentional killings. With a more or less accidental shooting like this one, we view the situation differently. Besides, we know the shooter, so there's no leads left to follow."

Seth felt the shock hit his face. "Two people killed, and it's an accident?" Then it hit him again. "You know who shot H.R. and Sue?"

"Just need a confession, but old Kenny is working on one. Right, Kenny?"

Kenny seemed more than pleased to re-enter the conversation. "It shouldn't be more than another day, unless he lawyers-up, and I doubt he has the good sense to do so. The trick is to read 'em their rights real fast. The hard part with backwoods folk like Lymon is catching 'em, but once you've got 'em in custody, it gets less complicated, if you know what I mean."

Seth's face came alive. His eyes raced from Deputy to Sheriff. The name Lymon leapt from his memory to his imagination. "When did you decide it was an accident and that this Lymon was the shooter?" As he spoke, Seth now realized why the cabin hadn't been secured as a crime scene.

"Although I'll admit it took two days to be sure, I had a good idea from when I saw the scene, you know, in the woods."

"What do you mean, sir?"

"Well, the first thing I noticed was where it happened. That part of the county sees a lot of hunting, and a lot of trespassing, too. Many of the landowners up there are absentee, like Mr. Garrison's cousin, so the locals take advantage of the situation during deer season, right Kenny?"

"Always have, Sheriff. Helped the game warden arrest a few up there."

"So, you've got a better than average chance of a stray bullet to begin with, right, Kenny?"

"I wouldn't hunt up there without a flak jacket myself, Sheriff."

"Anyway, when you look at the fact they were killed by a high-powered rifle, it adds more wood to the accidental fire, if you get my meaning." Seth nodded as if to grant the simplistic analogy the respect it wasn't due. "Then, you look at how we found no sign of footprints in the area, other than those of your friends and two Beagles. The shooter must have been a long ways off, which suggests to me a randomly fired bullet: you know, a stray." Another accommodating nod from Seth. "Given that only one bullet was fired, there's no escaping the conclusion this was a hunting accident."

The nodding stopped. Seth again appeared newly informed. "There was only one bullet?"

"I realize that don't sound quite possible, but the forensics boys up in Birmingham have already confirmed it. One projectile, as those boys like to say, killed 'em, uh, um, resulted in both deaths." Seth sat motionless. "Sounds like a one-in-a-million situation, but I guess that's the point. There ain't no way somebody could've done that on purpose, shooting one moving target through the throat, then another behind him in the head. Kenny, you ever known anyone good enough with a rifle to pull that one off?"

"Sheriff, I've been around guns and shooters for thirty years, and I've seen some good marksmen, and even some fine markswomen like my big sister, but I never seen anybody could make that shot from 200 yards or so."

Seth was trying not to seem amazed at the revelation of the one bullet. Now there was a new suggestion about how far away the shooter was. "Two-hundred yards? Why so far?"

"Well, like I said, we couldn't find any sign of strange footprints inside that radius, nothing but some old three-wheeler tread tracks, and the ground was damp. Besides, they were standing in an open area, and for a hunter out in the woods to have not seen or heard them, he must have been about that far away. You're talking 75 yards to the nearest tree line and, with those pines being thinned not long ago, I'd give it another hundred or a bit more for there to be enough trees available to block the shooter's sight line."

Baffled, a still polite Seth asked, "So, are you saying that, because the shooter was so far away, it was an accident, or that because it was an accident, the shooter was so far away?"

The Sheriff took a moment to stare at the ceiling. Deputy Yes-Man didn't seem focused on anything. The Sheriff tilted his head left, then right, while his lips moved silently before saying "Maybe both, I guess. Well anyway, if you consider . . . Now, what was I about to say?"

A look over at Kenny with the sharp-shooting sister was no help. "Oh, well, the long and short of it is that no one could place a round that exactly from 200 yards. It had to be an accident, or if we can make it stick, a reckless shooting, and as soon as we get old Lymon to fess up, this case'll be done. Then, you and Mrs. Longshore can rest easy knowing things are made right."

Seth skipped the circular reasoning issue and switched subjects. "So, you've got Lymon here at the jail?"

Kenny spoke with no success at hiding his pride. "Yep, picked him up this morning. The guy was making a painting. He's in there still working on it. I figured if you're good to a Lymon and let him keep up his hobbies in jail, then he'll trust you enough to cooperate."

Seth was astounded, but his mind had processed the revelation so fast that it scarcely registered.

With a grin the size of his waist, the Sheriff asked, "Would you like to see him?"

"Who?"

"Lymon." The Sheriff stood; Dolton too. "Come along, and I'll let you in the jail for a quick look."

Seth was too shaken to let the offer surprise him. He followed the Sheriff, who led Seth through the back of the office to the jail entrance. The three were admitted through the multiple checkpoints and into the jail, and Seth was soon infected with a case of the creeps. The damp cement stench and the strange auditory cocktail of wretched silence and desperate, unhappy noises invaded his senses.

The Sheriff stopped two cells short of Lymon's space and said in a whisper, "There he is, Lymon C. Bream. Two cells down on the left."

Dolton added more noise. "Unfortunately, he don't say much. He just paints and mumbles."

Seth raised his eyes from the cement floor and gazed at the inmate, who wore the standard jumpsuit over his thin, 5' 9" frame. His hair was cut short and slicked back. The jumpsuit was buttoned all the way to the top, gifting him with the look of propriety. Seth noted the calm intensity in the man's eyes as he studied the easel before him and made precise, delicate strokes with the brush. Deep in his own processes, Seth lost track of time.

Lymon looked back at him. Seth felt pierced. The look flew into his eyes, but kept traveling, much farther than Seth was emotionally prepared. Seth felt like a child was peering at him, pleading with him the way a small boy with a hurt foot looks up at his father. Seth inhaled, his eyes alive with realization. He wished he could see the painting.

He said, "I'm ready to go. I've seen him."

They made their way back to Sheriff Gibson's office. Seth avoided a chair. Gibson and Dolton found theirs, and Seth eyed the Sheriff from above him. "I have some things to tell you. No one else knows them." They both looked at Seth, then at each other. "After this happened, I found a note from H.R. It suggested he was involved in something, something risky."

Deputy Know-nothing couldn't restrain his ignorance. "You mean like gambling?"

Seth let that one go without recognizing it.

"It's something more local. I think it involves the law school. It also relates to a place H.R. sometimes visited."

The Sheriff was at least curious. "What kind of place?"

"The Nasty Tap. It's a nighttime establishment law students frequent."

"We know The Tap well," the two lawmen said together.

Deputy Dingbat gave way to the Sheriff. "We had to help out the city boys with a fight or two there. The place has some of the queerest loud music I've ever heard. What was that band's name playing there last month, Kenny?"

"Wasn't it the Bad Appetites, Sheriff?"

"Maybe, or was it the Bad Attitudes?"

"Yeah, that was it, Sheriff, and some of them frat boys had just that."

"Yeah, I remember the shiner one of them gave you, Kenny." Kenny's face fell two inches.

Even Seth had finite patience, so he interjected. "Anyway, something was going on at The Tap."

Sheriff Gibson leaned forward. "Just between us, and since his reputation is no longer a consideration, did H.R. have maybe, uh, a little recreational narcotic complication, um, kind'a like your buddies Rentzell and Hays did?"

Seth aimed his anger at Gibson, his reply a direct hit. "I knew him. He never even smoked a regular cigarette. He drank no more than any college student, and had only women on his mind when he did. And one more thing. Rumor says Rentzell and Hays passed post-mortem drug tests, something an average voter would expect you to know. H.R. heard that rumor. Why haven't you?"

The Sheriff retreated, both palms held shoulder high. "I don't doubt what you're saying, but do understand, I guess it's just law enforcement instincts taking over, but we're always inclined to ask certain questions." Seth's eyes remained frozen. The Sheriff continued, "For instance, my next natural question would be, because he had a healthy interest in women, could that explain his note? I've seen men feel sorry for prostitutes and try to save them from their pimps, and I've seen the pimps not take too kindly to their gals being saved."

"H.R. wouldn't pay for a woman. That would be like a caterpillar paying for another leg."

Deputy Dufus's apparent eagerness to inject stupidity knew no bounds. "Might depend on whether the legs he had were getting the job done."

A quick glare from the Sheriff cut Dolton off and limited the damage. Gibson began again, apparently intrigued. "Anything else suggest he was involved in something risky?"

"He left me $200,000 from a life insurance policy he took out soon before he was killed. I think I'm to use the money to follow up on whatever he'd discovered." The law boys sat back in their chairs. Seth saw an opening to make his points, but his voice weakened. "H.R. wasn't specific. The Birmingham attorney who did his will was supposed to fill me in on the details, but he can't tell me until later this week. One reason I'm here is to find out whether what you know and what I know match up."

"Well now, I don't see it. Lymon's not the type to be mixed up in any kind of scandal or intentional crime. He's just a country hick, kind of like something out of the movie *Deliverance*, but without the meanness. We found a .308 Weatherby hunting rifle hidden in the ceiling of his dog's house, and it matches the caliber of the fatal bullet. Ballistics is working on an exact match, and even though the bullet was a little damaged by the multiple impacts, I'd be willing to bet it came from Lymon's gun. The fact that it was a mushrooming bullet protected a few markings on the stem."

Resigned to the fact this meeting would reveal nothing helpful, Seth arose to leave but asked, "So, how are you so sure the rifle was Lymon's? How does a poor guy like him wind up with a nice Weatherby?"

Kenny couldn't resist. "I reckon he stole it."

Seth fired back, "Thought he wasn't the type."

The Sheriff wanted no arguments between one of his deputies and a friend of a victim, so he hoisted himself up and began to walk with Seth to the front door. "Now, Mr. Sentel, we're here to serve this county, and if it ever looks like old Lymon knows more than he's telling, I guarantee I'll find out what. Realize, though, that if the ballistics tests show a match and he confesses to being the only participant in an accidental shooting, then my hands are gonna be tied."

As Seth propped open the door with his back, he sensed a weak courage brewing within. "Fine Sheriff, but mine won't be."

Seth walked out, and the Receptionist said, "You know, Sheriff, I even like the way he talks."

The Sheriff shuffled back and mumbled, "Not sure *I* do."

CHAPTER TWENTY-SIX

For the student body, the first few days after the shooting were a wasteland of collective mourning. H.R. and Sue had become quite popular, courtesy of their loyalty, their friendly manner, their refreshing senses of humor, and their overall complete lack of law-school inspired arrogance. H.R. was a wayward Romeo, but a lovable and generous one. Sue was no legal genius, but to dislike her was impossible.

Monday, January 20, 1986 was MLK Day, so Asst. Dean Thurow called for a memorial service to be held at two p.m. Tuesday the 21st. in the moot court room. The funerals were set for Wednesday in Huntsville and Thursday in Texas. Because of the consensus about Rentzell and Hays's drug involvement, they never got a memorial. They were sent off with little more than a twenty-one rumor salute.

On this short notice, Thurow was inconsiderate enough to name Seth as one of four speakers. Still too shocked to be angry, Seth acquiesced. Thurow also named Cindi, Professor Goodfried--an obvious choice--and the uninspiring Professor Borland--a not-so-obvious choice--who nonetheless served the purpose of gender neutrality. Thurow had also invited a black Legal Beagles teammate to speak, but because he and H.R. were barely acquainted, he declined.

Citing freedom of the press, Thurow invited the local media to attend. Their presence only added to Seth's emotional overload. It also didn't help that he'd ignored Cindi since the murder, and as he sat next to her on the front row, he sensed her displeasure.

Goodfried eased toward the podium, his usual relaxed dress code only altered by the addition of a blue blazer.

The good professor began. "Death is a certainty. Ultimately, its nature isn't random. You may fight it, but only with the knowledge of its victory. So, how then does one born to die respond? How do we deal with an enigma more powerful than any being? One could consider what he or she leaves behind, a reputation, a professional contribution, and perhaps a small measure of wherewithal for one's dependents. All these are fine bequests.

Our friend H.R., however, has left us with an abundance of a different inheritance--the gifts of happiness, laughter, and the good memory of a likable presence. If we leave behind many who were happier and more loved with us, than they would have been without us, then we've left a special legacy."

A person who supports a man of the people has also fashioned a valuable remainder. For the sower of love needs the spirit to sow, and such a spirit best arises in the midst of encouragement. Thus, it is a certainty young Sue has also done well."

Goodfried paused and looked down a moment. "For those of us who remain, our task is to model the example of these two. To assist and protect others, and to appreciate the assister, are both fine callings. May we all seek to heed those callings. May we all agree to assume those legacies."

Goodfried strolled away, his suede, soft-soled shoes scarcely invading the silence that paid homage to his words. Seth glanced at the gathered and surmised their sad satisfaction with Goodfried's sensitive speech. Thurow had decreed that Cindi speak second, possibly calculating that, if a student followed each teacher, it would create the effect of the wiser, elder leader being echoed by his or her respectful pupil.

Cindi's words were those of a law student, but also those of a sorority girl who had lost a "sister." She spoke of H.R. with a fondness one might have for an old college chum. "He was my buddy," she declared with unabashed accentuation. The student body smiled at her casual wording. Seth was reminded of Cindi's endearing, sometimes childish, quality, a prominent feature of her unfathomable, yet magnetic, emotional makeup. He sought refuge in her perfect face and failed to comprehend another word she said.

There was one thing certain to deepen a young student's despondency, a monologue by Betty Borland. There was nothing girlish to sweeten the somber nature of her demeanor. Dressed in an overstated high-necked black dress, Borland approached the podium as if it were the coffins of the deceased. Her black hair was pulled tight against the white skin of her face, uncolored as it was with makeup or joy.

Professor Borland spoke glibly of meaning and its scarcity, truth and its escape, life and its brevity. She changed the subject, but no one among the sedate seemed to notice. She lectured on the importance of integrity, how its preservation was paramount, and why and when risk and sacrifice were in order. She droned on about the future of the law school and the profession.

Then she mentioned something else. "Mankind should be grateful to history for begetting its great leaders, and prayerful that history and its institutions will continue to bear the strong, principled leaders who will save them both."

Seth looked at his shoes and felt some strange stirring within his being, countering the psyche infection he'd been battling for the last five months. He thought he noted an odd harshness in how Cindi looked at Borland.

Few in attendance seemed to comprehend Borland's final sentences. "Universities, in large part, are for the young, to test them, to prepare them, and to acclimate them for more costly and meaningful endeavors. In the rare instance, however, the young must wrestle fate without sufficient training. That's when their character becomes everything."

Borland returned to her place beside Seth, who glanced at Cindi, who seemed to glare at him as if he was incompetent. Borland switched her gaze to him, a look only the grim reaper could duplicate, yet a look Seth thought reserved something special for him, something out of place on a ghostly facade.

A synthesis of hurt, confusion, and embarrassment crawled up his spine. He perceived that a pause had blanketed the room. Then, he realized it was his turn to speak.

Seth had over-prepared for his speech, but it hadn't helped. He reached the podium, fumbled with his notes, and looked at the scribbled pages. He panned the crowd with eyes that moved too fast, eyes that then rested upon Borland. Now, he had something to say.

"Someone killed a friend of mine." Every one of four hundred eyes shifted and pinned itself to the podium. "They killed a friend of mine and someone special to him." The eyes looked at each other, challenged and astonished. H.R.'s Casanova ways were well known. "H.R. and Sue had become engaged on the day they died, maybe only an hour before." He heard the whispers and gasps, but blocked them out and continued. "This wonderful, though unexpected, circumstance reveals a great deal."

The student body became a collective microphone. Borland eyed Seth. Goodfried's face, which rested in his right hand, appeared lively, yet calm. "This fact speaks volumes. The obvious implication is a profound change in H.R., not one to be confused with a Marrying Man. Something powerful must have affected H.R. A vague notion instructs me that it was not just Sue. It also suggests that, because of his new viewpoint, H.R.

was engaging in new behavior. He was taking new risks, and he was fighting new fights he once might have avoided. I believe he'd changed . . . and that it was change that killed him. H.R. and Sue's death was no accident. It was murder."

♦

Asst. Dean Thurow froze in mid-exhale. The last thing a man like him wanted was unfounded controversy and uncontrolled publicity, but he saw the crowd latched onto Seth, filtering his every word. He didn't cut him off. The unpopularity was too much to risk.

♦

"One more thing--I've heard that Rentzell and Hays passed drug tests, and unless somebody proves they were dealers, then the presumption of innocence should follow them to their graves. They should get a memorial service too."

Seth cut a glance at Thurow, then went on. "I've seen the man in custody regarding these deaths." The crowd looked at itself in awe. Jaws dropped; eyes widened. "I only had to see his face to know his innocence. He could kill no human, not even recklessly. He's an uneducated outcast, but he's also untouched by a world that can convert men into killers, and there was too much care in his eyes for him to be reckless."

Seth heard whispers. "How does he know?" "Who does he think he is?" "Who *is* he?" He saw the media's focused eyes, like those of wolves onto an injured prey.

Seth's last observation was to be his most powerful, the one that sent the media into hype-stage, the one that, if it weren't last, would have convinced Thurow to step in, the one that sent the rumor mill of a close-knit institution into overdrive.

"From what I know, and I admit a need to know more, I have compelling reasons to believe people associated with this law school are involved with these murders." He paused. "I hope these people are afraid."

Seth stopped and stepped toward the aisle. He'd been true to his friend. He'd done the right thing. He walked past everyone toward the big back door. He saw the crowd stare at itself for a clue about how to stare. Seth glanced over at Thurow, who seemed confused by the confusion, maybe unnerved by his failure to fathom the direction of the wind. Cindi knew Seth and his philosophical ways. Her face showed a futile embarrassment for him.

It was quiet as Seth still walked up the aisle. An initial clap of two hands bounced off the mock courtroom's walls. This sound bred other randomly dispersed claps, which soon combined to generate applause. The noise grew in volume and linkage, swallowing the room with a respectful ovation.

Seth sensed waves of nervous energy pouring over him. Cindi looked over at Goodfried, seemingly with admiration, as he continued to lead the respectful chorus of hands that he'd begun.

CHAPTER TWENTY-SEVEN

Seth was sleeping well that night, but at 4:30 a.m. on Wednesday morning, January 22, 1986, the *Birmingham News* hit the Chancellor's driveway. It skipped across the cement and into the flowerbed, as Seth had noted it always did, then came to rest three feet from Charlemagne. The big tomcat's head snatched up, and he bolted out to find a more peaceful bed.

Seth's head snatched up, too, but he had nowhere to run.

The paper landed heavy this morning, Seth realized. He considered whether to make a futile attempt to return to sleep. Today, Seth felt differently about life, as if there was something more important to fight than it. He knew the effort to sleep would be wasted, and with a long day ahead--packed with activities like criminal investigation, legal reading and analysis, and Ivy League dog walking--he rolled out of bed and yanked on a pair of jeans.

Throwing on a sweatshirt, he tried to ignore his guilt about not attending the funerals. He was in no state of mind to face Susan's mother again, so he sent flowers. He thought H.R. would understand if he went right to work on the investigation, so he made his apologies to the Garrisons and sent a large donation in H.R.'s name to the Texas Wildlife Fund, the charity named in H.R.'s will.

He ambled down the staircase, scooped up the rubber-banded paper, and walked through a cold darkness across the patio to the Number 11 kitchen. He started a pot of Columbian coffee, removed a carton of heavy cream from the commercial fridge and sat on the tiled countertop to scan the front page.

The lead story was boring: Yet another state politician had been indicted. He unfolded the paper and saw a sub-headline at the bottom, just above a photograph of some charred wreckage. *Local Attorney And Young Son Lost In Sunday Afternoon Plane Crash.* Elliot Gaston, nice guy lawyer, was dead. It had taken a few days to identify the bodies and notify the next of kin.

For seven seconds, Seth sat still, speed-reading about the deadly crash into a wooded area in Shelby County, one mile from a small airport adjacent to Interstate 65. Because the beat writer had taken an extra day to investigate, the story contained plenty of sad and scary details. Seth had never known such a personal manner of bad news on the doorstep. He'd never experienced this real brand of fear before daybreak. His hand shook while it gripped the coffeepot. He spilled seven drops. An eighth drop hung suspended, like a stalactite.

Seth felt the urge to find a hole and hide awhile. The last few days had been too much to risk an encounter with another human. He returned to his room, sat in the window seat, and absorbed the emerging daylight.

H.R.'s note rested halfway open on a nearby desk. Seth felt it pull him. The urge to re-read it seized him. He turned toward it, rubbed his left eye, and lifted it, then absorbed it with a mind relaxed. The mention of allegedly great people was meaningful. Myerson was the suspect only a fool would miss. Myerson was no doubt prominent, and not just at the law school. Myerson and H.R. were also proven natural adversaries, two men from opposing schools of attitude. He considered their past altercations, wondered what type conflict their philosophic differences might have bred.

He sat back and remembered. In every situation, Myerson hadn't shied from confronting H.R., and H.R. hadn't backed down, had even been ready to fight him that day after class. Maybe the final New Orleans altercation led to something beyond confrontation. The reference to The Tap had to be meaningful too, but how it might relate to Myerson would have to yield to research. Maybe H.R.'s social adventures had unmasked some ugly truth Myerson wished to preserve. The rest of the note Seth took as typical hyperbolic H.R.-speak, with the Rentzell-Hays reference a jigsaw puzzle piece that just didn't seem to fit. Then, there was no forgetting perhaps the most damning indicator of Myerson's possible involvement in something illicit, namely his firm pre-game reprimand: "We're here to play football, you two, not to play detective."

The intense focus produced a high, and Seth noticed his hurt and fear had disappeared, replaced by the nirvanic rush of a mind firing on all cylinders. In the past, he'd wanted to run away any time H.R. took on Myerson, or anyone else. His mind leapt to the day he and H.R. visited the local Burger King, the event H.R. mentioned in his last phone call.

◆

It was the Thursday of the first final exams week. The Contracts test was the following day, and every first-year legal mind was delving deep into the caverns of offer and acceptance, unconscionable agreements, and other subjects of grave disinterest.

Seth was in the Football Room, a small meeting room decorated with photographs of Coach Bryant, Joe Namath, and a wall full of other Alabama football legends. Guy students loved to study here. The football memorabilia somehow made the law go down a little easier; yet, today, Seth sat with his forehead in both hands, beating himself to an emotional pulp for not yet being a preeminent legal scholar.

Fortuitously, H.R. stopped by. "Hey, Seth!"

"Hey, H.R. What's up with the seventh wonder of the red-headed world?"

"My hunger index, Sethinator. Let's fly this solitary confinement and hunt up some lunch."

Seth threw on a khaki windbreaker. "Most excellent idea."

H.R. announced, "I'm hungry enough to eat a Kroger. Where should we go?"

"Well, H.R., flame-broiled thoughts of Burger King are invading my glucose-starved brain cells."

"Well, I've never thought of a Whopper as brain food, but, then again, why not?"

They left the building and, amid an overcast sky, entered the real world. The winds of early December wisped about, vibrating the needles of the nearby pines. Above them, a local hawk called out to the sleeping earth below. They spied him above, soaring on the wind currents.

"Well, he's up there, H.R--a wild, free bird, just like you. Reckon someday you'll be caught and no longer free to roam without purpose?"

"Hold on. I may roam, but never without purpose."

"What's the purpose?"

"To discover my purpose."

Seth smiled and asked, "Do you think Sue could become part of your purpose?"

"I doubt it. She's beginning to assume the qualities of static cling. What about you and Cindi? Are you two made for the long run?"

"Well, maybe I can visualize it, but it takes two to make a vision a reality."

"Nice original quote."

"Thanks."

"Might she conceivably dump a younger guy like you?"

Seth shook his head. "I think I'm losing my sense of what's possible and what ain't."

H.R. laughed a telling little laugh. "It's funny when you slang-up a sentence, Seth. It's so out of character."

Seth asked, "You think a woman can throw a man off character?"

"Do you really mean throw him off his personality?"

Seth looked at H.R., this time with serious eyes. "I hope so."

They climbed inside H.R.'s Jeep and headed for the Burger King on Fifteenth Street near Central High, south of the stadium.

H.R. seemed to sense he'd hit an unintended target. He turned the focus on himself. "Back to this commitment notion. I guess other men do step voluntarily, or at least fall involuntarily, into it."

"Well, both of our parents are not yet divorced, and they were committed enough to engender us."

"Hmm. Commitment isn't evil, because it led to me. Now, there's an idea difficult to critique." He said this with a little smile. Seth knew any arrogance was faux.

"So, H.R., why do most men fear commitment?"

"I could write an instructive paperback on it, *Avoiding Commitment: Why and How To*. Chapter One, *Television Sports: Do You Remember When?* Chapter Two, *Children: How To Finance Them With Retirement Funds*. Yikes!"

"Is it that bad?"

"Worse. You should see how even my dad, world-famous surgeon, allows my mom all sorts of irrational control just to maintain civility."

"Really?"

H.R. responded playfully. "Yeah, it kind of saddens the masculine heart, assuming there *is* such a thing." Seth's eyes rolled as if on autopilot.

They arrived at the BK. Both ordered Whoppers with no onions, large fries, and shakes--Seth a vanilla and H.R. a chocolate. Several high school kids had arrived on lunch-hour furloughs. It was a generous allowance of freedom, but most were using it to either cut up or light up.

Seth and H.R. took a booth and the commitment conversation continued. "My conclusion, Sethster, is that commitment should be entered into, but only after a long period of stubborn procrastination. Now, I don't favor rough or impolite treatment during this period; give them as little as possible to legitimately complain about. Lord knows, they complain about enough with no grounds at all. But I do favor stalling tactics. This method puts the male prey in the optimal bargaining position. By the end of his independence, he's at least been able to barter certain assurances out of the predator."

"Gee, H.R., something tells me the National Organization for Women has a different idea about who the predator and prey are."

"They have a lot of different ideas about a lot of things."

Seth smiled. "With me, commitment has always seemed a matter of *who*, not of when."

An apparent lack of comprehension contorted H.R.'s face. "Really?"

"My guess is, only a finite number of compatible women exist for each guy. So, if fate happens to deliver such a female, a guy should lock in his gain, to use Wall Street terminology, lest he exist another ten years before stumbling upon a second."

"Gee, Seth. If you didn't make so much sense, you'd be annoying. Anyway, does your approach explain why you've been so hung up on Cindi?"

"Maybe so. She's a good *who* for me, and I've never met such a *who*."

149

Perhaps to avoid Seth's logic, H.R. took a bite out of his Whopper. "UHG! Onions. They put onions on my burger."

"Take it back and swap it."

H.R. walked to the counter, Whopper in hand. "Excuse me, but I ordered a Whopper with no onions, and this one has onions on it."

A bratty looking kid, no more than nineteen, with dirty blonde hair in a ponytail, looked down at the open-face Whopper.

"Sorry, dude. Look, why not just take the onions off?"

"What I'd like is another Whopper. I don't mind waiting for it."

"But that would be kind of a waste, dude. Why don't you just take off the onions and eat it."

Seth noted the Herculean self-control as the redheaded wonder kid gave the pony-tailed guy a look of professional kindness and responded, "Look, friend, would you mind if I discussed this with your manager?"

"Sure, no sweat off of my nose. He's the one who says we can't give out new ones."

The manager arrived and seemed even less impressive than his assistant. It's just that his incompetence was aged. He was a puffy-cheeked man of about forty who, from the equatorial size of his waistline, was waffling down most of the profits at this particular franchise.

H.R. said, "Sir, this Whopper has onions on it."

The manager peeked over the counter at it and said with a matching fat accent, "I see it does."

"Well, I ordered mine with no onions, and I'd like another one."

"Hm. If you'll just hand it over, I'll remove the onions. Then they'll be gone."

"Yeah, but it'll still have onion flavor and residue on it."

"Well, we can't take yours back. You've already bitten into it."

"Well, you don't have to, Mister Manager; I just want another one."

"Okay, I'll take care of it." Puffy cheeks looked over his narrow shoulder and, with the authority of a child impersonating a four-star general, yelled, "One Whopper. No onions."

When the new Whopper arrived, the manager placed it into a bag and said, "That'll be $1.08."

H.R.: "What'd you say?"

"For the new Whopper, sir. That'll be one dollar and eight cents."

"You want me to pay for it?"

"Only if you wish to eat it." The manager emitted a self-satisfied laugh.

"Mister Manager, this is a *Burger King*. Whatever happened to *have it your way*?"

"Look, we're sorry this happened, but I can't just be giving out free Whoppers."

"I don't want a free Whopper. I want the Whopper I ordered and paid for with no onions on it. Haven't you ever heard of contract law? I'm sure they taught you about proper performance in your manager-training course at Hamburger High. You have *not* substantially performed, so please give me another Whopper or just refund my money."

The words were steady rolling out of H.R. He didn't sound angry, just clear and firm. Seth was anxious, but enjoying the show and wondering how this would be resolved.

"Now wait a minute, I don't like you making fun of my career choice."

"Oh, you don't like me making fun of what will be a *short* career when a stunned Burger King headquarters receives my complaint letter? Listen, what *I* don't like is a Whopper with onions. So, you see this one?" The Michelin Man of a manager nodded. "Look a little closer."

He leaned over. H.R. still had half of the Whopper in each hand and, before Mister Manager could react, H.R. slapped both halves into the chubby face, rubbing in the catsup and mayo like sun tan oil.

Seth's nerves gave way to laughter. The high school kids joined him. Even the pony-tailed employee couldn't control himself.

H.R. delivered his summation. "Now, I think I'll be seated and enjoy my fries and chocolate shake." He shook his head. "Geesh."

H.R. was welcomed to his table with light applause, a sign the mis-manager had long practiced his particular methods. Four minutes later, the pony-tailed assistant brought over a sizzling Whopper and said with an entertained grin, "One Whopper, with no onions. Compliments of the manager."

H.R. thanked him as if nothing unusual had happened, then asked Seth, "Now what were we discussing?"

Seth almost hated to remind him. "The *whos* and *whens* of women."

"Right. I have to admit Sue is a good *who* for me because she puts up with my multiple flaws, e.g., my tendency to talk when I shouldn't, drink when I shouldn't, and jump her bones when I shouldn't. I just won't admit it to her, at least not for years to come." Seth smiled at the accurate admission of weakness. "Of course, you, Seth Sentel, All-American Alabamian, have no glaring weaknesses. So, such a consideration would be irrelevant." Seth eyed his Whopper and took another bite. H.R. peered at him tilt-headed, a bite of onion-less Whopper in each cheek. "What are you thinking, Seth?"

"Maybe I have some not-so-glaring weaknesses."

"Like what?"

"Like I never could've handled that manager the way you did."

"Why not? Was I not justified?"

"Sure you were, but he's a manager and twenty years older than we are."

"I demur, i.e. so what? Age and position don't grant one the right to be a cheap jerk."

"But I just couldn't have."

"Seth, who taught you to disrespect yourself? God gave you one valuable mind, so you've *got to stop* worshipping authority. Seth shrugged. "You know the bad thing about authority, Seth?"

"What?"

"It's too easy to abuse. Look at Hitler. He abused it, and his own people wouldn't buck him. So, the world winds up with millions of people dead. In contrast, consider King George in the 1700's. He abused it, but John Hancock, Ben Franklin, and company stood up to him, and we get one heckuva place in which to grow up and succeed, a free country that kicked Hitler's keester and sent him packing to hell."

Seth sighed in grudging admission of H.R.'s rightness, but also in grudging admission of his well-entrenched, humbling upbringing.

"Seth, even parents are wrong sometimes and have to be told so."

"But aren't our elders better judges than we? They have more experience."

"Often, but not always. Sometimes they're just wrong, but not necessarily in an evil sense. Perhaps their assumptions are inaccurate or incomplete. Maybe their logic is faulty. The point is, when they're off base, shouldn't they know? When I was fifteen, my dad told me to respect him, but not to the point I worshiped him. He'd rather be challenged than continue in the glory of his own ignorance."

Seth sat silent, his face affixed on H.R.'s half-consumed, onion-less Whopper. H.R.'s words hadn't upset him. Rather, he was hypnotized by a truth hovering so new and large that its permeation would take time.

H.R. summed up his point with the voice of quiet concern. "Seth, it's enough to remember this: Neither age, size, money, beauty, position, nor violence can make someone *right*. Being right is a matter of mind and soul, and other stuff like that."

Put thusly, H.R.'s words took a shallow root. Seth followed with a question. "But what about will and desire? Isn't a search for truth aided by what football coaches call *want-to*?"

H.R., hiding a little smile of respect behind a look of reflection, added, "You mean to suggest that truth is elusive and don't come easy?"

Seth nodded. "Yeah. King Solomon said those who search for wisdom would find it, and it seems like only those who love it will search hard enough."

"What worries me is that some people love truth less than they love themselves." The right corner of H.R.'s mouth bent downward, as he finished. "You know, Seth, what also worries me is that, too often, such people are lawyers."

Seth paused, then whispered. "Maybe it's because lawyers are best equipped to convince themselves that what's false is somehow true."

H.R. looked right at Seth, as if searching for truth, as if he'd found it.

♦

Seth snapped out of his latest trance with a searching look of his own . . and with the memory of H.R.'s last phone call. He walked back to Number 11 and grabbed a quick English muffin breakfast, but skipped class and hung out in his room, reading his *Bible* and Ayn Rand's *Atlas Shrugged*. For once, he was both without the law and without the guilt.

♦

By eleven a.m., he drove to the student workout room, an old-fashioned iron-pumping enclave attached to the back of the natatorium. Because he'd been a scholarship athlete with team weight room access, he'd only visited this gym once, but as he walked inside, he noted a few of the serious bodybuilders, the kind of guys who entered contests and took steroids in the hip. He remembered the lack of air-conditioning and weight machines in a place ruled by barbells.

As Seth loaded a bench press bar, a dead lifter dropped five hundred pounds from knee-high. Seth's ears registered the noise, but his eyes never looked. They also registered the sounds of Van Halen on an old boom box in the corner, but he never paused to enjoy the chords. He popped up some three-hundred-pound bench presses, then snatched around loaded curl bars as if gravity had disappeared.

Two attractive women in Jane Fonda workout garb reflected in a wall-length mirror. He looked dead ahead, focused on Myerson. The old man needed a taste of himself, to be hit with his own bat, and to be hit soon. Too many people were dying.

Seth took a five-minute shower in three minutes, and in ten more, he walked into the Number 11 kitchen. François was putting up leftovers from lunch.

"I'll take some of that," Seth declared, pointing toward a platter of lukewarm London broil.

155

"Oh, you will?"

"Yeah, you got some wheat bread?"

"A bit short-mouthed today, aren't we, young student-assistant?"

"Yeah, and hungry, too."

Seth threw six strips of the magical marinated beef on a slice of Roman Meal, slung on a tomato, some Grey Poupon, and a slice of provolone, then proceeded to wolf it down with a skim milk chaser. "What's that carbo dish?"

"That carbo dish is my exquisite Potatoes au Suzanne, named after my late Aunt. I suppose you also wish to eat it without tasting it."

"Whatever."

François struck an insulted pose. He always gave generously of his surplus cuisine, but he always resented any failure to savor it.

"Young carnivore, if you must treat my art as mere sustenance, I'll leave the cleanup for you. Refrigerate any dish you fail to vacuum." François changed out of his white uniform, and, when halfway out the door, threw back, "I have a date with a Chardonnay and some *good* conversation."

Seth bused the kitchen and bounded up the stairs to his room. He skipped class preparation and instead read another fifty pages of *Atlas Shrugged*. Dagny Taggart was kicking socialist behind and taking names. He smiled and turned out the lights, then remembered to read his *Bible* and turned them back on. He opened it to the Beatitudes. *Blessed are the peacemakers* . . . He slapped it shut and slammed it onto the nightstand.

◆

After a decent six hours of sleep, he awoke the next day, January 22, 1986, skipped class again, and bee-lined it to the library. At the library double-doors, he had to dodge a wiry, red-bearded computer nerd of a man carrying a new monitor. His name was Myron Gustaf, but the students called him Redbeard. He drank Tab colas and didn't say much, but was apparently some sort of technological genius. Seth sneaked a glance at him, happy there were strange people who understood computers. Seth noted a proper cadence to Redbeard's erect walk, but ignored the observation and went inside to study.

He forgot to avoid H.R.'s abandoned cubicle, however, and seeing it, he stopped. It was covered with mementos, seemingly encased with reverence.

Seth looked at the wall opposite. The law school had discovered an inexpensive way to decorate the library's generous wall space--namely with photograph composites of each graduating class since the 1800's. As H.R. had explained to Hound Dog Hampton, his cubicle faced the class of 1961. Seth wondered what would happen when the wall space ran out.

Seth examined the members of the '61 class. In the past, the Class of '61 had seemed like eager young lawyers-to-be, ready to sue the world and make their fortunes. Now, they all looked frozen, like the sentinels guarding the Tomb of the Unknown Soldier. He sensed something lurking within the composite itself, but ignored it, focused only on making an unknown killer known.

Seth recalled H.R.'s final note. His friend's faith in him was alone inspiring. Seth closed his eyes and realized he'd never been the subject of faith. Lost in the inspiring cocktail of thought, zeal, and reverence, he walked away to his own cubicle. The property syllabus was taped to the inside wall. Myerson held office hours later that day at four p.m. Seth's version of Mr. Hyde was about to pay him a visit.

CHAPTER TWENTY-EIGHT

It was 4:30 when Seth reached Myerson's office door. Professor Borland, dressed in black again, lurched out. She gave Seth an odd gruesome glance. It stilled him. She also relayed a suppressed smile that lessened the shock. He looked away and reached to knock, but paused and peered down at the floor. Somehow, his Sethian instincts kicked in, instincts reminding him of Myerson's age, status, and bearing. His lips quivered, his heart quickened, and he was forced to take a deep breath. He stood there, a human statue of dread. The urge to walk away had a familiar strength, but an opposing force locked his feet in place.

He fought the picture of H.R.'s murdered image, the hopelessness of it, but he couldn't step away. An innate circuit breaker had forbidden this vision to materialize, but there it now was: H.R. lying there, twisted on a bed of dead grass and dead straw. Sue resting behind him, her cold hand reaching out.

Seth knocked.

"Yes?" Seth opened the door, walked inside. "Mr. Sentel, please come in." Seth sensed welcome in Myerson's tone, as if he hadn't received a student visitor all semester. Seth ignored himself.

"So, what rests upon such a fine mind this fine afternoon, Mr. Sentel?" Myerson smiled.

Seth didn't. "A great deal. Since H.R. was murdered."

Myerson dropped the smile. "I know you two were friends. I'm sorry for your loss, and for that of the law school." Seth stared at the last phrase. He hated obfuscation. Myerson moved his head left and looked at him with interest. "You have something quite definite on your mind then. Won't you sit down?"

Seth risked a quick glimpse around him and moved to the edge of an antique leather chair. Myerson's office was crowded, but organized. Books decorated most of the space, but there were framed diplomas from Harvard and Columbia, a signed eight by ten from Coach Bryant, a glass-front trophy case behind him, an original oil landscape, and a group of framed Korean War medals.

Seth spoke. "There's one thing I know for certain. One of you professors is involved in this. I'm not stupid enough to reveal how I know, but rest assured that I do, just as I know he wasn't one of your favorite students."

The implication settled. Myerson moved a few papers on his desk and leaned forward. "I was unable to attend the Memorial Service, but I'm aware of your speech, so perhaps I'm not caught off-guard by your words." Myerson took a breath. "Nonetheless, I am unsettled that any investigator, whether amateur or professional, could suspect me in such a situation. For your sake, I hope you're in possession of at least the most indirect manner of proof."

Myerson stopped, maybe to restrain his approach. Seth remained fixed at the leather chair, his eyes focused straight ahead. "Why don't you do this, Mr. Sentel? If you believe a murder has occurred, and if you believe some professor was involved in it, then go to the authorities. I say this as good counsel. Loose cannons can sometimes misfire."

"But sometimes they don't miss."

Myerson's eyes closed, and he shook his head. "Please don't set yourself up against me, Mr. Sentel, for your own good. It will yield no benefit."

Seth lifted his left hand and pointed. "No. Don't you set yourself up against me. I'm not giving way, not without a fight."

Seth's hands were on Myerson's desk, his true self somewhere else. Myerson was up, his own thick hands a mere six inches away.

From somewhere outside himself, Seth raised his voice. "My priority isn't to preserve your status, or your reputation, or anyone else's. To get to the bottom of this, I'll expose anyone I have to."

Myerson seemed to have lost his capacity to placate. "You can't expose nothingness. Can't you see? Someone is going to play the fool here."

"We'll see who that someone is. Maybe it'll be this entire law school. It's not as if Thurow carries himself like John Wayne."

At the reference to Asst. Dean Thurow, Myerson folded his arms, and, when he did, he just couldn't stop the smirk winding into his face. A silent little body laugh followed.

Seth replied, "I don't see one thing entertaining here."

"It was not . . ."

"Let me make my purpose clear." Seth reached across the desk and grabbed Myerson's tie just below the knot. "I'm *on* this case, and even if I have to blow off law school, I'll break it. You better pray to Abraham I don't find you involved."

Myerson stared hard. Then, his forearms shot up from the desk, breaking Seth's grip. He grabbed one of Seth's arms and spun him. He went for a chokehold, but Seth was too quick and had one hand free. He struck Myerson on the neck with the side of his fist. Myerson tried to lean away, his grip still firm. Seth swung again and again. He had no leverage; the blows were weak.

160

Blinded by intensity, neither noticed the door was open. Goodfried peered through it and charged in, forced himself between them.

"Enough! This is all over the hallway."

Now free, Seth cocked his right arm and fist. Goodfried stopped it in mid-air. "You're out of here, Seth!"

Goodfried seized Seth by the tops of his shoulders to ride him out. Seth broke free, grabbed a marble bookend from Myerson's desk, hurled it. Myerson dodged left. The bookend crashed into the oil painting behind him, ripping a hole through its center. They paused a half moment, considering the weight of the destruction. Goodfried pushed Seth hard toward the door. Myerson, beet-faced, adjusted his tie and hair.

The door was wide open, and Seth turned and flung more words. "You're the one who hated him, and if you're the one who killed him, I'm going to need one mean lawyer."

"Enough, I said!" Goodfried's voice was controlled, yet firm. "You've dug your hole deep enough, Seth. We're leaving before you're buried."

CHAPTER TWENTY-NINE

Goodfried had a gold 1986 Mercedes parked in the faculty lot. He opened the door for Seth, who had worked himself into a brooding silence. The comfort of the leather seats began the relaxation process.

Goodfried glanced over and declared, "You could use a drink."

Seth was cooling down, and he couldn't hide the muted surprise in his eyes. Goodfried *was* one heckuva nice guy. After all, Seth had just assaulted a fellow professor. Seth said nothing until they reached the University Club, a private dining club three blocks from the Warner House.

They walked up the front steps, and Goodfried, under-dressed in his usual faded Levis and tie-less Oxford cloth shirt, somehow seemed at home. A black maitre de in a white dinner jacket approached and addressed him as Mr. Goodfried. Seth sensed he spoke like an old friend. No mention was made of any dress code violations.

"Lonnie, how are you?"

"Just fine, sir. Would you like a table today?"

"No, my guest and I will just be having drinks in the bar. Lonnie, this is Seth, one of my finest students."

The definition of courtesy, Lonnie replied, "Pleased to meet you, Mr. Seth. What a fine Old Testament name, same as my grandfather's." Seth was still not quite available for conversation and mustered only an obligatory nod. Lonnie escorted them to the bar upstairs. "Will that be the usual, Mr. Goodfried?"

"Yes, and make one for Seth."

"Are you certain the young man is up to it?"

"No, but I'm certain he needs it."

Lonnie smiled in an appropriate manner. "Two it is."

They sat in red leather chairs, with Goodfried seated against the back wall under an original fox hunt painting. Seth remained silent, still settling back into himself. He moped like a man broken, but it was with eyes still afire.

Goodfried eased his chair against the wall and turned it to face the open area. He stretched out his legs, slumped in his chair, looked at Seth and asked, "So, young Seth, do you make a habit of slugging it out with law professors, or was this a new experience?"

Seth's eyes awakened. Goodfried seemed to notice. It was a glance punctuated with a whimsical, almost appreciative, smile. Seth exhaled and suppressed his own self-conscious grin.

Lonnie arrived with a stainless steel shaker and two large martini glasses.

"Here we are. Two, both extra dry with black olives." He poured with a practiced hand, yet gave Seth a quick look. "Would your guest care for something from our appetizer menu?"

As usual, the mention of sustenance brought further life to Seth's visage. No doubt the preceding struggle had accelerated his high metabolic rate.

"Why not bring us the crab claws, and perhaps some Swiss cheese on wheat crackers?"

"Yes, would there be anything else?"

Seth spoke, his voice hoarse from his first martini experience.

"Could I have a glass of ice water, too?"

Lonnie and Goodfried suppressed a joint grin.

"Bring my brave friend an Evian."

Lonnie returned to the kitchen.

"Seth, you might wish to wait until the appetizers arrive before the next gulp. It has quite a potent effect, if not cushioned with something." Goodfried drank another generous swallow from his own glass. Seth followed suit. "Is this your first visit to the Club, or has the Chancellor brought you before?"

Seth cleared his throat, the fire still raging within it. "No, it's my first visit. Why do you mention the Chancellor?"

"I saw him here once, and he told me all about your sweet little arrangement. You tend bar on occasion, walk the beloved Basset hounds, and act as part-time chauffeur. In return, you get the run of, not one, but two mansions. Not a bad trade for one still in school."

Seth was embarrassed by the regal nature of his living arrangements. "Well, I suppose I did walk into a favorable situation at the Warner House, but I'm trying not to take it for granted."

"Now there's a good attitude. Speaking of attitudes, I understand the Chancellor's chef has an eccentric one."

"You could say so." At the mention of François, Seth managed a mild attempt at a laugh. "He's quite the unique character. One great chef, though. I've gained three pounds this semester."

"Really? I could use a few pounds myself. Perhaps you might save me some leftovers one day."

Lonnie arrived with the crab claws, cheese, and aqua. Goodfried asked for another martini; Seth's glass was still half-full.

After Lonnie left to fetch the shaker, Goodfried, still stretched out in the red leather chair, took Seth in with his right eye and asked with obvious curiosity, "Because I came in late,

I didn't overhear what led up to your little difference of opinion moments ago. You know, it might not hurt if a disinterested third party understood your position."

Seth realized he hadn't heard the last of what had just happened. There would be explaining to do. He rubbed his eyebrow with the back of his hand, realized the chancellor might hear about the fight and institute eviction proceedings.

Seth paused a moment, slowed his thinking, then began. "Well, I meant what I said at the Memorial Service. H.R. and Sue weren't killed by accident."

"Ah, so it's related to that. But how does Myerson fit into the equation?"

Seth somehow felt willing to share his thoughts on this with someone older. It was the kind of confirmation that could do a restless mind good.

"H.R. and Myerson weren't exactly like father and son. They, too, almost came to blows."

"Of course, you and Myerson did come to blows, at least one of you did, anyway."

Seth had already been attempting to block out the struggle, and he sneaked a guilty grin at not only his attempt to do so, but also Goodfried's recognition of it. Seth then realized the attempt also confirmed what Goodfried had witnessed. Maybe if he opened up a little, Goodfried would see things his way.

"It was a normal reflex reaction. When someone has a hold of you like that, you're not apt to just take it. The way he was twisting my arm hurt."

Goodfried twirled his drink and said, "It would stand to reason that one would naturally resist being held against his will. Besides, you were in imminent fear he was about to strike you. I know I would have been."

Such a precise fear had never occurred to Seth, but he saw how it might do so. "Well, maybe in the heat of the struggle, I

HENSE R. ELLIS II

was instinctively protecting myself against attack. That would make sense."

"The important question, I think, is what motivated him to grab your arm. Had you already assaulted him?"

"No, not at all. We were arguing, but no one was taking a swing yet."

"Any pushing or fisticuffs yet?"

"No." Seth remembered none at this point.

"Where were you situated when he grabbed you?"

"Well, I was standing at his desk."

"Did you bump him with your chest?"

"No."

"Just the argument, a heated argument apparently, but still merely an argument?"

"I suppose so."

"Sounds like a clear case of initiation and response."

"Sir?"

"One party converted the verbal altercation to a physical struggle, and the other party responded in kind."

"Oh, I see."

"Look, if this comes to some sort of inquiry, I can state you were being physically and even painfully detained against your will and, because I'm the only unbiased witness, I just don't see this resulting in any substantial penalty for you."

Seth's face dropped. "Penalty? What would an insubstantial penalty be?"

"Well, even at the criminal level, we'd be dealing with misdemeanor assault, perhaps even reckless endangerment, which almost always just leaves the accused with a fine. Then, there's the law school's Honor Code." He made two quotation marks with his fingers. "The Code has some general language regarding behavior unbecoming a law student, which this could arguably represent, and also a rule against property destruction-

-I think you damaged something. But even if the Honor Court rules against you, the chances of expulsion would have to be miniscule."

Seth shifted and leaned away from the table. All things considered, it was a restrained reaction to being knifed by extreme fear.

"So, I could be accused and tried at school? The entire student body would know?"

"They'll know regardless, given how the place churns controversy."

Seth painted a picture of hopelessness with his chin and eyes. Goodfried pivoted and rested his hands on the table.

He lowered his voice to a near whisper. "Look, this may seem frightening now, but please don't doubt me when I say that I've seen worse over the years. One student embezzled Student Bar Association funds, yet he still graduated. Although I'd be shocked if your situation wasn't investigated, I'd be equally surprised if it resulted in expulsion or a criminal conviction."

Seth's eyes closed in relief.

Goodfried changed the subject to one Seth found less threatening. "You don't strike me as the type to pounce on a conclusion. Something other than a previous altercation must have led you to suspect Myerson's involvement."

Seth hesitated and looked down at his now empty martini glass. He hadn't mentioned H.R.'s note to anyone other than Elliot, Sheriff Gibson, and Deputy Do Nothing. Gibson and Dolton hadn't taken it seriously. Maybe Goodfried would, then perhaps others might.

"Well . . . there's a note. H.R. left it for me. I'm not sure what it means." It was Goodfried's turn to look surprised. "The references are vague, but he was involved in something that wasn't normal, and it somehow relates to the law school."

Goodfried shifted back to analytical mode as smoothly as he changed gears in his Mercedes. "Any idea what he was involved with? I doubt drugs or gambling."

"Not H.R. He said that he used to beat up guys who did drugs, just to teach them a lesson. Gambling, like sports betting or something? I don't think so. H.R. wasn't the type. He came from money and had no need to gamble to get it. My thinking? He stumbled onto something involving the school, maybe caught a professor cheating on his wife one night when he was out drinking."

Goodfried smiled. "I see. So you rule out the possibility he might have been involved in foul play himself. How can you be sure? I mean, even though Rentzell and Hays may have passed their drug tests, or at least their bodies may have, it doesn't mean they weren't involved in drugs."

Seth winced a bit, but was able to muster a strong enough reply. "For one, *I know him.*"

"But for how long?"

"It was only for five months, but I feel like, once you know someone, you know them."

"Fair enough."

"Besides, the tone of the letter suggested he'd discovered a secret. It read as if he was saying, *You wouldn't believe what's going on here, and who's involved in it.* What makes it worse is, the only people he was possibly specific with are both dead."

"Do you know who they are?"

"Yes. It's Sue and a lawyer in Birmingham."

"Okay then. Do you have anything else to go on? Have you talked to this lawyer's partners or secretary? Who *was* he anyway?"

"It was Elliot Gaston with Hampton & Hellums in Birmingham. I met with him once. Nice guy for a country club type. He's the lawyer who died in the plane crash."

"Right. I think it was in the papers."

"But I haven't followed up with any of his contacts."

"Might not be a bad idea. By the way, have you mentioned any of this to the Sheriff?"

"I did, but a lot of good it did me. They all but laughed at me. Stayed focused on their suspect."

"I'm not surprised they gave you an inadequate hearing. To have an open mind, one must first have a mind." They exchanged smiles. Goodfried followed up. "Did they mention anything about their prime suspect?" He posed the latter question with a seasoning of suitable sarcasm.

"They just said it was Lymon Bream, the guy who lived in the woods near H.R.'s place."

"Now that sounds true-to-form. Pick out some strange character to arrest, then close their investigation. Look, Seth, I'd look into whoever Gaston spoke to. They might help you. And keep me posted. Listen, the Myerson altercation hopefully won't be a big deal, so don't lose any sleep over it. Well, not too much sleep."

"I lose enough as it is, so I appreciate it."

"Thought you might."

Seth appeared relaxed. Goodfried eased up from his chair.

"Can you walk home to the Warner House, or would you like a lift?"

"It's only two blocks, and maybe the walk would do me good."

Lonnie brought the check. Goodfried put a generous tip on it, signed it, and jotted down his club number. He thanked Lonnie for the "usual excellent service," spoke to two different lawyers on the way out, always taking the time to introduce

Seth. He shook Seth's hand when he reached his Mercedes, then climbed in, rolled down his window.

"See, young Seth, there are few ills a Martini and some good appetizers can't cure."

Seth looked like a normal first-year student again, i.e. as if he were only partially paranoid. "Good advice never hurt either."

Goodfried put the car in gear. "Tis true, and there's plenty more where that came from. By the way, if I were you, I'd take my mind off this by spending more time with a certain girlfriend."

Seth waved and wondered how Goodfried knew about Cindi. The law school was one tiny enclave, he figured.

◆

He walked home with his hands in his pockets, and his mind in a flux. A cold winter wind dove through the mammoth dormant hardwoods of Pinehurst, swaying the limbs above and stirring leaves and dirt from the ground below. He heard a noise and looked back to see if anyone was following.

Behind him, a frightened, panting squirrel clung to an oak tree. A guilty black neighborhood cat crouched behind the monkey grass, snarling. Seth saw neither cat nor squirrel, but he could feel that old ugly mental acquaintance slipping back into his mindset, now stronger than ever.

CHAPTER THIRTY

Dr. Whitehurst, a measure of concern in his voice, dictated his notes from the second meeting with his new eating disorder patient.

<u>Session Two, Thursday, February 6, 1986</u>

Patient missed her last session, arrived late today, her hair disheveled, wearing faded jeans and an old sweatshirt. Claimed she'd been studying all morning. Patient smelled of cigarettes and alcohol. Patient sleepy and irritable.

Upon follow up questioning about her father, she said his death was traumatic, but not "as bad as you might think it could be." She hesitated a few moments before naming her best girlfriends, then reiterated she was close to her mother. She stated flippantly that she'd never dated any man longer than six months.

Regarding her early dating life, she provided some innocuous detail, then abruptly reported she'd been date raped at the age of fifteen. She didn't report the crime, but had someone "beat the guy up," saying she discovered you could pay people from Northwest Alabama to "do stuff like that." She hopes he somehow goes to prison, to be "raped to death."

My review of her undergrad transcripts revealed a marked inconsistency in her scores, with some semesters showing B's and B+'s, others showing either all A's or A's combined with C's, and one showing all C's and C+'s. Her law school grades were mostly excellent.

A perusal of her high school yearbooks revealed she was voted both Most Likely To Succeed and Best Dressed, yet, in two photographs, the same inconsistency in dress and appearance was obvious. In one, she was dressed in black and appeared overweight. She listed Karate as a favorite pastime. She won the school beauty pageant twice. She wasn't a class officer.

Related to her eating habits, she said she hates her body and wishes she had someone else's, "like maybe a model's or actresses." Her opinion was, "this whole thing is no big deal because, when I get good and hungry, I eat all I want" and "a person should be able to eat when and how they want to because it's their body to do with what they want."

At the final session, I intend to ask questions about her high school years and to probe other areas of behavior for possible causal connections and more serious patterns.

He sat still, microphone in hand. He considered how he had witnessed the lowest levels of human behavior and pondered how it was too easy for life to nudge one along an unnatural and dangerous path, if one hadn't been born upon it, that is.

CHAPTER THIRTY-ONE

With all the travails of the past few weeks, Seth had neglected his shoes, a classic pair of Cordovan laceups. Though the talk with Goodfried offered relief and Seth had recognized his overreaction to H.R.'s advice about authority, nothing had changed his basic status as an emotional zombie. Still, he'd recovered the presence of mind to note the scuffs, the dirt, and the dull that reflected nothing from the leather uppers. Putting them on Thursday morning, he grew distressed.

His mental linkages recalled the law school's cure for such a crisis of the particular man. It was 11:00 a.m., Monday, February 10, 1986, and Mozz's shine emporium was open for business. Seth made his way there and took a seat against the wall, taking in the catchy handmade sign above the big chair: *25 Cents Was a Good Tip in 1966, Not 1986.* Seth was third in line behind a third-year student and an assistant basketball coach from Coleman Coliseum next door.

Mozz cut him the usual bright glance and spoke. "How's you doing, young Sixth Sentel? Grab something to read, and we'll be right wid yuh."

Seth mustered a muttered "Thanks," leaned back in the cushioned chair, and closed his eyes. Something perfect was in the air: Gershwin playing quietly over a portable stereo system. Seth drifted into the last bars of "An American in Paris," and his mouth's right corner even managed to move upward when the "Porgy and Bess" medley began. It was perfect Mozz shoe-shining music, and after it eased in and around his eardrums, it

173

seeped deeper, as he slid down in the chair and opened his eyes.

He took in the law center's big back yard and spied another freight train easing down the tracks, almost hidden behind the row of cypress trees bordering the property line. He realized the grounds of the building were its best feature, the most therapeutic for sure.

"Next," Mozz said, pretending to speak to no one particular. Seth was the only customer left.

"Oh, sorry." Seth sprang toward the big inviting chair, surrounded as it now was by Gershwin's mesmerizing "Rhapsody in Blue," not to mention the day's newspapers, which hid the month's *Playboy*.

"Have a rest, Seth, my friend. Take in the day's news, take in the day's views, you've got nothing to lose . . by taking it all in."

Seth smiled as he gazed down at Mozz from above. "You know you're infectious, don't you."

"Just being me. Whatever I is, I is, to sort of quote Mr. Popeye."

"Well, I sort of need a shine."

Mozz looked down at the dirty wine-tinted leather and noted the challenge ahead.

"Uh, uh, uh, Mr. Seth. Where you been walking in these shoes?"

"Some places I don't normally go."

"Well, for the good of these saddle broughams, I suggest you don't visit those places no more."

Seth closed his eyes and rubbed both lids with the palms of his hands. "Wouldn't if I could, Mozz. Wouldn't if I could."

Mozz snickered a bit and went to work with a damp natural sponge. The dirt had to go first or else the polish wouldn't take well and the buffing would combine with the sand to leave lifelong scratches on a nice example of L.L. Bean's product line.

"Yeah, I imagine you been in some unusual places this semester, maybe like Sheriff's Offices and private clubs."

Seth looked at him, first with disbelief. Then, it made perfect sense. Old Mozz likely knew over fifty percent of Tuscaloosa's fine citizenry, and 100% of the not so fine. It wouldn't be so unusual for him to know Seth's recent whereabouts.

Seth spoke like he dreaded the future. "Yep. Quite unusual, and getting more so all the time."

Mozz, now involved in the polish application phase, said, "It's an unusual world, Mr. Seth. And you know, I've noticed some places are more unusual than others."

Seth was scanning the *Birmingham News* Sports section, but mumbled as he saw how Alabama's round ball team had lost a close game on the road. "What?"

"Yep. You know, I've shined at the Tuscaloosa Country Club, over in the First National Bank lobby on Greensboro, and even down in the courthouse basement, but the law school seems the most unusual."

"How?"

"Other than folks all of a sudden dying left and right, I couldn't quite say, don't quite know. It's a gut feeling. What do the womenfolk supposed to have a bunch of--imtuition?"

"You mean intuition."

"Yeah, that's it. You got a bunch of it, don't you, Mr. Seth."

Seth moved the paper to see Mozz was looking up at him, his eyes brimming over with messages. Seth's eyes meekly shifted to look at the brick wall opposite and its old framed British barrister cartoons.

"Ain't nothing wrong with it, Seth, that imtuition."

Seth dropped one hand off the paper and scratched the side of his face. "Think so?"

"Know so. I'm sure it saved my black self more trouble than I could handle, more times than I can count."

"Wonder why yours kicks in around the law school, and wonder what it means."

Mozz stopped shining just long enough to answer. "Don't know what it means, but people here sometimes look at each other a little funny, like they're guilty or scared, and sometimes, they don't look at each other at all, when it seems like they oughta." Seth nodded his assent, the negative vibes he'd been discerning now indirectly confirmed. "It wasn't this way ten years ago, but maybe now there's something funny in the tone of a voice or the pace of a walk. Maybe there's people saying things that don't make perfect sense, like Miss Cindi. Wonder why come she'd be critical of a solid citizen like you?"

"Critical? How?" Seth was curious and amused at a shoeshine man's interjection into his love life.

"Just happened to overhear some stray complaint, sure she didn't mean nothing by it, that sometimes you might be too studious and too committed."

"She complained about *that*?"

"Yeah, but I 'clare for God, I don't understand it."

"So what if I'm studious and committed?"

"Some ladies do love the outlaw, Mr. Seth. Except, you know what?"

"What?"

"They might not be deep-down ladies."

"Deep-down ladies?"

"Uh-huh, ladies all the way through, know what I mean?" Mozz dipped his bare finger in the polish and was rubbing it in along the edge of the sole.

176

"I want to say I do, but I'm not really sure."

"You might want to take a course on the subject while you're still in school, young Seth."

"Why do I feel I'm already enrolled in it?"

Mozz smiled. "Likely because you already is." He hesitated a moment. "Just remember to listen to the teacher."

Mozz glanced into the air above as if to share a secret with Seth in a special language.

Seth breathed in, recognized the spiritual reference. Mozz looked down and whipped out an old toothbrush, the bristles as black as his skin, and dipped it in a bottle of what had stained it. Then, he began tracing a perfect black path around the top of Seth's soles, framing the still dull upper. Seth watched as the liquid sunk into the stitching.

Mozz produced a soft cloth and started buffing. Seth tensed his feet a little to firm them on the metal shoe props. The Cordovan leather became a perfect contrast with the black outline of the freshly painted soles, a mirror before his eyes.

"Mozz, you make them shine so bright they could blind a man."

"No, no, no." The words rolled out like cane syrup. "Don't want to blind no man. Much rather a man *see*. If a good man has bad all around him, then he *better* see. Needs to see the good, needs to see the bad. Needs to know the difference."

Seth's mind slipped away a moment, considering what he saw, what he might not have, and what the difference was.

Mozz always ended a shine with a little snap of his buff cloth, and the sound drew Seth back into the surreal world of the law center. He stepped down without looking at Mozz and dug out his wallet. All he had was a couple of crisp ten-dollar bills. He slapped one into Mozz's worn palms.

"I think I can change that," Mozz said, as he sat on the plywood steps of the big leather chair and reached underneath for his tin cash box. Seth was already walking off. For once, Mozz was the one befuddled. "Mighty big tip, Mr. Seth. What fer?"

Seth, feeling a little cleaner, wheeled and spoke as he ambled away. "I'm not sure yet, but my imtuition tells me there's a reason."

Mozz stood, looked him eye to eye. "You mean intuition."

Seth managed a smile. "Right."

"Try to take better care of those well-made shoes, young Seth."

The appreciation in Seth's eyes looked back, his comprehension growing by the second. For a few precious minutes, he'd forgotten about the Myerson incident and the Honor Court. There was a minor misunderstanding with Cindi, but Mozz's *heads-up* would prepare him to fashion a plan to alleviate it. There was energy in Seth's shiny shoes as he strode away to the upbeat rhythm of Gershwin's "I Got Rhythm."

Things are looking up, he thought.

CHAPTER THIRTY-TWO

His shoes shiny as new, Seth was halfway down the brick-lined breezeway when he recalled he had a message box in the Coffee Room. He'd been so consumed with off-campus events that he hadn't checked that box in a week. He walked inside the Coffee Room, looked toward the back, noted a group of second-year guys he remembered from the Legal Beagles team. They were talking loud and grinning big while pontificating about their future lives in private practice.

The first one opined, "My mom does insurance defense, and she says the key is creative pleading. The more creative you are with the documents, the more hours you can bill!"

Another added his billable hour's worth. "My dad says sincerity is the key. Once you can fake *that*, you can print your own currency!"

Seth's eyes jumped away and landed on Katie Ryals's portrait. Somehow, the subject's serene face seemed out of place.

Inside his box, he found meaningless memos from Asst. Dean Thurow about the proper parking place for bicycles and the importance of "giving back to the law school." There was a note about this year's Barrister's Ball and an offer to reserve your place early. He dropped them in the trash and dug out the last piece of mail, a sealed envelope with a return address for the Law School Honor Court. Handwritten at the top was the name "Jack F. Tatum, Prosecutor."

Seth's knees twitched. He breathed a little faster, tried to swallow the whole revelation away. He stashed the envelope in his pants pocket, eased out into the hall. He sped to the library and hid in his cubicle. He looked around, then sat down and pulled his chair up tight. He stared at the envelope for five minutes, then opened it with his pocketknife. His shoulders hunched, he removed the paper and read.

This constitutes formal notice of accusation that the accused, Seth O. Sentel, has violated Chapter 3, Sections 2 and 12, of The University of Alabama Law School Honor Code. This accusation is premised upon a report the accused intentionally, or with reckless disregard, defaced or destroyed property belonging to a law school professor on January 22, 1986, by breaking such property in an attempt to assault such professor. A Probable Cause Hearing will be set and held in compliance with Chapter Eight of The Honor Code. Elected counsel for the accused is Martin Sylvest.

A shiver jolted him. A thousand little pinpricks scattered out from his heart and into his limbs and cheeks. His eyes blinked; his mouth twitched. His breathing went staccato. His body wanted to do something with itself. He stood and walked to the front desk. Head librarian Janie Jernigan was among the reserve stacks, stretching to re-shelve a hornbook. Redbeard the techno-nerd sat in the back of the room, wearing an olive army cap turned backward and tinkering with an IBM Selectric.

"Janie, may I use the phone?"

"Sure, Seth, what's . ." He vaulted over the counter. Her eyes refocused. "Is something wrong?"

He was already on the phone, dialing a number from the law school directory.

"Is Martin there?"

"I'm sorry, he's away at a Young Democrats convention."

Seth cringed. "Young Democrats? When will he return?"

"Late Sunday."

"Tell him to call Seth Sentel."

"Okay. I think he's been expecting your call."

"Alright . . . He has?"

"Yeah. I heard him mention your name."

"Just be sure he knows I called. Tell him I was in some kind of daze when I did it."

Seth hung up the phone and stared at it, as if it was a ghost. Janie stared at him, like *he* was a ghost. Redbeard rearranged his tool belt.

Seth called Cindi. She sounded miffed, but avoided criticism. Instead, she suggested he call Goodfried, who, within seconds, was on the line.

"Professor, this is Seth Sentel. There was an Honor Court notice in my mailbox today."

Goodfried sounded disappointed. "So soon? I'm sorry, Seth. Myerson apparently wasn't in a forgiving mood."

Seth's voice was weak. "I suppose not. Now what?"

"Well, you should avoid further contact with Myerson."

"That'll be easy."

"Have you spoken with the Honor Court defense counsel?"

"I called him at home, but his roommate said he was away at a Young Democrat's Convention."

"That *sounds* like Mr. Sylvest."

"I'll bet his heart will really be into representing a Republican like me."

Goodfried laughed almost imperceptibly and responded, "Remember Seth, advocates are obligated to, and most rather enjoy, zealously representing their clients."

"Even if they disagree with them on every possible issue?"

"I wouldn't worry about it. After all, an ambitious guy like Sylvest doesn't want a loser's reputation."

"I suppose you're right," Seth said, unconvinced.

"Look, Seth. Again, I'm involved with the Honor Court as an advisor. I shouldn't delve much into this, but I'll be there to watch over your situation and, wink-wink, give my private opinion to you and Martin."

"Really?"

"Between you and me and Denny Chimes, really."

"Thanks. Maybe I'll get four hours of sleep tonight."

"Don't you worry, young Seth." Goodfried spoke with assurance. "This situation will be handled, in one manner or another."

Seth wanted to stop and think, but his mood wouldn't grant his mind the time. Instead, he said "Thanks" and hung up.

He started down the long front breezeway with hope he'd soon clear the building. Asst. Dean Thurow called him from behind.

"Mr. Sentel, would you mind stepping into my office a moment?"

Seth went with him, and Thurow shut the door behind them. Five minutes later, Seth emerged red-faced and unsettled, having refused to confess error, apologize to Myerson, and purchase him a new oil painting.

He stormed out of the building, aching to feel safe and at home. At the side door, he bumped into two guys in dark suits and Ray Bans. They were too old to be students and seemed too serious to be lawyers away from the office. He turned and looked at them as if he didn't know them. They looked back, but as if they knew him, which added fuel to his fear fire. *What kind of men wore those suits, those shades, those looks, and that attitude?* He drove to Number 11 and parked in the middle garage. He needed a quick snack and a good joke from François.

Stacey announced. "Seth, you're wanted at the Chancellor's office."

"The office?"

"Yes. The Chancellor said for you to report immediately."

François was slicing artichokes at the speed of light and, at first, ceased only to offer a shrug of genuine concern. Then his head flicked to the right. "Use a lift, mate?"

"No thanks, I'll walk it alone .. but thanks."

Seth spun himself on a dime and began the three-block journey to absorb the day's next left hook.

François closed his eyes, shook his head, then mumbled, "Young Seth, always walking it alone. Always the *bienfaiteur*, never the *bénéficiaire*."

Seth walked because he was afraid he might wreck the Jeep. He walked fast, his head aimed at the pavement the entire trip. He arrived at the two-story brick office that more resembled a traditional-style home.

He waited ten minutes while Dr. Bausch completed a phone call. It was ten minutes that hurt, yet ten minutes he wished were ten thousand.

He walked into Dr. Bausch's office and saw the look on the man's face, the same look he'd seen on his knee surgeon's face, right before he told Seth he'd have to cut.

"Be seated, Mr. Sentel." It sounded like an order. Seth slid into the nearest leather chair. He wanted to stand, to run.

Dr. Bausch studied Seth as would a judge on sentencing day. Then, he constructed a monologue. "Seth, Mrs. Bausch and I are concerned. I've been informed of, shall we say, certain irregularities at the law center." Seth swallowed air. "It seems you may have . . . It seems there's an allegation of inappropriate conduct, conduct of an arguably violent and destructive nature."

Seth looked down and closed his eyes. "Seth, you do understand there are image concerns here? This is somewhat of a public appointment I hold, one subject to a noticeable degree of scrutiny." Dying to make his defense, but now too smart to risk a word, Seth nodded. "Now, given the otherwise good experience this office has had with you, and perhaps given my wife's fondness for your abilities, I'm willing to take a patient, inconclusive approach to this particular situation." Seth breathed, but too soon. "For the present time." Seth looked up from the floor. "I will, however, monitor this particular matter, and if it progresses in a manner embarrassing to this office, or, if other questionable situations come to my attention, certain adjustments in our current arrangements would be in order."

Seth gambled a few syllables. "Adjustments?"

"Yes. As you might imagine, the University, and this office in particular, couldn't be viewed as harboring anyone with what one might consider . . serious behavioral shortcomings." Dr. Bausch examined Seth as if attempting to glean indications of guilt. Seth shifted at the veiled accusation. "Is this understood?"

Well, with all the indirect references and generalities, Seth was uncertain whether he did understand, but to get the conversation over with, he answered, "Yes."

"That will be all." Seth had no urge to linger, so he directed his insulted frame out the door. "And one more item, Seth. Both of the cars are in need of a thorough cleaning. I feel certain one of your apparent energy could achieve that by ten a.m. tomorrow morning." He finished the last sentence with a raise of his eyebrows. Seth's eyes registered his unhappiness, but after he'd turned, Dr. Bausch betrayed his true intent with a little smile.

◆

Seth wandered back to Number 11, entered the kitchen. He looked around for which direction the next grenade would come. François, now slicing a mango melon, launched it. "Young Seth, you're quite the *homme populaire* this day. While you were away, there were two additional calls. Your father requested you phone him at his office, and a Dr. Falls also left a number."

Seth took a deep breath and closed his eyes a second. Stacey allowed him some privacy in her office adjacent to the kitchen, and François shut the door between the two rooms.

Seth drew another deep breath when his dad left a board meeting to take his call.

"Seth, your mother and I are a little worried. We've received word that matters in Tuscaloosa are spiraling out of control. Your mother wants you to consider withdrawing from school. I want you to know I assured her that would be unnecessary. In any case, we were in agreement that-"

"Dad, what's this about?"

"Well, we're aware you're under some type of disciplinary review, and we suspect your mission priorities merit a re-ordering. This weekend, why don't you come home?"

Seth raised his voice to interrupt. "My mission priorities? How do you know about some type of disciplinary review? I just found out today."

"There was something in the mail from the law school. It was addressed here to no particular individual. Your mother thought it might be a bill for school fees. It must have been mailed here by mistake. In any case, it upset her to read it."

Seth's face tightened. "Tell her not to worry. It's not what you think."

"Seth, this isn't about this one situation. You're entrenched in a murder investigation that's not your fight. How can you stay abreast of law school, work a part-time job, track down a killer, and also maintain a dating relationship?"

"I'm not certain how, dad. Maybe I'm smart enough, and maybe I just want it all enough."

"Don't allow your ambition to expand past the size of your trousers, son."

"Thank you so much for the encouragement, daddy, but the truth is, I made a promise to H.R., and if there's one lesson you taught me, it's to keep my promises."

"But I didn't teach you to make too *many* of them."

"Well, they're already made. They're *all* made, and now I have to get busy keeping them."

♦

The good-byes were uneasy. His dad hung up, then made an assurance call to the worried wife. After it, he stopped a moment and smiled, the first real smile he'd experienced since Reagan's re-election.

♦

Seth hung up and grabbed the message from Dr. Kenneth Falls. He speculated that some type of growth must have been belatedly noted on his last X-ray. A receptionist put him through to the doctor.

"Seth, my good Baptist friend. How's life treating one of the best pure runners God ever made?"

"Well, sir, it has him running."

"It'll never catch you, young Seth. Don't worry yourself, and the weary runner may be in for a respite. I received your message about taking me up on my Yacht Club offer. Jo Ann and I have made reservations for tomorrow night. How does that sound for you and your friend?"

"Perfect, sir. Please make the reservation, and if Cindi has a conflict, I'll phone in my regrets."

"Fair enough. Unless I hear from you, we'll see you at the Club dining room at seven."

"Thank you, sir. I can't express how much I need this."

"Good, Seth. Now let me return to this shoulder separation case. Seems one of our more colorful baseball players became intoxicated and allowed his Corvette to wander into a pecan tree."

Not even colorful athletes combined with the day's only good news could erase Seth's high anxiety. Maybe fresh tropical fruit would help. Seth walked out to assist François.

CHAPTER THIRTY-THREE

It was early Friday evening, February 14, 1986, a day for sweethearts. Seth was at Cindi's apartment. She'd made him a double Scotch, and, after Monday's barrage of bad news, he'd needed it. He noticed it worked, lessening the creepy ephemeral feeling he'd known since before the murder. The sensation shrunk from invisible fly buzzing around his psyche to more of an intermittently visible gnat. Why it remained at all he'd been too busy to ponder.

The couple had dispensed with another quick conversation about Seth's upcoming date with the Honor Court. He tried to convince her he had no real exposure, but terrible liar that he was; she'd just stared at the ceiling and walked off to her bedroom to ready herself for the big evening ahead.

He followed, scanned the bedroom contents, sneaked behind her, and asked, "What's up with these cigarettes and this box of Nasty Tap logo matches on your dresser?"

From her seat atop a cushion in front of a full-length mirror, she applied what little makeup she used, and replied, "Oh. Those belong to a girlfriend."

Seth's disbelief reflected in the mirror.

She looked up at his reaction, then observed, "It's not fair for a girl to have to go up against you and your sixth sense."

"Would be better if you didn't *have* to go up against me, *or* it."

"I only smoke for the heckuv it when I'm having a few beers."

"Why don't you peel your label instead? A recent Mayo clinic study concluded that label peeling causes cancer at a much lower rate than cigarette smoking."

She smiled and observed, "That's cute. You can be kind of funny when you're in the mood," as if he wasn't often enough.

He smiled. "Are you ready yet?"

Across the unmade bed lay her dress for the evening, a navy blue-and-white all-cotton-tube. She appeared every bit the angel in her white slip. The sight of her was a welcome diversion from his tortured life and savaged reputation. His eyes committed to her stylish totality. Their widening reaction came without warning.

"Never seen a girl putting on makeup?" she asked, turning only her head toward him, smiling in apparent self-awareness.

"Yes, but never in a way which threatened my ability to think," he admitted, reaching down to rub her shoulders while she did her eyelashes.

"You think too much sometimes," she childishly scolded.

"Assuming that's possible."

"It is, when it, along with your studies, your job, and a pointless quest for justice that's left you in boiling hot water interferes too often with having fun." She pronounced *fun* as would a twelve-year-old.

He eased down to the floor, took the cute protester in his arms from behind. The mirror before them reflected both faces as he placed his head on her right shoulder and swayed them both from side to side. They smiled at the beautiful couple, using the mirror as a conduit for their expressions.

"I can't yet guarantee how my *pointless quest* will end, but I can guarantee nothing will interfere with tonight's agenda of fabulous food and drink, and more fabulous conversation, amid an equally fabulous setting."

189

"One, I'll be happier when your pointless quest is over, and two, tell me again how you swung this dinner at the oh-so-private North River Yacht Club."

"My knee surgeon, who's a deacon at my church here, said I could go as his guest. I think he was trying to take my mind off losing H.R. See, going to church has its advantages."

"It has its disadvantages too."

"Which are?"

"Sleep deprivation, among others."

"You do love your sleep."

"It loves me too."

Taking in her cheekbones yet again, Seth replied, "No argument there."

She patted his arms still encircling her waist, sweetly announced that she had to finish dressing, and raised herself from the cushion. He watched her slip the dress over her head. He loved her confident, womanly movements. He loved how they filled his lungs with air.

◆

The North River Yacht Club was a scenic thirty-minute drive down country thoroughfares with names like New Watermelon Road. As they crossed the dam over the Black Warrior River, he scanned the stress-alleviating view of Lake Tuscaloosa.

Soon, they were inside the gates of the North River development, and Cindi got busy critiquing the nice homes along the golf course fairways.

"Will we have a place like that soon?" she asked, pointing out a white columned two-story.

The question startled Seth out of a daze. "Huh? Well, yeah, I guess."

Cindi seemed placated. Seth drove on.

They passed through the entrance, and Seth looked in wonder as the club's nautical theme unfolded before them. Sizable wooden dinghies and iron ship cannons were placed at intervals along the thoroughfares. There was even a fountain with a full statue of King Neptune himself, spear in hand, crown upon bearded head. The nautical god's expression announced a splendid control over all things oceanic.

They entered the club to wait for Dr. Falls to arrive and sign them in. Cindi convinced an uneasy Seth to explore the upper and lower levels of the unique clubhouse. Covering the upstairs walls were an array of wildlife watercolors and several massive oil paintings of the ocean brimming over with power or serenity. Down under they found the focal point of the lower level, the oil painting, "LePalais DeGlace," or "Rich People Skating," as Cindi renamed it.

Dr. Falls and his wife arrived, and, after everyone charmed each other for three minutes, the hostess sat them at separate tables, with Seth and Cindi in a private corner. They dined on gourmet cuisine. Seth had sautéed grouper with a pecan sauce. He drank the Chablis the waiter recommended. Cindi had a marinated steak and a Heineken. Then, she tried the lobster. Seth finished with key lime pie. Cindi chose something that flamed. Seth politely suggested to the waiter that the pecan sauce had been a hint too sweet. He returned with the chef, who confessed error and offered after-dinner drinks. Seth felt terrible about appearing critical. Cindi ordered a Kahlua.

After dinner, Seth felt compelled to read over some Property notes. Despite Cindi's wish to show off her dress at The Nasty Tap, they headed for her place.

CHAPTER THIRTY-FOUR

So, there they were, at 10:00 p.m. on a Friday night, lying in Cindi's king-size bed, buried under an electric blanket. Public radio surrounded them with Mozart's double concerto for viola and violin, a piece even Cindi had to admit was a perfect duel of strings. He stared out the open window at a full moon high in the late winter sky. Now and again, through the golden spotlight of the moon, a sliver of cloud wafted by, its outline made illuminate within the moonlight. The clouds seemed invisible until they passed through the light of the moon. They had been there all along, he realized; it just took light to see them.

Seth's back was to Cindi, and she rested against him from behind, her chin on his left shoulder.

Cindi stirred him, the tone of the Southern lover all over her voice. "So, how are you and Mr. Property II getting along?"

"I've spent a lot of time with Mr. Property II, and although I much dislike him, I think I'm developing a healthy respect."

"He's too mean to make true friends with, that's for sure."

"Maybe by Tuesday night I can at least say we've come to an understanding."

"A summary under my bed would make him much easier to deal with."

"Cindi, you know how I feel about using other people's summaries."

"Don't worry, Seth, this one's no dud. The guy who wrote it made a 4.0 and was Assistant Editor of the *Law Review*. He knew how to study for a Myerson exam."

"It's not about reliance on an inferior product. If I gained from someone else's work, I'd feel like a cheat."

"It's not cheating, Seth. If you're worried about the Honor Code, which under the current circumstances seems doubtful, it doesn't even mention summaries. You can even buy them at the Copy Shoppe."

"I know, but none of that changes the way I feel."

"Well, how are you going to feel when you get a 3.0, or even a 2.5, and your chief competitors are making 3.5's and 4.0's, sometimes because they horde materials, such as model answers from old tests?"

"I don't see it as having competitors. Besides, it won't happen. I have my own method of preparing for Myerson."

"Which is?"

"Which is much more rewarding than just memorizing someone else's summary. You have to believe, in the long run, I'll be a better lawyer for going solo."

"Yeah. You'll be solo, solo because no good firm will hire you with mediocre grades and an Honor Court rap hanging around your neck. Besides, damn it, in the long run, we'll all be dead."

He hesitated, battled a sinking feeling about Cindi, rushed to ignore it. "I'm doing just fine. Besides, I don't think it's a big deal to start with a huge salary. There's more to life than having a Beamer."

"What's *that* supposed to mean?" she asked.

Seth's face dropped as he remembered her 320 model. "I didn't mean it personally. I only mean it's never a bad idea to struggle a little when you're young."

"Well, I refuse to struggle. I want a better life starting out than my parents had. I want to be a member of a place like the Yacht Club, and your conscience could never afford it. It wasn't until-"

After a few heartbeats too many had passed, her voice softened, but maintained emphasis. "I'm trying to help your career, Seth, but you won't let me. You could be so good and go so far, if only you'd let yourself."

"Maybe I have to wonder, Cindi, who *are* you trying to help?"

Sometimes, it just didn't pay to have too many thoughts racing around in an overtaxed mind.

Her face coiled, then struck. "I can't *believe* you said that. I can't believe you'd even *think* it."

"Cindi, I didn't mean-"

"Don't try to back away from it now. Don't pull any lawyer bull on me." She jumped out of bed and slung her silk bathrobe on. The finger pointed at him seemed like a spear. "How dare you, Seth. After everything my mother and I have done for you. I've taken you shopping and to the beach. I've taken you into my bed. I've taken you around in my car. I've put up with your crazy ways of thinking, your stick-in-the-mud attitude, and your obsession with football and a perfect conscience. You won't even use an old summary, much less, well, never mind, but Good God, Seth, when are you going to wake up and join the *real* world? It's a wonder we've stayed together as long as we have."

"Wait, Cindi. This isn't such a big deal. You're overreacting."

"Don't you *dare* accuse me of that. It is *the* most juvenile male cop-out there is. Not a big deal? You call *me* selfish?" She snatched her head to the side and narrowed her eyes at him. "While I'm lying in bed half naked with you, worried about your grade point average. Then you say it's not a big deal?"

Seth's lips went into their distinctive quiver. The pitch of his voice reached higher. "Good grief, Cindi, it's not as if I don't appreciate you. You know I do. Where are you coming from with all this? Where are you going with it?"

Cindi paused, yanked a cigarette from her bag. To Seth, she yanked it like a French woman snatching stitches below a Charles Dickens guillotine. She lit it. To Seth, she lit it as if she'd lit ten thousand. "Right now, I'm going into that bathroom," she swung her cigarette down as if it was a knife, "and you better not to be here when I come out."

She slammed the door behind her. The noise banged through his eardrums. Seth breathed hard, ignored the sound. The shock and confusion of a perfect evening ruined climbed all over him. His jaw was set as he pondered a hushed apology through the closed door. He'd rather have defused his first bomb. He blamed himself, threw on his clothes and left, the familiar soul sickness in tow and now a heavier payload than ever.

It was late Friday evening, February 14, 1986, a day for sweethearts.

CHAPTER THIRTY-FIVE

It was Seth's worst night of sleep in six months. All night, he'd felt as if Cindi's anger was ricocheting inside him. He'd never witnessed such fury in his boyhood home. Having one more new thing with which he was ill equipped to cope wasn't good.

Lying completely under a blanket Saturday morning, he needed relief. He convinced himself she was just in a bad mood and that he'd just said the wrong things at the wrong time; he just wasn't quite sure what they were. After an hour of over-analysis, he decided to call her and offer a make-up breakfast. He couldn't bear another night on a bed of unresolved issues, and he figured a good night's sleep had worked to settle her down.

The perfect breakfast spot was the Waysider, a quaint, red clapboard landmark of a breakfast house, with great biscuits, good coffee, and kind service to set the mood. Plus, all the college football memorabilia on the walls always made Seth feel inspired and comfortable. He called her at 8:00 and spoke carefully.

"Hey, it's me."

"Don't call me this early again."

"Could we talk a little?"

"*Could* we?"

Her tone threw up a danger signal, but a nervous, hurried Seth spoke right past it. "Why don't you decide over breakfast at the Waysider? You'll enjoy the cheese biscuits, and I'll enjoy the view until you feel like talking."

She giggled: a strange, restrained giggle, and said, "I'll meet you there in thirty minutes."

Seth felt stung. It was the first time they hadn't driven to an eatery together. He shrugged it off as just more bizarre feminine behavior.

Seth arrived early, signed his name on the wait list for a table. He washed his hands in the tiny men's room. The mirror reflected Seth's usual well-pressed self: nice khakis, the now-glossy broughams, and a Land's End shirt. It refused, however, to lie about his face or what was beneath it. He waited outside twenty minutes, then reached for a pay phone. As he dropped in a quarter, she drove up. She wore jeans and a T-shirt. Her pulled-back hair bounced with each step of her uninviting walk. A hostess said, "Sentel, party of two." The four words were like an aria. He forgot about the quarter.

He ordered coffee and skipped the cream. She asked for decaf, seized the cream pitcher, then flipped her eyes at him as she ran a spoon around her cup. She pulled out the cigarettes again. He winced. He waited, but she failed to excuse her tardiness.

She just poured a stare down at the menu and added more half and half. "*You* wanted this little meeting as I recall."

"What way is that to start a conversation?"

"Hey, I'm here, ain't I?"

Seth's tone was already nervous. "Well, in body, at least."

"I started not to be here at all. You oughta feel lucky to even see me today."

Seth replied in bewildered defense. "Why?"

"If you don't know, then I'm not sure I *should* be here."

Seth's voice grew louder as it grew more frustrated. "Maybe I asked you here to find out."

Cindi's voice was steady and direct. "You ought to know from what I said last night."

197

"Maybe it didn't make a lot of sense."

"Maybe that's *your* problem."

Seth breathed in her smoke and stared at his coffee. It threw back a nauseous fear and a growing panic.

"Look, Cindi, I can see you're upset with me, and with good reason . . . I *guess*. I know I'm not perfect. I can see how my ways might frustrate, or even irritate, someone else."

"Boy, there's the Seth Sentel understatement of the year." She aimed a sour corner mouth grin at him. "You've frustrated me since the day we met."

He breathed deeply. It was only the second time she'd ever complained about anything he'd ever done or said. He threw more watery confessions onto the incomprehensible fire.

"I know I may overanalyze everything, and sometimes I don't control my thoughts and the way they bound out of me. I should have been more considerate of you and thought about what I was saying and not just about what I was thinking. Look, I'm learning here. I'm only twenty-three."

"I'm happy you at least know your age. For a moment, I suspected you thought you were forty." Seth recalled Mozz's inside information. She continued the pounding. "You seem to be able to convince yourself of almost anything."

With eyes widened, he asked, "What does that accusation have to do with anything?"

"With the way you take yourself."

"I thought we were talking about what I said last night."

"Maybe we were, but this may be a good time to explain *all* the reasons we *aren't* dating anymore."

The snarled words stabbed him. His mind went limp. He stared back, not knowing how to reply. His mental organization was shot. His appetite dropped like an anvil. His heart went down with it. His system gathered itself for a last-ditch effort at self-defense. His emotional energies were marshaled on instinct. They rose through him, but they uttered not a syllable. Instead, they assembled into an honest countenance.

Cindi blew out a puff of smoke, stared straight through the most righteous plea for mercy a mere mortal had ever evinced, and said, "You love like a little boy, Seth. You were just too *easy*." She tossed her napkin in her plate, grabbed three cheese biscuits, and walked out.

CHAPTER THIRTY-SIX

Seth left the Waysider confused and embarrassed: embarrassed about the stares of the other patrons in the cozy breakfast house, confused about whether to go home and kick himself, or just go home and hide. Unable to decide, he drove down Fifteenth Street to the empty Central High parking lot. He felt his face stiffen. He sat for five minutes and stared at himself. He felt as if he peered at nothing. He forced down part of his own breakfast-to-go and wondered what he'd done to go so fast from good times to bad. He escaped to better times, to an interesting first trip to meet Cindi's mom.

♦

Cindi's mother's house was in Montgomery in the Twin Lakes subdivision, a new development with two winding, swan-filled lakes that mystified its homes and complicated its golf course. Once through the gated entrance, Cindi said they moved there after her father had died. Her mom said she needed to escape the memories of their cozy wood-frame home in Montgomery's Old Cloverdale section.

A lake was on their left, and Seth admired how its rippled surface intimately glittered with the afternoon sun. When he mentioned the complex refraction, Cindi giggled and said it appeared as if a million magical diamonds had been cast atop the surface of the lake.

Diamonds were ever-present in Twin Lakes that Friday afternoon. Seth noticed a lot of them on the ears and wristwatch of Cindi's mother. She was a beautiful woman of 39, who was actually 45. Her golden hair had been styled and highlighted by a sculptor of skill. Her makeup was of the latest shades and her soft sundress was of a pastel blue Seth's appreciative eyes had never seen. She gave him a close warm hug that caught him off-guard. He wondered what Cindi had said about him.

They stayed home Friday night and dined on catered shrimp casserole and tossed salad with chopped walnuts and mandarin orange slices. Seth complimented the cuisine three times.

Mrs. Vicari took Seth on a quick, informal tour of the 3,500 square foot house with a view of the Bermuda grass fairways and the stilled, dark lake, now reflecting the setting autumn sun and its Crayola box of hues. She showed him a collection of family photographs, and Seth mentioned that Cindi's hair once seemed darker. Cindi looked at her mother and gave a little shoulders-shrugging grin. She'd changed it as a freshman for sorority rush and never looked back. Her mother told an old family joke about how the milkman must have been Spanish, given that both she and Cindi's father both had light hair.

In an older photograph of her, Seth noted that her nose seemed different. She explained about the "little work that was done after a car accident."

Seth asked which university Mrs. Vicari attended. She responded, "Alabama," but explained with seeming pride that, when she fell "madly in love" with a dashing third-year law student, she'd been inspired to "punt college."

Mrs. Vicari turned in early, leaving the two students alone. Seth wanted to study, but Cindi talked him into flipping channels for just "a few minutes." A re-run of *Smokey and The Bandit* was on one channel, with Jackie Gleason uttering his famous line about a complete lack of respect for the law. Seth smiled. Ole Gleason had a way with a good line. Cindi switched to ShowTime for *Jagged Edge*, an erotic thriller. They cuddled and sipped on Scandinavian Vodka tonics, drinks strong enough to assuage Seth's guilt.

After the movie, Seth kissed her at her bedroom door, and, anesthetized by the Vodka, he was ready to sleep. Five minutes after he'd rolled into bed, Cindi tapped on the door and rolled next to him. She asked to stay all night, but Seth was worried what her mother might think.

The next morning, which arrived at about 10:00 a.m. for everyone but Seth, Seth went for a run, then took a golf lesson while Cindi and her mother went shopping for a few hours. Mrs. Vicari paid for the lesson and hinted golf would enhance his career. The Club Pro said Seth had more natural feel with a putter and a sand wedge than anyone he'd ever seen.

Over a late lunch at the club, the well-dressed ladies with their matching cheekbones and Gucci bags discussed shopping, while Seth, in fading khakis and a polo shirt, mostly listened. There was the time they'd conquered an Atlanta shopping mall in the manner of Alexander the Great. When they returned home, they had spread the day's loot all over the furniture and circled it repeatedly in adoration. Then they laughed aloud as they recalled panicking to re-sack everything when Mr. Vicari pulled into the driveway.

Seth was tired, but he noted that the two women seemed to appreciate the idea of being a team.

After lunch, Cindi and her mother's gold card took Seth on a quick trip to a men's shop and helped him choose $500 worth of wardrobe additions. Then, she stormed an adjacent women's boutique and helped herself to yet another Gucci bag. The evening brought an informal gathering at the Vicari home with several of Cindi's friends from high school, college, and law school. The keg was placed out on the deck, and Cindi introduced Seth to everyone, placing her arm in his as she did.

He was flattered she seemed proud of him, but still wondered why.

When he left to fill their beer cups, Seth overheard her laughing at a classmate's observation. "Won't it be great to be lawyers? We'll get paid a *fortune* to manipulate and connive, something most of us would do for *free*." Seth looked over his shoulder and enjoyed her childish laugh and perfect jeans.

They skipped church on Sunday and drove home that afternoon, his hand in hers or upon her knee. He looked at her and told her he loved her. He saw her examine his face and slowly smile, before she replied in kind.

◆

He and the Jeep sat in the Central High parking lot fifteen more minutes. He wondered how he'd inspired her sudden hatred and tried to will away the creeping nausea, the creeping tears, and that expanding carpet stain of a feeling he'd had all along. He failed. His breakfast hit the pavement. As he stared at his new reality, seven drops of forehead perspiration soon followed; an eighth hung suspended, like a stalactite.

CHAPTER THIRTY-SEVEN

He wiped the sweat from his forehead with a Waysider napkin and decided to return to Pinehurst. He planned to study a few hours before working an afternoon Music School benefit at the Warner House. He left, and, with the radio on, tried not to sink too far into Don Henley's "Boys of Summer", but its melancholy, almost spooky, verses surrounded him. He encouraged himself to stop loving all good music, to despise any artistic piece with a premise.

He drove through a red light. A car slammed on brakes to miss him, but he was too gone to care. He saw the blue flashes behind him, pulled over, and slumped farther into the Jeep's worn seat. It was the Campus Police.

A tall officer looked him over, asked, "Have you been taking any controlled substances?"

Seth looked straight ahead and said with a sad note of realization, "No, sir."

The cop glanced at the Waysider takeout box in the passenger seat and seemed to relax. Seth had just left a favorite law enforcement coffee source, not a bar. After Seth explained he was on the way to the Chancellor's home to prepare for a fundraiser, the tall cop handed him a warning ticket and suggested he drink more coffee if he couldn't remain alert.

Once in his room, Seth's attempt at schoolwork failed. The pain fog asphyxiated his focus. He stood and looked out the open window. He gripped the little window handles. The idea of closing it entered his brain and fed down to his hands. One second later, he slammed it shut. Mrs. Bausch was outside watering some pansies. She looked up.

He walked to the Number 11 kitchen and joined the chef for some potent French roast coffee. With lifeless hands, Seth helped François fashion ten dozen hors d'oeuvres--assembly line style, but Seth fashioned no more than one dozen words. Once halfway out of his coma, he spent the rest of the morning as a chauffeur and general support person. There were rich people to ferry about, and chairs and musical equipment to position on porches, in living rooms, and upon the flat sections of rooftops. There were little Blue Nun wine stations to strategically place along the flow of pedestrian traffic as it moved between presentations.

Seth managed to accomplish his work without a hint of a smile, without any words unnecessary to the tasks at hand. The chef observed the change, and Seth observed the observation. François correctly surmised the cause, and Seth surmised he had. Both knew better than to speak.

Seth's most important task was to interrupt the flow of the traffic by facilitating the flow of the inebriate. He was to move from station to station and pour the cold Rheinhessen wine from the blue bottles, all now on ice in fisherman's coolers. There was Tanqueray and tonic under the pouring tables for Mrs. Bausch. François delivered her first of the day while she examined the household books in her office at Number 9. But for Seth's indelible sulk, he might have delegated the honor.

Everything was set when the 100 guests arrived, and it wasn't long before short, jovial speeches by the Chancellor and the Music School Dean had been applauded and the lively live music began. Mouret's stirring trumpet piece, "Rondreau", announced the festivities. Then, there was Mozart's "Turkish March", played on twin pianos in the Number 9 living room. A Bach minuet was performed by a sophomore clarinetist in the

Pagoda Garden. Upon the roof of Number 11, there was a spirited rendition of Louis Armstrong's "Long Gone, From Kentucky", sung by a duet of black students with smiles as big as the world.

Then, a full professor took the microphone and gave a believable impersonation of Tony Bennett singing "Put On A Happy Face". Solemn Seth ignored that one. He poured glass after peachy glass without spill, without eye contact.

Mrs. B. glided over during a presentation of Brahms's "Hungarian Dance" played from the Number 9 front porch, and as the guests listened from the front lawn, requested a refill.

"Are you enjoying the concert, Seth? This must be quite a treat for your refined ear."

Seth's mind darted back to his early love of the guitar, and how his father, afraid Seth might slip into the "drug infested netherworld of rock music", had taken Seth's six string away when Seth was thirteen--just when he was showing promise. Frown in place, tie and hair otherwise, Seth examined the tablecloth and efficiently overfilled Mrs. Bausch's glass with the good stuff.

"I suppose."

The two previous Tanquerays were beginning to take hold. "Is there no happy today on your handsome face? Is something the matter, young Seth? You don't seem yourself."

"Just tired, I guess."

"Try a few glasses of the wine when George isn't looking. It'll insure a good sleep afterward."

His lifeless hand rested on the table. As she turned, she touched her index finger to it.

He snatched his hand back, then snatched three soft words from his weary soul--"Don't touch me."

The Tanqueray bottle crashed on the tile porch floor. Gin and shards shot across a five-foot radius. Mrs. Bausch's face went from shock to fright to concern. Seth's froze in panic. Then, he found a weak fourth word. "Please."

The kitchen door flew open. François's buoyant mouth followed. "It's not a party 'till something's broke." In his hands were a broom, more Tanqueray, and three Blue Nun bottles. Mrs. B. smiled with hesitation, wandered away.

"How goes it, mate? Thought it might be time to refurbish the inventory. These rich drunks have quaffed enough Blue Nuns to populate a convent." François watched for Seth's reaction, but there was nothing more than a restrained creasing of the lips.

His voice trailed down. "Look, young Seth, after today's well-lubricated festivities, Dr. and Mrs. B. will jump the company plane to Florida. A former trustee is on his deathbed at his beach house, and Dr. B. is making a pitch for a will codicil. Why don't you help me tidy a few things at Number 9 before you walk the dogs? There might be a few primo leftovers available."

Seth knew his only alternative was to study, and he suspected it would be years before he was in the mood again. Physical tasks made avoidance and escape so much easier.

He answered like a wounded robot. "Okay."

Early afternoon soon turned late, and it wasn't long before he was driving the academic power couple to the tiny Tuscaloosa Airport.

He handed the bags over to the co-pilot, who whispered, "The University needs a new natatorium, and I hear the old guy was an avid swimmer."

Seth somehow managed to wish them all a safe trip.

♦

Mrs. Bausch managed to make a call from the on-board phone to François.

◆

Back at Number 9, Seth and the good chef put away a bottle of the sweet vino and munched on any leftover hors d'oeuvres they weren't feeding to the Bassets. Yale and Harvard whined and nodded at the gourmet pup treats. François whined and nodded back to accept the compliment.

The cleanup complete and the cuisine consumed, François motioned toward a small hallway. "Come, young Seth, there's a fringe benefit of which you may be unaware."

Seth followed and soon saw François peering into the Chancellor's open liqueur cabinet. François scratched his head and addressed the bottles like they were familiar faces.

"Hm. All my good friends are here. Tia Maria, I have you to thank for last summer with young Maria. Amaretto, ah, you sweet companion of the cheesecake. Courvoisier, you naughty boy. Do you remember that night in 1974?" His head moved sideways. "François not so sure he remembers. Ah! Finally, my favorite friend of all, Gran Marnier, France's finest export, and the one who yielded Marnie."

Seth smiled for the first time all day. The enchanting chef held an open bottle of the orange-laced cognac toward Seth, who breathed in the precious scent. François took a generous sip.

"You try."

Seth complied. His palate agreed with his olfactory sensors. The chef took another hit.

"Now, sample the Courvoisier. Gran Marnier minus the wild orange."

Seth complied and winced a little before he said with a rasp, "A bit strong."

The chef tilted his head, downed a jolt without effect, and handed over the Drambuii.

"Not bad," Seth commented, examining the label as he leaned his languid frame against the paneled wall. "Didn't know the Scots made a liqueur."

"So do the Italians. Amaretto Originalle?"

Seth took a good gulp of the Italian potion and passed it to François.

"Now, a taste of Jamaica." François took a hit from the Tia Maria and handed it to Seth.

Unsteady on their feet, they settled on the Gran Marnier and sat on the oak floor. Seth looked in his glass, and suddenly, without apparent relevance, a tear fell into it. He cried with hesitation, but he cried. The death, the hurt, the injustice, and the humiliation: they all finally trickled out.

François let the tears fall, long enough for them to bring true empathy to his voice. "Young Seth, maybe Mrs. B wouldn't object if you took a few days off. Maybe spend your nights on papa's boat at the lake. Get laid if you like. I'd supply you with gourmet sustenance and would even throw in a big ole thumper, if I didn't know you better."

Seth shut off his embarrassing tears and managed a liquored smile. "They'd kick me out of school. Not that that wouldn't be a blessing."

The chef chuckled. "Maybe so. It would be one less thing on your young shoulders."

"My God, I can't help it if my whole life is now about resolution."

The chef's eyes softened. "I have no problem with resolution, young Seth, but you shouldn't seek it solitaire. Life is a fun challenge, but it can outman you, surround you, outgun you. Even the scriptures say something like 'as each part of the body does its special work, it helps the other parts, so that the whole body is healthy and well-fed.' Hmm. Maybe I misquote, but I'm certain the same meaning lies somewhere in Ephesians.

Anyway, maybe it's worth the minute risk of choosing some *partenaires*. You're unique, *mon ami*, but you cannot defeat every enemy of life alone."

"Unique, huh?"

The chef nodded. "It's a good unique, Seth. A good unique."

"I think most people just think I'm weird, or even crazy. I'm trying to do what's right, yet no one cares. No one says *Go get 'em, Seth*, or *Godspeed, Seth*. They just stare at me with some form of worthless pity."

François stood, finally a little uneasy on his feet, and looked Seth in the eye. It wasn't worthless pity in the chef's face, and, numbed to life as Seth was, he could sense it.

"Come hither, young Seth. I'll walk you to your room and tell you a story." They ambled through the kitchen. "Don't worry yourself with the Bassets. I shall walk them tonight."

"Thanks."

"Listen, about eight years ago, I had a little brother. Now, I don't. He was murdered one rainy night when he was only sixteen. It was the evening of my parents' twenty-fifth wedding anniversary. He offered to close the family restaurant, then drop the cash pouch in the bank depository. He never left the back parking lot."

"I'm sorry."

Both of their slurred voices grew solemn.

"Eventually, so were *les bandits* who shot and stabbed him. I harassed the police and the district attorney and screamed for retribution, fearing they might not be zealous because we were immigrants. The French and Americans have sometimes experienced *e'taienten de'saccord*. I also went in search of the *attaquants* myself with my father's Belgium made shotgun. After my efforts yielded a black eye and confiscation of the weapon, my father found me out, and he had a better idea. We fed the police and the D.A. twice a week for six months. No doughnuts, nuhh! We sent real pastries for breakfast and special lunch boxes filled with good cheeses and éclairs.

"So, we let them do what they do well." He shrugged. "And we did what we do well." Not a bad arrangement. Vous comprenez?"

"*Vous comprenez* means *do you comprehend*, doesn't it?" Seth asked with the appropriate accent.

"Excellent, young Seth. Your French not so bad when you're *intoxique*. Last Spring, I was at this Holman Prison in Atmore when they strapped the bandit leader into a big yellow chair, how do you name it, the Big Yellow Mama?"

"Yeah, I've seen pictures of it."

"I stared at that devil until he stopped trembling. He was the only *l'entré* I ever wished to see well-done." Seth nodded. "Anyway, this Sheriff, he opposes you, so maybe you should choose some *partenaires* to assist you with this quest for justice. Perhaps someone with special knowledge to compliment your own."

"I'll consider it." He paused. "I'm glad we got the main *l'entré* for y'all, François, and I'm glad you're now citizens."

"Yes, I think my family has both learned and taught many things since we arrived long ago."

"Maybe I've learned something tonight."

"There's no shame in learning and no shame in pursuing a worthy goal, young Seth. Just don't let your zeal render you *stupide*. Play smart."

Seth's numb eyes looked down, seemed to gather themselves, then looked back. "I guess smart beats stupid every time, doesn't it?"

François smiled. "Yes. Life is a tragedy for he who feels, but merely a comedy for he who thinks. The moral, not-so-young Seth, is to always feel, but never forget to think."

Ten minutes later, Seth fell asleep, thinking.

CHAPTER THIRTY-EIGHT

Later that night, Seth found himself alone in a world of pure hate. He saw one of evil charisma standing alone in a field. Men approached this being from every side and attacked, but all were slain. None suspected what they were up against.

Seth ran to face him, approached him with only his special knowledge and his special fear. Seth stared through him, spoke into him, "I know who you are." The beast's big white eyes began to melt, as Seth burned them with his quivering courage. "I know who you are." The eyes of the beast melted faster, then caved inside its shrinking, ghoulish face from Hell.

♦

A disturbing wail leapt out of the night. The sound seemed spooky, even sinister, to a young Seth breaking free from a bad dream. Seth heard the second moment of it, noted the noise resembled the cry of a lost child.

♦

Charlemagne and the less regal black neighbor cat were fighting in the Chancellor's driveway. They awakened Seth at three a.m.

Instead of just lying in bed trying to will himself back to sleep, Seth turned a three-way lamp on low and began to read, first, another chapter of *Atlas Shrugged*, where the productive geniuses of the world had finally rebelled against socialism's slavery and begun a general strike. Then, he grabbed his *Bible* and stumbled on the verses in *Acts* about the world's first commune. So much for the new sleep strategy. Philosophic conflict was no cure for insomnia, but, this time, he smiled at the realization. Somehow, with the finality of losing Cindi complete, he felt lighter on his conscience and lighter on his feet. Arising, he walked in his pinstriped pajamas to the window for a look.

The fighting felines had scattered, taking their shrill wails and their wounded ears elsewhere. Even though dulled by expensive booze, Seth's ears would recover no sooner than theirs. As he sat in the window box and glanced out into the night below, he hit his internal replay button for the audio of the night's big fight. He wondered about the source of such an unearthly sound, such a natural, pugilistic prelude. He wondered what drove them to the fray with such zeal.

Instinct. Mozz had talked about it. It was such an ever-present, undeniable force. Feline instinct was a peculiar variant, but God was behind it. He knew this much to be true, and if God was behind it, then there was some reason for it.

Instinct. Gazing out without focus, he asked himself why H.R. had confidence in his peculiar variety, and what his peculiar variety really was.

He flipped on a clock radio, and Mozart's piano concerto "Number 20" politely entered the room. Seth had never heard this concerto before, but he somehow knew that the soloist, in his fervor, had missed a note by a half. Somehow, he also knew where the remainder of this typically playful Mozart work was going. There was one measure where Seth guessed wrong, and he was about to hate himself for doing so, but then he finally realized it. At last, he was too weary to miss it.

Seth threw his head back, and on this exhausted night, this new comprehension rushed through his mind like an airliner, then made a perfect landing. His guess would have been as good as Mozart's; different, but just as moving a variation.

He went as far as to place both hands on the metal window handles before he stopped. He thought about it. He was tempted to leave it closed, tempted to just ignore what was out there. Then, his eyes opened wide to the stars, all infinitesimal trillion of them. He closed his eyes, rubbed them. Then he realized how, to most people, the stars sparkled, but to him, each seemed to pulse, to not just wink at, but to reach out to their admirers. His eyes opened again, but now wider as he remembered he'd always perceived the stars this way.

He threw open the window. He stood there long enough this time, long enough to feel an awareness finding a home inside him. It felt proper. He looked over at Andrew Wyeth's "Christina's World" on the wall nearby, realized how intensely the subject perceived her world.

Seth ran a hand through his sleepy hair and looked around outside. He saw Charlemagne in a prowling, victorious catwalk below. He watched the big feline slip into the straw-laden flowerbed, crawl behind a bush, and fall asleep. Instinct. It struck Seth that his own was indeed a peculiar kind, but it struck him deeper that God was behind it. He knew this much to be true, and if God was behind it, then there must be a good reason for it. So, there was no reason to shut it out.

A powerful new realization had struck his center. The old saying was true; knowledge was indeed power . . . and a lot of it was a lot of power. Seth was afraid--afraid of himself, afraid of his future. He was also sad. King Solomon had also been correct. Knowledge did increase a man's sorrow.

He looked out the open window, drew in the cool Southern air sifting through the big oaks of Pinehurst. Good booze and thoughts of H.R., Sue, and law school sifted through his mind. One thought led to another and another, but now, somehow, there were no thoughts of Cindi, yet no loneliness either.

His head shifted. He would call Hound Dog Hampton. Seth nodded. He knew it was the right next thing to do, knew he belonged somewhere else, knew whatever made him different wasn't to be wasted.

It was four a.m. Sunday. Seth walked straight to his antique maple bed. He crawled in and fell asleep.

CHAPTER THIRTY-NINE

On Monday, February 17, 1986, Seth phoned Hound Dog Hampton from the Warner House. Hampton's secretary answered, explained Mr. Hampton was in depositions. She took a message.

Seth realized it might be days before Hound Dog could return his call, then followed his appetite to the Number 11 kitchen. There was a small luncheon for Mrs. Bausch's bridge club, and François was turning out crab cakes, cole slaw, and twice-baked potatoes. Seth walked over and offered François his services.

"Interesting timing, mate. Does your desire to assist in my kitchen only materialize shortly before meal time?"

"It's a mere coincidence, I promise. May I sample one of your heavenly rolls?" Seth motioned toward a lovely stash of home-baked yeast rolls in a basket covered with a white cloth napkin. François raised a knife, but he was too late. Seth was already applying the Land 'O Lakes. The chef responded with just the right dash of attitude. "While you're absorbing my finest workmanship, would you mind shredding this cabbage?"

"Just show me how."

The chef plopped a healthy head of cabbage onto an oak cutting board, removed the outer leaves, and made a few thin slices. Then, he sliced the slices a few times each and pulled them apart. "Don't slice it too fine. Make shredded cabbage, not grated cabbage."

"Okay. I'll try not to do a *grate* job."

François slung over one of his pleasant perturbed looks and replied, "Nothing like a hungry smart mouth to make a kitchen feel like home."

Seth finished the cabbage detail in time for the kitchen phone to ring.

"Warner House."

"May I speak with Seth Sentel? This is Leigh, Harry Hampton's secretary."

"Hey Leigh, this is Seth."

"So, what's this Warner House greeting?"

"It's the University Chancellor's residence. I actually live here. I'm in the kitchen assisting the chef."

She sounded envious. "You have a good life, Seth. I lived in Tutwiler Dorm when I went to school there."

Seth laughed. "Leigh, I have a question for you. Would Elliot Gaston's secretary have sat in on his client conferences?"

"I know her, and I don't think she'd have time. She works for three different tax attorneys here and always complains about all the long wills and trusts she has to type."

"I see."

"Anyway, here's Mr. Hampton on the line for you."

Hound Dog sounded friendly. "Seth, is that you? The last time I saw you was just before Mike Shula and Van Tiffen achieved football immortality."

"Yes, sir, it's me, Mr. Hampton. I hope I'm not interrupting anything."

"Nothing major. It's just *another day, another deposition*. By the way, you don't have to call me Mister. Makes me feel like a decrepit old barrister. Just call me Harold, or even Hound Dog, like everyone else has decided to do without my permission."

"Yes, sir, Mr. Harold. I guess it's just the way I was raised."

"Well, that's a fine way of growing up, but remember that, by now, you may be grown up too. Did anything particular prompt you to call, or did you only wish to give me the chance to size you up for a clerkship?"

With a near audible blush, Seth replied, "Oh, no sir, nothing like that. I just need a little advice."

"Alright then, what's the topic? Women, whiskey, law? I should warn you. I'm only an expert on whiskey."

Seth laughed. "No sir, nothing like that. It's related to the law school. I'm sure you heard the bad news about H.R. and Sue, my friends you met at the football game."

"Yes, and I felt awful about it. What a heartbreaking waste, a hunting-related situation, according to the paper. Sounds like negligent homicide. I think that's Section 13A-6-4 of the Code. Anyway, it must be a tough time for you and the entire school, especially after those other two students were murdered under more heinous circumstances. How can I help?"

"Well, there are things about this that don't make sense. I guess you know an attorney with your firm had drafted a will for H.R. shortly before he died."

"I remember. H.R. called me first, and I referred him to Elliot Gaston. It was terrible about Elliot and his little boy. I really liked Elliot. He was a good estate lawyer and a fine fellow. My Lord. Seems like death is all around us."

"He was quite a tennis player as well."

"So, you met him?"

"Shortly before he died. I spoke with him at his club. We set up a meeting about H.R.'s will, but we never had the chance to meet."

Hampton's tone grew curious. "Really? Keep talking, Seth."

"H.R. left me an inheritance, along with a vague note suggesting I speak with Mr. Gaston. The note suggested H.R.

had stumbled onto some type of suspicious activity involving the law school. He also mentioned a rumor that Rentzell and Hays had passed their drug tests."

There was a strange pause before Hampton spoke. "This is highly unusual, Seth. Have you gone to the Sheriff's Office about this?"

"I met with Sheriff Gibson, and he's already arrested a suspect, a man named Lymon who lived in a shack near the site of the shooting. H.R. knew about him because H.R. lived in his cousin's cabin out there."

"Well, I'll be."

"Gibson is convinced this Lymon man shot them accidentally. His chief deputy is trying to coerce a confession. I think Sue's mom is pressuring the Sheriff. Her husband is a trial judge in Madison County."

"What's the judge's last name?"

"Longshore."

"I know old Guy Longshore. He's fourth generation old money, so he's lazy as sin, a seat of the pants judge who never hits a lick at a law book."

"Well, Mrs. Longshore is probably calling Sheriff Gibson every day. He wasn't receptive to the idea of a more complex case."

"Complexity isn't Gibson's strong suit." He paused again. "This case badly needs a private investigator. I want you to call a friend of mine named Hugo Black. He's an ex-ABI guy, a real-world thinker who's somewhat unorthodox, but incredibly effective. I've put him to work on civil cases. He works cheap."

"I'll be able to pay Mr. Black's fee, once I receive the money H.R. left me."

"Okay. If need be, I'll up-front his fee. Then, we'll get square when the estate is closed. I'll have another attorney in the firm get right on the probate work."

Things were moving fast, and Seth's voice grew excited. "Yes, sir."

"One more thing, Seth. Hugo has had his, shall we say, little bumps in the road. He's been associated with some bad women and was once a drinker, but he gave it up. And there was even talk of some cannabis experimentation. Anyway, he's harmless, and like I said, he can be highly effective. Well, Seth, I better return to this dog-gone deposition, but y'all watch out for Sheriff Gibson's receptionist. She's trouble with a capital T."

Seth was a little apprehensive about Hugo, but he managed a laugh about the Sheriff's fully receptive receptionist.

He returned to the kitchen to help François with the luncheon, reminded him not to overwhelm the crab cake mixture with onion. Afterward, they dined sober on leftovers and had an interesting conversation about women. Well fed and well relaxed, Seth listened, then concluded that women never made any sense. François responded that that was the whole point.

◆

After lunch, Seth walked across the back patio toward his room, panned left at the lawn of rye grass and the circles of pansies around the mighty oaks. He sensed cleanliness in the cool air and the promise of a bright sun's warmth. The sky revealed itself in a perfect blue, a gorgeous day for good thinking. He made his way to the window box and read through a Contracts II assignment. He slowly considered the subject matter, allowed the ideas to steep without resistance.

He realized it felt good and right when something made sense, but he was honest with himself. Maybe it was mostly the warm François cuisine that brought comfort. His mind loped back to other good recent meals. On Wednesday, December 4, after the Alabama-Auburn game, he had lunch with H.R. and Sue at City Café in Northport. Something about that particular sustenance outing meant something. Somewhere in that day's conversation was a diamond of import. Like lightning, his instincts had sensed it then, but then, just as quickly, he'd moved it to his mental backburner. Maybe, if he replayed the entire scene, he could discover it again.

◆

It had been three weeks before Christmas, and all through the house, not a first-year student was happy, not even an H.R. For, in early December, the first-year had but two thoughts, final exams and studying for final exams. Seth and H.R. were hunkered down again in the Football Room.

"This is mega-suck territory, Sethster. No one warned us law school would be so torturous when they took our tuition checks. I have five exams and a 100-page summary to study for each. Only one of our sinister professors allows an open book test. My sanity is indebted to Barry Goodfried. It's the Christmas season, and the only warm-hearted teacher we have is a Jew."

"True, but so is our toughest. I was never around Jewish people growing up, and I'm a little confused."

"But there's nothing confusing about the evil Myerson. He has the compassion of a rattlesnake. I still hate how the jerk blasted me for having a little fun on Bourbon Street."

Seth lowered his voice. "Hey, you better keep the rhetoric at a lower volume."

"Maybe I wish he'd hear me. Maybe we should finally have it out." H.R. twisted his mouth. "By the way, is there a boxing gym around here where I can train?"

"H.R., you're a riot. The man isn't evil. He's old fashioned, but he's not Darth Vader in a three-piece suit."

H.R. looked disappointed. "I dunno. He doesn't even go easy on the female students."

Seth smiled. "Maybe he just believes women have an equal right to severe emotional distress."

"Maybe he just relishes preying on the weak."

"H.R. You're taking this anti-Myerson campaign all too seriously."

"Easy for you to say. You're not the one whose career he's trying to torpedo. Sometimes, I think you're somehow one of his favorites, Southern Protestant that you are."

"Don't forget. He hammered both of us in New Orleans for discussing Rentzell and Hays during the game. The most I can say is that we have an uneasy rapport."

"Beats an uneasy war," H.R. concluded, as he looked down at a Torts hornbook.

Seth refocused on his self-made Property summary. They studied until 11:20, when the growl in H.R.'s stomach acted as a dinner chime.

"H.R., your stomach sounds like it's caging a Bengal tiger."

"Must mean it's time to hit City Café."

Seth began putting on his coat. "Let's grab Sue and go. I don't want to wait outside for a table in this cold."

"How about Cindi?"

"She's in class."

They picked Susan up at her cubicle and left in H.R.'s Jeep, setting a course down University Boulevard. They passed Denny Chimes on the right, and H.R. had a relevant comment. "Well, there she is, the biggest phallic symbol on campus."

Seth asked, "Shouldn't you refer to a phallic symbol as a he?"

Sue asked, "What's a phallic symbol?"

H.R. couldn't resist. "Sue, it's a symbol of power and superior ability to lead."

Seth clarified through twisted lips. "In other words, it represents a man's thingamajiggy."

Sue was on her toes this day. "In which case, it must also represent a superior ability to *mis*lead."

Seth laughed. "She has you pegged, friend. I guess that's the downside of dating the same girl for over two months. They figure you out."

H.R. couldn't help but laugh with him. "I have to admit it, darling Susan: *that* was a good one." Sue smiled and crossed her arms.

They chatted until they reached the bridge across the Black Warrior River on the way to Northport. Seth stared down at the barges below. He wished he could recline on a barge deck and daydream December away. He wished he was Huck Finn.

Tom Sawyer broke his trance. "Wake up, Seth. We're about to enter meat and three vegetable heaven."

"Sorry, H.R., just escaping for a moment. Do you think finals will be as tough as the third-years say?"

"Aw, Seth, the third-years are just happy because we're suffering like they did two years ago. They're blowing it out of proportion. Right, Sue?"

Susan's pre-finals mentality had improved since the Alabama-Auburn game. The look of academic paranoia had disappeared from her soft cheeks. "I don't feel so bad about it, Seth. I mean, I know how serious it is, but I'm learning to take it one exam at a time."

H.R. nodded in encouragement. Seth was surprised at her complacency. "It's good to see a little relaxation in your face, Sue. It becomes you."

Sue's voice became slightly more rapid and emphatic. "Let's just say I have a new frame of mind. Worrying too much will only make matters worse. I'll do my best, then take what comes."

H.R. added. "Hey, Sethinator, if you keep hanging around us professional nonchalants, you just might lengthen your lifespan."

"I'll take that under advisement, counselor."

They turned beneath the bridge and past a religious billboard declaring that, in the end, only what's done for God will last. Seth expressed a fear taxes might also somehow last. Susan joked that cockroaches might too.

They arrived at City Café, a diner fit for the *Andy Griffith Show*. The place was a beehive of Southern dining activity. Waitresses busied themselves taking orders and delivering iced tea. Their server arrived in a white apron and a baby blue uniform dress, with generous matching eye shadow. They were early enough to secure a booth. Seth faced the back where an oversized heating unit hung from the ceiling and fought the weak Alabama cold like an ancient warrior. Below it hung a black wall phone with the dial on the wall piece. A sign below it read *Local Calls Only, One Minute Limit*. It looked like a prop from *In the Heat of the Night*.

Deer heads and signed Bear Bryant photos adorned the walls. An old black-and-white TV sat atop the bar, and that rerun of *Smokey and the Bandit* was going again, with Jackie Gleason delivering the same line about a complete lack of respect for the law. This time, the words struck Seth deep. He was led to extract some kind of meaning from them, yet as his mind began to wrap itself around them, a busboy dropped an armload of plates. His head snatched over to track the noise.

H.R. looked at the menu and observed, "I still can't believe you can get a meat and three veggies here for $2.50, including tea. This would cost six bucks in San Antonio."

Seth added, "But you can't get good Tex-Mex here."

"True, and I'm beginning to miss it. If Southwest Air were available, I'd fly home and retrieve some."

Seth picked up a *Wall Street Journal* someone had left behind and began his perusal ritual. He was worried about the dollar's value on world currency markets. It had tanked since a September central banker meeting at the Plaza Hotel.

Sue and H.R. looked at each other and announced together, "Here we go again."

H.R. continued. "Seth, you'd read a bubble gum wrapper if you found it on a sidewalk."

Already over to the stock pages, Seth's head snatched up. He asked, "What? Am I that bad?"

Susan pitied him. "Is he that bad? With the way you soak up and analyze information, you're like a human computer processor. Seth, you'd read a children's book if it was all a doctor's office had available, then you'd find some obtuse meaning in it. Tell us, what are you gleaning from that hand-me-down paper?"

"Well, we were discussing Southwest Air, so I thought I'd check out its trading patterns. Maybe it's a good buy."

H.R. and Susan laughed. Susan concluded with a fond smile. "You're so Seth'ish sometimes, Seth."

Seth looked up from the paper with a funky look of humility in his eyes. "Then again, who else'ish would I be?" They laughed as if they'd just been furloughed from prison.

The waitress interrupted to take their orders. "So, what's the joke? I've been on my feet all day and could use a laugh."

H.R. helped her out. "Nothing, really. Our friend Seth here is just a human mainframe." The waitress appeared perplexed. They laughed again at her comical, eye-shadowed face.

Sue added. "We're sorry, but it's final exam time, and we're a little weird during the few moments when we're not studying. I think I'd laugh if my dog was run over, and I don't even have a dog." That merited an encore laugh.

They got serious long enough to order. Unfortunately, the conversation turned to law school when Seth asked, "So, H.R., what's your study strategy for the next two weeks?"

"The Civil Procedure exam on Monday is first, and because it's multiple choice, it should be the easiest of the five."

"Agreed."

"I'll spend all day Sunday on it, but use Saturday as an extra day for Property, which should be the toughest test the world has ever known, and Tuesday for Torts on Wednesday, which is an open book exam. Contracts is Friday, but I feel so good about it, I may just wing it."

"As usual, you have more guts than I do. What about today and next week?"

"I'll spend part of next weekend in the exam recovery room at The Nasty Tap. Beginning Saturday afternoon, I'll put in more extra time for Property on Thursday morning. Criminal is Tuesday afternoon, and because it's also open note, there should be enough time for it Monday and the morning before the exam. Today, I'll use for this Wednesday's Torts exam, which is also open book. With Goodfried, it's all about understanding, not memorization."

"Right. If you can understand it and apply it creatively to the fact situations, you'll do well. That's why girls often do better in his classes. They're more naturally creative."

Sue grabbed the iced tea pitcher on the table and filled her glass. As she began to speak, Seth noticed a peculiar look on her face as if she was thinking under pressure. "I like what you two said about Goodfried's classes." She hesitated. "As a girl, I shouldn't have to spend as much time on Torts and Criminal."

Sensing some strange tension, Seth tried to be supportive. "I can see how Myerson and Dooley's finals could scare someone to death. Neither of them is liberal artsy. Plus, they both take the old school Socratic approach, which makes it more difficult to know what to study. Myerson knows psychology, but he rarely applies it in a positive manner."

H.R. said the expected. "You can say *that* again."

Ignoring him, Seth went on. "I wouldn't invest too much time in Contracts and Property, though. I hear Goodfried gives a challenging exam, and, if you don't prepare yourself, you could get killed."

The hungry three then proceeded to vacuum the hot food they'd unknowingly craved all week. After lunch, they drove across the river, then ran several errands to delay their appointments with academic servitude. Seth and H.R. went to work on Torts. Sue returned to her cubicle and her struggle with the Property summary Cindi had given her.

♦

Seth's head shook involuntarily. He had re-entered real time. His inner Seth contemplated Sue at the City Café. It honed in upon her demeanor, her reactions, her mannerisms, the general incongruity between what she'd said about her study strategy and how she'd said it. That's what had pricked his inner Seth alarm then, and now it rang it gently anew.

He considered his current milieu. He considered Lesley Peace, the student he'd seen jotting down grades at the Wailing Wall, the girl-next-door. Calling her was the right next thing to do.

CHAPTER FORTY

An hour after he'd spoken to Hound Dog, Seth called Leslie.

She answered on the fifth ring. "Hello?" The friendly voice sounded preoccupied.

"Yes, is Lesley Peace there?"

"This, oops . . . um, this is she." Seth thought he heard something bouncing on the floor behind her.

"This is Seth Sentel. I saw you a while back at the Wailing Wall. Did I call at a bad time?"

Her voice seemed to gather itself. "Oh no, not at all."

He could hear water running. "Should I just call back later?"

"No, I promise it's fine. Just washing my hands."

"Oh, okay. I was wondering if I could ask you about something. We could meet at Storyville this Saturday for brunch."

Seth sensed some hesitation as she replied, "Uh, I'm curious. Why would you want to talk to me?"

"Remember how you said you were going to run a few regressions on the first-year class test scores?"

"Yeah, and I remember the screwy look on your face when I mentioned it." Seth couldn't miss the pleasant hint of unhappy accusation in her voice.

Now, it was Seth who hesitated. "Really? What do you mean by screwy?"

Her tone beat a quick retreat. "You know, like you were unfamiliar with regression."

Seth's reply was stoic. "Well, perhaps I was. I should've taken Stat in undergrad, but kept avoiding it."

"So why do you want to meet at Storyville?"

"I hope you might explain what you're trying to accomplish by running regressions, and well, also exactly what regressions are."

"You do?"

"Yes, I said I did, didn't I?"

Seth suspected she was restraining herself after his last words as if she didn't trust what any man said.

She finally responded. "Alright, I'll meet you there Saturday at nine."

◆

She hung up, then searched the restroom floor for the bottle of hair coloring she'd dropped.

◆

Seth stared at the phone a full second, long enough to remember François's observation about women, before hanging it up.

◆

At any hour of any day, the lighting was dim in Storyville. It was no different on this particular Saturday morning. Seth arrived first and sat alone in the corner. He felt strange being there without Cindi. He thought about their first night together during the warmth of mid-September. It was chilly February now, and his best comfort was to dwell on her, the look of her, the way she'd touch him, the surprising things she'd say: one moment, the words of the serious professional, and the next, the childlike sentences of an eight-year-old. He ignored how she'd dumped him and crushed his spirit, and instead sickened himself with speculation she might have a new lover. He convinced himself she'd still be the type to make up in a rush.

Moments later, he noticed a blonde-haired girl waving at him from the entrance. His eyes strained to recognize her. The hostess seemed befuddled. A girl was claiming she was with a guy at a corner table, but the sleepy-eyed guy seemed not to know her. Plus, the same guy had just mentioned he was waiting on a brunette and to send her back upon arrival.

Seth's face finally registered recognition. He pushed himself up from his chair and waved Lesley over.

Less spoke as if she knew him well. "Are you daydreaming so early in the day?"

Despite the dark circles under them, his eyes were wide and his smile playful. His voice was apologetic. "I suppose so. Sorry. Plus, I didn't quite recognize you."

She gazed up at her bangs. "Why another strange facade on your sleepy face? Does it look so different?"

Because it did, he couldn't answer. "The question is, will your actions be any different. They say blondes are less inhibited."

"Maybe I will be; maybe I won't."

He smiled at her precocious manner and motioned for her to sit. Their waiter, a freckle-faced freshman named Eli, arrived, and in honor of H.R., Seth ordered a rare Irish coffee. Less ordered a Screwdriver and after three sips, suddenly seemed comfortable. They exchanged the usual college small-talk about undergrad majors and where they grew up. Less was from Fairhope, an artsy town on Mobile Bay. They spoke of their families, and what their parents did for a living. Less's dad had died of cancer, but had been a financial planner, and her mom was a teacher.

Less was kind of cute, Seth noticed, as the Smirnoff and Orange Juice relaxed her face. The light brown eyes were feminine, yet spunky. The newly lightened, medium length hair was fine and straight. Her facial features were narrow and

231

pretty, just not too pretty. Seth calculated she was 5'7," weighed no more than 110 pounds, and he'd already noticed she moved like an athlete.

They enjoyed Eggs Benedict, French toast, and breakfast inebriants. Less had never eaten at Storyville before and appeared to appreciate both the food and the atmosphere. Seth commented on her thin frame and eager appetite and playfully suggested she should eat out more often. She'd only say there was a good reason for her physique.

She then commented on how he wore his evident lack of sleep so well. "Lots of practice," he explained.

They ordered straight coffee and began talking Statistics. Less opened a compact notebook to reveal a series of equations. Seth soon saw that, by avoiding undergrad Stat, he'd not missed the greatest academic show on earth.

Less saw the look in his eye. "Regression analysis is not so complex. It's basically a search for a mathematical and statistical expression of a correlative relationship."

Though Seth was befuddled, he sensed she'd prepared extensively for this presentation. She made an honest effort to explain Stat in an organized fashion, but he feared she'd over-presumed the starting point of her pupil. Hating to disappoint her, he continued to listen while she spoke of "R2's" and correlation coefficients, and, whenever he asked a question, she made a valiant attempt to answer it, but only succeeded in stirring the early morning clouds of mental smoke in his head. He needed more coffee, so he motioned for Eli.

"Incidentally Eli, why the name Storyville?"

"It was the whorehouse district in old New Orleans."

"Oh." Seth sensed the revelation was meaningful, that someone was trying to tell him something important.

He shook it off, and, after five more minutes of Statistical disconnect, he asked Less, "Could you draw me a picture to compliment your most thorough explanation?"

An eager teacher, she hesitated, then said, "Okay. Let me get a pencil."

As she dug in her purse, Seth perused the neat, organized equations in her notebook. This made them no easier to organize in his head, so he looked at the ceiling and squinted. He looked back down when she ripped out a sheet of paper and began jotting dots all over it. She made a graph outside the confines of the dots and labeled one axis 'X', the other 'Y.' Once he re-focused on the multiple dots, he could discern a pattern to them.

She used her pencil as a pointer. "The goal is to determine how much of the change in the 'Y' variable is explained by changes in the 'X' variable. If these dots had somehow randomly combined to form a straight line, then we'd have a perfect correlation, but that's quite rare. Instead, what one sees is something scattered like this."

She pointed at the collection of pencil dots. "Now, what a Statistician would do is feed the 'X' and 'Y' input into a computer, which will then calculate an equation for a line approximating the relationship between the two variables. A graph of that line would probably run through the middle of the dots like this." She drew a line through the dots. "The fact that the line is approximate tells us the independent 'X' variable doesn't exactly explain the other dependent variable."

"By the way, always remember--correlation and causation are not identical concepts. They may coexist, but the existence of the former doesn't necessarily prove the existence of the latter."

Seth was catching on. "Then, there might be some other independent variable to explain the change?"

"Right. That's my next point. So, one can run several of these regression calculations to determine which of several different independent variables are most reliably associated with the change in the dependent variable."

Now half awake, Seth couldn't resist having a little fun with an un-fun subject matter. "So, let's say the 'Y' variable is the number of dates a guy has in a given year, and the 'X' variables are his gross income, inheritance, etc. We could run a regression to see how much a change in an 'X' variable affects the value of the 'Y' variable."

"Right." She stopped, dropped her hands to the table, and tried to fight the smirk creeping its way into her lips. "Well as I mentioned earlier, we can't forget that correlation doesn't necessitate causation. To be diligent researchers, we'd have to check for the impact of other variables, like upbringing, maturity, and politeness. There might even be cross-correlation between the 'X' variables."

Seth kept the game going. "In any case, I'd be willing to wager that, in my example, the resulting computer output would yield a *powerful* correlation."

Seth smiled, but she wasn't done yet, so said the small measure of sass in her voice. "Let's examine another example. Suppose we were attempting to correlate how many dates a girl has with how large her bosom is, or how willing she is to reveal it. I'd wager such a comparison would yield an R2 of .99."

Seth was seeking to control his laughter. "What would really be interesting, Less, would be to run some kind of double test between the dependent variable from my examples and the dependent variables from yours. I'd postulate the existence of some kind of double correlation. My variables would be correlated with yours and vice-versa."

Less at last showed a smile, both small and genuine, and concluded, "Yes, that's cross-correlation between the x and y variables. In theory, x and y could be causing each other." Seth tapped his chin on his fist. "Seth, I think you've grasped these regression concepts all too well."

Returning the smile, Seth observed, "You know, you *are* the 'girl-next-door'."

She reacted with a charming stare. "What's that supposed to mean?"

"Never mind. Just an inside joke you wouldn't understand."

Her eyes flipped to the corner of the ceiling and back. "What I also don't understand is why you even bother with this Stat stuff? I had to learn it to pass two courses, and now I just do it out of curiosity, but why do *you* care?"

Seth lowered his voice. "It's related to, um, a school project I'm working on."

"What project? Law school is about word games. Apparently, the only important numbers are class rank and starting salaries."

"This project isn't widely assigned."

She leaned a little closer. "So, you're not, uh, going to tell me what it is?"

Seth wondered why his heart had jumped a gear. "Maybe, maybe not. Actually, you may even unwittingly know something vital to it already."

"And I'm guessing you wish to know whatever I might know or can discover."

He paused, took a sip of coffee, rested his cup, and said, "Remember when I saw you copying everyone's grades?"

♦

Of course she remembered. In her mind, it was like having a private conversation with a movie star. "The day you looked at me like I was from Venus?"

♦

He took a deep breath and said, "That's the day."

"I have a vague recollection. You weren't so curious about Stat then."

Their eyes met. "Now, I have a reason to be curious." He paused. She was locked onto his gaze. "Did you know how good of friends H.R. and I were?" She appeared baffled. "We were best friends right out of the gate."

"I know the feeling, more or less." Her voice sounded shy.

"Well, a real friendship can generate powerful commitment." He noted the question marks in her eyes. "A commitment stronger than death."

She nodded. "That's a strong commitment."

"I'm committed to discovering who killed him, and-" He shrugged. "Who knows, maybe who killed Rentzell and Hays too. I'm going to need your help." She swallowed the little lump of disbelief in her throat. "I'm going to need some *commitment* from you, Less."

Hearing the magic 'C' word, her chest heaved, but her answer was a firm question. "How can I help you?"

A slight movement caused Seth to glance over his shoulder. Lance, the waiter with the whiskey, walked toward the reception desk. He stopped there with his back to them and picked up a phone.

CHAPTER FORTY-ONE

As Dr. Whitehurst dictated his notes from session three, his voice bore an air of concern.

Session Three; February 24, 1986

Patient arrived early and exhibited a normal appearance. Patient discussed her high school years and explained she quit cheerleading because she was tired of "having to deal with the other girls' problems." She claims to have had no interest in serving as a class officer and avoided answering whether she'd ever sought election, adding she was into "real world" achievement.

This discussion led to more questioning about her interests, which included shopping with her mother and going "out." She admitted driving while "a little drunk a few times", but only around campus, stating, "Besides, everyone does it." She smokes, but only when drinking, and "maybe after sex." Patient is apparently sexually active, "just like any college girl." She elaborated that dating around was a lot of fun. She answered a follow up question with, "After all, the men are gaming you, so why not game them back?"

Patient claims she is in love with another law student named Seth Sentel, but she doesn't view it as a permanent "situation". She described Mr. Sentel as "a good guy, like my dad" and again added "maybe too good." For the record, I know Seth Sentel, and his involvement with her causes me concern for his well being.

She wasn't interested in having children "for a long time." Patient has no pets and states they're "too much trouble, like kids are."

Concerning her eating habits, patient explained she ate out often, particularly at a "Chinese buffet place," but sometimes just didn't feel like eating, and "why should a girl eat if she doesn't feel like it?"

Patient never fasts for more than three days. It appears she's too self-aware to allow the fasting to prolong itself to a point of danger. The gorging sometimes yields a temporary problem with weight gain. Nonetheless, this pattern has persisted for years, so it remains troubling.

ACTION PLAN - Refer patient to an outside psychiatrist, preferably a female doctor. Suggest she develop a means to smooth out the patient's eating habits. Express my concern with other disturbing admissions and observations, *e.g.*, absence of normal emotional development, incessant over-justification, indicia patient lacks appropriate empathy responses. Review case of *Tarasoff v. California* for any possible right to disclose pertinent information to Mr. Sentel, who is conceivably in danger. (Disclosure is strongly preferred, but probably unauthorized.)

CHAPTER FORTY-TWO

Common sense tempted Seth to admit he hadn't the time for a murder investigation. Between attending and preparing for classes and his obligations to the Chancellor, he had to rush just to shave and dress every day. The only time-demands that had disappeared related to Cindi and the big firm job interviews. He didn't miss the latter: the interviews had only left him wanting to take a shower.

In any case, he created a spare hour at 4:30 p.m. on Monday, February 24, to meet with private investigator Hugo Black. Hugo's office was on the second floor of an old building located three blocks off the main street, but within walking distance of several small Tuscaloosa law firms, the primary source of his sporadic referral work. The door was open. Seth knocked anyway.

Seth heard a noise from a small door down a short hallway. "Just a minute. Be right out." The flush of a toilet punctuated the assurance. A tall, lanky man with curly blond hair and a big smile zipped his faded blue jeans as he stepped out and spoke. "Sorry, just a coffee exit. Hi, young man. Hugo Black's the name."

Seth's return smile was small, reticent. "I'm Seth Sentel. I'm here for a 4:30 appointment. Mr. Harry Hampton referred me."

"Appointment, huh. My part-time assistant neglected to inform me of any appointments. Don't have many. Don't make many either. I'm used to folks walking in, and folks are used to me doing the same. It's funny, most are either pleased to hear what I have to say or have no choice but to listen. Anyhow, come on back to the office." Hugo reached for an old metal coffeepot. "Coffee?" Seth politely declined. "How about an ice-cold Cokey Cola. Nothing better in the afternoon." He paused. "Well, I can think of one thing better."

Seth accepted the Coke with a subtle, entertained smile. Hugo poured himself a cup of strong Joe in a stained Cash's Liquors mug. Cash's was a combination strip joint/liquor store in Fort Walton Beach, Florida. Hugo's home brew was dark as new asphalt.

"So, old Hound Dog referred yuh. How do you know that rascal?" Seth started to explain, but Hugo was still talking. "You have to respect a comeback kid like Hound Dog Hampton. The public kicks his ass out of office, so he puts out a shingle and starts making millions. His first wife runs off with a doctor, so he sues the doctor for alienation of affection, then marries a young fashion buyer who's twice as pretty."

Seth's eyes said he was surprised about the Hound Dog revelations as he added, "He's quite a man. He spoke highly of your abilities, too. Said you were once an ABI man."

"The Alabama Bureau of Investigation. Yeah, I learned my trade there. They didn't take too kindly to some of my methods, though, not to mention some of my habits."

"Hound Dog seems to believe your methods can be quite effective."

"Especially if your check is quite good." Hugo's Paul Newman-blue eyes twinkled.

Seth dropped into a stare. "If you'll hear me out, you'll have the chance to be more effective than penicillin." Hugo straightened up in his chair.

Seth secured a promise of confidentiality then told Hugo the entire story: where H.R. liked to hang out and drink and how he'd gotten serious with Sue. He described the scene in the woods as best he could. He relayed what Gibson revealed about the one bullet, the distance it traveled, the one suspect in custody, and the lack of footprints near the scene. He showed him H.R.'s note and pointed out its vague references and misplaced mention of Rentzell and Hays. He described H.R.'s strange phone call to him the night before, his incoming messages, and his will and life insurance policy.

Hugo raised his eyebrows. Seth continued. There was the meeting with Elliot Gaston and the subsequent meeting cancelled by the plane crash.

Hugo smiled, maybe out of respect. Seth responded with a tentative question. "What do you think so far?"

"I'm an honest P.I. I'm not entirely dependable, but I'm more than honest. This situation sounds odd, no doubt. At the same time, it could be no more than coincidence." Seth breathed out, but his gaze was steady. Hugo added, "I doubt you wanted to hear that."

"H.R. had to be indicating something was very wrong."

"Maybe something is, but don't assume we'll pop the top on some grand conspiracy. It just may not happen. As inept as Sheriff Gibson is, his choice of the obvious suspect could amount to a correct lucky guess. A positive ballistics result could seal the deal."

Four months earlier, Seth would have caved in and walked out dejected. "I'll double your normal fee. There's a nice fat check coming to me within a week, and Hound Dog fronted me your retainer money and said he was good for more until my check clears. What's your usual fee?"

Hugo folded his arms and took a moment. He stood, paced behind his desk. He turned and nodded. "I suppose I could at least run background checks on a few folks at the law school."

"And try to find out more about the Rentzell-Hays situation?"

"I'm on good terms with a few of the city detectives, so, yeah, I could do that. By the way, my usual fee is $40 per hour, and because this shouldn't require many hours, I'll feel fine about $80 per hour, plus expenses. Just remember, there's a distinct impossibility that I'll discover anything worthwhile."

Seth pondered Hugo's quirky wording, appreciated the reality of the man. He removed five 100-dollar bills from an envelope. "Here's a small retainer. When can you start?"

CHAPTER FORTY-THREE

Seth and Less had fashioned a plan amid the low lights, slow Jazz, and gourmet brunch cuisine that was Storyville, but their plan needed raw material. They decided to work together to get it. Seth had the movie star facade and the screenwriter's vocabulary. Less had a face still innocent, and one powerful chocolate chip cookie recipe, a writing of tactical significance, given Chief Registrar Doris Knight's love of sweets.

They decided to approach Mrs. Knight on Friday morning, February 28. Fridays brought with them a more relaxed atmosphere at the school and, at ten a.m., Mrs. Knight would be receptive to the idea of a snack. Seth approached the registrar's counter first, wearing a perfect smile of distraction.

"Hello, Mrs. Knight. Is that a new dress?"

"Yes it is." Doris Knight spoke with the smooth, contrived confidence of one who had left a striking beauty behind almost twenty years and twenty pounds ago, but refused to accept it. Seth could see she remained a pleasant looking woman and noted the Cambridge gray of her eyes, the butter blonde of her soft hair, and how the new gray dress with the light white collar must have been carefully selected to bring out the most of both. She reminded him of Haley Mills.

"It seems so right for you, as if you were born for one another."

She allowed herself a slight blush, and he knew her attention was his. "Now, Seth."

"Well, it must be expensive. I'll bet your husband is successful enough to afford the best."

"Well, he's not a bad lawyer."

"I've heard there are a *few* lawyers left who aren't bad."

She laughed a touch, the revived lyrical laugh of a young college girl. "I mean his practice has done well."

"Oh, great. Any particular specialty?"

"Business law. He does a lot of Contracts and related litigation."

Less ambled into view, backpack slung over her right shoulder. "Hey, Seth, what are you up to?"

"Just hanging around the Registrar's desk, trying not to fall in love."

The blush was immense this time, and Mrs. Knight gave a little girl-to-girl look over to Less and said, "So, how do you law school ladies resist this young Cary Grant?"

Less hid the grimace well enough. "Oh, we manage. He makes it easier by assuming this faraway vacant appearance from time to time."

The last comment wasn't part of the script, but Seth weathered it with a look of puzzled virtue, then changed the subject. "Speaking of Contracts, I wonder what last semester's class average was."

Less returned to the script. "I've already figured it: a 3.10."

Seth gave his own minor horn a minor toot. "Hmm. I made a 4.0, you know."

Less spoke the words of the unimpressed. "Yeah, I heard. Wonder if Contracts II will have the same mean score?"

They were talking Mrs. Knight's shoptalk, and she had something to add. "It's normally a little higher. They curve grades here, but not on an absolute basis."

"Wonder if every course yields the same average?"

"Not usually. Myerson curves precious little, if at all. Often, his class's average is below the other courses, and, in the rare semester, it'll be above them."

Dean Clay slipped in the back door behind Mrs. Knight and contributed his two cents. "Yeah, he and the Thurow have had a few showdowns over the matter."

Seth and Less looked at each other and said, "Bet it was fun to watch."

Clay put his hands on his hips. "They were like gunslingers, 'cept it was words they were slinging."

"Wow!"

"Myerson wasn't going to give in to Thurow, dean or no dean."

Dean Clay began to walk away, so Less jumped in with a brainstorm. "Hey Dean Clay, I made some cookies last night."

She whipped a shiny red tin out of her backpack and had the soft, pecan-filled delicacies displayed on the counter within seconds. Seth felt sorry for Doris Knight, as she gave the cookies the fast glance of true love.

Clay ate the first one in three bites, the last of which remained inside his cheek, as he scrunched up his face and said, "These are mighty fine, Miss Less." He swallowed and said, "And you know what else?" He tapped the air with his second cookie. "You're starting to remind me of someone I used to know."

Less blinked two curious eyes. "Really? Who?"

He was walking away. "I don't remember."

Mrs. Knight's beautiful eyes switched from cookie tin to Less. The former was out of reach at the far end of the counter. Seth detected a gathering of water at the corners of those eyes. Seth's sympathy was getting the best of him. He was about to slide the tin toward her, but she spoke first, like a drug addict who was too honest to steal, but not too proud to beg.

"Is there anything you two students need today?" Less and Seth touched eyes; this was it. "Can the Registrar's Office help you in *any* way?"

Seth adjusted his backpack and spoke. "Not me. I just came by to chat."

Mrs. Knight's hopeful eyes moved to Less, who was busy putting the lid back on the cookie tin. A three-year-old would have seen how hope had just shifted to desperation.

Less stopped loading the tin into her backpack long enough to say, "I don't think so." She looked away, but then back at a saddened Doris Knight.

"Then again, there's this one project I'm working on, just out of curiosity."

Mrs. Knight spoke up with renewed hope. "Yes, can I help?"

Less leaned toward her, whispered, "Well, it's not an official school project, but it *is* interesting."

Twenty minutes later, the lithe Lesley Peace slid out the Registrar's office door, just another first-year student who'd dropped by to review the comments on her first semester exam answers. But just another first-year student wouldn't have a manila folder tucked in the dark recesses of her backpack where a cookie tin once was, a manila folder packed with copies. White-hot copies. Copies with the power of information.

CHAPTER FORTY-FOUR

It was eleven p.m. on Saturday, March 1, and Seth was already impatient to see what Less and her number crunching skills had produced. He and his mindset hated unfinished jigsaw puzzles, abhorred incomplete logical outlines. He felt a hunger for a new revelation, something with which his mental processes could work, and Hugo had yet to report.

Less had begun crunching her numbers, so Seth grabbed a phone and dialed.

Less answered. Her voice sounded scratchy. He backed the receiver off his ear.

"Less?"

"Yes."

"What's wrong with your voice? It sounds like your larynx is sand paper."

"Very funny. I have a bug. It even changed my mind about going out tonight."

Seth said with the necessary concern, "I'm not a doctor, but I once dated a nursing student. Should I bring some medication with me when I come by to read your printouts?"

"No!" Less sounded like an indignant piece of sand paper.

For once, Seth was unfazed by a woman's emotions. "No Sucrets, no warm salty water?"

"No, you can't come over. I look . . I feel like a corpse. You can't just call people up, invite yourself, and expect to be welcomed in the middle of the night."

247

"It's only 11:15, so it's not quite the middle, and I guess I have these small town habits. You know, just always willing to drive through a thunderstorm to visit an afflicted neighbor."

There was a slight pause. "Can't you at least wait until the morning to be neighborly? I'm wearing pajamas."

"Well, I'm curious about how all your little computer-generated figures look. I don't think I can sleep until I know."

◆

Less glanced down at her own figure. Perhaps her Minnie Mouse nightwear and obligatory furry slippers didn't make the most of it.

"You law school guys. You think you can just do what you want whenever you want."

◆

Seth felt pricked, but continued with spirit of purpose unabated. "Well, aren't you getting curious about this whole thing too?"

"It'll make a lot more sense if you could give me 45 minutes to clear my head, and my throat."

"Okay, just give me directions, and I won't drop by until twelve."

◆

Less's second floor apartment was in the secluded rear section of a twelve building complex near the campus. It was also within a few minutes of a Mexican fast food joint, the first McDonald's restaurant in the state, and a housing project.

Less's roommate, Jane Blue, was an MBA student who, according to Less, was either over at a boyfriend's or else drinking at Galette's in search of a new one. The two graduate students had chosen an upstairs two-bedroom to avoid footstep noise on the ceiling. Now in sweats, Reeboks, and a pink polo that went well with her new hair color, she heard the knock and let Seth in with a self-conscious smile.

♦

Seth knocked again on the now open door and realized how light and hollow newer apartment doors were. Then, he scanned the place and noticed one window was cracked, but the paper-thin curtains were closed. There wasn't much of a breeze, but the scent of picante' sauce in the air suggested the local taco place stayed open late.

His eyes moved to Less. "Does that smell ever get to you?"

He saw her eyes whirl upward at her chemical blonde hair. "What smell?"

"The Mexican food place down the street. That odor would make me dizzy."

"I have a head cold. I couldn't smell a brush fire. Hey, you can actually smell that place from here? You have some kind of bionic nose?"

"Yeah, I lost the original one playing Pee Wee football. I remember the old town doctor saying, *We can rebuild his nose. We have the technology.*"

She waved him in and walked toward the kitchen table shaking her head. "Good to see you haven't lost your stupid sense of humor."

Seth, somehow uncharacteristically comfortable in a new environment, replied, "Hey, be easy on me. I brought you some Sucrets and Nyquil."

His insomnia had been discussed at Storyville, so she observed, "You *would* have the Nyquil. Hope you've never OD'd on it."

They entered the kitchen, where two of four light bulbs were out, yielding a dim, relaxing light.

Less stopped and turned. "Well, thanks. I've never used this stuff, but I guess it might help me sleep, once I get a chance."

"Oh, sorry, but I shouldn't be here long, and, yeah, it'll knock you out like George Foreman."

She rolled the eyeballs at the sports association, then waved at the regression results spread out over her little Formica kitchen table.

"Okay, here's what I have so far."

Seth looked for five unfulfilling minutes at printout stacks with perforated edges, then asked, "What do you see so far?"

"A few different things."

"Such as?"

She flipped through the results. Her voice renewed by the Sucrets, she explained, "For instance, I see, starting eight years ago, a higher correlation between examinees who did well in Myerson's class and those who did well enough in Goodfried's. It's not as strong between any other combination. Also, after three years, it became stronger, but-" There was a knock at the door. They looked at each other a second. "Must be Jane back from Galette's. She always forgets her key and wakes me up."

Less walked from the kitchen and into the den toward the door. She was reaching for the knob when Seth saw a shadow behind the thin curtains move away from the door. He started to get up and say something, but she was already opening the door. He noted a butcher-block kitchen knife set on a nearby counter.

Less peered out. "That's odd. I don't see anyone."

"Less. Get away."

The first guy hit the door hard. The door hit Less. The chain lock held fast. Less went down faster. A second man pried at the screen. Seth stared in disbelief, then, with no time to fear, he reached for the cutlery. He flung a butcher knife under the chain lock and into an arm. Seth saw a mask, a decent plastic mug of Robert F. Kennedy, and heard a scream from behind it.

"Less. Get up!" Seth helped her up, pulled her toward the back bedroom, hoping for an alternate way out.

Wobbly at first, she got angry second. "God, I hate violence."

Seth looked over his right shoulder as he helped Less along. The guy at the window was having no luck. Seth could see his shadow and fired a meat cleaver at it. The blade stuck in the screen.

They hurried out. The shadow pulled the cleaver through. Now, it came back the other way, sawing a nice square hole in the screen. A Teddy Kennedy mask looked inside. A husky body in blue jeans followed it. Seth and Less stumbled into the bedroom. Seth heard the chain lock break, but was in no mood to look back again. He saw the door to a balcony and was out it when he realized Less had somehow bolted ahead of him. He pulled two bicycles in front of the door and wedged one under the doorknob.

She reached the edge of the stair-less balcony and stared back at him, her scratchy voice now on fire with fear. "What now?"

"We'll have to use the pole." Seth took in her face. Panic engulfed her delicate features. She looked down and showed no sign of wanting to do what she had to. "Watch how I do it."

Seth grabbed the balcony rail with both hands, swung both legs over, and wrapped his feet around the top of the support pole. He lowered his hands until they reached the pole, then slid down fireman style. He looked up and was shocked to see Less in full swing. He could also see the temporary doorstop about to give.

"Hurry, Less."

"I am."

Hurry she did, but her tiny hands couldn't keep a grip on the slick painted metal between the rail and pole. She flopped back as if she'd fainted.

Seth knew he had to catch her cradle style or else their heads could collide. He whirled to his left and snagged her with knees bent and eyes wide. Her eyes bore down on him. The look in those brown eyes, now mere inches from his, struck him like lightning. It was more of the same fear, but he sensed it wasn't just for herself.

"Go, Seth!"

He pulled his right arm out from under her legs. Her feet were running before they hit the ground, and her legs propelled her ahead of him toward the parking lot, the Taco joint, and the housing project. Seth looked up just long enough to see the back door burst open. He bolted out the starting gate.

Teddy in Levis yelled from above, "They're heading for the parking lot." Seth thought he recognized the voice.

Seth gained ground on Less, but not because she was slow. Seth's football memory recognized the natural grace of her stride.

His football ears knew footsteps. He made a quick glance over his left shoulder in time to see a Halloween version of JFK fall in behind them. It was a bad nightmare; this Kennedy was black and ran like Jesse Owens.

Seth hit full-stride and focused ahead. He saw a vehicle filled with fraternity pledges pull up and park twenty feet to his right. The driver's parking job was Budweiser inspired, and he left his red Chevy Blazer too close to a blue truck with extended side view mirrors. The pledge on Seth's left opened his door hard and dinged the big truck's fender. He pulled the door back as if nothing had happened and decided to exit out the opposite side. Seth saw a chance and took it. He veered toward the slim crease between the two vehicles.

He slowed until the Kennedy on wheels was almost close enough to jump him, then dodged the truck's mirror and simultaneously grabbed the Blazer's door handle. He turned his torso sideways, whipped the door around, then shifted into escape gear. JFK's brakes weren't good enough. His right kneecap slammed into the heavy Blazer door. His head bounced off the truck mirror. He bounced off the pavement.

Seth blazed out of the parking lot and veered toward Less, still in full gait. He heard the excruciating noise behind him and remembered when he'd torn up his own knee. A sliver of sympathy pain shot down his right leg. He ignored it, concentrated on catching Less. She glanced back, but appeared too scared to speak. He caught her a few moments later, then, side-by-side, they ran another quarter mile, with no noise except the sound of their footsteps, a barking dog, and a random car horn in the distance.

They stopped behind the taco joint to gulp down oxygen. The place had just closed its drive-thru window and turned off the outside lights. The two survivors leaned their backs against the dirty back wall of the place and grabbed for air. Seth's nostrils bridled at the synthesized odors of fast food grease, chili sauce, and well aged dumpster garbage. They breathed deep and hard, and in sync.

He didn't look at her, but said to his Nikes instead, "You picked a nice time to learn how to move like a cheetah. I'd like to see you run when you're not sick as a horse."

Less took compliments from Seth any way she could get them. "Thanks. It doesn't hurt to have a dead politician chasing you." Seth looked over and smiled out of the corner of his eye. "I ran cross-country in high school." Her eyes cut around each side of the building between breaths, but seemed to see nothing. It was a no-show night for the moon. "Wonder where all those Kennedys are?"

Seth responded, "Well, there's no need to worry about JFK catching up with us."

"Was that him screaming?"

"Yeah, his days of record hundred yard dash times may be over."

"So, he was fast?"

"Yeah."

"Faster than you?"

"Maybe, but he wasn't quick, at least not quick enough."

"What's the difference between fast and quick?"

"Go ask him."

Their faces connected again and smiled the right smiles, the smiles of two people who had just outsmarted danger.

Then, Seth saw Less's countenance grow uncertain, and she said, "I guess it's okay when the bad guys get hurt."

"In the end, they're always supposed to. You just have to wait them out."

She replied with a little more assurance, "The waiting is the hardest part, isn't it?"

He thought on that one a moment, a moment interrupted. From nowhere, he heard a *basso profundo* voice, the kind that belonged on a Temptations song. "What are yall doing here?"

To the side of the small stucco building, there stood a couple of big black guys in jeans and black leather jackets.

Still too scared to be nervous, Seth's accent changed to a street version on a dime. "Hey, man, we're just resting. Don't mean no harm."

The eldest of the two men spoke like his house had been the one invaded. "You picked a strange place to rest in the middle of the night."

The younger man added, "Most folks have beds, you know."

"We had to leave home unexpectedly. You know how it is sometimes."

The elder one pried on, "Who *are* you anyway? You look a little familiar and you run pretty good . . . for a *white* guy."

Seth didn't see any weapon-related bulges on the two big black men, so he risked a little truth. "We're students. Law school." He wished he'd left out the last detail. "We're not lawyers yet, so don't suspect us on account of that."

The older one said, "You been around here awhile though, haven't you? You look like some kind of athlete."

"I guess. I was on the football team here. Didn't play much."

"What's your name?" the younger one asked.

"Seth. Seth Sentel."

Between her apparent fear and her amazement at Seth's ambidextrous social skills, Less kept quiet, but appeared on alert for the need to run again.

The younger guy, who was built like a block of granite, continued, "Yeah, I remember you. You made a great tackle on a kickoff against Auburn."

The older one now seemed entertained by his companion. "Cousin, you watch too much football. If you worked at your job as hard as you keep up with football, you'd be mayor by now." Then, the elder spokesman looked at Seth, curiosity in his eyes. "I guess you played for the Bear a few years."

"I played for *The Man*." Seth said it with just the right touch of respect for the no-longer-living legend.

"You know, my uncle used to drive for him awhile back."

Seth nodded. "Your uncle was a fortunate man."

"Say, what had you running tonight? Have a fight with your roommate or something?"

"No, there were uninvited visitors. We didn't know 'em, and they had on masks."

The younger guy broke in. "Is that them cruising by in that old black Camaro?"

It *was* them, slinking around, car in second gear, rumbling like a short track special, masks in place, looking right at them. Not one cubic inch of the younger guy's 6'5," 265 pound self was impressed. He walked a straight line at the Kennedy pretenders as the two-door Chevy idled on across his path a mere fifty yards away.

Seth watched his strides, like those of a big, black lion. He saw the big, black paw slip behind and under the big, black leather jacket. The gun was big and black, too, a Ruger .44 mag., Seth figured. It was six inches long and dangled from his big, black, hand like a big, black meat hook. Less found a door well and disappeared.

Seth's soul alarm went on alert stage. The Kennedy boys had slowed the Camaro to a slither, their potential targets in sight. Big and black stalking toward them, now within thirty paces. Someone had to make a quick decision. Teddy the driver must have changed his focus because the Camaro's big engine went almost numb. Teddy didn't have to look long, though. Seth could see he was now having a hurried discussion with RFK. Seth read his lips. There were four words, one with four letters.

With a sudden jolt, the Camaro's tires were burning, producing a peculiar combination of sound and smell that Seth always hated. The big guy and the Ruger stood at twenty-five yards. Big guy stopped, took a stance, raised his arm, and roared once. The big bullet caught the '0' of a 30-mph speed limit sign tacked to a light pole ahead of the Chevy. The car hit third gear, barked its Firestones again.

Big and black turned and walked back. As his face turned to Seth's, it was all business, as was his voice. "I'm a cop."

Seth had big respect for big, black cops with big, black, accurate guns.

"Nice shot, Officer."

Less whispered, "God, I hate guns."

CHAPTER FORTY-FIVE

It was a short trip back to Less's place in an unmarked police car, marked as it was by the blackwall tires and dark blue finish. Less sank in the back seat and hoped there would be no more unscheduled political events at her apartment.

Big and black had a name, Wilbur Johnson. One of the first black detectives on the Tuscaloosa Police force and the youngest to ever make detective, Big Wilbur showed the same big badge to the four patrol officers who'd been summoned to the scene by an old man from a nearby building.

Seth watched Wilbur survey the torn screen, as his eyes went straight down to the now sticky droplets of blood on the small cement front porch and to the silver and red butcher knife. He stepped over the blood, peered in and saw the cleaver resting on the cheap green carpet. The stare he cast over to Less and Seth was an insoluble mixture of wonderment, suspicion, and respect. He entered the front door and scanned the great big mess that once was Less's highly organized flat. Her purse was overturned, but still rested on the end table nearest the kitchen, and her twenty-inch TV was still atop her yard sale brand entertainment center.

Every drawer, however, was open, and the contents of most lay on the floor beneath them. Half the kitchen cabinets were open, and several plates lay broken on the counter and floor. The printouts were as gone as geese in winter. Fortunately, she'd hidden the rough data from Mrs. Knight inside the freezer.

Wilbur's uncle, Johnny Ray, took a sorrowful look at Less and asked, "You have any renter's insurance?" Like most renters, she didn't, but at least she kept from crying about it.

After Detective Johnson viewed a bedroom with an overturned nightstand, a tossed mattress, and an open door to the deck, he walked over to Less and asked, "So, what's missing?"

Seth spoke at high volume, because it somehow made it easier to lie. "I haven't noticed anything, which would be weird wouldn't it?"

Seth aimed the first part of his answer to Less, along with a sentence worth of eye talk. Less caught the hint, but her eyes were already tearing as she gazed at her once cozy apartment, now decorated in "Early Ransack." Seth realized Johnson, no stranger to strange words in strange situations, looked like he knew Seth was lying and seemed impressed that Seth was awful at it. Johnson asked Less the same question again, this time a little softer.

Less conjured up a nice compromise answer. "Well, my purse and TV and my cheap stereo are all here. I'm wearing my watch, so I can't imagine what they wanted." An impressive verbal concoction, considering she was almost lying and almost crying at the same time.

Wilbur responded with a deep breath and a little rub of his big dark eyes. "Well, *I* can't imagine either. Wonder why they picked your place to have a little breaking and entering party?"

Less looked at Seth and went mute.

Seth said with a shrug, "Maybe it was an act of random vandalism."

Wilbur glanced at Less. Seth noted pity in the man's eyes. Wilbur turned and spoke to Johnny Ray. "You know what I can't figure, Cousin Johnny?"

"What?"

"Why, all of sudden, the police band is full of random law school victims."

"Uh-huh."

"I mean, first of all, we hear about two being randomly shot in the back of their random heads, then another two die in a random hunting accident, and now, we hear about two more being the victim of a random burglary."

"Yeah."

"Well, I tell you what, Miss Lesley, if you have any more random visitors, or if you, Mr. Seth, former Alabama football player who runs like a black man, get any idea who these random visitors randomly were, why don't y'all give me a random call."

Big Wilbur handed over a couple of business cards, and, after collecting a blood sample from the front door, he had the patrol units load up and clear out.

Seth helped Less put new sheets on her bed. She slept in her jeans and Nikes. She didn't want to be sporting Minnie Mouse if she had to run for her life again. Seth slept on Less's couch, the meat cleaver on the floor beside him.

CHAPTER FORTY-SIX

It was cold outside at eight p.m. on Sunday, March 2, 1986, a good night to gather in the upstairs warmth of Hugo's office. Seth had phoned Hugo about the assault on Less's apartment and the missing statistical output. Now, Hugo had reason to take Seth seriously, not to mention reason to bill out a few more hours.

When Seth arrived, he saw Less waiting in Hugo's parking lot. She was wearing a wine and gray argyle sweater and a pair of gray wool slacks. She would've appeared attractive, at least to any male who wasn't obsessed with an old girlfriend and a multiple murder case.

As she entered in front of Seth, Hugo stood. "Well, Miss Lesley, nice to meet you. Seth failed to mention you'd be the picture of loveliness."

"Thank you, Mister Hugo. I dressed up a little for night church. I thought my grades could benefit from divine intervention."

Hugo was gracious. "Just call me Hugo. I'm no Mister anything."

Seth stepped into the conversation. "I apologize, but we'll need to make this meeting short. I haven't had a chance to study for Contracts tomorrow, and I need to get started on Tuesday's Property assignment."

Seemingly unimpressed, Hugo said, "Okay, studious one. We'll be certain to get you back in time for homework." A trace of bewilderment crept across Seth's face.

Hugo eased behind his desk and sat his long legs down behind a coffee cup with a large deer on it. Seth could make out the words imprinted below the deer: *The Buck Starts Here*.

Hugo reached behind him and poured Seth a cup in a Bear Bryant mug.

Less watched Seth take the potent java, asked as assertively as she was able, "Is there enough for me?"

Hugo was the perfect host with the least. "Sure, Miss Lesley, and when this runs out, there's more Maxwell House in the can."

♦

Less got stuck with the only mug left, the yucky Cash's Liquors model. She got over the lack of cream, glanced over at Seth to see if he appreciated her appreciation for bad coffee, then took a sip. Her face drew up, but she hid the grimace well enough by running her hand through her soft, brown-again hair.

♦

Hugo hid a smile, then brought the meeting to order. "Well, since Seth has more important things to do, let's get to the itinerary."

Seth spoke up. "I want to know who owns The Tap."

"A logical place to start, Mr. Sentel. How would you find out?"

"I could use what I learned in Property Law to research it." Less nodded and stared into Seth's eyes.

Hugo countered, "Well, yeah. Or, you could just ask the guy who runs the place."

"Oh. Right. I hadn't thought about that."

"Well, the great thing about *that method* is that you might luck up on some *co-lateral* info."

Seth put his hand on his chin. "Collateral info? Like what, for example?"

"Like, I don't know, for example, but see, that's what makes this type work interesting. You never quite know what you'll find, nor when and where you'll find it, but the more places you look, the more stuff you stumble onto, or into, depending on where you're looking."

Seth knew Hugo made sense. He noticed Less was watching him. Their eyes met. She shrugged and tilted her head, likely to show it made sense to her too.

Hugo continued, "How about you, Miss Lesley? Having any luck with your repression stuff?"

She froze, perhaps wondering how he knew about her crush on Seth, then recovered and said, "Oh, I guess you mean regression stuff."

"Repression, regression. Like I know the difference."

"Well, anyway, Hugo, I haven't had any huge discovery yet, but the more computer models I run, the more I need to run more of them."

Hugo was too old to appreciate the use of computers for investigative purposes, but he replied as if he was already fond of Less. "You just keep on running 'em, Miss Lesley, and maybe the more of 'em you run, the more stuff you'll find."

Seth tapped his shoe. "What have you come up with, Hugo?"

"First, I bought breakfast for a couple of the city boys who are working the Rentzell-Hays case, and, between the three of us and these designer coffee cups, the dope found at their apartment wasn't the quantity a dealer might have on hand, and the stuff wasn't the pride of Columbia either. Sure, it was coke, but it was old; it was stale, and it had been cut more than once."

Seth's eyes honed in on the new facts. "That suggest anything, Hugo?"

"Look at it this way: If anyone had the right to be angry about getting the short end of a drug deal, it was Rentzell and Hays. If they bought this stuff, I hope they didn't pay market price."

Less had a thought. "Couldn't one also guess that this was expendable product, the kind of stuff you didn't mind losing if you wanted to set somebody up?"

Hugo shrugged, flipped his palms open, and tilted his head right. "And maybe in turn, if you wanted to change the investigative focus."

Seth nodded, cut an appreciative glance Less's way, then continued, "How about the various professors? Anything interesting on them?"

"I've completed background checks on all professors and Asst. Dean Thurow. Why don't I talk the highlights, then give you the detailed reports to read later as your demanding schedule permits?"

Seth looked at Hugo then down at the floor, realizing he'd been perceived as a smart aleck.

Less helped. "Sounds great, Hugo. I'm curious about why they're all so *weird*."

Hugo leaned back and grinned. "Okay. Let's start with Mr. Sentel's favorite suspect, Professor Myerson." Hugo picked up a file folder and opened it. "Jacob Benjamin Myerson. Born in 1930 to middle-income Jewish immigrant parents and raised in New York City. Attended Columbia University on a scholarship and graduated summa cum laude. Fought in Korea and earned a Silver Star. Then, he was an honor student again at Harvard Law School.

"Practiced law in New York with one of them big Wall Street firms until 1958, when he became involved in the Civil Rights Movement down here. He moved to Alabama to marry his wife, then practiced for ten years with a Birmingham firm doing a lot of property and estate law. In '69, he accepted an associate professor job at the law school here, and, in 1975, was tenured in what is apparently record time. Teaches Property and Ethics.

"Has three children, two girls in college at Tulane, and one son who's a football star at Tuscaloosa Academy. Goes to the gym five days a week to run and do weights." Hugo shook his head and lit a cigarette. "Gee, glad I'm not him. Anyway, he's often seen at a conservative synagogue, and in the last few years, has spent his summer breaks in Europe: Switzerland, Luxemburg."

Seth asked, "What was the name of his law firm in Birmingham?"

Hugo flipped through some notes while Less tried to take another sip of coffee and avoid breathing in the smoke. "Silverstein, Berkowitz, and Greenberg. Hmm. I doubt anyone mistook them for a predominantly Catholic firm."

Less glanced at Seth and winked. Hugo's sense of humor was golden.

"Patrick Dooley. Born 1945, an early baby boomer. Grew up in Georgia. Both degrees from the University thereof. Been at Alabama since 1975. Teaches Contracts and upper level commercial law courses. Big sports fan. Officer in the Georgia Bulldog alumni club. Says he's a distant relative of Georgia Coach Vince Dooley, which might explain his officer status. Found out he has box seats at Fulton County Stadium. Huh, I might want to get to know him before my next trip to a Braves game. Methodist, but rarely attends church, likely because it interferes with sporting event attendance."

Seth and Less nodded their agreement. So far, there had been nothing surprising.

"Betty Borland. Born in Arizona, but later moved to San Francisco. Only forty-two-years old." Hugo held up a photograph of her and frowned. "Good Lord. The woman could pass for fifty-two. Anyway, she went to the University of California-Berkeley for undergrad, then she worked for Senator Ted Kennedy one year between undergraduate and law school at Georgetown. Next she worked for a Consumer Rights group in D.C. for several years before joining the faculty here in '82.

"In a contradictory role, she's a past President of the local *Young* Democrats chapter. Young. Huh. She drives a little Peugeot and likes to eat health food. Registered Agnostic, but is a member of MENSA." Hugo fashioned a charming smirk. "Guess she won't be wife number three."

Under the relentless pressure, Seth cracked a smile. "What about Goodfried? I've always been curious about his past."

Hugo picked up another folder. "Barry Goodfried. From Philadelphia, best I could tell. Penn undergrad. Cal-Berkley Law School. Graduated from there in 1965. So, he'd be how old, about 45?"

Seth and Less looked at each other, and Less spoke their thoughts. "He looks much younger."

"Maybe it's the blue jeans and long curly hair," suggested Seth.

Hugo went on. "He taught at a small law school in California and did some work for the ACLU for years, then came here in 1978. He's also Jewish, but never attends services. Spends his Saturdays and other spare time either reading for the blind or running a free legal clinic for the poor located on the Strip. Gee, if I'd known him before my divorces, I would 'a saved a fortune on lawyer fees."

Less smiled at Seth. Everyone paused to drink from their mugs.

♦

Hugo had billed out twenty-five hours already, and, with the idea of steady money beginning to inspire him, he was out of reasons not to bill more. "Um, anything else you want me to research, Mr. Sentel?"

♦

"Not now. Something tells me we'll need you later for more important matters."

Hugo, looking curious, glanced at his paperwork, nodded, said, "Alright."

Seth stood, reached over for the biography folders, turned to leave.

Hugo wasn't finished. "Wait a minute. How about Asst. Dean Thurow?"

Less answered, "Oh, we know he's just a harmless jerk with an inferiority complex."

"Well, that's about what my research of his inferior self discovered."

They took turns smiling at each other. Seth was walking to the door.

"Wait a minute, boss." Hugo smiled. "There's three other pieces of news you'd be interested in, one bad, one interesting, and one good. The bad news is the ballistics on Lymon's rifle came back positive." Seth stopped and slumped. Hugo switched to the interesting news. "I checked with a buddy down at Forensics Sciences. The drug tests on Rentzell and Hays definitely came back negative." Seth raised an eyebrow, knowing that didn't preclude them from being dealers. Hugo hurried straight to the good. "The good news is." His voice took a turn toward business-like. "I can get us inside the jail to interview Lymon."

Seth wheeled. His face latched onto Hugo's. Hugo nodded. "Yep."

Seth was excited. "How soon can we get in?"

"Just tell me your schedule, and I'll try to work out a time with the Sheriff's Office."

"Anytime will do."

Hugo laughed. "How about day after tomorrow around noonish?"

"Fine. Later on, we'll visit The Tap to speak with the management."

Hesitation ruled Hugo's voice. "Are you sure you want me to go with you to The Tap?"

"I just felt you'd have a way with people who run bars."

"Not sure how to take that, but I'll go anyway. Guess I could bill another hour."

When Seth reached the Jeep, he realized Hugo's last words were those of the disinclined.

CHAPTER FORTY-SEVEN

Hugo had been around a long time, long enough to have the goods on a few people whose reputations were their livelihood. Case in point: Sheriff Gibson. Hugo knew Gibson had a son by a black woman who cleaned his mother's house during his college days, a circumstance that might not endear him with the rural contingent of the county's electorate. Therefore, the fat lawman begrudgingly extended Hugo the favor of a private talk with Lymon. It was a good lesson for a Seth. It paid to pay people who knew people, who knew them *very* well.

At noon on Tuesday, March 4, the unkempt Sheriff Gibson, *Columbo without the brains*, as Hugo referred to him, made sure he was dining at City Café when Hugo visited, so he could blame someone else if things went wrong. Deputy Dolton was supervising a search party for a county jail escapee. God help the citizenry.

Seth met Hugo outside his office.

"Okay, Seth, how should we extract information from Lymon? Maybe we should threaten him, or maybe we should use the old good cop, bad cop routine to slowly suck him dry. You look like you'd make a *good* good cop."

Seth's face responded with disbelief. "Are those the only options?"

"Well, college boy, because you're so experienced at interrogation, what methodology do you suggest? I'm all ears."

Seth tried not to snicker because Hugo did have larger than normal ears. They protruded from his head like those of a cartoon mouse.

Hugo must've realized the joke. He responded like an insulted teenager. "Funny. So funny. But you know what? There's not much these ears don't hear, even if it's approaching from behind." He pointed his finger curiously at Seth.

Seth shook his head a bit in apology. "I'm sorry. It was just the look on your face. Back to Lymon, maybe there *is* another way."

Hugo tugged at both his ears and said, "I'm listening."

"What if we communicate that we believe he's innocent and that we'll help clear him? Then, maybe he'll cooperate."

"Oh, so we should *lie* to him?"

Speechless, Seth turned and walked to Hugo's truck.

Five minutes later, they entered the Sheriff's Office. Gibson's receptionist was on the phone again, flipping through a Victoria's Secret catalogue. Her bedroom smile revealed a more than casual familiarity with Hugo, who had maintained a measure of outdoorsy good looks, thanks to his good skin and full head of blond hair.

Seth wore a hat, horn rim glasses, and an old overcoat that allowed him to slide into the Sheriff's Office unnoticed. Hugo had informed the Sheriff he was bringing an assistant to take notes. The receptionist seemed too busy eyeing Hugo to recognize Seth.

Hugo signaled Seth to walk with him to the back door leading to the jail entrance. An efficient young jail keeper took the two good cops down a cement walkway past a row of cells filled with the usual suspects: three hookers whose evening had been interrupted early and an apparent drug addict who sat at the edge of his bed, dripping steady beads of sweat and a vacant stare onto the absorbent floor.

The dull yellow cement block walls still insulted Seth's sense of color. The putrid aroma of the place hadn't changed either. Seth kept his own eyes forward, thinking at the speed of light.

Then he saw Lymon, who seemed to be taking jail life well. In his early forties, he had the thin face a thin man should, with bony, but pleasant features. Somehow, he'd maintained a close shave while incarcerated, and his cropped haircut exuded military-type propriety. Although his oil canvass boasted at least ten different colors, his white jail-issue jumpsuit reflected only one.

Seth saw nothing animated about Lymon, not in his movements, not in his appearance. He still saw only the same pure, uneducated innocence.

As the jail keeper worked the lock, Seth watched Lymon work the canvass, seemingly unaware of their presence. Even as they entered, Lymon didn't appear to notice. Instead, he stood facing the corner where his easel now was. He held the brush like it was a sixth finger.

Seth knew little about art, but he knew a lot about beauty. He entered and realized God had somehow hidden a nouveau impressionist in rural west Alabama. He had a sincere question. "Hello, Mr. Lymon. Who taught you to paint so well?"

Intent on his canvass, it took Lymon fifteen seconds to answer. His mouth opened as if bracing for an effort of courage. He never turned from his work in progress, but replied, "I, I, I just paint. Didn't have n-n-no teaching."

Lymon stuttered, but not in a manner that could frustrate a Seth, perhaps because, with each word, Lymon seemed to apologize for his impediment.

They had a thirty-minute time limit, so Seth approached the easel and posed another question. "Have you sold any of these yet?"

"Hadn't done no seh-seh-ling. They all ah-ah-ah thuh cabin. Ain't nobody try and buy one yet."

"Maybe that's because no one has seen them. I know I'll buy one."

Lymon raised a lowered head in time to see the sincerity in Seth's eyes.

Hugo spoke and gestured toward the bed. "Mind if we have a seat?"

"You mean you-you wanna stay?"

Seth and Hugo looked at each other, not certain if Lymon was making a joke. Seth smiled, having decided he was.

Hugo continued, "Nah, we just wanted to chat a spell. Wouldn't want to be a hindrance."

"I gots all day, not going anywhere. What you want to ch-ch-chat about?"

Seth broke in and eased toward the point, being sure to intone his doubts about Lymon's guilt. "We heard about why they have you in here. Wonder why they think you could've goofed up and shot someone?"

Lymon re-focused on his painting, effectively absent from the room. With a sense of color reminiscent of Monet, he'd already painted a clearing covered with golden grass and deep red pine straw. There was a backdrop of forest green pines, with the center trees lower than those on the edge. The sky was a mesmerizing combination of grays, blues, and sunset hues. Lymon chose a smaller brush and began making some fine curved lines in the sky above the shorter trees.

The conversation stopped: Hugo and Seth exchanged their concern without a word. Seth's eyes returned to the canvass. He realized that the finer lines in the sky were birds.

He waited for Lymon to pause his brush, then spoke, "I'm wondering why the middle pines are lower than the others. It seems like I've seen paintings with the taller things in the middle, kind of like they're pointing toward something above 'em or framing something between 'em."

"Not just painting things up."

Lymon made eye contact again. Seth knew understanding when he saw it, and his return gaze couldn't cover his own realization of it. Lymon returned to his work. Hugo rolled his eyes, no doubt wondering where this waste of time was headed.

Seth inhaled, then said, "H.R. was my friend, a guy I could trust." Lymon resumed painting. Seth elaborated, "I was H.R.'s friend, and I wanna be yours." Seth sensed tension in Lymon's lips. "I want to get you out of this hole, Lymon. I know they're trying to trick you into saying you shot H.R. I know you haven't shot anyone. Men like you don't have hunting accidents. If you shot anyone or anything, it would be because you meant to, and there's no reason you'd have meant to. I'll hire you a good lawyer."

Seth held his breath for a response. Lymon made a series of smooth brush strokes.

"No reason to shoot no one. I liked H.-H.-H.R. He was f-f-funny."

Seth looked down, smiled at the pleasant memory. Hugo just sat there all big-eared, his hands in his pockets, his back leaned against the hard jail wall.

Lymon worked out a few more words. "He was good to me, gave me a cheese b-b-burger."

Seth smiled. "And a beer?"

Lymon looked embarrassed, like an underage drinker who'd been caught. Now, even Hugo smiled.

Seth sensed the relaxing atmosphere, then asked, "Will you help us get the real bad guys here, Mr. Lymon?"

Lymon swallowed, looked back at his painting. Seth and Hugo looked at each other.

Then, his words sprang from nowhere. "I-I was in a tree."

Seth liked the tone of the sentence. Hugo leaned off the wall.

"Okay, what were you doing? Were you hunting from a tree stand?"

"I was looking for muh dog."

Seth asked, "Alright, what's your dog's name?"

"Pesky, except he's not as pesky anymore 'cause he's getting old."

"Okay, you're looking for Pesky, and what else did you see?"

"Saw H.R. a coming."

"Did you see a girl with him?"

"Yep."

"Had you been up there for long?"

"Not long."

"A few minutes?" He nodded. "Did you have your Weatherby rifle?"

"No, my gun done been st-st. Somebody took it."

"The one the Sheriff has now?"

"Yeah."

"But the Sheriff didn't steal it, did he?"

"No, before the Sheriff took it away, somebody put it back."

"Someone stole it, then put it back in your dog's house?"

"No, they put it under the bed, but 'cause they knew where I kept it, I hid it where the Sheriff found it."

Now there was an explanation for the ballistics match and the concealed rifle, a far-fetched one, but a reason nonetheless.

"Where did your gun come from?"

"Old Doc Griffin gave it to me."

Hugo sounded incredulous. "Dr. Ralph Griffin gave you a Weatherby? What for?"

"I fixed his old flintlock rifle when no one else could."

Hugo continued. "What kind of bullets do you use with your rifle? Do you use mushrooming bullets?"

"I don't use no mushrooming bullets."

"But don't they work better? Don't they get bigger at impact?"

"If I shoot a deer, I always sh-sh-shoot it in the head. Don't need a bullet that gets bigger if you're shooting them in the head."

Hugo looked at Seth. This guy could shoot.

Hugo kept asking smart questions. "Alright then, when you saw H.R. and a girl, who was walking out front?"

"H.R. was."

"Then what happened?"

Lymon waited a second, lowered his voice. "Then, I h-h-heard a shot."

Seth took a slow breath and asked, "Just one?"

"Just one."

"Where from?"

"From the left."

"Know which direction, like north or south?"

"Be the north. The sun was facing me."

"How far?"

"Close in. I could see 'em."

"You mean H.R. and Sue?"

"No, I means the sh, sh, shooter, too."

Hugo arose from his seat and said, "You saw the shooter?"

As if he heard Hugo's unspoken disbelief, Lymon said with assurance. "Yep. Looked like a Viking, 'cept he had on an old green coat, like an Army man wears."

"Would you know him if you saw him again?"

"Too fer away to know his face."

Hugo bit his lip.

Seth pressed on. "What did the shooter do?"

"Crunked up his buggy."

"His buggy?"

Seth looked over at Hugo, who asked, "You mean, he was riding on something, Lymon?"

"Yep, a three-wheeled buggy."

"Buggy. What color was this buggy?"

"Red."

"Where did he go in this buggy?"

"Didn't leave right off."

"Oh, sorry."

Lymon looked satisfied and said, "The Viking man got off to look for something, but never found it. He got back on his buggy, rode in a little circle awhile, then he leaved off."

Hugo's question was reluctant. "Which way did he go?"

"Reckon back the way he come from, which'd be north, I s'pose." Seth noticed the stuttering disappeared as Lymon's confidence grew.

"Why do you guess north?"

"The best cover was there. You need cover if you want to sneak up and stay hid."

Hugo piped up again, "So you don't think it was an accident?"

"Weren't no deer out there, and H.R. didn't look like one. He wuz wearing an orange hat; the girl, too. Plus, the Viking took the time to ride in a short circle before he left. He road over to where he'd just walked, then left without looking for what he shot at. Don't seem like no accident."

Hugo glanced at Seth and said, "No, it doesn't sound like no accident."

♦

Seth and Hugo sneaked out almost unnoticed, while Sheriff Gibson's receptionist, that voluptuous outlier on the libido curve, filled up a bottom filing cabinet. Hugo glanced over, seemed to restrain himself, then ambled out with Seth in tow.

On the way to the truck, Hugo shook his low-hung head to clear it of confusion, then asked, "Vikings, buggies with three wheels. How can such an idiot make so much sense?"

"Maybe he just has a funny way of expressing himself. It's not like he has a PhD. in Linguistics." A silent Hugo missed the meaning, perhaps because he thought linguistics was a pasta dish. Seth's voice was hurried. "There's no denying, though, that, one, he didn't do it, and two, he saw it happen. I'll bet the shooter was looking for a shell casing, and I'll bet the guy rode in a circle to cover his footprints."

Hugo's face reconfigured itself. "Well, maybe his story is nutty enough to be true. If he *did* see something, we better be careful as a cat about who we mention this to."

Seth had never seen such a dead serious look on a man's face, but he sensed it wasn't the first time Hugo had borne it.

CHAPTER FORTY-EIGHT

Hugo's first hunch was to examine the scene of the crime. Maybe Seth was right and a shell casing had been left behind. On Wednesday, March 5, he looked two hours with a metal detector and found nothing. Next, on the outside chance Lymon really saw a "buggy," Hugo made phone calls to every all-terrain vehicle dealership in the Tuscaloosa and Birmingham areas. If Lymon's "Viking" shooter had used a stolen rifle, then maybe he'd also used a stolen ATV. After five calls, he hit possible pay dirt with the manager of a Birmingham dealership.

"Yes, sir, this is Hugo Black. I'm a private investigator down in Tuscaloosa who's looking into a series of thefts, things like go-carts, ATV's, and motorcycles. Any chance your dealership has experienced any recent thefts?"

"Funny you ask. A few months ago, one of our new salesmen left a three-wheeler outside the gate with the key still in it. It was gone the next morning, so we reported it. We just got a call from the Tuscaloosa cops yesterday saying it had been found at an old dirt pit. We're sending a truck to get it today."

"Here in Tuscaloosa you said?"

"Right. It was the police, not the Sheriff's Office, because the dirt pit where they found it was within the city limits."

"Really? Have the cops taken it into possession?"

"No. They didn't bother once they knew it had been stolen from us. They figured college kids took it to joyride the thing, and we said we'd pick it up there and save them the trouble."

"I see. So maybe no one has messed with it since it was abandoned."

"As far as we know. Then again, by now, another group of delinquents might have commandeered it!"

They shared a little laugh, then Hugo asked, "You wouldn't mind if I checked it out, would you? My insurance company client is trying to see if there's any pattern to a series of thefts in the Southeast. I doubt yours was taken by any kind of theft ring, but I'd like to check it out for statistical purposes."

"Statistical purposes, huh? Whatever that means."

Hugo improvised, "I ain't sure I know either, but those big-city insurance boys seem to throw such words around a lot, as if they're real important."

Another shared laugh, then the manager said, "You go right ahead. It's no sweat off our nose, and if y'all are trying to stop a show-nuff organized theft ring, then more power to you. I guess the mob will steal anything these days."

"Anything they can resell for 33% of retail. Look, thanks for your help. Where is it?"

"It's in an old north-side dirt pit on the way to Cottondale, on a road not far from the last Tuscaloosa I-59 exit."

"Yep, I know the place. I did some night riding there when I was a teenager, but I wasn't riding no three-wheeler!"

Another laugh, and now they were old friends. Hugo wrote down the manager's name and phone number as well as the date the ATV had disappeared.

Hugo had one final question. "By the way, what color is this three-wheeler?"

"Red."

Hugo recalled Lymon's description. He felt a rush, an energy he hadn't felt in years. He soon found the ATV parked under an old tin-roofed shed that maybe had kept the rain from diluting any fingerprints.

He stepped out of his truck, fingerprint kit in hand. He started dusting. There was nothing on the mirror. None around the handles or on the key either. He checked the gas tank cap, but still came up empty. As he unscrewed the cap to check fuel content, he noted one strange item. With a pair of tweezers, he reached down in a crevice where a little oil had gathered dust and pulled up one strand of red hair. He placed it in a baggie and sealed it.

He looked for more, but was disappointed until he saw a brass item reflecting off the glow of his penlight. He smiled. With the same tweezers, he retrieved a spent rifle cartridge, .308 caliber. The news got even better. A quick dusting of the cartridge uncovered a near-perfect index fingerprint and a three-quarters thumbprint.

He shook his head, knowing he didn't believe the sudden dose of good luck, knowing he and Seth might be in business. He walked to his truck and something hit him. He walked back and collected a couple of dried dirt samples off a tire fender. They didn't match the pit dirt.

CHAPTER FORTY-NINE

On Saturday evening, March 8, the special anti-crime task force of Sentel, Black, and Peace weren't at the movies or a nice restaurant. Instead, they gathered again around Hugo's bad coffee and Bama Bino's good pizza, an impromptu meeting prompted and financed by Seth.

Hugo sat slumped in his old cracked leather chair and spoke with a commanding air of inertia. "Well, where in creation are we on this crazy case? We got a . . ." He hesitated just long enough to roll his eyes. "A bunch of oddball professors, a Viking in army fatigues driving a stupid three-wheeler, and two fingerprints off a rifle cartridge, but nobody who made them."

Seth requested a status update. "Did you get anything back yet from your Fed contacts on the fingerprints?"

"Sorry, nothing yet."

Hugo took a slug of his industrial strength Maxwell House and continued, "We got a folder full of law school exam data of questionable value and obtained under questionable circumstances, with skills of questionable origin." Hugo's mouth crinkled at the last phrase, a prideful recognition of his co-conspirators chicanery.

Less asked, "May I say something?" Hearing no response, she added, "I'm still experimenting with the data. It may still hold a clue. I have this feeling something's there."

Hugo tried to hide his lack of faith. "You're more than welcome to continue doing your thing with those numbers, Miss Lesley. It's not like it'll hurt anything."

Seth tried to encourage her. "Sometimes it helps me to put something aside, then return to it later with brand new eyes."

"Okay." Her eyes did appear brand new; they were looking into Seth's again.

Seth went on. "What doesn't make sense is this Viking reference. I wish we could talk to Lymon again."

"Not gonna happen," Hugo announced, shaking his head. "His attorney, thanks to the soft heart and fat wallet of Seth 'Big Bucks' Sentel, has muzzled him."

Seth sounded regretful. "Alright, I know, but hey, I felt for the guy, especially because he had to deal with that Deputy Dimwit every day. So we'll just have to work with what we've got. Lymon said the guy was a Viking. What could a Lymon have meant?"

Hugo chipped in his usual good-natured derision. "A strange bird like Lymon? Good Lord, he could've meant the guy looked like a Minnesota Vikings football player."

Less said with a pinch of animation, "Maybe he had a battle axe and an animal fur overcoat."

Seth closed his eyes and smiled, but he was also imagining Lymon's viewpoint. There wouldn't have been much to focus upon, given that the shooter was wearing loose army fatigues. Seth first recalled the cadenced walk of someone he had encountered. He recalled that Lymon knew colors. He next realized that, if the Viking was wearing a hat, then Lymon would have barely been able to notice the color of his-

Seth's voice was charged. "Wouldn't you expect a real Viking to have long hair?"

Less offered a woman's opinion. "I would, and a beard, too."

Hugo added skeptically, "And didn't some Vikings have red hair, like the one I found on the three-wheeler?"

Seth's head snapped over. "You found a red hair?"

Hugo pulled a baggy out of his top drawer. "I forgot to mention it."

"Many Vikings had red hair," Less added.

Seth continued, "In fact, the most famous Viking of all was redheaded, right?"

"Eric the Red," Less and Hugo said together. Seth let a moment of silence trail by.

Less looked right at him. Seth could see her eyes ignite with the fire of realization, along with some other fire he didn't recognize. "You don't think . . ." Seth held her gaze, as his mind replayed the way a certain redheaded man walked. "Seth, it couldn't be."

"Oh, don't tell me. There's some nerdy professor at the school who has red hair and a beard."

"No, but there's a nerdy computer geek."

Hugo shook his head. "Sorry, guys, but I can't imagine a nerdy, army-fatigued dude out in the backwoods riding a three-wheeler and shooting at folks with a high-powered rifle."

Less's voice accelerated. "Maybe he's not a nerd. Maybe it's just his cover."

Faced with the amazing resilience of youth, Hugo closed his eyes.

Seth sensed Hugo's doubt, and figured a combo of bad grammar and honesty was one way to deal with it. "It's the best we got, Hugo."

After a deep breath, Hugo gave in. "Alright, can you get his prints off something?"

Less was quick to back Seth. "I know just the thing."

♦

Securing the Tab cola can was easy enough. Gustaf left them all over the building's administrative areas. Fortunately, only Gustaf and an anorexic first-year ever drank Tab colas. Early Sunday afternoon, Seth found a can next to a copy machine Gustaf had likely serviced. Pursuant to Hugo's advice, Seth picked up the pink can with a pair of Hugo's tweezers and dropped it into a paper bag.

♦

When he returned to Hugo's office at six p.m., Hugo had his fingerprint kit laid out on an old card table. Less was back at the B-school running more numbers on a mainframe.

"Time for you to engage in some practical learning, young student assistant."

After over a semester of law school, Seth had no objection to practicality. Hugo had his powders, brushes and tape scattered about. Beside the table, there was an old wooden case the size of a boot box.

Hugo seemed casual. "Now you see this powdery stuff?"

"Yeah."

"I'm gonna use one of these brushes to dust this can with it, and I'll use different color powder for the top of the can because it's a lighter color."

"Okay."

"And I'll just keep dusting until something shows up." A still moment passed as Hugo meticulously dusted. "Ah, there's one."

Seth could see the outlines of a latent fingerprint emerging against the contrasting powder. "Is that a thumbprint, Hugo?"

"Uh-huh. Now let's check the top of the can."

Hugo found a good, smaller print on the top of the can and a few other partial prints scattered about the sides. Then, as if he were handling rare diamonds, he lifted each of the two full prints with some special tape from his kit. Next, he pulled an old microscope from the wooden case.

"Now, I'll examine one print, then the next, and then I'll look at 'em side by side." Hugo examined the first print.

"Okay, with this print, we have a definite plain arch pattern, and, with this thumb print, there's more of a loop."

"Now let's see what the cartridge print comparables have for us."

Hugo slid the print from the cartridge under the microscope. His expression jumped from relaxed to stunned. He flung both thumb prints under and looked again. Seth noted a higher adrenaline level in Hugo's face.

Hugo looked at Seth, pursed his lips, put his hands on his hips, and said, "You are one *unusual* student assistant. How did you *know*?"

"Know what?"

Hugo sat down in a nearby metal chair and waved Seth toward the microscope. "Go ahead. Look for yourself and get it over with."

Seth leaned over, peered into Hugo's antique instrument of magnification, then observed as would a kid, "They look a lot alike to me."

"No kidding. At least ten points of identification match up, same dots, same islands, same ridges, and same bifurcation. I'd bet what's left of my reputation *you were sure about it the whole time*."

"Well, I kind'a had a feeling." Seth looked up at Hugo. His attempt to fight back a smile failed miserably.

"Yeah, I felt like you had a feeling." Hugo's voice climbed a few decibels, as he looked Seth dead-on and declared, "You're one of them people who *knows stuff* and don't know how he knows it, *ain't you*?"

"Huh?" Seth tried to appear innocent and ignorant, a task for which he was only halfway equipped.

"Oh Lord, Seth Sentel. Never dog-gone mind."

Seth was having a hard time hiding his burgeoning bliss. He thought tweaking the subject might help Hugo deal better with being wrong. "So, Hugo, what do we do now?"

Hugo moved over behind the desk and plopped down in the ancient leather chair that magically conformed to his lanky physique. An unlit cigarette dangled from his mouth. "I want to think about it. I hadn't considered the chance anything quite like this might arise."

Seth fell into the old couch. "Wow. We're getting somewhere. I was becoming accustomed to dead ends."

"Well, academic amigo, I assure you that this end is *totally alive*."

"Guess so."

"I have an idea, clairvoyant one. Given how you've been so right lately, why don't we also follow your advice to Miss Less and sleep on this little revelation. Then, maybe we can come at it from another angle. It's getting late anyway."

"Are you hungry, Hugo? I don't think H.R. would mind me feeding the hungry help with a small portion of the kitty."

Hugo stared at a roach crawling toward a big Charles's Potato Chips can beside his desk. The can served admirably as an office wastebasket. He wondered aloud to Seth, "You think old H.R. would mind if the hungry help wanted steak?"

"Considering the fact he was from Texas and appreciated a good cut of beef, not at all, Hugo Black, not at all."

As they walked out together, Hugo observed, "So, he wouldn't muzzle the ox whilst he was a treadin'." Hugo nodded. "I think I would've liked ole H.R. Sounds like the kind'a guy who'd make a great character for a novel."

CHAPTER FIFTY

The next Saturday morning, March 15, at 8:30, Hugo called Seth.

"Seth, a question has come to my caffeine-soaked brain."

"Okay."

"Before you visited Less's apartment several nights back, did you speak with her in person or on the phone? And Lord, Seth, did you tell her what this is all really about?"

"Well, she feels like she's in this with us now, and I want her to feel I think she's in it too."

Hugo smiled a knowing private investigator smile. "Uh-huh. How'd you tell her?"

"By phone."

Hugo had his answer, but now he was hungry, and his bony body could stand another free meal.

"I always wondered what the Warner House looked like from the inside. Anyone there today?"

"Well, the Chancellor and maybe the chef. The Chancellor's wife is visiting their son in New York. The social director and the housekeepers don't usually work on weekends unless there's a big event."

"Call the chef. Tell him you pay well, and you'd like to have company for lunch."

◆

It didn't take long to find the wiretaps, all three of them, one in the office phone, one in the bar phone, and one on Seth's garage apartment phone. It also didn't take long to discover that a few door locks had been picked. By 11:45, they were done. Hugo didn't tell Seth he purposely left the bug on his room phone.

◆

François was working, prepping early for the next night's annual athletic department dinner. There would be twelve head coaches and two athletic directors searching for ore d'oeuvres and free drinks, then dining on beef tenderloin. François knew Seth had bitten off more than he could chew these days and didn't mind serving him and his P.I. friend a treat, in this case, grilled Mackerel sandwiches, wild rice, and spinach salad. Besides, he was suspicious his girlfriend Marnie, a preacher's kid, was fooling around, and he wanted Hugo's sage advice about such matters of the heart.

The lunch went well. François hired Hugo for a cut rate and a promise to cook for him and a lady friend to be named later. Hugo resisted the Pinot Grigio, but not the Gevalia Amaretto coffee. Seth noted how the rare exposure of fine cuisine to Hugo's blue-collar palate seemed to inspire this real-world comrade. In fact, after dessert, Seth saw Hugo's eyeballs roll to their top right corners. Then, having imbibed two glasses of wine, Seth headed upstairs for a pre-announced, well-deserved nap.

CHAPTER FIFTY-ONE

Hugo called Seth about forty-five minutes later, long enough, he figured, for a good insomniac's siesta. Any longer and Seth would never get to sleep at night. Besides, if he was still groggy when the phone rang, the call would sound more natural, and Seth would be too sleepy to mention the bugs they had found earlier over the tapped line.

Seth awoke to the ring he loathed, his straining voice a mixture of dissonance.

"Uh, yeah, I mean, hello?"

"Sentel, look, I think I need to trip out to Lymon's place early tonight. I doubt he'd care if I took a look."

"His lawyer might, but likely not Lymon. Why go there?"

"I just remembered something important he mentioned and wanted to check it out."

"It'll take a couple of minutes to wake up, I mean, to get ready." Seth glanced over at the clock; it was almost three p.m.

"Don't worry about it. Grab a few more winks. I can handle this alone."

Seth wished he were going. "You sure?"

Hugo was reassuring. "Yeah, it's just a quick errand I'm going to run after supper tonight. Wanted to examine a detail that hit me after lunch when I was fumbling for my last cigarette."

"Well, okay."

"Hey, Sethy boy, this is what you're paying me for."

"You sure you want to go out there alone at night, given you're a convicted felon who can't carry a gun?"

"Well, I'll just have to be careful," Hugo said, faking his concern for his own safety. He continued with a little lecture. "Look, leave this one to me, Seth. You need to go out and do something a normal college boy would do. Call a girl. If you ain't got one to call, go to The Nasty Tap. Of course, if I were in your boots, I'd call little Miss Lesley."

Seth's mind was waking up. "I forgot I was paying you for social advice."

"Big money'll do that to you, young Seth. When you're cash heavy, the memory cells are the second to go, right after the humility cells."

"Losing memory cells. There's an interesting observation, coming from an old alchy."

They both smiled and hung up. Seth arose and hunted for iced tea. François handed him the twenty-ounce tumbler.

♦

Hugo did some paperwork, then went to the restroom, reached behind the toilet, and pulled out the gun he didn't have. It was an old stainless revolver, a .41 caliber Smith, a virtual jackhammer to hold. He hid a speed loader, and a few other important items, on his person.

CHAPTER FIFTY-TWO

At four o'clock, Hugo began the thirty-minute drive out to Lymon's old shack. Even though Seth had posted Lymon's bail, the accused wouldn't be there. The judge had insisted Lymon be released into the custody of his Aunt Wynona, a retired schoolteacher with a stern manner, but a soft heart. She'd look after ole Lymon until his case was tried or settled.

Hugo didn't drive the entire distance to Lymon's shack. He parked at Thomas Garrison's cabin and considered how pleasant the fifteen-minute walk to Lymon's would be for most people, but he wasn't most people. As he began his trek along the narrow footpaths, the sun was in retreat, casting multiple shades of crimson, yellow, and lavender across the God blue background above.

Hugo, with his Levis still pulled up an inch too high and his belt off-center, was no work of art; however, in his toffee-colored field coat, weathered chamois shirt, and Chippewa hunting boots, he was in his element.

He had scant company for this walk, just a few crows heading for home overhead, a lone gobbler turkey slipping across his path, a bluebird couple tweeting and fluttering from bush to bush, and the .41.

About halfway there, he paused to remove his straw cowboy hat and give his shaggy blond hair a shake. Admiring how the sky signaled the change from day to night, he couldn't help but notice it wasn't a bad day to die. After all, his old familiar emptiness remained, and he knew what he once filled it with was his poison. He touched the .41 to verify it was still there.

He remembered the lyrics from that Huey Lewis and the News song, and wondered if he'd ever find his own new drug. The mesmerizing call of an early hoot owl stole his attention, made him realize someone had gone to a lot of trouble to make all this. Then, he gazed at the beautiful sky, and for the first time in years, he sensed the beating of his heart. It wasn't a bad day to live either, he surmised. Why not give fate a chance? He put his hat on and walked forward, promising that, on Sunday, he'd get his ass into any church that would have him.

He spied Lymon's rural residence just ahead. A few small sweet gum limbs and a double handful of pine cones sat still on the porch roof. A beautiful fox squirrel extracted seeds from a cone. The door wasn't locked; in fact, it didn't even have a lock. No TV's or stereos to steal from this place; just some rough hewn wood furniture and a gallery of original outdoor art. There were only three rooms to the place, one large one for sleeping and painting, a small kitchen, and a bath with an old claw-foot tub. The floor was a jewel, though. Thick pine, unfinished and a little rough, but the folks living around the Yacht Club would have been jealous.

Hugo crept toward a closet door where Lymon had attached one of his most inspired efforts, a horizontal landscape depicting a lush meadow between two tree-covered hills cradling the morning sun between them. Below, a gathering of Whitetail deer grazed along the dew-lightened grass: ten does, a small buck, and a cuddle of fawns, one kicking up her heels to celebrate the new day.

What caught Hugo's uncultured eye was the lady in white. She drifted among the herd, her arms held out to her side, each a splendid wave of flowing lace and silk. Her hair and eyes were of a luminous golden hue that Hugo, and no other man, had ever seen. He marveled at her, the floating lady of the meadow.

Thinking it was a good place to wait for trouble to arrive, Hugo opened the closet door, still gazing at the deer goddess.

He should have looked straight ahead. A hard stick and a scream from hell burst from the closet. The door nipped Hugo on the right foot and the forehead, and the stick caught him just below the sternum. There was so much pain Hugo couldn't yell, and he wasn't sure where to hurt. The charge knocked him off both feet and launched him to the splintered pine floor. More pain shot up his arm and back as an exposed nail tore at the left sleeve of his field coat, and the bulky .41 sandwiched itself between his back and the hard floor.

His eyes strained past the hurt. A red-haired warrior in army fatigues stared down at him. He wielded a shiny black MP's baton above his right shoulder. The hair was as wild as the eyes and hung a full six inches past his ears, Redbeard without the ponytail, and without the sanity.

The second battle cry snapped Hugo out of his throbbing woe. Redbeard stalked forward for an overhead smash. Hugo rolled left in time to save his head, but ripped his left sleeve and the arm underneath it. He sensed the blood trickling down his arm, felt it gather on his forehead. He didn't want to bleed from any other body parts, so he sprang to his feet as Redbeard recovered.

The Celtic warrior was only four feet away, rearing back for cut number three. He opened his mouth to snarl. Spit and drool went everywhere, but it just gave Hugo a good place to aim. He drew a can of mace from his pocket and gave it to him like breath spray.

Redbeard released a scream from hell and covered his face, turned his back, and stumbled several steps away. He clung to his oak baton. Hugo could see it sticking up above the wild man's head. Then, both arms of the beast dropped, and he let out a maddening, paralyzing noise. Hugo knew the language, the war cry of a gladiator who wanted more of the fight.

He charged Hugo as would a wounded wildebeest, nostrils flaring, stick twirling, eyes on fire with a hate for life and a willingness to end it. Hugo stared and thought fast. This was no criminal mastermind; this was someone's pet on a long leash. Maybe he was a dog that could talk. He stepped once to his left, ran to meet the monster, then went horizontal and aimed his right boot at a locked right knee, drove it straight back until something broke and something else tore. They both went down and fell four feet apart. Redbeard's face bit hard into the pine planks, but he still turned to find his prey. His rich brawler's blood made a gruesome roadmap down the background of his yellow-maced facade.

Despite a broken kneecap and a torn ligament, Redbeard crawled toward Hugo, who had landed wrong on his hip. The fall stilled Hugo's reflexes a second too long, for the ogre was now upon him, straddling him with legs, baton, and animal eyes.

Another shot of the hot stuff added fuel to the fire. A desperate Hugo tried to reverse out, to knee the madman off him, to bust his solar plexus with the now empty can, but this fighting machine had too much training. He'd been in too many contests. He blocked every shot Hugo threw.

Then, he cocked his right arm to place the head splitter in the slot. Hugo just stared right at him and insulted him slowly. "I figured you for a wimpy Kung Fool fighter."

Eric the Red froze for a sufficient second. He tilted his head and paused long enough to become further deranged. Hugo needed the distraction, and he whipped Plan B from his right coat pocket, stuck it to the groin area, and hit the red button. Redbeard's entire body shuddered.

Not everyone carried a compact cattle prod, but Hugo thought it was a must-have for the aspiring P.I., and the uncontrolled convulsions of a redheaded commando proved him right. The voltage neutralized Gustaf's vocal cords, and his limbs. He only managed a pain-tinged, repetitive vowel noise.

Hugo let up a second or two, just long enough to climb away, and, when the mercenary of death fell on his back, Hugo jolted him again to the heart and lungs, a piercing charge that knocked him out hot.

He lay there stiff and ugly. Gustaf was war on two legs, but he was no match for four 'D' size Evereadys and a world-wise P.I. who didn't want to die.

CHAPTER FIFTY-THREE

Hugo peered at the ugly, idled fighting machine below his feet. Even in an electrically-induced slumber, the crumpled maniac looked a menace. A shoulder holster was now visible below Redbeard's left arm, and Hugo removed a .22 caliber Browning semi-auto, the executioner's weapon of choice. *Might get a match on the Rentzell and Hays projectiles*, Hugo figured.

He found some rope and tied Redbeard's hands behind his back, then took off the army boots and leaned the man's back against the wall. In another five minutes, the wild man awoke to the sight of a .41 caliber dangling from the hand of a Hugo with an attitude.

Redbeard's voice was flat. "You won't kill me. You're hoping I'll tell you something."

Hugo respected the viewpoint, but had already thought through this conversation. "I'd rather prod you into talking, then shoot you if you won't."

"You know torture won't work on me."

"Maybe I'd do it just to do it."

"You don't seem like the kind. Besides, that thing leaves a burn mark, and I'd sue you for the cruelty."

Hugo shook his head. "And what an appealing plaintiff you'd make. I'm sure the trial boys downtown would be lining up to take your case."

"Maybe I'd just have you prosecuted for attempted murder."

"Maybe the DA would wink and look the other way."

"Maybe I know someone who knows the DA."

"Maybe you might want to play let's make a deal and tell us who this person might be."

"Take me in, get me a lawyer, and maybe I will."

Hugo paused long enough to examine this man with the multiple personalities, half-animal, half-nerd, a bloodied barbarian who knew his constitutional rights. Why would this strange conglomeration of human flesh insist on protection?

Hugo's stare landed between the pair of red and yellow eyes and asked, "Who would a marauder like you be afraid of?"

The stare came back at him, but evaporated a moment later. Hugo couldn't discern if it was fear or shame. He did know torture wouldn't ultimately work. The man was Marine tough, and if he was afraid of someone, he'd probably rather be tortured than to talk and die. Besides, Hugo would enjoy bringing in such a ferocious prime suspect to "Sheriff Codumbo" and "Deputy Do-nothing." Proving them wrong would be better than a stiff drink, definitely better than suicide.

Hugo forced his captive to walk in his socks to the truck. If the madman of technical support wanted to run, he'd have to bloody his feet in the process. A softie at heart, Hugo gave him a walking cane Lymon had apparently carved. They reached the truck in thirty minutes, and after loading him in the truck bed, Hugo tied him up like the animal he was. He reminded its hindquarter about the cattle prod, tied the feet together, then curled them backward till Redbeard admitted he believed in God. He then tied the hands to the feet. The way the constricted beast lay on his side and writhed, he resembled a wounded animal taken on Safari.

It was 6:30, time to interrupt the Sheriff's supper. Hugo used a CB radio to get a message to Gibson. "Tell him I'm on my way in with a guilty-looking suspect in the law student murders. He can hold him on attempted murder, trespassing, and wiretapping charges."

Ten minutes later, Sheriff Gibson, who was eyeing dessert, came in loud and clear over Hugo's radio.

"This better be good, Hugo Black."

"It's show nuff better than what you've got: an introverted woodsman who shoots nothing but his food? C'mon!"

"Who do *you* got?"

"He's a computer expert from the law school, and if I had to guess, he was a Special Forces grunt in another life. He didn't go down easy."

The Sheriff still sounded bothered. "You P.I. types always have to work at night?"

"Well Sheriff, I worry more about results than working conditions. I consider my profession a public service. Hey, you should consider serving the public. It's a high calling."

"Enough of your smart ex-felon mouth. My wife and I are having company, and you're spoiling the party."

"It must be time for dessert. What are you having, sweet potato pie? Did your extra son's mother make it for you?"

"No, it's a lemon cus . . . It's none of your frigging business."

"Look, Sheriff, I'll be at the jail in thirty minutes. If you want to meet me and the reporters I'm about to notify, you should leave now. I'm sure the wife will save you a big fat piece of lemon custard."

◆

Hugo arrived on time, and three reporters, one from the local news station, one from the *Tuscaloosa News*, and one from student newspaper *The Crimson White*, were all there. Sheriff Gibson and Deputy Dimwit were already talking with them, explaining like a trustworthy uncle and his polite son how the Sheriff's Office had been working with Mr. Black on a possible second suspect.

The reporters gathered around the truck to ogle Hugo's catch. The little frizzy-haired coed journalist and the others were impressed and frightened by the squirming red-haired man, all bloody and hog-tied, with the length of his body resting against the inside of the tailgate. They fired a few questions at a humble Hugo. He declined to answer, saying it wouldn't be right to comment on what was now official Sheriff's Office business.

The Sheriff called the reporters over to begin his re-election campaign, then led them into a discussion about his love of his office and the general profession of law enforcement. It was a phony "thin blue line" type speech, enough to nauseate any real man with a shield. Hugo stood at the front of his truck, while Deputy Dufus began to untie Redbeard, likely to cuff him and wrestle him to the door in front of the cameras.

Hugo looked over at the Sheriff, who had his back to him as he plied his trade on the three unsuspecting journalists.

♦

Dufus was busy trying to loosen Hugo's elaborate rope-a-dope job. He wasn't having much luck with the various knots, so he took the expensive self-defense knife he kept in his boot and decided to just cut through the rope. He went at it haphazardly, only intending to cut the rope running from feet to hands, then cut the feet loose. Dolton cut the connecting rope, but he cut just enough of the hand rope, too. Then, he sawed through the foot tie.

Out of the edge of his eye, Hugo saw what had happened, but, by the time he decided to care, it was too late.

Redbeard kicked Dolton hard. The blow came donkey-style with the foot of his good leg. Dolton took it on the chin, and the back of his big head hit the asphalt below. Like red lightning, Redbeard was off the back of the truck. He pounded Dolton's midsection with the good knee, the whole while wriggling to get his hands free. He separated his right hand and snatched Dolton's revolver. Screaming to cover the pain, he spun on his knees and beaded in on the largest target in view, the lawman who loved pork chops and desserts.

◆

Hugo hadn't been a highway patrolman in fifteen years. His old instincts still ignited. He drew the .41, saw Gustaf below him, and fired from hip point. A round bit Redbeard high on the forehead. Redbeard got a round off too, one last assault in one last battle. It put out a street light in the parking lot.

Deputy Dimwit was taken to Druid City Hospital. His shattered jaw would be justly wired shut the next morning. Two reporters and another deputy pulled Gibson from the pavement. Hugo figured Gibson was happy to be alive, fortunate he'd survived to eat another day, but maybe unsure if owing Hugo another favor was worth it.

Hugo dropped his head, sighed, and exhaled. Just when his team had finally earned a huge break on this nebulous, mysterious case, a dumb Deputy had blown it in five seconds. They had finally found something they could get their hands around; now, it was dead and gone. He'd just saved the Sheriff's life, but wasn't sure it was worth it.

CHAPTER FIFTY-FOUR

It was early April now, and after worrying about his dying investigation for weeks, it was time for Seth to worry about mid-May's final exams too. He was behind on his self-made summaries and looked forward to catching up soon. Now, however, he had catching up to do at Hugo's office. Maybe he and the old P.I. could jumpstart a stalled investigation.

Seth looked at Hugo and realized the man had a quirky way of peering at a third cup of coffee. Seth eyed Hugo's cocked head and squinting eyes. Heck, the scarecrow of a P.I. had a quirky way of doing most everything. With Gustaf caught and heroically slain, and with the Rentzell-Hays murders possibly solved, Seth had also realized Hugo had a quirky way of knowing exactly what he was doing. Unfortunately, the slaying of the nerd-beast had also slain their investigation. Gustaf knew something he never got to tell. At least the incident had resulted in dismissal of the indictments against Lymon, but neither Seth nor Hugo was ready to quit.

Seth leaned back in his chair, adjusted the bill of his L.L. Bean cap, and, given how they were fresh out of leads and suspects, asked a question to help stir Hugo's real-world mind. "So Hugo Black, what's our next move?"

Hugo required another slug of high-test java to consider the inquiry. "You know, Sethy boy, you ever noticed how this here third world concoction remedies the effects of both my boozing and your insomnia?" Seth couldn't argue the point, candid as it was. "Anyway, it seems like maybe, if there's some kind of conspiracy behind all this, then maybe old H.R--still wish I could've met him--wasn't the first one it killed, assuming Rentzell and Hays weren't the first, that is."

Up under his cap, Seth closed his eyes, still unaccustomed to hearing the words *H.R.* and *killed* in the same sentence, but his ears remained receptive.

Hugo must have sensed Seth's slight discomfort. "Well, this grand conspiracy could've been born years ago, and I have a hunch it might've affected someone else, maybe another student." Seth's head nodded an inch. "Have you heard of any students who've been unfortunate in one way or another?" Seth considered it with the usual rapidity and initially recalled none. Hugo prodded on as if he was onto something and knew he was sitting across from a genius. "I mean, anyone ever get beaten up? Anyone destroyed when their secrets were disclosed? Any poor soul been in an accident?"

Seth lost the room for a moment, crossing his feet at the ankles and pulling the cap's stiff cotton bill even farther over his eyes. There wasn't much to connect this idea with yet.

Hugo leaned in a little. When Seth removed his cap and uncrossed his feet, Hugo knew he'd sent out the right probe.

"Anybody else ever die over there, Seth?"

"There's Rentzell and Hays, of course, but nothing new has come up on them lately, right?"

"Not lately. It's probably Gustaf, but no results back yet on the Gustaf pistol ballistics. Has anyone else ever died or been waylaid, for *any* reason?"

Seth rolled his eyes around as he pondered the query, then pointed them right back at Hugo. "Well, there's this Coffee Room gal."

Hugo's face showed appreciation for Seth's humble manner of securing truth. "Coffee Room gal? If she likes coffee, she must be alright."

"No, Hugo. The coffee room's named after her . . as a memorial."

Hugo's hand fell from the side of his face. "If it's a memorial, then she must be dead. Any idea as to *why*?"

"I've never heard. No one ever talks about her."

"When did she die? I mean, is it a black and white photo with her dressed like 1950? You know, with short bangs and a string of pearls?"

"No, the portrait appears more recent, but I've noticed she's dressed conservatively, and she seems so-"

"Well, so what, my friend?"

Seth noticed the reference tagged onto the end of the sentence, but was riding too smooth a train of thought to detour. "So, so good."

Hugo's entire upper body nodded on impulse before it halted, and he asked, "So *good*?"

"Yeah. Goodness is just all over her." Seth was smiling a little now, as he explained without explaining. Hugo had his left index finger in his ear and was working it around to lessen the cranial pressure caused by Seth's exasperating intuition.

"Look, Senior Sixth Sense. Why don't you ask around and find out some actual, cold, hard facts about this Coffee Room gal. For instance, where's she from? Who were her friends? How did she meet her untimely death?"

Hugo peered down at his empty *Buck Starts Here* mug. Seth arose. He had to study at least a little this week. "Hey, Hugo. Do you want me to find out about her being *good*, too?"

Hugo must have given up. "Yeah, find that out, too," he said. Seth was walking out the door and putting his cap back on, when he detected Hugo's smoky tone of concern. "Sentel, be careful with this one. Don't ask just *anybody* about this good gal. Nobody with authority, and I might not ask any students at all. Schools can be efficient rumor mills. Ask someone ordinary."

Seth suspected no one was ordinary in law school, *any* law school, but he kept thinking . . . maybe there was at least one.

CHAPTER FIFTY-FIVE

Daniel Clay, known around the school as Dean Clay, was nothing if not ordinary, just an ordinary guy who still lived in the Wild West. In charge of every facet of a 140,000 square foot, state-of-the-art educational facility, he wore pressed khakis with his dress Cowboy boots. He took care of the school building like it was his home, and did so in an amiable, business-like manner.

His small office was on the lower level, the painted block walls decorated with a photo of Dallas Cowboys Head Coach Tom Landry and an action-filled Western print of a real cowboy, with twirling rope poised and chaps and hat flying, about to rope a big runaway Longhorn.

Not many students knew where his office was, nor had they taken the time to know him, but the few who knew him well were glad they did. Seth always spoke to Clay, ever since he'd walked up on Clay and H.R. discussing boots and Texas. Dean Clay had grown up near H.R.'s family ranch in the Texas hill country, "God's vacation home," according to Clay.

It was Monday, April 7, 1986. Dean Clay's office door was open, but Seth knocked on the metal door well anyway. Clay, dressed in a nice check shirt, rose from the manual he was reading and greeted Seth like an old saddle pal.

"Hi yuh, Seth. No need to knock."

"Hello, Dean Clay. Could you spare a minute or two?"

Motioning to an oversized wicker chair, the fifty-year-old Texan with a stocky build and short-cropped black hair, replied with a welcome grin. "Lordy mercy, I'd be lying if I said I couldn't. I think my tired old eyes could use a breather from this HVAC maintenance book."

It was nine a.m., and Seth's sharp eyes and high-powered olfactory nerves were drawn to the red light of the coffee maker resting on a Formica credenza behind Clay's left shoulder. Reading Seth's mind with a little sideways grin, Dean Clay turned and poured Seth an oversized Styrofoam cup's worth of perfect coffee.

Seth sipped it and noted it was a superior brew. "This is excellent. What is it?"

"A good little grind I pick up when I travel through Louisiana. Mozz's coffee is fine, but this stuff is special."

Seth took a slight detour. "You know, the Coffee Room is quite a place, when you think about it, isn't it?"

"Well, I'm not in there often, unless it's to check behind housekeeping or see about new furniture, so what do you mean?"

"I'm not sure I know. There's so much activity every morning, all the discussion and arguing and joke telling and gambling."

"Well, I've seen money change hands, now that I consider it."

"And then there's the portrait of the honest-faced girl, Katie someone, looking over the whole of it, like a guardian angel."

The old Cowboy-turned-manager chuckled a little before adding, "Yeah, I guess even a saloon needs a guardian angel." Seth returned the slight laugh. "I can tell you this, Seth, no saloon could have a finer angel over it. Katie Ryals is looking down, from heaven to be exact, because there's never been a better example of a good gal in a bad profession. No offense."

Becoming more suspicious of the law every day, Seth replied with assurance, "None taken."

Dean Clay continued, "Katie was as well brought up as a girl could be. Always polite, always volunteering to help folks out. Never a big partier like some of her gender around here." Dean Clay raised his right eyebrow.

"Yes, sir, I've visited the Kit-Kat House."

"Well, I've never visited the Kit-Kat House, except maybe the one outside El Paso, but I've sure heard the stories about it." Seth laughed and confirmed the stories. "Anyway, Katie liked horses, not hunchy punch, or whatever y'all call it."

"Yeah? Was she from Texas, too?"

"No, but she should've been. Well, she was from the Southwest, but it's southwest Alabama, Clarke County area, I believe, not far from the Tombigbee River. She took me down there one time over the Christmas holidays to ride horses and meet her folks. Fine people. My wife and I were having a spat at the time, so I was fending for myself. Now what was the name of the nearest town?"

"Grove Hill?"

"Nah. It was farther west," he said, as Seth watched him take a gulp of the good Louisiana joe.

"It wasn't Coffeeville, AL was it?"

"Doggone if it wasn't. How did you know?" He peered at Seth with an odd look of amazement.

"Just a guess, I guess."

"Well, she had this beautiful Appaloosa, then they had a couple of Chestnut quarter horses and the proverbial old gray mare that'd be perfect for a child's birthday party or something."

"Sounds nice. We have a few quarter horses and a converted Tennessee Walker we use to round cows up with."

"No kidding. Sounds like it's time for another marital spat!"

Seth smiled. "Anytime you're ready to ride."

"Anyway, the nice thing was how Katie insisted I ride her Appaloosa. Said the quarter horses didn't take to strangers very quick like."

"What a good sort of girl. Wonder what happened to her. There's no explanation under the Coffee Room portrait. No plaque or anything."

Seth watched as the grown man across from him transformed into a sad cowboy. Seth was moved to silence when Dean Clay closed his eyes and shook his head. Seth looked down, swirled his half-empty cup, wishing hard he'd left his question unasked.

The silence was overwhelming, so Clay said, "I still don't believe it." Then he looked at Seth as if Seth could somehow answer his question. "Why would a girl who lived to help others want to take her own life?"

There was no hiding Seth's shock, no covering his wide eyes. Seth had hoped she'd maybe died in a car accident. "I'm sorry, sir. Maybe she was torn up about something no one knew about."

Dean Clay rested his sun-weathered forehead on his thick left hand, halfway closed his eyes a few seconds, and looked at his desk. "But a girl like her, who made friends just by waking up each morning, could've taken any problem to any of them. Even to me."

Seth was looking at a real man caught somewhere between frustration, sadness, and some sort of unjustified guilt, and he perceived something. It was like waking to a bump in the night and wondering if you truly heard it. Something unfamiliar inspired a response more appropriate than Seth knew. "Sometimes, I guess a person just doesn't have time."

The way the Texan moved his head and closed his left eye spoke to a well-warranted bewilderment. Seth finished the good coffee. The wicker chair creaked when he stood to explain he was almost late for class, so Dean Clay rose, too, and now seemingly recovered, offered a hearty handshake. Seth felt a little embarrassed about how serious the conversation had become.

Dean Clay scratched the back of his head and looked up at the ceiling, perhaps wondering why Seth had dropped by.

Seth walked away and realized he might've discovered all he was afraid of.

HENSE R. ELLIS II

CHAPTER FIFTY-SIX

Seth left Dean Clay's office, headed up the east stairwell toward the library, then turned right. There were two sounds he wasn't quite ready to hear, an explosion of thunder . . . and a voice. The thunder was loud; the voice was powerful: it cut through the heavenly rumble and his cloud of concentration, yanked his eyes away from the glass wall and the beginning of a typical Southern storm of light, noise, and water. The voice nibbled first at the edge of audibility, then somehow subtly invaded his comprehension.

"Seth, Seth!"

It was the uncharacteristic font of desperation that, as he continued forward, caused his head to tilt. The voice and the tone didn't match.

"Well, are you just going to walk away?"

The voice was tinged with a distinctive spice grain of childlike hurt.

He stopped and turned. She'd materialized out of thin air, but there she stood, just inside the glass door separating the breezeway from the front porch. He looked at her, or perhaps only at where she stood, noted there wasn't a drop of rain on her, and, outside of a measure of fear, felt nothing, knew he felt nothing, was surprised he felt nothing.

The next sentence from her sneaked a little further into his personal space. "I hear you've been busy, but are you too busy to even speak with someone who cares about you?" Her voice trailed off into an affectionate tone, one he'd heard before, just before she'd dropped her arm amid that wondrous soft glow that only two large candles could give.

He was tempted to wonder why her arm had chosen to drop, but only an immortal could avoid recalling how pleasing that sight had been. Seth couldn't resist replaying it, his imagined version as vivid as the live one. Within seconds, he'd relived the whole experience, the warmth of the water, her overwhelming perfection and its pull upon his being, the sense she welcomed his every touch, yet seemed to lead any moment he felt uncertain. Seth's ability to remember was special, almost as much it was honest. He remembered as well the feeling at the end, as his body soaked in the smooth tub and his eyes soaked in the red tile surrounding him, that unrecognizable suggestion he'd stepped upon the hot sands of a dry desert, that painful aloneness.

He stood still. The tinge of fear grew stronger, assuming an icy-hot quality that weakened his focus. He needed a place to run, or a sudden source of strength, or at least a convenient distraction. His panicked eyes began moving, shifting first left, then right. When they moved down, she stepped forward. He knew where her eyes were and what they said, but he steered his own away from them, and they made a desperate landing over her left shoulder, 75 feet away down the endless breezeway.

There stood something without threat. Perhaps it was soaking wet, but it was a welcome sight of genuine concern, a powerful message of devotion that asked nothing of him in return . . . the exact expression one might expect from a girl-next-door.

Seth had only to recognize it for what it was, to contact it and convey his gratitude, then to take one deep breath, lock in upon the eyes before him, and ask, "I can't remember when you *ever* cared about me."

Surprise overtook her face. She swallowed hard, walked away harder, wearing what he realized was a brand new look for her, an unbecoming façade of disappointment, failure, and confusion. He stood still and watched her walk the length of the inner porch and turn toward the faculty elevator, feeling safer because he was no longer drawn to follow her. It was a rainy day; it was a Monday, but she couldn't get him down.

There was one pull he did feel, however, as it led him through the glass door to the faculty lot. Casting a glance of impending detection over his left shoulder, he stepped to her car to see which professor's name was on the parking sign before it. Seeing the name, and sensing the left edge of his mouth rise, Seth thought, *Gee, he really is a nice guy. He even allows students to use his parking space, that good friend of a Professor, Barry Goodfried.*

CHAPTER FIFTY-SEVEN

Barbwire and pine forests. There were about 140 miles of both between Tuscaloosa and Coffeeville, located just a long stone's throw from the Mississippi line. The Thursday, April 10 weekday car ride took Seth down Interstate 59 West for thirty miles or so, then onto US Highway 53, where he passed two mobile homes and three logging trucks. Seth traveled through, or near, a world of towns with unique names: the Greek sounding Demopolis, not far from the famous Faunsdale Bar and Grille, the Jersey-sounding Hoboken, and towns with Indian-based names like Naheola and Choctaw. There was even one named Hugo on the map. Seth wondered if it was populated with quirky P.I.'s who were on the wagon.

The Ryals family had been surprised by his call. Seth had told them only that he was a law student who had lost a friend and wanted to talk to them about the loss of their daughter. He tried not to be specific when they asked why. Instead, he steered the conversation to topics like the appeal of non-urban existence. They invited him for lunch.

The long drive gave Seth needed time to think, but he wasted the first hour with the radio off, fighting Cindi withdrawal symptoms, wondering if it had been right to quit her cold turkey, wondering if he should feel a little guilty about obeying his first impression. Then, he switched to beating himself up a bit for not yet avenging H.R.'s murder. Maybe he should've followed up on the funny feeling he'd had about the Rentzell and Hays murders and his realization that actual drug dealers usually didn't ask a lot of questions. Fortuitously, the

Jeep's fuel gauge was on empty, and he was forced to stop at a Linden, AL Texaco.

He filled up the car and bought a Diet Coke. Left of the station, he saw a group of high school cheerleaders having a bake sale.

One of the girls yelled in Seth's direction. "Hey, Mr. Good Looking! Would you please buy some cookies?"

Her friends broke out in laughter, and one of them called her crazy and gave her a nudge. Craving diversion, Seth walked over and watched the girls' eyes grow excited.

The cutest girl said, "Hey, Mister, I'm Pamela. We're just trying to raise money for new uniforms, and we've got some great stuff!"

"Okay. What would go best with a Diet Coke?"

Pamela mannerismed her way through a quick listing. "Well, we've got chocolate chip with pecans, and we've got some great oatmeal cookies, chocolate oatmeal actually, and some M & M cookies, and also some chocolate cake."

Seth nodded. "It's interesting that everything has chocolate in it."

She gazed back, her smile infectious. "Maybe we do have a way of making what we like. Anyway, which would you like?"

"I'll have the chocolate oatmeal. At least it has some semblance of nutrition." Seth gave them five bucks for a two-dollar bag, a gesture that threw them into extra giddy mode. He'd walked halfway to the Jeep when he heard Pamela yell, "Hope those cheer you up, mister. You're too handsome to be pouty faced!"

Seth paused a half-second, but never turned. Instead, he walked to the Jeep and drove away, a convicted man. He turned the radio on, found an eighties alternative music station. He got a heckuva kick out of some outside-the-box rock--Peter Gabriel's "Shock the Monkey," Thomas Dolby's "She Blinded

Me With Science," and The Talking Heads' mournful "Take Me To The River." Then, he dug out Wagner's powerful "Ride of the Valkyries" from the glove box, loaded it in the stereo, and considered how the invigorating piece propelled his brain cells into cruising gear. He spent the rest of the drive analyzing the case and how to approach the Ryals.

CHAPTER FIFTY-EIGHT

The Ryals' home was a modest stained-wood ranch set in the middle of a pasture. A postcard-worthy blend of hardwoods, loblollies, and flowering pear trees encompassed the home, and two evergreen trees towering twenty feet high attested to how long they'd lived there. The white mailbox attached to a painted mule plow hinted at a genuine neighborhood pride, even though theirs was the only home in a two-mile stretch.

Seth parked in the back and saw a man in farm Khakis and a blue-jean shirt carrying a bucket to a trough. Katie's Appaloosa bounded toward the bucket of sweet feed. The quarter horses and the gray mare were out in the greater pasture munching on fresh hay. A pickup truck and a white sedan sat under a shed, both cleaner than any country vehicle should've been.

He walked around to the front and rang the bell. A mature version of Katie Ryals' portrait welcomed him with a smile. There was no hiding the effect of the angelic likeness, and Seth saw how her eyes swished left at his surprise.

"I'm Seth. Seth Sentel. I guess I wasn't aware of the resemblance. You and your daughter were likely mistaken for twins." Appearing bashful and self-conscious, Mrs. Ryals turned her cheeks away and invited Seth into the definition of a home. The hearty scent of fresh cornbread sealed the feeling of warmth he sensed overcoming his mood.

"I hope you like homemade vegetable soup, Seth. It seemed like a cool enough day for it, and I wanted to use up some of the items we put away from last year's garden."

The cuisine smelled of heaven, and Seth asked, "Is it chicken vegetable?"

As she led him to the table, she glanced back to inquire, "How could you guess?"

Seth shrugged and replied, "I don't know."

She motioned to a place at one side of the table. "Wait just a moment, and I'll get the tea from the kitchen. Jerry is feeding Gipper."

"I'm guessing again, but Gipper was your daughter's horse?"

"Yes. The three of us were watching an old Ronald Reagan movie soon after we bought Gipper. Jerry was going to name him Tonto, but Katie liked President Reagan, and the movie inspired her to name him Gipper."

"Catchy name for a horse, and there's never been a better president."

"We think so, too, but I think Katie liked Reagan because he liked horses. There's still a photograph of him in her room, out for a ride, wearing a white hat and a big smile."

"He does smile a lot. I hear he has as wonderful a sense of humor in private as he does in public."

Katie's dad entered and said, "No kidding?"

Seth hesitated to answer, but said, "My dad has been a County Republican Chairman for twenty years or so, and he met him at a fundraiser."

Seth was introduced to Mr. Ryals and his big rural Alabama smile. "Have a seat, Mr. Sentel. Let's see what's for dinner. Maybe it's soup and corn bread."

"Oh, you peeked, Jerry. Seth here just knew somehow, even guessing what was in the soup. He must have ESP."

Seth shrugged again and looked down. "No, just a lucky guess."

They sat down and Mr. Ryals blessed the food, thanking God for it and for blessing them with Katie as long as He had.

Seth placed his napkin in his lap and spoke up. "I've often looked at your daughter's portrait and wondered."

Mrs. Ryals smiled and explained, "Oh. We had it commissioned through the owner of a local art gallery in Tuscaloosa, Zack Greyson. Mr. Grayson was so nice. He works with the finest artist named Niccolo Caracciolo. Katie's portrait was painted in Florence."

"And we don't mean Florence, Alabama," Mr. Ryals said with a smile, a reference to a northwest Alabama city known for producing more gangsters than artists.

"Jerry!"

Seth offered his observation. "I could see it was a fine portrait, and the artist's name suggested he wasn't local. Was it expensive?"

"Well, it might have been, but Mr. Greyson said if we'd just pay enough to cover Nicky's travel expenses to the States, then he'd do it. The church took up a special collection to help us with it."

Mr. Ryals commented, "Yeah, Nicky--we all called him by his first name because we never could pronounce his last--was coming over for a showing anyway, so he painted Katie from some photographs and brought it over on the plane."

"They invited us to the show and treated us like we were dignitaries." Seth could sense Mrs. Ryals was reliving a special moment.

Mr. Ryals wedged back in. "They'd already framed her portrait, and it was part of the show. So many people asked about it that they had to put a little 'Not For Sale' card at the bottom of it."

"We were so flattered I almost drank too much champagne," Mrs. Ryals admitted. "Many of the folks there, and they were all high society types, were commenting on how she shone through the portrait like an-"

"Like an angel," Seth said without thinking.

Both stopped and looked at Seth, who was having another spoonful of the blue-ribbon vegetable soup.

Mr. Ryals looked at his wife, then at Seth. "That's what they said. You weren't there, were you?"

"No, sir. It just seemed like what they'd say. I mean, it was the first thought in my mind when I saw it."

Mrs. Ryals put her spoon down. She accentuated each word. "Well, that's the nicest thing to think about our Katie, especially when you never met her."

"Well, I'm sure she made a special first impression in person. Forgive me for being curious, but could you tell me more about her?"

"Katie was a tender-hearted girl, so helpful to anyone with a need."

Mr. Ryals contributed detail. "And any animal, too. She was always taking in stray cats and dogs. For a while, I thought we were running a foster home for felines and cur dogs."

"Oh, hush, Jerry. Anyway, we didn't see Katie as a lawyer, but there she was, in her third-year of law school, one month from graduating, when we lost her."

Seth went logical. "How did she become interested in the law, instead of say, animal science?"

"Well, the local judge was a deacon at our church, and he knew Katie was good with words. She was always reading and even wrote some poetry, including a kind one about the Gipper."

Seth asked with a smile. "The horse or the president?"

"Both, we think."

Mr. Ryals put in his take, "So Judge Espy encouraged her to sit for the entrance exam and to apply during her senior year at Samford, where she studied marketing and made decent grades. Her entrance score was good enough, and with the judge's recommendation, she was accepted. The judge even made us aware of a scholarship she qualified for, some type of good citizen-type award. I was just glad to see it after funding four years of private college."

While the discussion proceeded, Seth had another piece of cornbread and continued to ask seemingly unimportant questions. "So, how was law school for her, and how long ago would she have graduated?"

"She'd have graduated almost three years ago," Mr. Ryals said.

Mr. Ryals added, "She was doing just fine. I think only thirty percent of the folks were ahead of her."

Mrs. Ryals said, "Judge Espy said she'd make a great judge. She didn't *think* she was too smart, he said, and she had a fine sense of right and wrong."

Mr. Ryals took his turn again. "It made sense, once we thought about it. We weren't too keen on her being a lawyer, but being a judge sounded right. Katie wasn't mean enough to be an actual lawyer . . . no offense."

Seth waved off the apology, then asked, "Did she have any particular friends or maybe a boyfriend at law school?"

"Well, there was no one in her class, but I think she befriended a few girls in the classes behind her. Two came here to stay one weekend."

"She was like a big sister to those younger girls. They seemed to look up to her," Mrs. Ryals said.

"What about guys?"

"She didn't mingle with the law school guys much."

Mr. Ryals offered, "She thought they were too single-minded for her. Single-minded about money or about parties."

Mrs. Ryals looked at Seth a moment, then back at her half-empty bowl. "I'm sure she wouldn't have thought such about Mr. Sentel, Jerry."

"Course not. No offense, Mr. Sentel."

"None taken, and it's just Seth."

After another thirty minutes at the table and another 30 in the den, Mr. Ryals took Seth out to see the horses.

As they ambled down the gravel drive toward the horse pen, Seth looked over at the old wooden barn and mentioned in a neighborly tone, "There's something serious I wanted to speak with you about, sir."

"I thought there might be. I made the trips to Birmingham and Tuscaloosa quite a few times when she was in school, and it's too long a drive just to chat and eat homemade soup."

"Well, it was mighty savory soup, sir, but there are some, well, other questions I was hoping to ask you, to ask you with respect." The fine man nodded. "When I spoke with Dean Clay, he mentioned how you lost your daughter. He didn't seem to quite believe it."

"Well, we've accepted it. I'm not sure we believe it all, or that we've put it all together, but we've learned not to think about it."

"I'm not sure I can put it together either, sir, and, well, I've never learned not to think about things I don't yet understand."

There was a comfortable pause, and for once in his life, Seth waited patiently.

The farmer's voice weakened. "I never should have given it to her, and we should've taken her to one more doctor for the pain. Maybe another guy up at UAB Hospital. I fear our local doc was out of his league, even for maintenance care."

"I don't understand, sir."

"Back before we bought the Appaloosa, she had another horse; Spunky was his name." He shook his head and stared at the good, dark dirt below his boots. "That crazy horse. It wasn't that he was bad, you see. He just had too much energy, too much spunk. One day, and a God-awful day it was, he took her under some trees too fast. A big oak limb caught her before she could duck." Seth felt a shiver of nervousness jump inside him. "Then, when she fell off, her shoulder hit a stump."

Seth closed his eyes. "I'm sorry she went through that."

"Well, the sad thing was she just never got over it. The headaches were bad, real bad. They'd come and go, but were awful when they came." Seth shook his head in genuine sadness, but couldn't muster a word at the thought of such a sweet girl in such misery. "They never did line her shoulder up either, and her neck was twisted when the limb struck her, so she had a banged-up disc. Anyway, we took her to several doctors, but didn't have much luck. She still needed those damn merciless pills."

Seth knew it was instructive for this mild mannered man to utter profanity. "Pain pills?"

Mr. Ryals nodded. "She'd try not to take them, and, about when this happened, she'd cut down a good bit. She was getting some physical therapy through the University athletic department, somehow for free."

Seth nodded, his football past having experienced its own wealth of physical therapy. Nothing was said for a few seconds while the first part of the conversation settled in, and Seth gathered himself by drawing tiny circles in the dirt and straw with his foot.

Empathy in his voice, Seth said, "As I mentioned on the phone, I lost two law school friends. A few things about the way it happened never made sense. I think a few things about Katie's situation aren't making sense to you."

The 55-year-old family man who had lost half his family looked at the 23-year-old student who had lost half his friends and said, "Her roommate, who'd been to a concert after she found two free tickets in the mailbox, found Katie with too much pain killer inside her, and with the gun I had given her nearby." Seth shook his head and unknowingly reinforced Mr. Ryals' revived disbelief. "The investigators said it was an obvious suicide, that she wanted to be sure she succeeded, and that she must've been unable to bear the pain anymore."

"Well, sir, what else is obvious is how she was close to finishing school. The timing doesn't fit."

His tone now a little less grieved and a little more angry, Mr. Ryals said, "Not to mention how we were a close family, yet she never mentioned any severe recent bouts with pain or with anything else, just before it happened." Then he waved his arm over the countryside. "You can't help being real close when you live out in the middle of nowhere."

"About the gun, Mr. Ryals. I have a few myself. Some for hunting, one or two just for protection. I don't hear of many girls who have them, though."

"Well, I couldn't afford the nicest place on campus for her to live, so we did the best we could and found her an apartment in a well-kept complex near the school. Because it was just a little close to a suspect neighborhood, I gave her my old 38. Katie had a permit, and I taught her to plink tin cans when she was in grammar school."

"Was she living near a taco place?"

"Right. How'd you know?"

"I have friends there. It's a popular place for law students," Seth added, and thought about Less and the uninvited politicos from Hyannis Port.

"After they found her, I wished I had just bought her some mace or a whistle."

Seth caught him right in the eyes again and said, "It's not your fault, sir."

Seth saw something real and material in the older man's eyes, and it said the man saw something in his. He knew not what, but it was unmistakable.

By the time Mr. Ryals spoke again, his voice had found another channel. "You're not so sure about what happened to your friends. We heard it was a hunting accident."

"So, you've heard about it."

He smiled a little. "Heard about those two Mobile boys being murdered, too. We live in the country, but not in *another* country."

Seth made eye contact and nodded. "I have reasons to believe, seriously good reasons to believe, it was no accident at all."

Mr. Ryals returned the eye contact. "Now you know our story. Just please call if you find out anything else about Katie?"

Seth answered, "Yes, sir, and I won't tell anyone who's not working with me about this."

Ryals's gaze was good as gold. "I'm working *with* yuh, Mr. Sentel."

Mrs. Ryals sent Seth off with a paper sack filled with cornbread and a Tupperware container of soup. During the return trip, Seth listened to a series of Chopin piano Impromptus. They played their classical magic on his mind. He realized the world had lost a large measure of genuine goodness when Katie Ryals died. When H.R. died, it lost a mover and a shaker; however, with Katie, it lost a giver and a helper. He also knew Katie studied Marketing.

CHAPTER FIFTY-NINE

It was late afternoon the next Friday April 11, and the curtain was closing on another spring day. The sun was slip-sliding away, and, at this hour, there wasn't much company in the Coffee Room. Just the two gambling addicts playing chess for three bucks a throw, the anorexic first-year girl arguing with a salad, and a small, obsessive, study group enthralled with themselves and their love of the law.

Seth bought a tasty, ice-cold Frostie root beer and sat his dreary self near the same window where his life had just begun to unravel. Seth couldn't tolerate too much noise, but whenever life became too quiet, despondency could sometimes threaten a nasty comeback. The honeybees were leaving the clover of the school's big back yard. He thought about that morning when Less had found the huge key ring and H.R. had met Sue. The whole episode had opened the door to Sue's young heart, and maybe, if Seth's instincts were correct, H.R. had lost his own life when he tried to protect hers. He recalled H.R.'s quotation from the Song of Solomon: *For Love is as strong as death.* With H.R., it had, at least, been stronger than the fear of death.

He sipped root beer and pondered on. It wasn't supposed to be this way. Heroes weren't supposed to die. In Springtime, they were supposed to be spending time with their buddies, outside turkey hunting or at home watching Jack Nicklaus win another Masters, instead of abandoning their friends to their own depressing devices.

Seth looked up, focused on Katie's portrait. He'd missed something about her face, a face casting a Southern Mona Lisa smile over the gray linoleum and painted cinderblock below. He'd noted an innocence and simplicity every man needed to often see. Seth rubbed his ear a little and ran her glow of happy, quiet confidence through his mental photo album. He hadn't seen it enough since he left Fawnlund for college. He faintly remembered seeing it recently but was too tired to realize where.

Seth's focus fell deeper into Niccolo's painting and considered what Dean Clay and Katie's parents had said about her. She loved horses. She studied marketing in undergrad. She was a conscientious student. She'd have been a fine judge, and she was empathetic to a fault. She just had more pain than she could handle, and her roommate returned from a concert to find Katie had taken the widest available exit. He wondered what her roommate's name was and exactly what a Marketing curriculum entailed.

He looked at her face once more and gently tapped the now empty soda can on the tabletop. His lips yielded a small smile. Niccolo was the best: he could even paint hope.

CHAPTER SIXTY

The next Monday morning, Seth phoned Dr. Alfred Thigpen, the head of Samford University's Marketing Department. He asked what the study of Marketing was about, thinking it involved only sales and retail merchandising. He was wrong, it was also about numbers. He asked Dr. Thigpen if he remembered Katie Ryals. Thigpen said "Of course" and recalled her willingness to pour herself into every aspect of her major, as if she enjoyed learning for the sake of itself. She had a habit of staying late in the computer lab to run extra, unassigned regressions, trying to figure out what drove certain people to buy certain products. She once even spotted a cross-correlation he'd missed.

He hung up the phone and called Mr. Ryals.

"Mr. Ryals, this is Seth Sentel."

"Hello, Seth. It's good to hear from you."

"Well, sir, this isn't just a social call."

"I was hoping it wasn't. Yesterday, I wondered from my tractor seat if you had an update."

"I have a few new answers, and they're begging more questions, which are begging for more answers. I was hoping you might know them."

"Like I said, I'm working with yuh."

Seth remembered not only that he'd said it, but the effect of his voice when he did. Seth's voice slipped into a more direct tone. "Did she ever mention she was working on a special project, maybe an extracurricular activity?"

"I'll ask her mother later, but I can't recall any."

"Could you say she appeared overworked or stressed right before you lost her?"

"If so, it would be difficult to notice. She always took school too seriously, I remember thinking. She was so conscientious."

"Did she ever bring up a peculiar subject or ask any questions you couldn't comprehend the reason for?"

"I'm sorry, Seth, but, no, I don't- Well, this may be unimportant, but there was this one call when, out of nowhere, she seemed worried about us. She was asking if we'd received anything in the mail we didn't understand, or if we had had any surprise visitors, like someone whose car broke down in front of the house. I remember shaking my head afterwards. Heck, she was as worried about us as we always were about her. I think her mother and I even had a little chuckle about it, though we appreciated the concern."

"Were there any such visitors?"

"Nope. Trust me, it's been a few years, but we have so few visitors out here, I'd recollect any unusual ones."

"That may be a good thing. And your house was never broken into or never worked on by a new or strange-acting repairman?"

"I'm the repairman here, and except for an occasional sleepwalk, there's no strange behavior to see."

"Do you still have all of Katie's school things and any papers she might have kept?"

"They're all boxed up and sitting in an old top-loading freezer in the horse barn."

"Good. Could I look through them?"

"We'd love to have you over again, Seth. Why don't you plan to spend the night this time?"

"A generous offer, sir, but I'm feeling a little rushed these days. One other question, who was her roommate in law school?"

The answer hit Seth hard, froze his overactive mind in place, for once.

♦

He drove back to Coffeeville where Mr. Ryals showed him Katie's school things. There was a shoebox filled with papers, old checking account statements, her law school acceptance letter, and a Copy Shoppe business card. There was a matchbox with a familiar logo, too. He picked it up, noted the logo and the street address on the back, and recalled H.R.'s note and their last phone call, plus what Dean Clay had said about Katie's social habits. Then he looked Mr. Ryals in the eye.

"Katie didn't even drink, did she?"

CHAPTER SIXTY-ONE

The next day, April 15, Seth marched up the stairs to Hugo's office. With everything his research had yielded, Seth, for once, was happy with Seth.

He looked through the door without knocking and saw Hugo waving him in with a Marlboro.

Hugo announced, "Well, if it ain't Captain Stupid Head." Seth's face fell two inches. "The idiotic genius of book learning."

Seth tried to rally in the face of the surprise attack. "Hey, I've had a decent week of investigating."

"A good week of *being* investigated would be more like it."

Seth's voice stuttered. "What's up, Hugo? All I did was walk in here an invited guest."

"Hey, all you did was about get your head blown off. Didn't I say we needed to be careful as cats?"

Curiosity and shock made for an interesting mixture on a twenty-three-year-old face. Hugo now spoke with a pause between each word. "Did you ever think even *once* that, when the same old black truck follows you down a lonesome lower Alabama road for almost 100 miles, someone might be following you?"

Seth sat across from Hugo and the Bear Bryant mug and assumed a silent, slumping, idiot position. The Socratic tongue-lashing went on. "Please tell me yes, Seth. Did you even notice them back there? Remember the old woman with the long, curly, dark hair, who maybe was a man with a wig?"

A man of mercy, Hugo gave him a chance to answer. Seth thought back, running a file check through his gray cells for records of long, dark hair. None found. He did recall, however, seeing an old black, seemingly vacant truck parked across from the Texaco.

"Well, I did see an old black truck near a Texaco in Linden, and yeah, now that I think about it, I might have seen it behind me once, but good grief, Hugo, there's nothing unusual about old trucks on a country road."

Hugo just shook his head. "There is if they follow you clean from Tuscaloosa to Grove Hill, then turn around and head home."

Seth couldn't help but agree, but he also couldn't help but think. "Hey, how do you know where it turned around? Was this some kind of test? Was it you in a wig following me or something?"

"No, Mr. Juris Doctorate in daydreaming, I was following the follower. If you had had just one foot in the real world, you would've noticed me behind her, or him."

"So, why do you think she might be a he, and, hey, why were *you* following me?"

Hugo wasn't about to answer the last one honestly. "The question is, why was *someone else* following you?"

Seth's head budged side to side. "I just don't know, Hugo."

"Someone knew where you were going, or at least that you were going somewhere, and I doubt someone would follow a scatter-brained law student 24 hours a day for nothing."

"How could they know?"

"Did you tell anyone you had a trip planned?"

"I just told Less I had a good lead and was leaving that day to check it out."

"Where did you call her from?" Hugo had already dropped by Seth's place and removed the bug on that phone while Seth was fetching coffee.

"The library."

"Where everyone, including the dear departed Redbeard, knows you practically live during the week."

"So, another phone is bugged?"

"Probably."

"I feel like I've been gang-violated."

"You should try getting gang divorced. It feels the same."

"No thanks. Anyway, Hugo, after what I found out in Coffeeville, I have to know who owns The Tap building."

"Fine, but searching title ain't my specialty. Let's try my direct method, and if that fails, I'll let you deal with the maze of deed books all alone."

"What time will you be ready to drop by The Tap?"

"How about 4:30? The place will be open, but empty." Hugo's voice weakened.

"Hugo. Look, I didn't mean anything by suggesting you'd be comfortable there. If you aren't, then just let me know."

"Come to think of it, maybe I should go ahead and find out if I can handle it."

"Alright then, and Hugo-"

"Yeah, Seth?"

"I'll be there."

"Thanks. It would sound awful if I called my AA partner for help from a bar."

♦

The afternoon visit to The Tap with Hugo was as strange as it was unproductive. With Huey Lewis on a lowered-volume MTV still wanting a new drug months after his hit song had been released, they ordered coffee and started asking questions. The assistant manager went mute. The guy had been around, he knew Hugo was a P.I. with charming methods. After a second cup at the bar, Hugo walked to the rest room. Built into the back wall, tucked behind an old jukebox decorated with dust and cobwebs, was an old brass mail chute slot. Hugo touched the lid, the one place where there was no cobwebs and little dust.

Fifteen minutes later, they left. Seth was disappointed the visit had yielded none of the random info to which Hugo had once referred, and he still wondered what was under the stairwell. He resolved to do the courthouse research the next day.

CHAPTER SIXTY-TWO

The Tuscaloosa County Courthouse was a good example of 1970's architecture. Seth parked on a side street and bounded up the stairs. He took a wild guess and started with the Probate Office, telling a nice older lady he was a law student working on a title research project. With a misplaced grin, the lady directed him to the Mapping Office down the hall.

A pretty girl who appeared about nineteen sat at a small desk, almost hidden behind a large counter serving as a freestanding book depository. There were rows and columns of ledger-sized books stacked on roller shelves in the counter. More books lined the walls and the shelves behind her. Her oversized desk calendar read April 16, 1986.

She looked up, all smiles and enthusiasm. "I'm Sissy Snowden. May I help you?"

Seth saw the glow in her eyes and wasn't sure what it meant, but the girl was indeed pretty, even though her fashion erred to the rural side.

"I'm a law student working on a school project. I'm trying to learn how to determine property ownership when I only know the address. Another Miss Snowden next door suggested I start with you."

The girl's facial expression indicated first that something like this had happened before, then registered that it wasn't a bad something. "Oh, she's my grandmother. She's the sweetest person."

"She seemed willing to help but thought I should begin here."

Sissy smiled and shrugged as she examined Seth's shoulders. "Guess my family likes to help people."

Seth tried to ignore the fact she wore Obsession, the same perfume as Cindi, then gave her the street address of The Tap. "Just take this address, for instance. How would I research who owns it?"

"Well, there must be tons of ways to do so, but the easiest might be to start over here." She walked to the counter and pulled out a large, heavy, black book with the words *Bond Ownership Map* and the year 1985 embossed on the front. "If we can find the street name, then all we'll need to do is locate the number." She flipped over the mammoth pages until she reached University Boulevard, the real name of the Strip. She made a circling motion with her index finger just above the page, then dropped it down with a little thud. "Here we are."

The look in the corner of her eye suggested Seth had permission to draw closer and look over her shoulder. "This gives us not only the parcel number, which you really don't want to get into, but also the owner's name and the deed book and page where a copy of the deed granting to this owner is found."

"Great. Who does it say the owner is?"

"Lottie Moon Corp. Hey, that's weird. Lottie Moon is the name of a Baptist charity."

"Well, there's nothing Baptist about this address. It's a bar."

She giggled and asked, "Are you Baptist too?"

"I grew up next door to the church."

Her eyes seemed to swell with joy. "Did you sing in the choir?"

"Sorry, I didn't, but they asked me to. Hey, is this all there is to this? It seems too simple."

"You may want to go the Probate Record Room and check for recent deeds. Come on, I'll take you."

They walked down the hallway, and Seth could see her grandmother's Baptist eyes glancing up to check the progress of her latest missionary venture.

"In here are all the deed books. Since you wanna know if this Lottie Moon Corp still owns the property, you'll need to check what's called the Die-rect Index."

Seth paused and smiled at her pronunciation. "Direct Index?"

"Yeah, that one has the deeds listed by the grantor's name. If Lottie Moon sold the property, then you'd find the deed under its name in the newest book."

They walked past several of the large freestanding counters--with even larger books on roller shelves below them--to the end of one counter.

She looked down in mild despair. "The right book is always on the bottom. Would you mind?"

"Oh, not at all." Seth rolled the heavy red book out of its bottom slot and plopped it down on top of the counter. She opened it and began to flip. "Thank God they don't use permanent binding so that these deeds can be alphabetized."

"See anything?"

She flipped a few more pages. "No deeds under Lottie Moon Corp. Means they must still own it. Imagine that, a bar owned by a company with a Baptist-sounding name."

"Maybe it's supposed to be some kind of joke. By the way, can we look up the deed where Lottie Moon became the owner? I brought the numbers with me."

"Sure." She smiled, gazing at Seth as if she was willing to do this all day. They walked toward another counter. "Here we are. Book 482, Page 762. Looks like Lottie Moon bought the place from Elijah, Inc. Gee, I never realized so many corporations owned property around here."

"Well, bars get sued sometimes when drunk people leave and get into car wrecks. It's called a dram shop suit. Anyway, to keep from losing their personal assets in such a suit, the smart owners put the place in a corporation."

"Wow, you're smart. I like that in a guy."

Seth, now wise to the scheme of the Snowden women, tried to hide his embarrassment. "Thanks. And thanks for all the help."

"One more thing, but I'll need to borrow your notepad."

"Sure."

♦

She scribbled a number down on the pad. "If you have any more questions, just call me." She looked at him and gave him one last smile, and after he left, she checked in with her grandmother.

Grandma looked up from a romance novel. "How did it go with him, Sissy?"

Sissy's bottom lip protruded. "Well, grandma, I'll bet he'll be just like that red-headed Texas guy and never call."

♦

As Seth drove away, Professor Borland walked into the Mapping Room.

Sissy was back at her post, and at the sight of Borland's grim façade, Sissy's voice became unsettled. "Um, may I help you?"

CHAPTER SIXTY-THREE

Ten minutes later, Seth called Hugo and gave him the new info on The Tap ownership. A few hours later, Hugo called him back.

"Guess what, Seth Sentel?" Hugo seemed to be fighting off an explosion of laughter. "I called a friend in the Secretary of State's office, and your mystery building is owned by a corporation wholly owned by a little old Baptist lady. Her name is Wilma Holman. My mom used to play dominoes with her. Bet she gives half the rent money to the Lottie Moon charity to alleviate the guilt of leasing to a bar!"

Seth was crushed. "Oh."

"Just goes to show how things ain't always what they seem."

Enlightenment spiced Seth's voice. "Yeah. Seems I've heard that before."

"Anyway, something tells me Wilma's not our murderer."

"Well, if it were a multiple choice question, I'd eliminate her first."

"What now, Joe Student?"

"Let me think about it."

"Call me if you need me. Um, has your inheritance landed? The retainer is long gone."

"Send me a bill."

CHAPTER SIXTY-FOUR

It was past mid-April now, the home stretch of the second semester. Seth was in his room trying to keep up with his Property II reading. The not-so-ancient law of condominiums was eating into his investigative time. Myerson had assigned the entire *Alabama Code* chapter on the subject. The phone rang loud, like a town crier with breaking news. Seth's head popped up. He pounced on the hated device to silence it.

"Hello?"

"Seth, it's me."

"Hey Less. Sorry if I sounded tense. This condo law assignment has overtaxed my nerves. How are you faring with it?"

"I'm not. I hit on something more important."

Seth scrambled out of his chair, his voice flew into exhilaration gear. "No joke?"

"Sometimes you're just too transparent, Seth Sentel."

"What?"

"Never mind."

"There's an unusually strong relationship between Myerson's exam scores and Goodfried's."

"What do you mean?"

"As a group, the people who make a 3.0 or better in Myerson's class also score higher on average in Goodfried's. Isn't that a little strange? I also found a strong and slightly increasing correlation between Torts and Criminal, but that makes more sense."

Seth was nodding. "Yeah, Property is an entirely different area of the law than the other two, both of which are all about who to blame for what."

"As in Property law is for the detail person, and Torts and Criminal are for the creative thinker."

"As in Property is for the legally insane, but tell me more about what you see."

"Consider it this way, there aren't enough students who made a 3.0 or better in Goodfried's classes who also made below a 3.0 in Myerson's class."

"Alright. Find anything else?"

"Myerson's overall class grade point average has shown a slight but steady increase over the past seven years or so, but Goodfried's has remained almost constant."

Seth tapped his pencil on his forehead, then Less asked, "Are you thinking the same unthinkable I'm thinking?"

"I think so, and it would match up with a reference in H.R.'s note, not to mention with some other facts I can't quite recall."

"And it would explain why a high average on Goodfried's exams, which are taken before Myerson's, would correlate with a high average on Myerson's."

"Because someone who felt confident about Myerson's test wouldn't have to study for it until after Goodfried's two tests were over."

"Take me," Less said. "Out of sheer fear, I know I started studying early for Myerson's exam."

"Precisely."

"But how would H.R. find out about the arrangement?"

"I'm not certain, but I do know he used to glean all types of information when he was hanging out at-" Seth stopped a second as it hit him.

She said it. "The Tap."

"I still can't believe it's owned by a little old lady, and I wish I knew more about who runs it."

"Try sleeping on it, then look at it another way."

"*Trying* to sleep is never a problem. The actual sleeping is where I so miserably fail."

Her voice softened. "Then try not trying so hard."

CHAPTER SIXTY-FIVE

The next morning, Myerson was in lecture mode, a nice break from his usual Socratic swordplay. Apparently, there were few cases from the Middle Ages on the subject of condominium law which, in Alabama, was established by statute in 1964. Instead of choosing a random young mind, then electrocuting it, Myerson soliloquized on the complications of creating an entire new body of law, the need to placate various groups with an interest in the legislation and to foresee potential misinterpretation. Seth sat and stewed. Then, Myerson jarred his senses.

"Mr. Sentel. What case from last semester foreshadowed the arrival of the condominium?"

Seth's lungs filled; his eyes darted. Was Myerson trying to humiliate him? After exams, Seth had pulled the plug on last semester's material. His thoughts raced, searching for a connection, not wishing to be embarrassed by his nemesis. What was condo law all about? He replayed the code sections he'd read only eight hours before. His brain switched to scan function and came up with individual ownership of certain spaces and common ownership of other, usually larger and more open spaces. Maybe Myerson asked him because he'd called on him to discuss such a case last semester.

"*In re Ellenborough Park?*"

"Mr. Sentel is correct." A few students shot looks of awe over or up at Seth. Seth saw only suspicion.

Myerson concluded. "Now, for our next class, I've placed a compilation of reading materials at an establishment well known as The Copy Shoppe. Its proprietor, Mr. Geiger, will, with pleasure, allow each of you to purchase this packet, which contains two Alabama cases related to the law of condominiums, the *Callahan* and *Howell* cases, and three cases from other jurisdictions. Be prepared to discuss how the courts have treated the condominium construct in various situations. Furthermore, I'll require the assistance of one student on the important question of-'*For what purpose may a condominium be established*?' Class dismissed."

♦

Campus Grinch Vincent Geiger didn't do anything with pleasure for students, even though they paid his rent and fed his family. He had a virtual monopoly on the local copy business, which also explained his tendency to overprice. Seth walked into Geiger's shop and saw the owner working on a copier behind one end of the counter. Seth took one look at Geiger's no-nonsense face and was convinced to approach a meek-looking student-employee wearing an apron. He ordered the Myerson materials and watched as Geiger appeared to grow agitated with the broken copier. Behind Geiger, he saw a built-in ladder on the wall.

"What's up with the ladder?" Seth asked the student, who returned with the Myerson handout.

"It leads to the upstairs."

Seth avoided saying *No kidding*, and instead asked, "What's up there?"

"Just stuff."

"Stuff?"

"Yeah, like extra boxes and a few old machines. It looks like it used to be another store, though."

Seth paid and was about to leave, when Geiger lit into his apron-clad assistant. "Warren, you devil. Didn't I say loose staples could *ruin* a copy machine?" Warren the assistant

343

appeared as if *he* was ruined, or, alternatively, as if he had just met the devil. "I ought to fire you, Warren. I ought to fire you yesterday!"

Seth bolted before the fireworks spread. He pushed through the door and turned left in front of the stairwell to The Tap, just in time to collide with another student and drop his packet and books.

He reached down to retrieve everything. His pupils dilated. There was a cement base beneath the bottom plank of the empty structure supporting The Tap. He saw a vague numerical imprint in the cement. He wrote down the number: it was one digit lower than the street number on Katie's Nasty Tap matchbox. In the middle of the sidewalk, he snatched out the Alabama condo statutes. On page two in the fifth code section, he found the answer to Myerson's question about potential purposes for establishing a condo . . . for *"any purpose,"* it said.

CHAPTER SIXTY-SIX

He phoned Hugo from Number 11, his words tripping all over themselves. "Hugo, I may have something. Would you call your contact at the Secretary of State's office again?"

"I wouldn't mind driving down to see her. She's a mother of two, reportedly has never destroyed any man's self-worth, and isn't bad looking either."

"I'm in a hurry here."

"Sure you're not just impatient?"

Seth spoke as if his hair was on fire. "No, I'm not sure. Anyway, find out who's on the articles of incorporation for Elijah, Inc."

Hugo sounded entertained by Seth's excited voice. "I'll have you paged at the Warner House when I know something."

"Funny."

After lunch, Hugo called. Seth was in his room studying Torts II. "Hold onto your backpack, college boy. Elijah, Inc., which, by the way, lists New Orleans as its headquarters, had three original shareholders, namely Gabriel Elijah, Gabriel Elijah, Jr., and guess who?"

"Huey Long? Hell, how should I know?"

Hugo, grinning at the first time he'd heard Seth inspired to curse, replied, "Benjamin Myerson."

Seth felt the air around him freeze.

"Seth, are you there?"

"I'm here. I'm wondering who still signs the property tax checks on anything still owned by Elijah, Inc."

"Tough one, Seth. We don't know which bank they use nor even what state it's in. Besides, we can't get bank records or corporate records without a subpoena, and to get the subpoena, we'd have to go through Sheriff Gibson."

Seth cursed again, this time as if he always did it.

"Such language for a choir boy."

"Daddy wouldn't let me join the choir."

Hugo must have remembered the mail chute he'd seen behind the old jukebox at The Tap. "Let me think about it, Seth. There may be another way to get to the bottom of this, so to speak, something to do with co-lateral info."

♦

At eleven p.m., Hugo called. "Seth, do you have any experience as a felon?"

"None that I know of."

"Want some? It's highly underrated."

"What?"

"Well, you just don't want too much of it. Me, I've had my measure. Maybe you should take a turn. Do you recall what H.R.'s note said about the truth?"

"Nope."

Seth heard papers rattling.

"See if this refreshes your memory. To quote, *Sometimes, it's also-*" Hugo said it, but Seth was mouthing the words. "*Right up under your feet.*"

The silence was appropriately odd. Seth's weak voice emerged. "Hugo, let's meet tomorrow morning. I'm not sure yet, but I just might be in the right mood to break the law, and I just might need the benefit of your unlawful experience."

CHAPTER SIXTY-SEVEN

April 18, 1986. People are supposed to be happy on Fridays, but for a Seth Sentel, there was depression--and no depression was worse than the depression of anxiety. When it hovered over Seth and poured down on his temperament, no shelter would suffice to protect his weary countenance. That old funny feeling from before the murders had made a nasty partial comeback, working its way up his soul. It was as if a neutron bomb had detonated in range, and he could find no escape from its penetrating ions. At times like these, he often wandered, and, on this afternoon, he wandered around the inside of the library, pretending to be going somewhere, taking rapid strides of phony purpose.

Although he had no intention of ending up any place, his subconscious pulled him around like a lazy horse, like a horse too drunk to think. After two trips around the room, it slowed him just in time. He stopped and recognized something for the first time in months. Like those stars outside his bedroom window, it pulsed toward him, yet scared him right down his center.

He placed his hands on each side of H.R.'s old chair. The little wreaths and mementos remained, some with handwritten messages taped to the front of the three-sided wooden box. Over the little open tomb, the old composite photograph still stood watch: seventy-five coat-and-tied soldiers of the law, watching in serious silence. Seth wished they could have somehow protected H.R., wished he could have too. Then, he became angry with himself for not being supernaturally there for his friend.

He gazed again at the not-so-merry graduates of 1961. Why were they looking at *him*? He was doing all he could. He'd even blocked out Cindi for this. He'd hired Hugo and been willing to let Less help too. He'd managed to put at risk his relationship with anyone and everyone who could crush him. He'd risked his reputation as a top student and a stable, reliable guy. He'd given up about everything but his principles for this mission.

The old narrow-lapel suits, each underlined by its three names of pretense, had given up nothing, hadn't helped at all . . . well, except for Hound Dog Hampton, whose resolute face looked on from the third row. Then, he saw Cindi's father's face in the same composite, and, from the first glance, knew he was the kind of principled man who would've done something too. The face also reminded Seth that Cindi seemed so much like her mom, except for Cindi's naturally dark hair.

Seth began to scan around this antique picture of pictures. He couldn't help it. He took a mental photograph of the entire frame, then began perusing it row-by-row, just scanning, but not for nothing. Something gently led his eyes.

This type pursuit was easy when he searched for a downed deer. He'd lock in the desired colors, shapes, and textures, then broadcast the vision until a match appeared on his inner video screen. This search was different, he had nothing real to input, just the pure suggestion of some strange subtlety of the utmost least.

He scanned each row of photos like his eyes were fast-sequence cameras, starting at the top and moving left to right. He panned faster, until his inner gauge registered a stronger signal, like a metal detector nearing a buried treasure. He blew through the rows one by one, now almost leaping from end to end. At the end of row seven, something stopped him.

His pupils braked, then reversed five photographs. The image was unfamiliar, but only vaguely so, and what remained was enough to lock in his focus. His eyes encircled it. His pulse reeled. He blinked a quick blink and leaned backward for a different angle--just to be certain. At last, he confirmed the name, a name his instincts had already generated: Gabriel Elijah, Jr.

He reconsidered Less's remark about Redbeard and his "cover." He seriously reconsidered cross-correlation. Stat was boring, but, apparently, God had let humans invent it for a reason. Now, it was the key to truth. His heart leaped at the unveiling of all mysteries, mysteries both outside and in. Now, he knew one reason his internal sensors had been flashing a red alert for months. He reconsidered the *Bible* verse from Matthew about flashy false prophets, as it entered the front door of his mind. Another realization about the shape of Elijah's face tapped at its back door. Seth ran away from it and hurried outside.

CHAPTER SIXTY-EIGHT

By Monday, April 21, 1986, Seth had reconsidered his principles. He whispered into the Coffee Room phone, his back turned to the open room. "Less, you know I have to go in there."

"Seth! Don't you know what curiosity did to the cat?"

"I don't have a whole lot of choice here, in case you've forgotten."

"Okay, but let me go with you, so I can be a witness to what happens. Who knows what they'll accuse you of if you're caught inside that old building."

"Hey, I'm going to be doing the catching and accusing here."

"You don't know that for sure. You only have what's in your head." She said it with kindness.

It didn't matter to Seth. "Thanks for the confidence in my intelligence."

"I didn't mean to sound unconfident."

"Try to understand that logic is about all I have to rely on, that, God, and maybe a few close friends."

"I thought you didn't want me there."

"I don't. Curiosity need not kill the cat and his friends."

"Okay. I give in. Seth, sometimes, you're like a mule and a cat. At least our research shows that any evidence you steal can't be excluded in court."

"True, and please be careful with your wording. I don't need any more reminders I'm about to commit a crime."

"What time are you going in? Doesn't The Tap only close after someone's been shot?"

"I leave the library at 10:30. Then, I'll wait until 2:30 a.m. to be sure the place has closed. It's Monday night, so they won't be open as late. Don't you *dare* show up."

"Yeah, yeah. But don't expect me to come claim you at the county jail."

"Would you claim me at the county morgue?"

"Would you please shut up?"

"Good idea. I better go. Someone's coming."

"Seth." She hesitated, and her voice drifted into warm concern. "Would you *please* watch your smart little ass?"

He got serious half a moment. "I may be curious as a cat, but I'll be careful as one too, as Hugo says, careful as one with eight lives lost." The half moment was long enough for Seth to feel out of character again. "Oh, by the way, if someone *were* in jail, or in the morgue, then someone might miss *your* smart little ass."

She blushed and said "Bye" with the sweetest air of fake outrage a girl could radiate.

CHAPTER SIXTY-NINE

He arrived in Pinehurst at 10:30 p.m., pulled out his L.L. Bean backpack, and packed everything Hugo had loaned him: the lock picking tools, the miniature camera, and a small tape recorder. He also packed his Walther PPK .380 handgun.

As he checked the weapon, a troublesome realization sneaked into his overactive mind--if he took that gun inside late at night, it'd look real bad, and if he were convicted of burglary, he'd get a minimum sentence of twenty years. He practiced ignoring this realization, repeating to himself— "*Killers just weren't supposed to get away.*"

He put on his darkest jeans and jacket and laced up some hiking boots. He'd already asked Walter to meet him behind The Tap and had already hoped Walter would make an exception and arrive on time.

From midnight to 2:45 a.m., he stared at the darkness from the window box and covered his eyes. The guilt and fear wouldn't leave by themselves. He tried to block them out and tried not to feel guilty about doing so. He didn't like doing this stupid stuff at this stupid hour all alone, and he thought about Hugo's response when he'd begged him to go along: *I'm old, Seth; you're young, and the best thing about being young is you don't know for sure you'll fail at whatever crazy thing you're trying to do*. Seth worried that he was young, yet remained paranoid about failure. He worried himself into thirty minutes of needed sleep.

At 3:15, he slipped out. If Lesley, or anyone monitoring a phone tap, showed up uninvited at 2:30 and saw no sign of him, maybe they'd conclude he'd changed his mind, and maybe they'd leave the area before he arrived. He'd walk the six blocks from Pinehurst to the Tap, stay off the street. The backpack would look suspicious at this hour.

He eased from house to house, jumped behind trees and shrubs when a rare car drove by. He broke across University Boulevard from the bushes, bolting so fast and smooth that the freshman dressing herself in a fraternity house window must have thought he was an alcoholic vision.

He walked the back alley behind the buildings on The Strip. He knew there were rats about, and he noted among the brown dumpsters and silver cans that a few big stray cats were crouching like lions, hunting a live meal.

He looked at a huge one and whispered, "Happy hunting, Tom."

He heard the occasional buzz of flies, an appropriate background noise for this particular walk in the dark. His nose detected the signature aroma of most any back alley, a heavy combination of decaying food and warm over-fermented beer, mixed with partially digested portions of both.

Though dark, he could see the paint-less backsides of the two-story buildings. He noted the dingy gray of exposed mortar and wood. A few had rusted railings surrounding stained and chipped cement stairways. He stepped on a beer can, cringed, paused, but there was no reaction, no sound but his own breathing. He quickened his pace. The Tap was the next to the last building in a row of eight, another thirty-yard walk through darkness.

He'd walked through the woods in pitch-blackness before, but he sensed something strange about this nighttime stroll. He felt this was the only dark enclave in an otherwise bright setting. He sensed a focus upon both him and his locale. He shook his head a little and wished his mind was less unusual.

Now he needed an entrance. The problem? There wasn't one. The backside of the lower level was all dull cement and worn, thick boards. Thinking there might be a storm cellar-type entrance from outside, he examined the grounds. No luck. He fought frustration's urge and made himself think. He eliminated all impossible options, tried to picture what remained as a possible. He re-read H.R.'s note in his head. What was the part about Seth and his weird imagination?

Lost in thought, his head jerked. Someone was close, real close, but out of sight. The sound didn't match Walter's booted feet. It was too delicate. He scanned, feeling vulnerable in the open alley. There was little cover other than a couple of dumpsters, and the closest was thirty feet away.

The voice came from behind an old mimosa tree. "The way in may be next door. He owns the Copy Shoppe building too." Seth's shoulders slumped. He heard the voice again, and the footsteps resumed, "Is it clear? I saw some cops driving down University a few minutes ago."

Seth shook his head, waved Less over, more concerned for her safety than disturbed by her persistence. A nice girl like her didn't belong in a felony like this.

"Less, you don't follow instructions well," and as she neared, he added, "At least you wore black. It looks good with your new real hair color, you know."

"Thanks, two compliments in one breath." It seemed she tried not to whisper and sound sarcastic at the same time.

"What are you doing here? I even told you the wrong time just to throw you off." He tried not to whisper and sound exasperated at the same time.

"I kept waiting, and well, I suspected you might be fibbing a little. Guess you're a big fat liar, huh, Mr. Integrity."

"Just trying to protect the so-called weaker sex from a death wish, and I noticed you were here on time, in case I wasn't lying."

"I was hoping law school wasn't teaching you any bad habits. Besides, you lied with such ease."

"Funny one, Less. Maybe I'm becoming more skilled at it under pressure." She replied only with her warm, persistent eyes. "Less, how do you know he owns the Copy Shoppe? That Yankee sure acts like he owns it, along with the rest of the campus."

"Geiger only owns the franchise. He leases the building. Apparently, when you checked title chains, you didn't check the Copy Shoppe titles. Then, I found this note in my box after you called." She handed over a typed note on yellow legal paper. "It says, *Incidentally, he owns the Copy Shoppe building too.* Weird, huh?"

Frustrated and undecided, Seth said, "You were supposed to just crunch numbers, and now you're getting mysterious notes in your box."

"Crunching numbers gets boring."

"And committing a crime doesn't, I suppose."

"Well, that may depend on the circumstances. Besides, you may need some help in there."

"Oh. How's the girl who abhors guns and violence planning on protecting me?"

"You just never know what a female law student might do."

He exhaled, accepting this now obvious truth. He considered the tone she'd used to say it. There was fear and uncertainty in her voice, but enough determination pushed through to evoke his pity. He looked around for Walter, but as expected, ole slowpoke was nowhere to be seen. Seth had tried to trick him into punctuality by telling him to meet at 3:00.

He closed his eyes a second and asked, "Why are you even here? Why do you care?"

Her eyes seized his. "Seth, it's because you've got the guts to be good, even if it means being bad."

His eyes hung with hers, too long to avoid the initiation of a new impulse, but his tone was that of the resolute. "We'll have to break in the Copy Shoppe now." He shook his head and added, "Guess one crime deserves another. C'mon, I have a lock to pick," he concluded, handing her the flashlight. "If I can find a door."

♦

Fortunately, the Copy Shoppe had a back door, and there was no sign of an alarm system. Pondering the image of the hard-hearted Yank testifying against him at his burglary trial, Seth took fifteen minutes to pick the back deadbolt. It had taken six hours to learn the trade, but Hugo and a local locksmith had been good teachers. Seth hadn't even known it took two tools to pick a lock--one to move the pins off the tumbler and one to turn the tumbler itself--but his touch with both tools was soon evident.

They entered. Their feet caressed the hardwood floor. She stayed close. After three steps inside, Seth whispered that he smelled cat litter. Less reminded him he was weird.

"Didn't you think to bring your own flashlight?" he asked.

"Sorry, can't I just live off your light for awhile?"

Seth ignored the syrupy implication. Instead, his mind rolled around some interesting questions. "If this is how he makes his entrance, doesn't he worry about Geiger walking in on him after hours?"

"Maybe he always enters well after hours."

They looked for an entrance door between the Copy Shoppe and the bottom of The Tap building. Seth even used a hydraulic pallet jack to pull a heavy bookcase out from the paneled adjoining wall, but there was no door. Seth looked in the back of the room, lit only by the light of a Coke machine. He heard a loud bonk behind him. His ears locked on the sound. He wheeled, the flashlight in one hand, the Walther in the other. He saw nothing, but his eyes imitated a robot's. Then, he spied a sudden blur in the dark, a movement down low, black with a flash of white, angling toward him and to his right. He stepped behind a stack of copy paper and shut off his light. A few seconds later, he saw another flash, this time from the right.

The culprit didn't notice Seth behind the stacks of Georgia Pacific letter size. She was a small cat. Seth eased out for a better view. She returned with a gray kitten in her mouth and sped on to parts unknown, a likely acquaintance of Big Tom's.

Seth peered around and saw a wicker kitty basket with a country blue pillow and two more kits inside. Mom was abandoning the store-bought bed for something more natural. Near the basket was that permanent ladder he'd noticed before, embedded in the outside wall. It led to an attic door with hinges on one end and a big Master padlock on the other. He went to retrieve Less, who had discovered the new kitty residence.

"Isn't he cute? Their eyes aren't even open." Less had a blind, black kitty in the palm of her hand.

Seth allowed a small, quick smile and said, "Hmm, she found a nest more to her liking." An empty box sat atop two other full ones parked against the wall. An old University of Alabama sweatshirt in the bottom of it formed the new bed lining. "Nothing like raising your young in a positive environment." Less's shoulders slumped. Seth changed the subject. "Come on, Less. I think I found the way in."

They reached the wall where the ladder rested. The area was now bereft of infant felines. Mommy cat was prancing away like a Clydesdale with the last.

Less glanced at the ladder. "It's on the wrong wall, and it's pointing in the wrong direction."

Seth stalked up it anyway, and now in good burglarizing rhythm, had the padlock picked in a few minutes. It was 4:00 a.m. There was little in the attic, just a few old machines, a box of leftover ceiling tiles, and some old pink insulation. A strip of carpet led from one end to the other end, the Tap end. They saw it and looked at each other with anticipation--this could be it. Then, they looked again with fear--*this could be it.*

At The Tap end of the walkway, there was a small, square door in the wall with a silver latch. When it was open, they put their heads in together for a look. They peered inside of a room the narrow width of the stairwell and half the depth of the building, with a hatch door in its floor. Inside the little room to their right was the wall facing the top of the stairwell that led to the Tap.

Less breathed a deep one. Her face had never been this close to Seth's. "How did you know it was here?"

"The cat made me think. Maybe it moved those kittens because someone had recently been using the ladder above the kitty bed. Besides, it made too much sense for the entrance to come from the Copy Shoppe level, and nothing about any of this has ever made sense."

They climbed into the narrow room and opened the hatch door. Down the hole was another permanent ladder leading back down to ground level. They climbed down the ladder and looked up. The underside of the stairwell was above them and to the right. Now, he finally knew what was under the stairwell to the Tap: a narrow secret room, one that led to the apparently abandoned condo below the TAP. They heard a thump from the Copy Shoppe. They froze.

Less inquired, "Seth, could the Yankee be the type to open early?"

"Yep, but I hope it was just the cat. We never put the bookcase back in place."

They waited, but the thump went unconfirmed. Seth's flashlight illuminated another door: this one led to the room below the Tap. He picked the lock on it. It took both of them leaning on it to push it open. Small wonder, the inside of the door, like the walls around it, was padded and there was an end chair up against it.

"Soundproofing," Less observed.

Seth whispered. "Is it to keep The Tap noise out, or the noise from here in?"

She shuddered as if an unpleasant, grubby feeling had beset her. Then, a funny thought relieved her. "Seth, if it's soundproof, then why are you whispering?"

Seth cut his eyes to the ceiling. Less smiled under her breath.

They eased along. Seth pointed his flashlight out front. Lesley stuck close behind with a finger in his belt loop. He looked back a second. She seemed to touch him as if relying on him, a nice feeling, he had to admit. He thought maybe the Walther in his back pocket made her feel safer.

They entered an apparent office. A roll-top desk to the left faced out into the room. A couple of dining room-type chairs faced the desk, and a green loveseat sat opposite where they'd entered. On the wall behind the desk was a twenty-five-year-old oversized map of the city, outlined on each end by two windows. Every pane was painted black, making the boards on the other side invisible.

On the opposite wall were two framed prints depicting scenes from Tuscaloosa city life over twenty years before, and in the middle of them was a large mirror. Seth shone his light at the office floor. It swept across the mirror. The reflection was weak.

Seth re-examined the floor. The intense demeanor evident in the glow of his flashlight said he was looking for something. Then he eased toward a door to who knows where. He turned the glass doorknob. It was a bedroom. An old king-size four-poster displaced half the room. Other old pieces, including a large, marble-top dresser, sat against the walls.

He got down on one knee near the bed and took a Swiss army knife from his backpack. With the smallest blade, he poked between the boards of the hardwood floor.

Less asked, "What are you looking for?"

Seth said nothing, just kept prying. When a four by three-foot piece of the hardwood floor popped up, he answered. "This." It was an oversized floor safe.

"Nice. How'd you know?"

"I first thought that if there was one, it'd be in the office where most people would put a floor safe. Then I remembered how he goes about everything in a unique manner, probably with intent to be unique. He put this in the bedroom because most people would look in the office, then stop looking."

"In other words, he forces himself to examine a situation as would an average person, then modifies most everything to take advantage of that."

"Uh-huh. Good way to put it, Less. Few would look for a hideaway under a popular bar."

She glanced down at the safe, then put her watch up under the light. It was well past 4:00, but cracking this safe was more challenging and time consuming than picking a couple of padlocks. It took thirty perspiration-filled minutes. They looked at each other. Darkness was getting scarce.

Inside the safe was a journal with 1985-1986 printed on a leather cover. It bore student initials and secret exam numbers on the left margin, then numbers appearing to be grades, with debit and credit columns farther to the right. At the right margin was a column entitled Special Credits.

Seth shook his head at the warped play on words. Most of the entries in this column were beside the initials of female students; many he recognized. A pencil entry next to Suzy's initials had been erased, a sign of a tentative arrangement, Seth figured. The initials of Rentzell and Hays had been slashed through, and "*U. cover*," typed next to their names. Seth stared down and wondered. *U. cover? Under cover? Under cover for whom?*

He wondered how a guy could earn a Special Credit. He counted five guys who had done so, and the initials of three rang a bell, the two goons from the Kit-Kat House party and the Honor Court prosecutor. Maybe the former had been two of the midnight guests at Less's place. Maybe they'd received passing grades in exchange for enforcement work.

Two older ledgers and some Cuban cigar boxes remained inside, more than he'd expected. He snapped a few photos with Hugo's mini-cam, then had a better idea. He unhooked a ledger at the left margin and presented Less with a stack of green sheets, along with his backpack to carry them.

"The copiers next door will be faster. I'll keep going through this stuff and photo the pieces that are too big."

She raced up the ladder and headed to the Copy Shoppe.

He searched deeper inside the safe. There must have been seven ledgers. He was afraid to find out whose names were in the older ones: many were probably in state government by now. He pulled them and photographed the inside and outside covers and the first page of each. There were a few cassettes and videotapes. He put them in his backpack. When he opened the first cigar box, he recognized the smell of money. Most of it was in stacks of hundreds and twenties, but there were a few fives.

"I guess the fives are for making change," he whispered.

"Nah," a voice answered. "There was this female student who strip-danced in Atlanta on weekends. She paid in fives, for some reason. Always wished she'd come up shy so she could pay in kind. Alas, she never did."

There was no need to even glance at him. Seth knew the all too kind voice, but its plastic tone was brand new. His hand twitched, and now, nothing mattered but how to survive and how to protect Lesley. Did the voice know she was there?

"Wondering how I made my way in here? Somehow, I fear you won't be taking the alternate entrance out, so you might as well know. There's a passage from my Legal Aid office next door. It leads to a back room." He pointed to an open wooden door over his shoulder. "As for the access you discovered through the Copy Shoppe, it's not even the primary entrance, but I'm impressed you located it. It's such a shame your relentless mind is going to waste, Seth." He shook his head in fake pity, then paused. "Maybe, just maybe, it can still be salvaged, Mr. Sentel. What would you say to one more lecture plus a follow-up discussion? It wouldn't harm a young scholar, would it?"

Seth raised his head for what was a veiled challenge. He'd already made the calculations. Goodfried was standing over him at the end of the bed. There was a big damn revolver in his left hand. Seth remembered Goodfried used his left hand to "shoot" Dooley. This complicated Goodfried's shooting angle--he'd have to shoot over the corner of the bed. Seth's Walther was still on the floor under the bed, but he resisted a glance. If he could distract Goodfried, Seth felt he could get off the first round.

Goodfried continued. "Now if I were a hard case, like Professor Myerson, then I'd just go ahead and shoot you now. After all, you're in my premises, and although you haven't threatened me, you've opened my safe to steal my belongings, and if your defense of weapons in Criminal Law is an indicator, you have a gun under your coat. If not, I could always supply your body with one."

Seth considered a shot through the bed. It would give him the advantage of surprise, but the bullet could be deflected by a spring.

Goodfried went on. "Now, I have an idea. You remain seated at my feet, and I'll lecture from up here. I'll use this Smith and Wesson Model 686 as my pointer. With its six-inch barrel, it's amply long for a pointer. A long barrel makes a gun more accurate, does it not, Mr. Sentel? I yield to your expertise on matters of firearms."

Thinking a measure of discourse might distract, Seth responded. Hugo's voice-activated recorder might gather some valuable evidence. "True Professor, a long barrel, all else equal, does render firearms more precise at ranges over ten feet. It's about increased sighting radius. A small movement of the hand has less effect because there's more distance between the front and rear sights."

Goodfried tilted his head back, folded his arms like he'd learned something, then said, "So, I have in my hand what must be a pistol whose tendencies are far less random than a similar revolver with a three-inch barrel, or even a well-fashioned automatic." Seth guessed Goodfried had made his own determination of who had the advantage and was trying to convince Seth to surrender any thoughts of resistance.

Goodfried continued, "So, with those factors in mind, let us continue this learning experience on a less mechanical plane." He switched subject matter. "I suppose the goal of engaging in these various illegal acts is to collect circumstantial evidence of certain activities, whose criminal nature is arguable at best."

Seth countered. "Although the applicability of the Illegal Assistance statute to your activities is subject to debate, that of the Extortion and Rape statutes isn't, not to mention the Murder code sections. You've breached at least five Ethical canons as well."

"A challenging statement, Mr. Sentel. This could be interesting. Hmm. To take your last point first, only the uninitiated lawyer adheres to Ethical rules. Most real attorneys consider Ethics a nuisance, a subterfuge necessary to bolster the bar's public image. After all, it's the *appearance* of propriety that matters, not the actual existence. When push comes to shove, the rules of Ethics are often, well, shoved. In my view, they're advisory-only, except to the extent they establish a lawyer's duty to zealously maximize injustice. Isn't it awesome to be so low in character, yet so high in repute?

As for your initial assertions, let us not forget that with any crime, the prosecutors, and those unauthorized to assist them-- such as you--have a great deal of proving to do. As a practical matter, extortion is quite difficult to prove, especially when those alleged to be victims never complain of it. Would the students cited in that ledger complain they were victimized?"

"There's one who would, and did."

"Hypotheticals are superb learning tools, but their value in the real world--especially when their existence appears to be scarce--is quite minimal. Except in old foreign films like *Rashomon*, only the living can testify. Correct?"

The coldness of his reference to Sue combined with the falsified warmness of his voice lit Seth's internal pilot light. He shifted on the hard floor.

"Would those ledgers you've stolen, even if admissible, constitute sufficient proof of extortion? They're a mere list of initials with meaningless marks beside them. If the so-called parties listed within claim no meaning, how can the State show they're anything more than fiction? Because they're all in block letters, how could it show who even prepared them?

"Moreover, you broke into my building and opened my safe. Who's to say someone else didn't do the same and plant those ledgers? Maybe they were concocted to frame someone. Maybe they belong to someone else who didn't want to store them on his or her own property, so they hid them in an abandoned building."

"But what about my testimony?"

"To what could you testify? Have you ever witnessed me demanding money or some less tangible benefit from any student in exchange for a higher score? How about threatening to harm a student for not meeting an obligation? Have you ever seen me provide special assistance to any law student? Besides, you may soon become a hypothetical yourself."

Seth closed his eyes . . . but kept fighting. "What about the pattern in your exam scores? I suppose you'll just beg coincidence?"

"Of course, what else? Besides, the pattern is a tenuous one at best. It took little Miss Lesley weeks of hard number crunching to decipher it. Oh, incidentally, she's set to receive another unexpected visit tonight, this time by a man quite skilled at staging suicides."

Seth perceived Goodfried was enjoying himself, reveling in the idea of the perfect criminal enterprise. Seth tossed out more easy bait. "And how about your expanded office hours? And your willingness to teach two sections of two subjects and stay long after class is over? And the way you spend so much time with students outside school? Isn't it all about expanding your market by discovering who's interested in your arrangement?"

"Come, come, Seth. You're smarter than that. Remember what I said after I shot ole Dooley: 'People play roles in the real world, just as they do upon the stage.' My reputation as a student's professor is too wide, too deep. No one would believe my motives were illicit. The groundwork I've laid over the years is firm. It would take an act of God--whoever He is--to shift it."

"Well then, what about how your system perpetrates a great big lie, a fat false statement about a student's competence? *Doesn't truth mean anything?*"

"Truth?" Goodfried shook his head. "Oh my, Seth, don't get desperate. Remember: we're all lawyers here. First, the students I helped in the past are now some of the most effective attorneys in the state, men and women willing to do what's *necessary* to win." He glanced up a moment. "*Indeed.* Give me your greedy, your heartless, your Nietzsches and your nihilistic--I'll make great lawyers of them all!

"Second, to paraphrase the good Pilate, *What in Hell is truth*? Well, I know truth. Truth is what the *lawyer says it is!* Truth is our child, Seth. We create it, and we *own* it. So, we can bend it, twist it, *even rape it*, if we wish. Truth isn't a sacred cow, young Seth. Truth is a *cash* cow. We milk and herd it to finance our lifestyle. We're paid for every pound of verbal garbage we generate. *Indeed*, truth is a mere capitalistic construct, and, after all, this is the 1980's, and your conservative President Reagan is in the White House. Man, oh man! I love *my* decades because they proved that nothing is absolutely wrong, and I love *yours* because it proves the man with the cold hard cash is *always* Mr. Right." He smiled. "Yuh know, you gotta love that Madonna and her material world."

Seth took a deep breath and tried to appear defeated. It was the sickening challenge of Seth's adult life, but he must have met it. Goodfried gave pause and stared at his idea of an under-matched opponent. His facade altered. He switched off the tone of intellectual rivalry.

"Look, Seth, what are you trying to accomplish here? I'm a lawyer doing what lawyers do. You can't change that. Converting an entire profession is a monumental task, even for one as innocent and well-equipped as you." Goodfried downshifted again, now to a pleading tone. "Just let us be! Let us do what we do. Why couldn't you just forget what you think may have happened to H.R. and move on to a deserving future? Of course, that choice would make your life difficult, plus I might never trust you to remain practical. In any case, will you never learn that moral distinctions are so paralyzing, so complicating, and so limiting? One who avoids them has a more relaxed life. He sleeps better. Don't you ever want to just stop fighting yourself?"

Goodfried gazed down at Seth as if he was a pathetic child he had just whipped, but would now soothe with fatherly attention. He lowered his voice one last notch. "Seth, for you, for the genius who located this place, there's a more appealing alternative. You can join a quest with purpose, one that's productive. Furthermore, my arrangement produces the immeasurable feeling that goes with helping those who won't help themselves. Call it affirmative action for the underachiever. Think about it: my little grade-enhancing system is the perfect combination of your decade of greed with my decades of ease." Seth exhaled.

Goodfried continued the chase. "Listen, Seth. I'm not here to destroy you. I'm here to issue an invitation. You can become a part of a new family. I'm not a self-centered soul. Sharing what I've built over the years wouldn't come hard to me-- especially with one in whom I have confidence. In fact, I picture myself taking on a consulting role soon. Being your mentor and watching you become a professor and expand the enterprise would provide me as much pleasure as I derive from operating it now.

"You'd be taken care of; the security element would be powerful. Again, I don't just mean financial security, even though--at fifty thou per or maybe a percentage of future earnings--the financial security is beginning to add up. Other less concrete modes of security are also available. You've learned how painful it is to lose what you value, but haven't you noticed how the more aggressive and self-focused a man is, the more attractive he is to women? Your days of pain would be over!"

Goodfried waved the gun for emphasis, but never loosened his grip. Seth stared back, his hands braced against the floor. He must have appeared subdued.

Goodfried volleyed a hopeful glint from the corner of his right eye and moved in to capitalize. "Seth, this is the rare situation where all parties involved would benefit. It's not a zero sum game. Men like us shouldn't be encapsulated by manmade arbitrary rules. After all, who are *mere men* to govern those such as you and me?"

A pause set in; it seemed to belong. Seth felt the urge to give, to just sit there and be overcome. The mere consideration of it felt so easy, so relaxing. The feeling reminded him of his first night with Cindi, how it felt to feel so wanted.

Then, he blinked. His mind slashed ahead to that sickening morning at The Waysider. He tried to avoid the memory, tried to roadblock the pain, then breathed faster as it morphed into anger.

Now he considered the entirety of that creeping feeling he'd so long ignored, he slid his right hand under the bed. He had the Walther in his hand and the safety off without a sound. He cocked the hammer and heard a vague click escaping into the uncarpeted room. Goodfried heard it, too, but didn't recognize it soon enough.

Seth had to move. He snapped off the first round. The bedspread frayed. Goodfried shuddered, struck in the upper left shoulder. He jerked backward and counter-clockwise, only his right side now exposed. Seth fired again. The bullet shattered the framed print to the right, sending a small shard of glass into Goodfried's neck. He jerked his head at the floor. His cold eyes bored down on Seth, his face as red as his blood. Seth tried to move, but there wasn't time. Goodfried aimed and fired with hate. A .357 slug bored through Seth's left thigh.

The shock of the impact jolted Seth's heart, and the pain burned through him like a hot ice pick. He sensed blood escaping both sides of his leg. He grabbed the upper wound with his left hand and pulled the rest of himself under the bed, using his elbows for propulsion. He fired again as he scampered toward the headboard and to the other side.

Goodfried returned the favor. The round ripped through the mattress where Seth had just fired. Seth could determine a rough angle of entry. Goodfried had moved to his right and was near the foot of the bed. Seth fired back.

Goodfried spoke, his words those of a proper madman. "You're two out of four, but the last was a mere graze. I've fired just twice, so I have two more rounds left than you. Why don't I be a gent and even the odds?"

He fired again and again, apparent random guesses about Seth's position under the big bed. One was off to Seth's right. The other splintered the wood between his knees.

"Seth, you still there? Now, we each have two rounds."

Seth was weary of the chatter. He hurled more lead. The blast missed and hit the blackened window at chest level to the professor's right.

"Nice shooting. The height was well calibrated, but sorry, you were wide. I shan't say to which side. Hmmm. If I were you, I'd wonder where I'll move next. Will I try another shot through the bed? Will I move to one side or the other and fire up under? The bed spread should be long enough to hide my feet until they're at the edge."

Goodfried removed his shoes. A strange silence absorbed a strange moment. Seth knew a shoeless Goodfried could move about the room in virtual silence. Seth committed all his auditory cilia to the detection of footsteps, but the multiple percussions were deadening his hyperactive ears. He situated himself parallel to the headboard. If the next shot came up under the bed, he'd be less of a target than if lying end-to-end.

More silence passed. Seth sensed movement, but from where, and to where, he wasn't sure. Then, like a nightmare from Hell, he first smelled feet, then saw it, stainless steel, all six inches of it, two inches from his head. There was a smooth metal click. He flinched once as the chamber revolved, then once more at the report. The blast racked his right ear, stunned the attached brain cells. The odor of gunpowder struck him. He tried not to jerk, but failed. His right arm flew back, and he returned fire behind his head. This one bored just below the professor's right hip. Seth heard him groan and stumble against the wall.

Goodfried pushed himself off the bloodied wall, the Smith & Wesson still gripped like a throat in his hand.

The plastic tone had evaporated, replaced with a tone of fatalism. "Your gun is empty, Mr. Sentel. I have one round remaining. Class is dismissed." There was a pregnant pause. "Isn't the Latin word *finito*?"

His ears ringing, Seth could now only feel the vibrations of an unhurried shuffle back toward the bed. Seth knew his last shot had done more damage and about where it was inflicted. Seth also knew his Walther carried eight rounds.

Goodfried would likely kneel down and peer under the bed from the right side. Seth had already made a 180-degree turn to face him, and he had the Walther poised on his navel to pivot it and fire.

His throbbing thigh threatened to alter his aim. Goodfried reached the bed. Seth caught his scent, but Goodfried wasn't on the floor yet. Seth waited to see his face, waited to kill for the first time.

The pause was cruel, the stillness unfair.

Two explosions ripped through the air. Seth shook. The shots were too soon, too many, and too soft.

The bed sunk at the middle. A few pieces of glass fell to the floor. He saw blood trailing down the bedspread and onto the hardwood planks. He pulled half his body out the opposite side with both arms. He saw nothing and heard less, until the sound of footsteps. He had to search for what to do, so he did nothing. The footsteps approached the bedside. Seth was still as a newborn fawn. He heard a sound on the other side, but saw no face. He heard a feminine gasp. He felt consciousness fading, yet sensed the sound of footsteps rushing toward him.

The pain reverberated from his leg to his upper body, but he readied himself for whatever came next. He was dizzy, even nauseous now, but he knew that, through the fog of his mind and body, he could see a small pistol hanging down in front of him, pointed toward the floor. He wanted to level his gun at whatever was attached to it, but his hand seemed to take forever to move. Then he heard a small voice, commanding, yet comforting.

"Don't try anything. I may be afraid of guns, but I know how to use one."

Lesley hovered over him, then knelt by his side. He could make out the small pistol.

His voice was weak. "An old Derringer?"

"It was a weird ex-boyfriend's idea of a Valentine's Day gift. And it's not just a Derringer; it's a .38 Derringer."

Seth dropped his head. "How romantic." Then, he raised an eyebrow. "You have an ex-boyfriend?"

"If you don't hush, I'll have an ex-friend."

Seth issued a wise compliment. "Nice shooting, sis. Is he-"

"I haven't checked for a pulse. Thought I'd get one on you first. Are you certain you still have one?"

"Thanks."

He managed a painful smile, tried to suppress a few tears that the physical pain, the un-subsided fear, and the joy of hearing a soothing voice had combined to yield.

"Less, what happened? I heard two shots and some breaking glass." ·

"I was making copies when I heard the first shot. Once I mustered the stupefying courage, I climbed down the ladder, but I kept hearing gunshots. I was about to burst in when I noticed I could see him through the wall."

"Through the wall?"

"Well, no. There's a two-way mirror between the office and here. I shot him through it so I wouldn't enter the room and risk alerting him. I had noticed something odd about the way your light barely reflected off it when we were snooping around the office. He looked right at me once, maybe to admire himself, but he couldn't see me."

Seth turned to Goodfried's dead body sprawled across the white, and now red, bedspread.

"*Alors, la verite existe. Verite d'avantage.*"

Less's translation was solemn. "Thus, truth exists. Advantage truth." She paused, then said, "Seth, I didn't know you spoke French."

Seth nodded, added, "Look, it'll be daybreak soon. Let's figure out what to do next."

"Oh, sure, with your leg bleeding out of both sides, I'm sure we need to sit down over coffee and strategize. You're *way* too much sometime, Seth Sentel. The first priority is to get you out of here and into Druid City Hospital."

She sterilized his wounds with some Stolichnaya she found in Goodfried's desk, then applied a tourniquet made from her sweatshirt and helped him to his feet.

Seth rose from the floor, and a brutal noise rose out of his pain. "Ugh! I feel like an extra from *Gone With The Wind*. I'll never make it up that steep ladder."

"Maybe we could use the door for a change."

"Remember, they're all boarded up."

"Then how are we getting out of this slice of Hell tonight?" she queried, obviously not interested in sleeping in a bed now occupied by a bloody dead man.

"Such language for a choir girl."

She cut her eyes over at him as he leaned on her for support. "Would a has-been athlete like another game leg?"

He managed a grin and added, "Okay. Okay. Not to change the subject, but before we inflicted multiple gunshot wounds on his person, Professor Badfried was good enough to mention there was another way out of here from the back room. He said it led to his legal aid office next door."

Seth hobbled into the back room, looked for the other secret entrance, leaned on Lesley when the pain struck. He saw no sign of an exit and collapsed onto the couch. The throbbing pain in his leg was evil. He wanted to drink the rest of the vodka. He tapped his forehead with his hands and stared at the floor.

Then he noticed it. The outline was vague, but he could make out the muddy pattern of a Converse tennis shoe on the floor below. They moved the lightweight couch and found a big trap door behind it. They removed the door and saw permanent stairs that were much less steep than the wall ladder leading from the Copy Shoppe attic.

"Less, you better go down first in case I slip and fall." She looked back at him, obviously scared silly. "Don't worry. I'll try to fall on you gently."

"Thanks."

They eased down and found themselves in a narrow tunnel. The bottom was lined with wooden planks, but the dirt around them was cold and damp, thus the footprint upstairs. Water and power lines ran against the walls, thus no utility bills attached to the hideout. It was a short walk underground to Goodfried's legal aid office. They climbed another stairwell and entered a walk-in closet through a regular upright door.

Just before they entered, Seth thought he heard the faint sound of an automobile engine, maybe a German make. Then, farther away, there was another engine noise, this one from a Ford. When the noises abated, he blamed them on his battered eardrums. Once inside, they could see how the door blended into the wall and was camouflaged by a row of old hanging clothes.

Seth breathed heavily, weakening with every step. They found a back exit. It would be another long short walk from there to Less's car parked ninety feet away on a side street. They pushed on the door with Less still leading. A dumpster stood to the left. Seth hobbled forward, but hesitated a moment beside the dumpster, as a new burst of pain shot through his frame. Less stood in front of him, held onto his arm.

Then it happened.

He saw the shadow of yellow and steel, slashing from behind the dumpster. His body tried to move, but his reflexes were cooked. He felt the sharp pain rip through his ribs before he ever heard the gunshot. He tried to stop himself from falling forward to the pavement. He wondered whether gunshot noise always lagged so far behind a bullet. A hazy vision fell with him. He wondered why someone else was falling, as he broke his own fall with his hands and the right side of his face.

He fought for consciousness. His existence jumbled, he struggled to decipher the vision beside him: blonde hair, bright clothing, a thick bottom lip with red lip gloss running below it, a right eye closing as he looked straight into it. High cheekbones--just like those of a model. Wedging its way into his thoughts was H.R.'s caveat about the beautiful and the bizarre. His mind closed in on the last remnant of the same strange feeling that had trailed him for months, that sick sense of being in the wrong place, with the wrong people.

His eyes closed first.

CHAPTER SEVENTY

August 22, 1986. Tuscaloosa, Alabama, a university town. A good place. And as good a place as any for good things to happen

Maybe the calendar claimed it was still summer, but now, the wind blew a little cooler and a little less humid, especially at six p.m. Seth surveyed the Bermuda grass football field. It wasn't the same lush green it'd been in April. The relentless summer heat had turned it a worn bluish hue, but to Seth's sensitive eyes, it seemed to cling to its original shade. Seth rubbed those eyes and decided that, deep in Alabama, the grass just didn't want to die.

In June, his classmates had scattered across the Southeast on summer clerkships. At firms large and small, they trained for the mad dash: the race for the billable hour, the plaintiff with damages both real and huge, and for that rarest of criminal defendants--the one who hadn't confessed.

Meanwhile, Seth, after posting a miraculous 3.4 second semester GPA, had spent his spare time in doctors' office waiting rooms and rehab clinic whirlpool tubs, time he'd used to learn the facts of life. There was the fact it now hurt to run, the fact Asst. Dean Thurow had threatened to expel him, the fact Goodfried's football game date had been Katie Ryals's roommate--and a co-conspirator in her murder, the fact that the FBI had been suspicious enough about what was going down at the school to set Rentzell and Hays up as undercover agents. They just died before they could connect things to Goodfried.

Then there was the real drug dealer, the recently arrested one claiming that mother Vicari had paid him to kill her husband, the aptly named Nolte Vicari. Then, there was the fact that Cindi, the psychological minefield he'd loved with every ounce of his soul, had tried to kill him. The fact his best friend Walter had shot her dead. The fact Cindi's *real* father, your "good friend" Goodfried, had tried to kill him, too. At least his own father had stopped giving him orders, and started giving him advice.

Although Seth's wealth of time was healing all his wounds, it would never heal *all* his facts. He could never live with Cindi and Goodfried's romantic affair--not only because of what it said about them--but because of what it said about life, how it had somehow fashioned such a double evil and somehow lured him close to both sides of it: a seller of success and his chief recruiter, two sociopaths, both born of lies, vanity, and death. He had, however, learned to live with how the invisible, omnipresent *cohorte'* was looking out for him, bailing him out of his stupid mistakes, and teaching him a few real truths along the way.

Maybe life still frightened him, but now he was confident he and God could frighten it back. It helped that his year-long battle with internal malaise was now over. He knew he didn't belong in law school, and, most important, he now knew precisely why. Conquering the chief embodiments of the problem hadn't hurt his spirits either.

As the day wore on, the swelling orange sun began to drop toward the tops of the granddaddy pines that bordered the field, and another set of dark eyes peered down from a nearby parking lot. All eyes watched as a little black running back took a pitchout and loped to his right. The defense flowed toward him like a tiny wall of water from a tiny dam break.

Then, with insufficient time for thought, he stopped and reversed course. The wall collapsed on itself, as little feet slid under little bodies and little helmets bounced against the soft grass. There was a defender on his left with a face full of distress. The little ball carrier aimed at him. He faked hard left and ducked right, just under the swipe of a befuddled arm. He veered back left to the sideline. Twenty little antelope strides later, another made a desperation dive at his feet. He hurdled him. Another grabbed high. He shook him off. Forty yards down the field, the far defensive back still had a chance, but the little runner ran as if he was alone.

He planted his left foot and spun a tight counter-clockwise circle. His pursuer couldn't stop and collided with an evergreen tree just beyond the sideline. The little running man laughed his way to the goal line.

Seth blew his whistle, extracted the shaken defensive back from the Christmas tree, then made a welcome announcement. "Take ten. Water break."

Seth slapped the half-pint halfback on the rear. "Nice running, Jack."

The little twelve-year-old walked backwards, his head tilted to the left. An abundance of curiosity, along with a little irritation, was evident on his face.

"Coach, how come you don't call me by my real name, Kennedy? I was named after a President, you know."

"Because, now I knows you, so I gots to nickname you. You run like a jackrabbit, so I like to call you Jack, okay?"

"Well, I reckon that's okay."

"Jack" broke off and ran to the water faucet, passing every player on the team.

Walking toward Seth and ten yards away, Myerson spoke. "It appears you have a young superstar on your hands, Coach Sentel."

"I hope I can keep his ego in check."

"Yes, the world is never so wicked as when genius turns to folly."

"Yes, I've seen it happen," Seth replied.

Myerson smiled. "Well, you seem to control your own ego, so just teach him your secret."

Seth asked, "Can a man be *too* humble?"

"Life is a search for happy mediums, Mr. Sentel. Just keep looking."

Seth nodded. "So, sir, what brings you here this afternoon?"

"Just to answer some questions and perhaps ask a few."

"I don't have many questions left."

Myerson allowed himself a light, good-natured chuckle. "Men like you tend to have questions until they vanish."

"Fair enough. Because you know the answers, what are the questions?"

"Goodfried, we now know, was once named Gabriel Elijah. As your man Hugo may have discovered, Gabriel Elijah was named after his father, my former client. Unbeknownst to me until late in the game, Gabriel, Sr. was a less than legitimate real estate developer. Gabriel, Jr. was invited to turn state's evidence against his father, who hadn't yet been arrested, in December of 1960, during Jr.'s last year of law school here. Jr. agreed, but, after recalling his father's tenacity, decided to escape his civic duty."

Myerson's voice became hesitant for the next sentence. "He was also running from fatherhood." He waited for Seth's reaction, then went on. "The Feds found him living near the beach in California, doped up and still unwilling to testify. To motivate a reconsideration, the Feds packed him off to Vietnam in 1962 as one of those so-called advisors we then deployed.

379

"Two years into his Asian vacation, during which he met Myron Gustaf, also known as Redbeard, Gabriel, Jr. returned home in 1964 to face his fate. His father was tried, and Jr.'s uniformed testimony was so impressive that, in December of 1964, the jury convicted on all counts, including arson, tax fraud, and conspiracy to commit murder.

"Two months later, we heard Jr. died in combat. Actually, he went into the Witness Protection Program. The Feds were so grateful that they allowed him to have some of his father's assets, including all shares in Elijah, Inc., a corporation owning some new Tuscaloosa commercial property set up as condominiums under that September 1, 1964 legislative act I helped draft. Finally, I was often a token shareholder in my client's corporations because the law required three, and I was a convenient depository."

Seth nodded again.

"Well, the Feds cashed out a few units at Jr.'s request and even collected rent and paid the taxes for him on the others. They also permitted him to finish his final year of law school at the university of his choosing, California-Berkley, in May of 1965. As an aside, he jilted Professor Borland there. An instinctive woman, she recognized Goodfried shortly after joining the faculty here, and it seems she and Katie Ryals were once involved in some form of joint effort. Thus, she assisted again by doing some title research for me and delivering a note with her findings to Miss Peace's box."

"How did you know what we were looking for?"

"I've been around this rather large small town for many years, Mr. Sentel, and I've made a few friends."

"Friends are good."

"True. Anyway, his father died in prison, and in 1975, with a new surgeon-adjusted facade and a new name, Jr. felt safe enough to return here to teach and corrupt."

Seth's head moved left to right. "How does one live when almost *nothing* is *really* the way it seems?"

"Carefully, Seth, carefully."

Seth closed his eyes a second and nodded. "In any case, you filled in a few gaps. Thanks."

"Thank you as well." Seth's eyes flipped over, seeking meaning. "I'm a Yankee Jew, thus, I'm not supposed to love this place. Yet, I do. You've made it a better place. And that, Mr. Sentel, is good."

Seth's eyes swung over again. "It's a good place, sir. I love it, too."

"Good indeed. Now, there's one more item of possible interest. Asst. Dean Thurow, who was disappointed when I demanded he call off the Honor Court, desires your return for next semester. He can't fathom how you'd put so much at risk, but he's pleased now that you did. He says that you're an outstanding credit to your law school. All is forgiven, and you'll be reinstated as if none of this distasteful set of events ever transpired. Hm. Perhaps Mr. Thurow has had a talk with his superior."

Seth dissected Thurow's words. "I doubt he could fathom the depth of a washtub. I'll wager he's pleased I performed the dirty work he didn't have the guts to do himself. I'm certain he hates me for discovering something he didn't. Plus, I know there's no way in hell, heaven, or earth that life will ever be as if none of this ever happened. Anyway, I'm not sure it's my law school anymore."

"I can't answer that for you."

"And you wouldn't if you could. You'd make me think it out for myself."

"Yes. For your betterment, and hence, for the betterment of all."

Seth took in a slow breath. "I've considered some other options."

"That's fine, but remember that time walks among us."

"Sometimes, it seems more like it runs after us."

"Wait until you reach fifty, Seth", Myerson said, as he smiled and began to walk away.

"Professor," Seth called out. Myerson turned. "If I enroll, would you be up for discussing Isaiah Chapter 53?" Myerson smiled, nodded his assent, indicating he was game to debate what this intriguing scripture foretold.

Seth smiled at the nod, and realized, that for once, Myerson had called a student by his first name.

A few moments later, the team of twelve-year-olds returned and a familiar gray Toyota pulled up and parked at the edge of the field. In the back seat was the neo-impressionist painting she'd retrieved from a frame shop--"Deer Angel" by Lymon Bream. She handed it to Myerson.

Meanwhile, the day's football practice was complete, except for the dreaded wind sprints. The players all moaned like the children they were. The customary cries rang out, "Aw, coach," and "do we have to?"

Seth blew the whistle at half-volume and offered a bargain. "You can run six of 'em at full speed or ten of 'em without trying. What's it gonna be?"

With the unison of the Vienna Boy's Choir, their high-pitched voices cried, "Six!"

"Okay, but if even one of you goofs off, we'll add two each time Miss Peace or I notice."

"Deal!" was the energized response.

Several of the sweaty Pee Wees looked back at Miss Peace while they walked to the chalk starting line for six forty-yard dashes. Two walked up beside "Jack" and warned him not to goof off.

Seth got out in front of them and injected a little motivation. "Who's gonna die in the fourth quarter next week?"

"*Nobody!*"

"Alright. Let's go." He blew his whistle, and the young wanna be All Pros ran like greyhound pups.

The routine was repeated six times. "Who's gonna quit when it hurts a little bit?"

"*Nobody!*"

Genetics dictated that Jack finished first all six times. Seth let them get more water.

Less walked closer and said, "So will you ever get a paying job?"

He looked at her and smiled. "We'll discuss that after practice. There are young lives to be molded here. By the way, Mozz visited me in the hospital and told me his nickname for you, little Miss 'Less-is-more'." She smiled. He looked at her and added, "Um, I've misinterpreted a few people. I'm sorry you were one of them. I feel stupid."

She looked back, but he'd already walked forward to address the team. She spoke anyway. "You weren't stupid. You were just young."

The players assembled before him, still blowing hard from the wind sprints. Most also cast a curious eye toward the coach's new "assistant."

"Not a bad practice today. We still need to work on our downfield blocking on offense, and on our tendency to overreact on defense, but I'm pleased with your progress. I have ample reason to believe you'll be ready for your first game."

A tall redheaded kid raised his hand halfway and asked, "Coach, what do overreact and ample mean?"

Seth nodded, realized his faulty word choice. "Well, overreact is like when you run too hard to one side of the field to tackle a ball carrier, then he hands off to another on the reverse, and you're left to feel like a dummy. You'll learn all about overreactions and feeling like a dummy when you start spending more time with girls." Several players cringed and murmured, "*Girls*. Ooh, yuk." He smiled and looked out of the corner of his left eye at Less, who smirked playfully. "Ample means plenty, or a bunch." The gathering of young minds nodded its collective head.

"Now listen up guys. I know it gets hot out here, and I know y'all get tired, but remember, the tough stuff you go through now is what makes it easy when you get in a real game. Games are fun, more fun when you win. In fact, if y'all keep working hard and you win next week, there's gonna be pizza and Frostie root beer for everyone, courtesy of me and Miss Peace over there," Seth promised, pointing his thumb toward Less.

She overheard and had a big-eyed *I didn't know about that one* look. The boys laughed like boys.

"All right, guys, try to stay out of trouble this weekend. Strike that, *do* stay out of trouble this weekend, and I'll see you here tomorrow at four o'clock. Now huddle up."

The players formed a huddle and stuck their hands in the middle. They broke the huddle with the energy of wild ponies, then scampered off to the moms and dads who waited in the parking lot.

She walked near him. He relaxed. He took a deep breath, then said, "I learned a few things from H.R., and one of them was to take life with a smile and a grain of salt. Sometimes, I wish I could just do this forever."

"I wish you could, too, you know. Football does seem so much more real, so much more legitimate than law."

"Never thought about it that way. Maybe I just felt it."

384

"Well, Sixth Sentel, maybe if you keep wishing and say your prayers, everything will work out."

"Maybe so. Myerson just told me the law school wants me back for the fall."

"I guess Asst. Dean Thurow is a great guy after all."

He smiled. "Right. And so was Hitler."

She smiled back. "Do you think you can give up the dream of being a lawyer?"

Seth shook his head. "Sometimes it all seems like a fool's dream. Sometimes I think, with what I've seen of the law, I'd rather be without it." She nodded. He went on. "Jackie Gleason might say I have a lack of respect for it." A smile crept onto both their faces. "Besides, the Birmingham Police Department wants me for their Internal Affairs unit. My father, who, for once, seems proud of me, called a Congressional contact about the FBI and the CIA. They want to talk, but said I'd be better off if I finished law school first."

She looked away, then back. "You know what, Seth, I like the idea of finishing law school at the top of your class, then telling the legal profession--whatever exactly it's professional at--to drop dead. Plus, you'd have two more years to play both Legal Beagles football *and* your new guitar."

His eyes came alive at the mention of the good things in life. He remembered one more. "Not to mention two more years to learn about Statistics."

Seth saw her look away into the distance. He noted the healthy blush beginning to settle into her cheeks. Her honest lips creased, then an understated smile slowly crept into the most tranquil face he'd ever seen.

As he slipped into some rarified zone of true bliss, he considered how, in one short year, so many things had changed; yet, how some things, like knowing you did the right thing, would last forever.

Made in the USA
Charleston, SC
08 June 2012